Sigh with the Tide

Sally Redmayne

Bloomington, IN Milton Keynes, UK

authorHOUSE®

AuthorHouse™
1663 Liberty Drive, Suite 200
Bloomington, IN 47403
www.authorhouse.com
Phone: 1-800-839-8640

AuthorHouse™ *UK Ltd.*
500 Avebury Boulevard
Central Milton Keynes, MK9 2BE
www.authorhouse.co.uk
Phone: 08001974150

First published by AuthorHouse 12/4/2006

ISBN: 978-1-4259-5014-9 (sc)

Printed in the United States of America
Bloomington, Indiana

This book is printed on acid-free paper.

Acknowledgements

The author would like to acknowledge the encouragement of her creative writing tutor Pam Burrow.

The author would also like to acknowledge some ideas for the storyline of this novel from Gladys Simms, also of Radcliffe, Greater Manchester. Thank you, Gladys.

Front cover photograph of Blackpool Tower in the early 1900's by kind permission of the author, taken from the book "*Blackpool Tower*" by Bill Curtis, published 1988 by Terence Dalton Limited.

Chapter One

She was hurrying down the bottom flight of stairs when she heard the rattle of the letter box. Her heart pounding, her errand forgotten, Janet wrenched open the vestibule door. She didn't need to stoop before recognising the familiar hand under the French postmark. Snatching up the envelope, she tore it open, pulling out the letter. The paper was of poor quality but she knew it was all he could get at the Front.

He had told her in his last letter from France that supplies of any kind were very hard to come by. That letter had arrived three months ago and since then she had been worried sick about his safety. Neither she nor Ellen, his mother next door, had had any news from the Front. They had tried to comfort each other with the thought that they hadn't had any bad news either. After four years of worrying and waiting, neither would admit to the other the possibility that Harry hadn't come through the fighting at this late hour when everyone was saying that the War couldn't go on much longer.

Feverishly scanning the letter, the words jumped out at her, "I shall be with you at the beginning of June – invalided out – nothing to worry about – just a cough – the gassing – we'll be married as soon as I get home."

Janet tried to take in what she was reading. It seemed that not only was he safe – he was coming home to her in June! Why, she realised, it was nearly the end of April now!

Through tears of relief and joy, she tried to read the letter through from start to finish. She discovered that Harry had, in fact, been away from the fighting for nearly two months. He mentioned writing to her from the convalescent home, telling her that he had been gassed in the early March offensive. She had never received that letter. If Harry had written to his mother at the same time, it looked as if that consignment of mail had gone astray somewhere along the line from France. Putting the letter to her lips, she breathed, "Harry, my darling, you're coming back to me! I'm going to touch you and kiss you – soon I'm going to be your wife!" As the full realisation of what that meant hit her, she felt a surge of pure panic. Although they were betrothed, she and Harry had not yet been lovers. She had always felt that the right time for lovemaking was their wedding night and she knew that Harry respected her for that. When she considered it, Harry had never been passionately demanding but when they were married he would expect her to be his wife in every sense of the word.

Her mother had never talked to her about the physical side of marriage. Evidently she felt the subject was too embarrassing to discuss with her daughter. Janet couldn't help wondering what union with Harry would be like. The very thought of undressing in front of a man, even Harry, brought the colour to her face in a wave of hot anticipation. Would she be able to put modesty aside for Harry and embrace him in the way a good wife should?

Of course, she wanted children and there would be plenty of room for a nursery in Ellen's house, where they would make their home for a while. Harry had some savings towards getting a home of their own in the future, but it was no use looking too far ahead. He would have to be completely fit before he thought about going back to his job at the carpentry shop.

She, too, had been preparing for the day when she would have her own house. The mahogany tallboy in her bedroom at the back of the boarding house, was full now of household linen which she had embroidered and embellished in her spare hours. In the top drawer lay the finest cotton petticoats, trimmed with lace, and the delicate nightgowns she had cut from the piece of French silk Harry had brought her on that least leave, when they had got engaged. The household linen would have to stay there a while longer, but soon the contents of the top drawer would be taken out and put into service. The idea of wearing those nightgowns and sleeping in the same bed as Harry brought the hot colour racing back again. Did every woman feel apprehensive about her wedding night – even panic about it? She couldn't really guess. All she knew was that she loved Harry, had loved him ever since she had been a young girl at school – and afterwards when she had left school at fourteen and begun helping her mother in the boarding house, there had been nobody but Harry.

The boarding houses, part of a long, red-brick terrace which lay just behind the promenade, were tall, three-storeyed buildings. The ground floor windows boasted stone bays, each displaying its potted aspidistra, supplemented by signs advertising "Vacancies' or 'Bed and Breakfast." Janet's mother, Sarah Crossley, took in paying guests from spring right through until October, as did Ellen Tomlinson, Harry's mother, next door. Normally, their rooms would be full all season but the

War had changed all that. As she stood, reading through the letter once more to convince herself that it was true, a shaft of spring sunshine, brilliant with promise, slanted down through the vestibule window, setting her red-gold head aflame. Thick and full, her hair cascaded in rich, coppery waves over her shoulders, almost to her waist. The round face was dusted across the nose and cheeks with freckles but the eyes, a clear sea-green, lifted the face above the ordinary.

As she finally folded the paper and picked up the envelope, it came to her that she had been on some errand before she had picked up the letter. Of course! She had been going down to the scullery to see how her mother was coping with the baking. Sarah had been suffering from a very bad cold and Janet was worried about her. The letter clutched tightly in her hand, she ran along the lobby, past the visitors' dining-room and the back parlour, into the big kitchen which overlooked the paved back yard.

This wonderful news should cheer her up. Now there would be a wedding to look forward to for both families and her mother would want to play her full part in it. Janet glowed as she visualised herself, on her father's arm, walking down the aisle at St. Luke's. Harry would be waiting for her there, at the altar, tall and smart, just as she remembered him. Thank God he hadn't been maimed like thousands of other men who had returned from the battlefields. The gassing had evidently left him weak and chesty, in fact with a persistent cough but, otherwise, the letter said, he hadn't been injured.

She found Sarah standing by the window in front of the shallow stone sink which held a large enamel washing-up bowl. At its side was fitted a wooden draining-board. Alongside this a smooth slab of stone served for pastry-making. She had just finished rolling out the dough for her apple pies in preparation for the next influx of visitors into the house. They would have two families staying next week, so they would all be busy. A new-looking gas stove on curved iron legs stood to the right of the sink. It had been turned up to a good heat ready for the pies and the kitchen was already filled with the delicious smell of newly-baked cakes, which were cooling now on wire trays set on the big deal table in the middle of the room.

Rushing over to her mother, waving the letter excitedly, Janet cried, "Harry's safe, Mother! He's safe and he's coming home at the beginning of June! I can't believe it yet." She handed the letter to Sarah, who took it in astonishment and with enormous relief.

"Thank God for that, dear, this makes up for all our sleepless nights. I see he's nearly ready for leaving the convalescent home. He can't be all that bad, then, and once he comes home, we'll soon have him on his feet again. I'm so happy for you, dear." Sarah glanced up from the letter to find her daughter gathering together used crockery.

"It's no use, Mother, I'll just have to keep busy. I'm so excited, I can't keep still."

"No wonder, with this marvellous news arriving, at last. We'll have a wedding to be thinking about, too, but if anyone deserves a bit of happiness, it's you, dear."

How fortunate she had been, Sarah was thinking, to have a daughter like Janet, who had been her constant help and companion in the boarding-house since she had left school. She had shared her happiness when she had become engaged to her childhood sweetheart and her despair when he had left to become a young soldier at the beginning of the War. Now, at twenty-three, he was a man and ready for the responsibilities of a wife and some day, a family. She knew that Ellen, Harry's mother, felt the same about this marriage. They had both been delighted, if not surprised, when Janet and Harry had finally become engaged and now it looked as if the wedding would be quite soon.

As she handed back the letter to Janet and turned quickly to pick up one of the pie plates from the table, she felt the room beginning to revolve around her. She stopped herself from falling by grabbing the edge of the table and holding on hard, leaning her head on her arm as the dizziness persisted. The next moment Janet was by her side.

"Whatever's the matter, Mother?"

Sarah lifter up her dark head gingerly. "It – it's nothing, dear. I just went a bit dizzy, that's all. It's going off now. Perhaps I'll go and sit down for a minute or two." Her face colourless as she took Janet's arm, she managed to walk on wobbly legs into the back parlour, but Janet must not know how weak she really felt. She didn't intend spoiling in any way Janet's happiness over Harry's letter.

As they entered the cosy parlour, Janet said, "That cold isn't clearing up, you know, and you're doing far too much work. I don't like to see you off-colour, like this. I wish you'd see Dr. Fraser."

"Now, don't fuss, Janet, I'll be alright. It will go in its own good time, I reckon. I'll put my feet up for an hour before we start on the dinners."

"That's better, now you're being sensible. I'll finish the pies but I'll bring you a cup of tea in here first."

"That would be nice, dear." Sarah had to admit to herself that the only thing she wanted to do was to lie down. She quickly slipped off her shoes before lifting her legs onto the black horsehair sofa. Her head dropped onto the long roll cushion at the couch's head. That was much better! The back of the sofa was draped with a bright shawl made of knitted squares, stitched together. Pulling it over herself, she thankfully closed her eyes. How she wished she could throw off this wretched cold! Janet was right – it wasn't getting any better and after waiting all this time for Janet's wedding, she wanted to be perfectly fit when her daughter made her vows. There was so much they would all have to do – so much would need organising. Just now, though, she felt like doing nothing at all ....

Returning to the parlour five minutes later with a strong cup of tea, Janet found her mother asleep. Oh, well, she wouldn't waken her. It would do her good to have a little nap. She could see that a little colour had returned to Sarah's face, but she was going to have to persuade her mother to do a bit less in the house. Rose, Janet's younger sister and Arthur, her young brother, would have to help, too. Rose, at twelve years old, was already familiar with the routine of the house and Arthur, nearing fourteen, had been trained by their mother to do most of the jobs around the house when they weren't at school, including washing-up and clearing the tables.

Robert Crossley, their father, was the only one excused duties in the boarding-house. He worked long shifts in Riley's bakehouse around the corner at the back of the house. He had to be up at four in the mornings and get some sleep during the day. His income, supplemented by the products of the bakery, had been their mainstay all through the lean years of the War.

Janet carried the tea back into the kitchen and began lining the pie plates with dough. As she filled each one with the tangy apples and the soft brown sugar, her emotions swung this way and that. They ranged from sweet anticipation of her fiancé's return to anxiety and speculation about her mother. If Sarah wasn't able to cope with the work in the kitchen, she herself would have to do more. But, then, if she was kept busy all the time with work in the house <u>and</u> the kitchen, the next few weeks would go by quickly. Oh, Harry, darling, she thought, how am I going to get through another month before I see you?

Putting the apple pies into the hot oven, it came to her suddenly that she should at least start making plans for her wedding. By the time Harry arrived she would have some ideas about clothes and receptions. She must decide soon, too, on who should be invited. There were so many things to think about and the work of the house would have to go on whilst all the arrangements for the wedding were being made.

On one thing Janet was determined. If her mother was no better soon, she would insist on her seeing Dr. Fraser. At this stage Janet didn't want to worry her father. In the past Sarah had thrown off with ease any little ailment and she seemed confident that this would be no different. Her mind settled on this point, Janet checked the oven before going through to the front door. She must pop round next door to see if Ellen, too, had received Harry's wonderful news. It didn't look like it, or she would surely have been round to tell them before now. Eager to put Ellen's mind at rest, Janet went out into the warm spring sunshine, which seemed to her almost like a benediction. It was going to be a wonderful summer for them all, she thought, as she pushed open Ellen's vestibule door, wondering idly which visitors would be coming from over the Pennines to stay in the boarding-houses this season....

Chapter Two

The Yorkshire mill town of Bradfield nestled in folds of the high moors just across the Pennines. Its woollen mills and engineering works crowded the centre of the town, down in the river valley. From this centre radiated long terraces of dun coloured stone houses, mainly two up and two down buildings. Built right onto the street, they had yards at the backs containing an outside privy and a coalhouse. Heavily grimed by the smoke from numerous chimneys in the valley, they climbed, rank upon rank, up the grey hills which surrounded the town.

Some of the terraces reached as far as the moors but others petered out half-way up, as if building had been abandoned suddenly. In one of these cottages the Boothroyd family were packing for their summer holiday – one week in the seaside town of Blackpool, over on the Lancashire coast.

Joe Boothroyd, a moulder in the local iron foundry, was always in work. Even so, it had been a struggle for his wife, Mary, to save enough to take them all away for a week in July when Joe had his Wakes week holiday. Some of the families on the row had as many as six children, so they never went away. She herself had only two. Alice had been the first and then, much later, her brother George, had arrived.

At seventeen, Alice was working full-time now in Foster's mill so they had an extra wage coming into the house. The only trouble was that Alice was fond of getting herself dolled up and she demanded a new dress now and then. George, too, was forever needing bigger clothes. Sometimes she managed to get him cast-offs from neighbours but often she had to buy him new things. Fortunately, she and her husband needed few clothes. Joe seemed always to be in his working overalls and she herself had learned to make do with little. By now, Mary had stowed away all the luggage in one bag or another, including two cheap suitcases which were strapped, ready for carrying.

"I don't know how we're going to get all this stuff on the tram," Joe grumbled, as his wife placed a large carrier-bag near the suitcase.

"We need to take some food with us to Blackpool. We're only having the use of the cruet, you know, we're not boarding. We shall have to buy some when we get there, and it's a lot dearer in Blackpool. Mrs. Tomlinson says she's put a new gas cooker in the kitchen, although I'm used to the old parlour range. I expect it's to save the visitors going into their parlour. "Alice! She called to her daughter, "come and take one of these bags. You'd stand there all day titivating your face in that mirror."

Reluctantly, Alice tore herself away from the oval mirror which hung over the bungalow range, with its side oven and deep fireplace. The result completed the effect of pale, slender beauty, darkly crowned by the black, wavy hair. The soft pink dress she had on had been given to Mary by little Mrs. Ollerenshaw, the ironmonger's wife, for whom Mary did occasional cleaning and washing. The dress had been too small for her but it had fitted her daughter a treat. Alice, she knew only too well, wasn't keen on hand-me-downs but in this instance she hadn't argued when her mother had bought her a new navy coat to go over it. Mrs. Greenhalgh at the local dress shop had let Mary pay for it on a weekly basis, like most of the new clothes she bought.

"We've got to carry all this stuff between us. Where's George?" Mary's exasperated voice was sharp. Handing one of the carriers to Alice she said, "Just wait 'til I get my hands on him," as she went all over the house, checking the sash windows and the back door.

"He wanted to spend one of his holiday ha'pennies, Mum, at the corner shop." Alice stole another look at herself in the rather mould-spotted mirror before picking up a brown paper bag from the strip of linoleum which edged a thin needlecord carpet.

"He'll have no money left at this rate," Mary complained.

"The trouble is, you spoil that lad," Joe said, as the boy burst into the room, cheeks bulging, carrying a paper toffee bag.

"How much have you spent?" Mary demanded.

"Only a ha'penny, Mum."

"You'd better give the rest to me, then, to mind for you. Here, take one of these bags and watch you don't let anything fall out of it."

"Have we got everything? What are we waiting for?" Joe asked impatiently, eager to get started on his holiday. Hoisting the two suitcases from the oilcloth, he moved swiftly to the door with them, followed by Alice and George, who recognised the signs that their father was beginning to lose patience. Mary brought up the rear of the little party, quickly locking the door as she struggled with two large bags.

"Pick your feet up, George," Mary shouted to her son, "and don't swing that bag or you'll have the stuff falling out."

"He's excited 'cos he's going to Blackpool." Alice was generous in this instance towards her brother. "He'll behave – you'll see."

"He'd better, or he'll know about it."

The family, with all their baggage, boarded the tram on Cunningham Lane, one of the main roads into the town, after a short walk along Moscar Street, where their house stood. It clanked its noisy way down from the heights of the moor with a great grinding and crashing of gears, warning bell clanging. At the railway station, they found they were in plenty of time, after all, and they found a compartment all to themselves. The cases and bags were stowed away up on the luggage racks with the hats and coats and the family settled down to wait for the train to start.

Joe relaxed on the long bench seat, stretched out his legs and took out his pipe. Of only average height, he had a depth of chest and a muscularity which spoke of heavy work. Although in his early forties, he had no paunch and his face was unlined, if pallid, through long hours in the foundry. The slight droop of his lips betrayed his occasional bad temper and the vivid blue eyes were alert and watchful. They were not much lighter than Alice's and just as striking. The still-black hair, too, mirrored his daughter's, waving strongly in spite of the shortness of the haircut.

He pulled happily at his pipe as he held a match to it, smiling across at Mary. She and Alice had installed themselves on the opposite side of the compartment. He was thinking, with some satisfaction, that his wife, in her best blue frock, was still every bit as attractive as his daughter. Although she had turned forty now, she looked ten years younger......

"I want to wee, Mum." His son's voice interrupted the flow of his thoughts.

"I thought you went before we set off!" Mary regarded her son with suspicion.

"I want to go again, Mum." George wriggled about on his seat to emphasise his point.

"I told you you shouldn't have had that glass of lemonade. Anyway, there's no lavatory on the train – you'll have to go on the platform. I'll take you but you'll have to be quick or the train will go off without us, then you won't be needing that new bucket and spade I promised you."

After five hurried minutes, Mary returned with her son to the compartment, warning him that he'd better behave himself on the journey.

"C'n I have a toffee, then," he asked, hopefully, sitting down meekly in the far corner by the window.

"For goodness sake, get that bag out of my pocket up on the rack, will you, Alice. We'll all have one." She passed round the sweets to the whole family, while Alice got out a small powder compact and mirror.

"You'll see Old Nick in that mirror, one of these days," Joe teased her.

"Oh, go on, Dad. You know you like to see me looking nice."

"You don't need that stuff on your face. Your mother doesn't use any and she's one of the best-looking lasses in Yorkshire," Joe said proudly, slapping his wife affectionately on the buttocks as she reached up to replace the sweets.

The train had by now moved out of Bradfield station to pull slowly uphill between the gasworks and the Brittania Mill, past works yards and scrap heaps. Soon, however, the industrial clutter of the town thinned out. Fields and stone-built farms replaced the ugly town sprawl then, these, too were left behind for the high, bleak moors.

"I hope Dad will be alright staying with our Ivy," Mary addressed her husband doubtfully. "They don't get on all that well, you know."

"Stop worrying! The Old Man will be alright. It's about time she took a turn at looking after him. He'll last longer than me at this rate – the way you go round there seeing to him all the time."

"Well, someone's got to do it since Mum died, and our Ivy lives too far away."

"She's made sure she does." Joe compressed his lips. "Anyway, bugger the Old Man – we're going away on holiday and a week at Thornhill with your Ivy won't do him any harm. Let's forget about it."

"I wish you wouldn't swear like that, love. Little pitchers have big ears – I keep telling you."

"What's wrong with a strong word now and then?" Joe puffed out a cloud of noxious smoke from his pipe. The thick twist was the strongest he could buy. "You don't want him to grow up a cissie, do you?"

To which Mary had no ready reply. Glancing at her son, she could see that the novelty of the train ride was already beginning to wear off.

"Keep your feet off the seats," she ordered him, "and leave that window-strap alone."

"Just look at that sunshine," Joe said, "laid on specially for us."

As he spoke, the train plunged into the Low Moor tunnel, the sun disappeared and they were left in deep blackness.

"Oooo…" George cried, "I don't like it …."

"Don't be so soft," his father said, "we'll be out in a minute. There's nothing to be frightened of."

As he finished speaking, the train emerged again into dazzling light. It really was a beautiful July morning – just the right kind of morning to be going away on holiday. Thin veils of blown cloud hung high up in the pale vault of the sky. Against this, the drab grey-browns of the moor were etched, fold upon fold, until the train reached the summit of Otterthwaite Fell and emerged onto a small plateau. Here the train picked up speed, running parallel with the narrow road and passing the reservoir which provided the town with its water. Its blue-black surface reflected the sun in every ripple along its elevated length before it, too, disappeared. The train, running downhill now and through yet another tunnel, sped along the westerly flanks of the Pennines towards the coastal plain.

On this side the foothills were greener and the few farms clung precariously to the hillsides. Then the land flattened and broadened. Fields, divided by dry stone-walls enclosing sheep and cattle flashed by. There were a couple of small stations before the train arrived at Preston – quite a large railway junction and a town of some size. Here they had to change trains, which caused the family quite a bit of disruption but, eventually, they managed to stow themselves onto the Blackpool train. Mary was surprised that they were again able to secure a compartment to themselves. It looked as if the holiday traffic wasn't yet back to normal.

The journey from Preston was only a short one and after passing through the flat, green landscape of the Fylde, George suddenly shouted, "Look – I can see the Tower!" He jumped up and down by the window in his excitement. "See – over there!"

"Where?" asked his father, moving over to take a look at George's side. Taking hold of the leather strap, he let the window fully down, leaning out his head and getting a lungful of clean, sharp air.

He could now see the famous landmark, looking from this distance like a Meccano toy. Near it stood the Big Wheel, a huge structure, almost as high. Last year he and George had ridden on it, but he wasn't going to repeat the experience! The two structures appeared tiny still, but they grew bigger with every mile until they were blotted out from view as the train reached the outskirts of the town and intervening streets and houses closed in around them.

Nelson Street, where they were staying, was a little further south than Central Station, where the train came to a final stop. From here, the promenade with its trams, was only a short step across the road. Outside the station, parked by the kerb, stood a rank of half-a-dozen landaus – open carriages, each with its beribboned horse. One or two people from off the train were now negotiating with the drivers for fares.

"Look, Mum, can we go in one of them?" asked George, in a loud voice.

"No, we can't. We're going on the tram – it's cheaper." Mary gave her son a shove. "Follow your Dad, and be quiet!"

As they crossed the road towards the tram track, Mary noticed that the shrimp stalls, peep shows and souvenir shops were doing a good trade and strollers on the Central Pier looked like a multi-coloured moving kaleidoscope. As the Boothroyd family stood waiting for the tram, they were already savouring the clean, champagne-like air – a northern vintage, perhaps, but heady, just the same.

Mary tucked her arm happily in her husband's as they sat together on the wooden seats, the children in front so that Mary could keep her eye on George. "I wonder who'll be in at number Fourteen this year?" she asked Joe.

"I don't know, lass, but *we're* going to have a bloody good time here, never mind about anybody else."

"Of course we are, but I can't help wondering if there'll be some nice people in. Mrs. Tomlinson said in her letter that her son, Harry, was coming home from France. Being invalided out, she said. I suppose that nice girl Janet, from next door, will be getting her trousseau ready. They'd just got engaged when we came last year. She showed me her engagement ring. D'you remember?"

"Well, if they make as good a go of it as we have, Mary, lass, they'll not do too bad." Joe squeezed his wife's hand – now in his. He was feeling good now that he had arrived in Blackpool and his holiday was starting. "You've earned this holiday as much as I have, lass, and we're going to see that we both have a bloody good time while we're here."

Chapter Three

Harry Tomlinson had been home from France for just over a month. He was sitting in the July sunshine outside the bay window of Fourteen Nelson Street, in Blackpool, reading the day's newspapers. He was a handsome man, although the rigours of the War had left him lean – even gaunt – in the face. His hair was fair and very fine, with a soft wave in it which fell forward over his deep forehead. This, combined with the light complexion and clean-shaven chin, gave him an air of boyishness. Like his mother and his sister, Maud, he was tall and lanky. His eyes were a very light grey and when his mouth relaxed into a slow smile, they came alive. At the moment, they were concentrated on a newspaper.

He was occupying the ornamental bench under the bay window of the front sitting-room. It was placed there for the benefit of visitors but today, being a Saturday, he had it all to himself. The last week's complement of guests had packed their bags and were well on their way home. His mother and sister were now awaiting the new intake who were due in after mid-day.

The front garden was paved, like all the others in the street. In the corners, one or two wooden tubs held evergreen shrubs. Thick, creamy lace curtains at the windows were draped to reveal a sign which indicated 'Vacancies' and which also displayed a potted aspidistra. Railings divided up the fronts and along the pavement a low brick wall held a wrought-iron gate.

Harry was taking in lungfulls of the ozone, which wafted up from the sea-front just around the corner from the end of the street. He had been one of the lucky ones. The Army doctors had decided that the Blackpool air would be therapeutic and had sent him home quickly from the convalescent home. It was hard for him to believe that he was away from the horrors of the War for good and he harboured a guilty feeling that he should be reporting back to his unit. All that was finished now, though. The doctors had told him that his lungs had been affected by the mustard gas and they couldn't say to what degree. Sometimes, though, breathing was agony and he couldn't stop coughing.

Here at home, he was trying to get used to the soft beds, the good food and the constant attention which surrounded him, day and night. His mother and his sister, for instance, had never stopped waiting on him since he had arrived home. And as for Janet…. Well, he didn't want to try to define exactly how he felt at this moment about his fiancée! During the fighting he had thought about her constantly. Her far-off image had been like a bright beacon in a dark world. But now that the dream of home was realised, he felt disillusioned in some strange way, but he couldn't say why. On that last leave, twelve months ago, when they had become officially engaged, he had been too weary to notice that the young companion he had left behind four years ago had matured into a twenty-year-old woman! Of course, he had always acknowledged that she would make him a wonderful wife, and it had seemed the natural thing to ask her to marry him. When he'd gone away to the War he'd known that she would wait for him – he'd have someone to come back to – to survive for.

The trouble was, thought, now that he *had* come back to her, he wasn't sure exactly how he felt about it…. Oh, to hell with it! Janet was expecting to be married. She had been waiting for him to name the day ever since he had arrived home. What was holding him back, making him use his illness as a delaying tactic? He would have to make the move soon, though, everyone was expecting him to. And she had everything ready!

He became aware of footsteps halting at the gate and he heard the latch being lifted. Glancing up from his paper, he saw a short, broad-shouldered man pushing open the gate. On his head was a cloth cap and his suit was of rough tweed. Under this a matching waistcoat was visible, over a stiffly starched collar. The man was carrying two cheap suitcases which he was manoeuvring through the gateway. Behind him came a woman whom Harry took to be his wife. She was attractively plump and dressed in a blue frock under a grey coat. Under the grey hat, her hair was fair and fluffy.

But it was the third member of the party who captured Harry's full attention. She looked about seventeen, eighteen at the most, and he thought he had never seen such an attractive girl. Her saucy hat, worn at just the right angle, matched the pink dress which showed under the dark coat as she approached. As she walked towards him, she smiled and he noticed that her eyes were a very dark blue – an unusual combination with the black hair. The eyes held his for a moment longer than was strictly necessary before they looked away.

Some emotion deep inside him stirred, but it was fleeting, and the next moment a boy came running up the path. He looked about seven or eight years old. His short trousers had evidently been bought large enough to allow for growth. He was fair and freckled and, like his mother, he had fair, curly hair. As Joe Boothroyd's family moved towards the open front door, Harry stood up, held out his hand and introduced himself. "Welcome to number Fourteen," he said. "I'm Harry Tomlinson. Come on inside and I'll tell Ma you're here."

An hour later, Alice Boothroyd stood at her bedroom window on the first floor of number Fourteen, to the side of the bay. She was gazing down into the street. One or two children were playing on the opposite side of the road in front of houses similar to this one, but she didn't really see them. Her mind was elsewhere, back in Bradfield. She was thinking what a shame it was that she'd had to come away on this particular week, just when she'd been out for the first time with Jimmy Briggs. All the other girls at Foster's Mill had been madly jealous when she'd told them he'd asked her. He was a real heartthrob, was Jimmy!

Of course, she hadn't told her mother she was going out with him. Mary's idea of a suitable young man was David Ollerenshaw, from the ironmonger's shop. Admittedly she had let him take her to the pictures once and he paid for her, as well. But he was so *soppy*! She hadn't gone out with him again. Alice knew that it was Mrs. Ollerenshaw she had to thank for her new pink dress, but she didn't owe David anything! A scornful smile twisted Alice's lips as she pictured his pink, embarrassed face as he'd stammered out an invitation to the pictures. And he hadn't even tried to kiss her! Most of the boys she'd been out with had tried to kiss her almost at once. Jimmy Briggs, for instance, had walked her down Pottery Fields in the warm, dusky twilight, and they had lain on the dusty grass and talked for only a short while before he had suddenly leaned over her, kissing her full on the mouth and putting his hand over her breast.

She had pushed him away, rolling from him and telling him she had to get home. But that had only been the first time and she hadn't wanted him to think she was one of those girls who are 'easy'. When she had told him she couldn't see him again until she came back from Blackpool, he had promised that he wouldn't look at another girl while she was away. Alice wondered, though, whether he was, at this very minute, arranging to meet someone else tonight. The sooner she got back from this holiday, the better!

Lifting up the bottom sash of the window to let in some sea air, she put her elbows on the sill and leaned out. Around the chimney pots of the houses seagulls wheeled and dipped, their raucous cries mingling with the shouts of children playing. On the seat below, Harry Tomlinson had once more stationed himself, paper spread out. The sound of the opening window brought his head round and upwards to meet the gaze of the girl he had admired earlier. He hadn't been wrong in his judgement! Without the hat her hair, smoothly waved and shiny, framed the pale oval of the face. The deep blue eyes were large, and the brows, slightly lifted, gave the face piquancy. The rosy bow of the mouth was beautifully drawn, whether by nature or by art, he couldn't tell. Her arms were bare, slender, but shapely and as she leaned over the sill, the swelling of the breasts beneath the light dress was accentuated. He found he couldn't tear his eyes away and she showed no signs of moving.

"Hallo," she called down.

"Have you settled in, then?" he asked.

"Oh, yes, thanks. I've put all my things away. There's plenty of room in the wardrobe and our George's things haven't taken up much room. He's just gone into Mum and Dad's room to mither them."

"Oh, well," Harry laughed, "I shouldn't think they'll be ready yet for coming down to make tea."

"No. I was wondering whether to have a walk along the Front until they're ready."

"Would you like me to walk with you?" Harry didn't quite know why he had offered.

"Alright, then, I'll just go and tell Mum where I'm going."

As the girl disappeared into the room, Harry asked himself what had possessed him to offer. Was it because he knew that Janet would be fully occupied next door in the preparation of tea? Well, what of it, anyway? He was only showing a friendly interest. After all, the Boothroyds were his mother's paying guests. Whistling, he went into the house to put on his jacket – it could be cool on the promenade – before re-appearing in the doorway to wait for the girl.

Walking along the promenade by her side, he felt lucky to be escorting such a pretty girl. He hadn't missed the admiring glances she elicited from other men as they passed. The tide was fully in and a huge swell was dashing green waves against the sea-wall, sending up plumes of foamy spray. Alice gave a little cry as one of these showers fell beside her. She stepped hastily aside and Harry caught her to him, out of harm's way.

"How silly I am," she laughed a little breathlessly. "I shall have to watch where I'm walking."

He let her go and they sauntered towards the Victoria Pier – the most southerly of the three.

"Have you stayed here before, then?" he asked.

"Oh, yes, we were here for the first time last year. You weren't here, then."

"No, I was in the Army, in France."

"Have you got to go back again?"

"No, I'm home for good, now."

"Oh, I'm glad. We're here for a week, so perhaps we could go for a walk another day?"

"Perhaps we could," he agreed.

He must be quite a bit older than me, Alice decided, as they strolled along the promenade towards the pier, but he wasn't treating her as a child. "I've been working in the mill full-time for two years," she said, wanting to sound grown-up and mature. "I was glad to get into Foster's mill. I never liked school and I'm running six looms now and earning quite good money."

"I wasn't keen on lessons, either," he admitted, "but the arithmetic came in handy later when I started my apprenticeship at the carpentry shop. I expect I shall go back to it when the doctors sign me off."

"Do you make furniture, then?" she asked, interested.

"Yes, I made a dresser for Ma – the one in the dining-room – before I went into the Army."

"Was it very bad, in the War?" Alice asked, looking up into his eyes as he glanced down at her.

"Yes, it was. So bad that I try to forget it, when I can."

"Oh, I'm sorry! I didn't mean to upset you," Alice cried, seizing his arm in her dismay. "If you don't want to talk about it I wouldn't dream of making you."

"Don't worry about it." He was very aware that her arm was now in his. "It might do me good to get some of it off my chest. I don't seem to have been able to talk about it much to anyone before."

They had now reached the entrance to the pier and here they turned, to walk back to Nelson Street, Alice listening intently as he related some of the experiences he'd had. He couldn't understand why he felt so much at ease with this girl. They had only just met and yet, here he was, telling her things he had never told another soul. He couldn't help admiring, too, as he talked, the long curve of the black lashes and the symmetrical sweep of her dark eyebrows as he glanced down at her.

"Goodness, we're nearly back already," she said, as they approached number Fourteen. As they went through the gate he noticed that she withdrew her arm but they were still deep in conversation as they reached the front door and stepped inside.

Setting tables in the dining –room, next door, Janet spied her fiancée as he walked up the path with Alice. She was intrigued to see that he was talking so animatedly. The girl was evidently one of Ellen's visitors and very young, she could see. Perhaps Harry had been showing her around the district? Dear Harry, how caring he was – always so kind and helpful. He was going to be a wonderful husband to her, quiet and gentle as he was by nature. He had never been aggressive or forceful, like some men. Life on the battlefields must have been terrible for him and he had never wanted to tell her about his experiences as a stretcher bearer with the Royal Army Medical Corps.

She wondered, yet again, why he hadn't asked her to fix a definite date for the wedding. His health was improving all the time, so she supposed that when he felt fit enough he would ask her to name the day. Let it be soon, she breathed, as she left the dining room to return to the kitchen for the table napkins.

Over tea in the parlour with his mother, Harry found himself thinking about the walk with Alice, going over what had been said on both sides. Ellen noticed her son's preoccupation, but she didn't comment. She was a straight-backed, angularly-built woman, with handsome features which mirrored Harry's. Her baby-fine, greying hair was severely sculptured into a knot on the back of her head, while her high-necked dress, dark and plain, was set off by a white crocheted lace collar.

Her fine grey eyes were thoughtful as she studied her son's face. He was a grown man now, and she couldn't try to tell him how he should run his life. As a child he had come to her for everything. Maud, his elder sister, had been the self-sufficient one. Was it the War that had created this gulf between them or did this happen to all mothers when their sons grew up? Perhaps if his father had been alive, things would have been different....

How she wished he would marry Janet soon. She found herself unable, though, to ask why he was waiting. Physically he was looking a lot better but she hadn't missed the worried frown which had creased his forehead lately. Oh, well, it was something he would have to work out for himself, she decided, as she asked him if he wanted more tea, getting up to refill the teapot from a large iron kettle singing over the bars of the open range fire.

"No, I think I've had enough, Ma," he replied, absently. "Perhaps I'll go next door for an hour." Why should he have this feeling of guilt? He had merely walked and talked with Alice on a purely social level. All the same, he knew that it wasn't as simple as that....

"Alright," his mother was saying, "if you could just bring in some coal to fill the scuttles before you go?"

"Of course, Ma." He got up, going through the kitchen and out of the back door into the yard. Here stood the coal-house and the tippler lavatory which served the whole of the house.

He shovelled up the gleaming cobs of best trencherbone coal into a bucket, then, leaning over a little with the weight, he hauled the fuel into the house. Filling the parlour scuttle first, he went through into the visitors' dining room. This also served as a front parlour when the tables were cleared. Three sets of tables and chairs filled the space, one placed against the window, the others occupying the centre of the room. Against the back wall, a long hard sofa sporting bright cushions created a splash of colour. The tables were covered by snowy damask tablecloths, each with its polished silver cruet and its vase of fresh roses. On the side wall stood Harry's dresser, which served as a sideboard for crockery and dishes. In the far corner an upright piano held vases and photographs. The air was fresh with ozone from the open window and sweet with the scent of the flowers.

At the table nearest the door a family of four – a couple with two children – were sitting. Joe Boothroyd, sitting with his own family at the window table, had already introduced himself to his fellow-guests. It appeared that the Baileys were also staying for a week. Tea, having just finished, the two families remained at their tables talking and getting to know each other.

As Harry entered the room with the bucket of coal, he glanced across to the window, his eyes holding Alice's before he quickly said, "Ma thought you'd like a fire laying in here. It can get cold later on." Bending, he placed the gleaming cobs on top of the paper and sticks already in the grate before hurrying from the room.

From the window table, Alice Boothroyd smiled. In Harry's eyes she had seen all she needed to know. She turned towards the dresser which he had made during his apprenticeship. Like all the other furniture in the house it was large and solid, the mahogany French-polished to a rich ruby-red shade. Alice couldn't help comparing the quality of Mrs. Tomlinson's furniture with the contents of her own home in Bradfield, where cheapness had been the main consideration when the items had been purchased. In fact, she thought, glancing round at the curtains, the carpets and the sparkling tableware, everything here was of good quality. Even though the contents of her own home were cheap and shabby, Alice could recognise a good thing when she saw it.

She wondered how soon Harry would ask her to go out with him again for another walk. Probably tomorrow, she imagined, smiling at her mother as Mary started gathering up plates and dishes from the table and placing them on a tray, ready to take them into the kitchen for washing-up. "I'll give you a hand with those, Mum," she offered, taking the tray from her mother.

Mary looked hard at her daughter. She usually had to be pressed into doing these little jobs. The Blackpool air must be doing her good already. Before they came away, Mary had suspected that Alice wasn't too keen on coming here for her holiday. She must have been wrong about that because here was her daughter, bright and happy tonight and offering to do the pots. Let's hope this keeps up all week, she thought, as she followed her daughter through into the scullery. Her mind, always on the alert where her children were concerned, slipped into a lower gear as she relaxed her guard in pleasant anticipation of the week's holiday in front of her.

Next door in number Sixteen, Sarah Crossley and her daughter were also in the scullery at the kitchen sink, washing-up.

"Here, let me do that," Janet insisted. "You have a sit-down – you look all-in."

"Yes, dear, I do feel a bit tired. I'll try to get up to bed a bit earlier tonight."

"Yes, you do that, Mother. I'll see to the suppers."

"Thanks Janet. Did you say that Harry is coming round tonight?"

"I don't really know. I expect so. I haven't seen him today, we've been so busy."

Sarah had found it hard this last couple of weeks to restrain herself from asking Harry himself about his marriage plans. She couldn't understand why the couple were waiting. On the other hand, she knew that she should not interfere. It had been a touchy subject between herself and Janet ever since he had come home. Sarah had expected the couple to start planning their wedding soon after his return, or at least set a date. She, too, had seen that Harry was looking better, so what could be delaying it? There didn't seem to be any obvious reason and Janet couldn't give her a proper answer, at all.

Carefully putting crockery into the big cabinet which hung on the kitchen wall, Janet was as puzzled as her mother. She had no more idea than Sarah what was stopping her fiancée from naming the day. She, like her mother, had seen that he wasn't coughing as much and that his colour was better. But, then, it was only July and they had the whole of the summer in front of them. After all, what was a few more weeks when she had already waited four long, weary years?

Going next door later in the evening, Harry found Janet in the back parlour, sewing.

Getting up from the sofa, she came to him, putting her plump arms around his neck and kissing him lightly. "Mother's having a rest for an hour," she said. "Her cold just won't clear up. It seems to have gone onto her chest now and she's been using Friar's Balsam and camphorated oil trying to clear it up. I can't think what else we can do." She pulled him down to sit beside her, moving the sewing-basket out of the way.

"Has she seen the doctor?" Harry asked.

"No, she won't hear of it. She keeps saying it will take its own time, but it keeps dragging on. If it doesn't clear up soon, I shall insist. What have you been doing today, Harry?"

"Nothing much, really." He wondered whether she had, in fact, seen him from the front window, coming up the path with Alice.

"How are you feeling then, dear?" she asked, changing the subject.

"Better. The cough isn't all that bad, now."

"Well then, do you think that we should start to make plans for the wedding? Set the date, perhaps? Even if we decide on a definite date, it will take four weeks for the banns to be read."

Janet hadn't meant to push her fiancée, but some instinctive urge had prompted her to make the first move. She was horrified to find that her face had flushed and that she couldn't meet his eyes.

"Of course, Janet," he said quickly. "I'm feeling a lot better. You go ahead and decide on a date. There's nothing stopping us now that I can see."

"Oh, Harry, I'm so glad you feel well enough to settle on it now. Shall we talk it over, then?" she plunged on, unable to stop herself from following up her advantage.

"It's up to you now, Janet. Make whatever arrangements you want. Women know more about these things than men. I'll fall in with anything you decide."

As he let himself in to number Fourteen, he told himself that he was doing the right thing. Once the wedding date was settled he would be fully committed. He could settle his mind to the fact that his childhood sweetheart, now grown into a woman, would make him a perfect wife in every way. She was kind and affectionate and he knew she loved him dearly. The fact that she had waited patiently all this time proved that. As a woman she was desirable, although he had never gone beyond holding and kissing her. He had tacitly understood that she did not expect more until they were actually married. And she would be a wonderful housewife and mother. Her training next door had guaranteed that. Yet, while the logical part of his mind was telling him all this, he knew in his heart that it wasn't enough.

Kissing his fiancée goodnight, he returned next door to his bed, but he found he couldn't sleep. After some time, he did doze off, only to dream and to re-awaken suddenly. After that, it was no use. He couldn't get off to sleep again. Harry got out of bed and stood by the window, looking out. The moon was obscured by drifting clouds and only a soft circle of light from the gas lamp across the street glowed in the darkness. He could hear the pounding of the sea. In this town the sea was always present – sonorous, never silent – but the streets were quiet. By two o'clock everyone, visitor and native alike, was in bed, asleep. All, that was, but himself, he thought. A face, it seemed, was haunting his dreams – a pale oval face which smiled up at him, a face with deep pools for eyes, wide and wise as a child's.

He reached into the drawer for the bottle of spirits and drank. Wearily getting back into bed, he pulled up the cover. If he slept, he hoped that the dream would recur......

Chapter Four

Although she wasn't feeling at all well, Janet's mother sat, the following morning, over a cup of tea in Ellen Tomlinson's parlour to talk over the good news about the wedding. And about time, too, she was thinking privately! A delicious smell of roasting beef was already filling the back of the house so Ellen was evidently preparing a meal for one of her families. It must be the Baileys because she could see Mrs. Boothroyd now, in the kitchen, getting used to the new gas stove. Ellen, she knew, was used to cooking her joints in the old parlour range, where a whole meal could be cooked with very little attention. A creamy rice pudding, too, was probably sitting on the bottom of the oven, baking slowly with the beef.

"What date is the wedding to be then?" Ellen asked, as she lowered her angular frame into a wooden rocking chair near the fireplace.

"Four weeks on Saturday, according to Janet. Just time to call the banns," Sarah said, with a satisfied smile.

"Is it to be at St. Luke's, then?"

"Oh, yes, with both of them going to the Sunday School there. She's a sensible girl. She wants a small affair, with just the two bridesmaids – our Rose and your Maud. Then the family and one or two friends, and from what she says, Harry agrees with that."

"Well then, we'll have to be thinking about new clothes. I've had my eye on a grey marocain dress and coat in Bartons, knowing I might need something smart soon. I'll have to be looking for a nice hat to go with it."

"Yes," Sarah agreed, "and I shall have to try to get something in town. I don't seem to have had any energy for buying clothes, lately, but I mustn't let Janet down now the date's fixed for a month on Saturday. I've waited so long to see her married to Harry, I must do her proud."

"It's Harry who's the lucky one," Ellen told her. "Janet will settle him down and get him back to his old self – he's seemed so restless since he came home. And there's plenty of room here for them until they get a place of their own."

"Yes," Sarah agreed, "and there's no need for him to be running back to his old job until he's properly fit, when Greenwoods are keeping it open for him. You were wise, Ellen, paying for him to be apprenticed when he left school. With the shortage of skilled carpenters now, I should think he could get a job anywhere."

Coughing painfully, she got up to return to her work in number Sixteen. It had been harder, this last few days, to carry on. Only the news about the wedding had now given her the incentive.

"Harry's taken that Boothroyd girl onto the promenade," Ellen said, as she accompanied her old friend to the door. "He said he was going to show her the Pleasure Beach. She's only a child," she added, as Sarah took her leave.

Harry took hold of Alice's arm as he guided her through the entrance to the Pleasure Beach. As he had returned from the newspaper shop earlier in the morning, she had been standing in the front garden, next door, admiring the flowering shrubs.

"Hallo," he had said, "did you sleep well? It usually takes a day or two to settle in a strange bed."

"Oh, yes, thanks, except for our George snoring in the other bed, but I'm used to that," she had replied.

Harry had laughed, preparing to go back into his own house, yet reluctant to leave her.

Quickly, she had asked him before he could go inside, "Do you know the Pleasure Beach? We went last year, but Dad says we're not going this time. Our George wanted to go on everything and he spent all his holiday pennies. Dad's not giving him the chance, this time."

"Well, it is a big temptation for children," Harry had agreed. "It's a lot cheaper going on the sands with a bucket and spade."

"That's what Mum said, but *I'd* like to go, even if they're not. We're not going out till this afternoon so I could go this morning, if you wanted to take me."

The deep blue eyes had been innocent and appealing and he had told himself that he had nothing to do this morning, anyway, except to read his paper, and that he could do later. Janet would be fully occupied next door until noon, after which she had arranged to take him out for a picnic. A walk with Alice would while away the morning hours, he had decided.

"Alright, just give me a few minutes and I'll be with you," he'd said, his heart beating unevenly as he had walked into the house to put on his jacket.

Now they entered the Pleasure Beach after strolling along the promenade towards the south, chatting companionably,

Harry wondering again why this girl affected him so much. She didn't look much older than a schoolgirl! Why should she have this magical power of lightening his heart and making him feel young again?

They were now walking on sand and, to their left, stood an ornamental rock garden. Beyond this, a rough track made of railway sleepers had been put down to form an entrance road into the Pleasure Beach proper. Alice trod daintily on the weather-beaten logs with Harry's arm supporting her. Now and again, her small feet slipped into one of the grooves between the logs and he had to hold her tight to stop her tripping.

"Oh, dear," she gasped, laughing a little. "I don't seem to be able to keep my feet."

"Don't worry – I won't let you fall."

As he tightened his arm around her waist, she smiled up at him, snuggling closer to his side. The wooden road slanted diagonally to the right across the fairground, flanked on the shore side by the Velvet Coaster. As the cars climbed the high crests and dropped into the dips of the ride, loud shrieks and cries drifted down from the heights. These mingled with all the other noises of the fairground. To their left rose the Bowl Slide, a very fair copy of a lighthouse. Here riders slid down on cocoanut matting into the dark interior. From here, too, cries and laughter issued as people were jostled together inside.

Opposite the Slide were a few cocoanut shies, the stallkeeper giving away fluffy toys and dolls as prizes. Further along, a tent advertised, 'Madame Rosalie – Your Hand Read for 6d.'

"Oh, I'd love to go in to see the gypsy." Alice gazed up at Harry, eyes shining. "I think I'll go and spend 6d. of my holiday money."

"No, I'll treat you," said Harry, smiling, "and while you go in, I'll see if I can win you something on the Rifle Range."

Madame Rosalie had a customer just leaving, so Alice went inside the small booth, with its drawn curtain and sat on a stool, waiting for the fortune-teller to reappear.

Harry wandered across to the Rifle Range, picking up one of the rifles from the heavy wooden counter. The old familiar feel of the stock against his shoulder brought back all the memories he had been pushing away from his mind since he had got back from the War. He lifted the sights, levelling the rifle at a row of metal ducks which were moving across the back of the booth. He fired and one of the birds lay flat as the pellets found their mark. After repeating the successful shot three times, the barker handed him a doll in a cardboard box with a cellophane lid. "You bin' in the Army, mate?" he asked, as Harry accepted the prize.

Tucking the box under his arm, Harry made his way back to the gypsy's tent. Alice was evidently still inside, so stood watching the carefree crowds as they strolled around the fairground, spending their hard-earned money.

There was a movement at the back of the booth before the curtains parted and Madame Rosalie appeared. She was a very old lady, brown and wrinkled as a walnut. Around her head she was wearing the traditional gold filet strung with numerous gold coins which held in place a thin half veil covering the back of her head and shoulders. Two large hoped earrings glinted beneath the filmy stuff of the head-dress. Around her neck, amongst sundry gold chains hung a five-pointed star enclosed within a circle. Tiny and slightly stooped, she moved towards the low table where she sat opposite Alice, gazing intently at her.

"Give me your hand, child," she commanded in a clear, resonant voice. Nervous yet fascinated, Alice held out her own slim young hand, palm upwards and looked into the gypsy's eyes. They were intensely black, yet very bright, in the wrinkled old face. Alice shivered a little as the old woman began to speak.

"You have a very pretty face, my dear. You've had a lot of admirers already and you've had a few kisses from them, but you haven't yet had a lover. You're going to have one very soon, now. I have to tell you that he will only bring you brief happiness, my dear. You must say goodbye to him – he's not the one for you. If you do accept him, you'll have to pay later on. We all have to pay, you know, if we take something we shouldn't have. There is always a price to pay, some day. Perhaps you'll take a chance, though. Young girls always think they know best!

I see a soldier in uniform and he is showing me a wedding ring. Does that mean anything to you?"

"No," replied Alice, bemused.

"Well, you are going to meet someone very soon, if you haven't already met him, and all I can say to you is, turn away! He won't bring you much happiness my dear. Do you live here, or are you on holiday?"

"On holiday,"

"Oh, well, the danger is here, in this town. Perhaps you have a chance of escaping your fate if you can get away soon enough. If you've already met this man, bid him goodbye before it's too late! That's all I can see for you, dear. You can put the silver into my hand now."

Alice placed the 6d. piece in the gypsy's heavily-veined hand. What had she been talking about? Getting up from the stool, she lifted the curtain and stepped outside.

The din of the fairground closed around her and she saw Harry there, waiting outside. How could she have been so stupid? Her mind hadn't really registered all that the old woman had been saying. The eyes had had an hypnotic effect, but now she remembered that she had something about a soldier. Did she mean Harry? And what had she said about a wedding ring?

Harry smiled as he joined her, saying, "I've won this for you. Do you like it?"

He handed her the cardboard box and Alice promptly forgot everything the old woman had said as she took hold of it, lifting the transparent lid. "Oh, what a beautiful doll," she exclaimed, eyes round with delight. "It's got a lovely dress on and proper little shoes to match. I'll stand it up on the dressing-table when I get back. You must be very clever to win it."

"Not really," Harry laughed. "Just a good shot, that's all."

"Well, I think you're clever, anyway.

"Alright, if you say so." Harry felt a rush of pleasure – a sensation he hadn't felt for a very long time. "And what did Madame Rosalie have to tell you?" he asked, amused that she should believe in such things as predictions.

"Oh, nothing, really. She said I should get away from here, but that's silly. I've only just come, and I'm just beginning to enjoy myself." She looked up at him with a pleased smile. "The rest was just rubbish. Anyway, it's gone now – I can't remember." Dismissing the prophecy from her mind, she tucked her arm into Harry's, the cardboard box under the other.

Escorting Alice through the clamour of the Pleasure Beach, the realisation came to Harry that he too was enjoying himself – he was happy, when he had thought happiness was a thing of the past – something he had left behind when he had set off, a naïve young boy, for the War. But he was also coming to terms with the fact that his light-heartedness was induced by the presence of this slip of a girl.

He glanced down at her flushed, smiling face and his arm tightened on hers.

Sunday dinner was in progress in both houses when Alice walked into number Fourteen. The Bailey family were being served their meal by Maud, Harry's sister. A little older than her brother, Maud was still a spinster. Tall and angular like her mother, yet not as handsome, Maud had a plain, raw-boned face, the nose too big and the eyes too small. She had none of that feminine appeal necessary for the marriage stakes, and she knew it. Resigned to her role in the boarding house, she performed her work efficiently but with an air of general sufferance. The only man she cared for was her brother. She wanted to see him happy and she felt that it wasn't just his health now that was troubling him. He'd had a restless air about him ever since he had come home but, surely, once he was married he would settle down here and pick up the threads of his life again.

Maud considered that Janet, his bride-to-be, had all the virtues any man could wish for in a wife. Harry couldn't do better than Janet and she herself was looking forward to having her for a sister-in-law. Even though she had lived next door for so long, Janet hadn't been a close friend of Maud's. She seemed to confide more in Ellen, Harry's mother, but Maud was sure that when the couple were living as part of the Tomlinson household her relationship with Janet would be closer.

As she served vegetables to the Baileys, Maud speculated on what colour of dress Janet would want her to wear as her bridesmaid. The wedding would be a high spot in all their lives, especially her own, and she was going to make the very most of it!

In the kitchen, stationed in front of the new gas stove, Mary Boothroyd had just returned from serving her depleted family a first course of fluffy Yorkshire pudding. It was covered with rich gravy from the beef she had cooked and it was one of Joe's favourites. She was just ready to take out of the oven a dish of golden-brown potatoes and the tender joint of meat. These she now placed on a tray, together with a tureen of vegetables, ready to carry into the dining room. Alice walked happily into the kitchen, still clutching the doll in its box and offered to help her mother carry in the food.

"You're a bit late, aren't you?" You nearly missed your dinner." Mary didn't hide her annoyance. "And don't you think you're seeing a bit too much of that young man?" He's being married soon, you know. I heard them talking about it earlier this morning – Janet's mother and Mrs. Tomlinson."

"Well, he likes me, Mum, and look – he won me a doll on the Pleasure Beach."

"Very nice, I'm sure, but I shouldn't think Janet would be very pleased about you going out with him while she's working," said Mary.

"Why should she mind? It's only for company. He only took me on the Pleasure Beach and won me a doll."

"Well, they're going out together this afternoon, anyway," said Mary. "Janet was in here before you came back, talking to his mother, telling her that she's taking him out for a picnic. They're going to Fairhaven Lake, at Lytham."

"Alright, Mum, I don't want to upset anyone, but I think he's at a loose end, sitting there on his own, with everybody else working. He doesn't seem to have many friends coming to the house that I've seen."

"Well, it's not your place to keep him company," Mary told Alice firmly, carrying the tray out of the kitchen.

"No, Mum," replied Alice meekly, trailing after her mother and through into the dining room, as Maud came out with the Bailey's used dinner plates. As Maud passed Alice she glanced briefly at the girl, who was still clutching the doll in its box. Maud barely managed to hide her disdain. She's as empty-headed as that doll she's carrying, Maud thought. She had learned though, through years of waiting on visitors, that they must all be treated as welcome guests, some more welcome than others, of course. Maud was glad that she wasn't having to serve at the Boothroyd's table. Having to wait on the Baileys was bad enough, he was only a self-made plumber, but the Boothroyds made no pretence at all at refinement. The girl was attractive to men, no doubt. If she were the girl's mother, she would be keeping a very sharp eye on that one! Her lips drawn tightly together, Maud deposited the dirty dishes by the sink and turned to remove the steamed jam pudding from its basin. It had been boiling slowly for a couple of hours, so it should be just ready.

Dismissing Alice and the Boothroyds from her mind as of no possible consequence to her, Maud got on with her work.

Chapter Five

True to her word, Janet had taken Harry out for a picnic in the afternoon to Fairhaven Lake, at Lytham, just along the coast. A picnic basket was open by her side as they sat on a plaid blanket, spread on the springy grass. As she laid out the daintily prepared sandwiches, sultana buns and lemonade jug on a spotless green and white checked cloth, she thought that Harry seemed a little preoccupied but now that the wedding date was settled, he probably had a lot on his mind. She, too, had been deep in thought about her wedding plans. She had decided to have her dress and coat made by Miss Walker, who had sewn for her before. Miss Walker would also make Rose's dress. Janet had decided that lilac would suit her sister very well. Rose's colouring was very much like her own and she would be able to wear the dress afterwards for Sunday best. Her own dress was to be amethyst, and Maud's a very pretty shade of mauve crepe. With Maud's mousy-fair hair and rather colourless appearance, she knew it would be more flattering than the fawns and browns she usually wore.

Janet had explained to Miss Walker that she wanted something quite plain and she felt that her new grey shoes would do perfectly well if she managed to find a hat to match them. She had put the church arrangements in hand at St. Luke's, the guest list was nearly complete and the wedding breakfast at the Co-operative Rooms was going ahead.

Passing across a plate of sandwiches to Harry, who took one absently, she asked him, "What are you thinking about, dear?"

"Oh, nothing special."

Why did he feel so guilty? He couldn't stop his mind from dwelling on the morning's excursion with Alice and he was finding it hard to concentrate on what Janet was saying.

"I know we have a lot to decide," he heard her say, "but don't worry, everything will be alright."

Of course it would be alright! Everything she did would be perfectly planned and executed – but – was it what he wanted, anyway? He knew that something was very wrong about the whole situation. Something very important was missing between them and she seemed to have no inkling of the way he was feeling about her. She was happily going on, making all these arrangements when he was unsure about the whole thing. But what could he do when he had committed himself irrevocably to the wedding? An overwhelming wave of guilt and despair made him exclaim, "I wish it was all over and done with."

"Oh, Harry, I'm sorry. I should have realised that you wouldn't want to bother with all these arrangements I've been making. Don't worry about a thing, dear. All you'll have to do is turn up for the ceremony," she laughed. "You can leave everything else to me."

As she spoke, Harry's chaotic thoughts crystallised into a firm decision. He knew what he had to do.

"Would you like some more lemonade before we walk round the gardens?" she asked him, unstoppering the jug.

"If you like."

It didn't matter whether the thing was right or wrong. He knew he had to do it and do it soon, no matter what anyone else thought. But he needed the right opportunity. He couldn't tell her now, while she was so full of all these plans for the wedding. And yet, wouldn't it be better to let her know straight away before she made any more arrangements?

Taking the basket from her after she had packed everything tidily away, he followed as she led the way round the edge of the lake in the direction of the rose gardens, meaning to speak to her but not managing to find the right words.

For her part, Janet was happy to think that Harry, although very quiet, seemed satisfied with the way she was forwarding their plans. He appeared thoughtful but, like most other men, he must be feeling a bit tense now that the big day was approaching. She must remember that and make allowances. She herself had had a few nervous flutters whenever she thought about making her vows. It would be the most important moment in both their lives and she herself was not going into marriage lightly. It was a lifetime commitment as far as she was concerned and she had no reason to think that Harry felt any differently about it. Her spirits rose as she told herself that in another month she would be Mrs. Harry Tomlinson and that all her rosy daydreams would have come true.

It was just gone six-thirty as Alice Boothroyd sat by the dining-room window in number Fourteen, watching the front gate. Half-an-hour earlier she had seen Harry's mother and sister, dressed in their Sunday clothes, depart for the church. The rest of Alice's family had gone out onto the promenade after tea but Alice had made an excuse. She had told her mother she had a headache and would go up to her room to lie down. Except for the Baileys, who had gone upstairs to put the children to bed, she was alone in the house.

Watching the sun sinking slowly behind the houses opposite, she waited. Harry must come back from the park soon – he must! Her heart thumped wildly as they came into view, walking along by the wall of number Sixteen and she saw them stop by the gate, Harry handing over the picnic basket to his fiancée. So, he wasn't going into the house with Janet! Alert for the moment he entered his own door, she got up swiftly from the window seat as she heard the lobby door open. In a flash she was through the dining room managing to bump right into him as he stepped into the lobby.

"Oh, you gave me a surprise," she cried, as his arm came around her to steady her. His eyes looked directly into hers before he pulled her to him. Putting her own slender arms around his neck, she closed her eyes for his kiss. The strength and passion of it took her by surprise. His lips closed over hers and stayed there. She found she could scarcely breathe and yet she didn't want him to stop. She was gasping when he let her go.

"I'm sorry," he said, regarding her intently.

"No, you're not – you wanted to kiss me!" She was breathing hard.

"Alright, then, I did. What are we going to do about it?"

"Well, we can't talk here. The Baileys are putting the children to bed but they could come down again any time. Everyone else has gone out."

"Walk quietly past their door, then. We'll go up to the attic. Their room's too near mine," he added.

Harry walked ahead, up the softly-carpeted stairs, Alice following on tip-toe. Passing the Bailey's closed door they could hear Lily Bailey reading to the children but no other sound so it looked as if they were already going off to sleep.

Harry led the way until they reached the steps which led up to the attic. The door was kept unlocked and it gave noiselessly and easily to his touch. She crept inside after him, her eyes widening as she looked around at the collection of miscellaneous bric-a-brac and surplus furniture. There were several spare mattresses on the floor, over by the wall, one above the other. Leading her over to them, he pulled her down beside him onto the softness of the flocks.

He kissed her tenderly this time and her response was instant. His hands sought her breasts under the thin stuff of her dress and he caressed them gently, not wanting to upset her. Then his tongue insinuated itself between her small, white teeth. He felt her stiffen for a moment but the next second she relaxed in his arms and became responsive under his hands. Her body moved to meet his and he knew that he would have to restrain himself. This was not the time – not yet.

She was clinging to him, returning kiss for kiss. He could not stop his hands from moving down to her thighs. Above her stockings, his hands caressed the firm, smooth flesh before moving up to her groin under the flimsy cotton underwear. She gave a little cry as his searching fingers found the sensitive area, but soon she began to respond to the slow, stroking movements and her body arched in enjoyment.

He was surprised at the strength of his own response. What would it be like to be inside her then? He wondered whether she was a virgin and whether this was her first experience of love-making. He had never made love to Janet although he'd had several women in France, mostly professionals. Janet had never encouraged him to touch her much and he had respected her feeling that the marriage bed was the right place for making love. Alice, then, had no such inhibiting scruples, but he meant to treat her with respect, as well as with love. In spite of his strong erection and the demands his body was making, he managed to restrain himself from trying to enter her.

She opened her eyes, looking up at him in wonder. This was quite different from anything she had experienced with the local boys back at home. They had often kissed her and one or two of them had gone further than that. She had allowed it because she was still curious about sex. She had wanted to find out what it was like, but she hadn't felt much pleasure in the kind of furtive groping they had wanted to indulge in and she had never allowed anyone to have actual intercourse with her.

There hadn't been anyone who had really aroused her sexually until now. Now, Johnny Briggs and the others faded from her mind, as if they had never existed. Lying here with Harry, a wonderful new world had opened up for her. She felt as if, for the first time, her body had come alive. It had been Harry's touch which had aroused in her these feelings of intense pleasure. His lips had awakened desire. She had not known that she was capable of such a response.

Kissing her gently again, he whispered, "Let's just stay here together for a while before we go down," and she snuggled up to him like a child, putting her head on his shoulder, as his lips caressed her hair.

"I love you, Alice," he said. "I've only just met you, but I knew the moment you walked up our path that this would happen. Do you feel the same?"

"Oh, yes, I do, Harry."

"My little love," he breathed softly, as he cradled her in his arms and she sighed with contentment.

"What about Janet?" she asked him, at last.

"Let's not talk about Janet just now. Let's make the most of being here – Just the two of us."

His lips moved hungrily over her mouth again, preventing her from answering and she instantly responded. It was as if every touch, every kiss, lit a little flame which ran exquisitely along her nerves, bringing her whole body alive with tingling pleasure. She gave herself up completely to the overwhelming enjoyment of his hardness against her body, his hands on her thighs, and she forgot the things she had been going to ask him about Janet, about everything. Nothing seemed to matter except being here, with Harry.

The street below was quiet, the sun sinking low and, noticing the quality of the light, Harry whispered that they must go downstairs before they were discovered. The others would surely be returning soon. They clung together for a long moment before leaving the security of the attic and he kissed her again, murmuring, "Until tomorrow, my little love."

There was stillness in the Bailey's room as they slipped past, hand-in-hand. On the landing they clung together before parting, she to go to her bedroom and he to seek the emptiness of the back parlour, there to sort out his turbulent thoughts and feelings.

It's not like Alice to be complaining about headaches, Mary Boothroyd was thinking as she came in a little while later with her husband and son. They had enjoyed a pleasant walk along the promenade and George had behaved himself. The clean, strong air, combined with the running about he had done during the day, seemed to have tired him out at last, and he was ready for bed.

"How's your headache?" Mary asked, as she poured water from the flowered jug on the wash-stand into the bowl. She dipped a flannel into it, soaping it liberally before handing it to her son, reminding him to include his ears in the washing. "I thought you might be in bed when we came back. There's not much point in your getting up now." Mary, noticing her daughter's flushed face and over-bright eyes, added, "I hope you're not sickening for something. Are you feeling alright?"

"Of course I am, Mum, I feel much better now." Alice raised herself from the pillow and swung her legs down from the bed. "I do love Blackpool and I wish we could stay here forever," she announced.

"Well we can't love, much as we'd like to, your Dad's got to go back to work next week, and so have you."

What's got into the girl, Mary wondered? There was something here she couldn't quite put her finger on and there wasn't much that Mary missed where her children were concerned. "Go and put the kettle on love, if you're feeling better, while I see to our George. He'll never get into bed at this rate."

"Alright, Mum." Alice jumped to her feet and ran downstairs as lightly as a young gazelle.

Well, thought Mary, there's nothing much wrong with her now! One minute she's wanting to go and lie down and the next running about full of energy! Had she herself been like this at seventeen? That time seemed so long ago that she couldn't remember. It seemed now that she had been lucky. She was happily married, with a home and two children, one of them grown up and nearly ready herself for marriage. Joe had proved to be everything that a woman could want in a man. He had been a good provider, a faithful lover and a caring father. Perhaps he did shout a bit if things didn't suit him, but Mary couldn't imagine life now without Joe and she knew he felt the same way about her. She wanted for Alice someone who would have the same qualities, but there was plenty of time. Alice was very young yet, much too young to be thinking about a husband, in Mary's opinion.

Early the following day, Ellen asked her son if he would make the journey up the coast to Fleetwood. The Blackpool landladies were fortunate in having the small fishing port right on their doorsteps. Ellen had fish delivered from the fish-market there once a week.

"It's not good enough," she said. "The catch comes in every day so there's no excuse. This last couple of weeks I haven't been satisfied at all." Ellen prided herself on her catering, insisting on the freshest meat and fish available.

His mother had asked him to bring her several items from the market there as well as a couple of things from shops in the town. The tram track had recently been extended to run all the way up to the port so Harry travelled on the 'toast rack' as these open, single-decker trams were known locally. Once en route he knew he would be committed for the day. As his ticket was punched, Harry resigned himself to the fact that it would be teatime before he returned. After that, Janet would expect him to call on her in the evening for more discussions about the wedding arrangements. Why couldn't he tell her straight that it was no use, he couldn't go through with it? He should have stopped her from making all these plans. It wasn't fair to her to let her go on thinking that everything was alright.

As he sat on the slow-moving tram he cursed himself for not telling her then and there, on the picnic, that he couldn't marry her, after all. He didn't want to hurt her – he didn't want to hurt anybody – but it was no use, how could he go through with it when he loved another girl? Because he knew now that he did love Alice with his whole being. He had never felt like this about Janet, but how could he explain it to her? He could visualise her shocked, incredulous face, hear her tearful protests. And it wasn't just Janet. Both of their families were preparing for the wedding. His mother would be devastated. The repercussions were too awful to contemplate. He couldn't do it – not today, anyway!

Arriving back at Nelson Street later in the day, laden with his purchases, he made excuses to check the coal scuttles in the dining-room, but it was empty, the visitors having all eaten and gone out. After his own meal, delaying the moment he would have to go in to Janet, he was, after all, spared the effort. He had only been upstairs a few moments when there was a tapping on his bedroom door and his mother's voice called to him, "Can you come down, Harry? Janet's here to see us."

"Of course, right away," he said, wondering what had prompted this visit. His guilty mind jumped straight away to the conclusion that she suspected something but he told himself not to be a fool. She couldn't! No one but he and Alice knew about the attic. Perhaps it was some detail about the wedding arrangements? Hell! He must scrape up the courage to tell her soon. He couldn't go on deceiving her like this.

She was standing in the parlour looking pale and anxious. A worried frown appeared between her green eyes and she came to him, taking his hand and speaking quickly. "Oh, Harry, I'm so worried. I've just been telling your mother and Maud about it. We thought that Mother just had a very bad cold. You know that she hasn't been well for the last week or so. Today, though, just after tea, her legs seemed to give way and she fell onto the kitchen floor. Dad and I managed to get her up to bed right away and we sent for Dr. Fraser. She wouldn't let us before. He says the fall hasn't really hurt her, but he says she must stay in bed for at least a week. She told him that she was aching all over and that she felt awful." Her troubled eyes met his. "It's so unlike her to be ill." Her lips were trembling.

"You should have come for me." Harry said.

"No, it's alright, dear. Dad was in and we managed to get her upstairs between us."

"Robert must be worried," Ellen said, "I can't remember Sarah going down like this before."

"No, she's had such good health," Janet said. "Dad's staying with her. He won't go in to work tomorrow. He's going to wait and see how she goes on."

"I'll come round right away," Ellen offered. "Don't worry, dear, we'll work something out between us, doing the jobs. You're going to be busy looking after your mother for the next week."

"Thank you. Ellen, you're very good." Turning back to Harry, Janet said, "It looks as if I shalln't be seeing much of you for a few days. I'll pop in when I can. Don't come in to see her yourself. It wouldn't do for you to catch this flu or whatever it is Mother's got when you're feeling so much better yourself."

He nodded mutely, so that she wouldn't see the relief he felt. He wouldn't have to go in there for a few days! He wouldn't have to keep up the pretence of co-operating with the wedding arrangements!

Upon this thought came another. He would now have more opportunity of seeing Alice! With Janet and his mother fully occupied next door, and Maud supervising here at number Fourteen, they wouldn't have time to notice his own comings and goings!

Janet left very soon for next door, accompanied by his mother, Maud deciding to go through into the kitchen to check on requirements for the following day's menus. He was left alone in the parlour with only the solemn ticking of the grandfather clock to disturb his thoughts. It was quite plain that he was not going to see his love this evening. He would have to be content with working something out for the following day.

At the moment when Harry was thinking things out, Alice was walking along the Victoria Pier against a light evening breeze. She was with her family, George and Joe well ahead. Joe was doing his best to stop his son from running off to look at the swivel telescopes, the peep show machines and the rock stalls which abounded on the pier. Swinging along behind his son, happy and relaxed, Joe was enjoying his holiday. A week wasn't long but it was better than nothing. Working long hours in the foundry, he had thought that it would never come. He had on his best trousers, worn low over his slim hips because he flatly refused to wear braces, preferring a leather belt. The day having been quite warm, he had left his jacket in the wardrobe and had rolled up his shirt-sleeves. The stiff collar, too, had been abandoned for the duration of the holiday. He might be persuaded to wear it going home, but now he was letting the breeze play over his deep chest where he had unbuttoned the neck of his shirt.

Foundry work was hard and dirty but it was the only thing he had done since he'd left school at fourteen and been apprenticed there. It was a man's job and no namby-pamby could do it. Joe prided himself on his toughness and stamina. Looking at his son, though, he doubted whether George would follow him into the work – the boy was too much like his mother. In George he couldn't see that hard, tough streak he himself had inherited from his own father, a coal miner. Well, the foundry was better than the pit, so why shouldn't his own son go one better than he had? Wasn't that, after all, one of the things he was working for? His son deserved a better chance in life than either he, or his father, had had. By all accounts, George was showing promise at school. Alice, now, had never made any pretence at learning, but then she didn't need to. In Joe's opinion girls were wasting their time at school, especially those as pretty as Alice.

He caught up with George, who had spotted another moving picture machine and was jumping up, trying to see through the viewer. It was no use, he wasn't tall enough. Joe took a penny and let it drop into the slot provided, stooping and putting his eye to the viewer. Pictures of scantily-clad ladies in frilly underwear flickered by on the small screen until the machine clicked and then stopped.

"Lift me up, Dad," George shouted, at his elbow.

"Sorry son, it wasn't working properly."

"C'n I have some rock, then?" George looked hopefully at his father as he spotted a rock stall ahead.

"You can have a penny one and that's the last thing you're having today. And don't chomp it all up at once. Suck it slowly, then it will last."

Strolling behind her husband and son, Mary was asking her daughter, "What's the matter with you, Alice. You've been very quiet all day and you didn't want much tea, either."

"I wish you wouldn't go on about it, Mum. There's nothing wrong with me."

"Well then, try to look as if you're enjoying yourself. That's what we've come here for. Yesterday you said you wanted to live here. What's changed your mind?"

"I haven't changed my mind. I just didn't want to come out tonight, that's all."

"Don't be silly, the walk and the fresh air will do you good. You've been moping about all afternoon."

Alice didn't answer her mother because hot tears were pricking her eyes. She had by now accepted that she wasn't going to see Harry today after all. That hour in the attic had been the only thing in her mind all day. She had been constantly reliving every second of it. She could still feel his lips on hers and his hands on her body. Warm desire arose in her and the only thing she wanted was to be with him again. The afternoon had dragged on and on and she only hoped and prayed that she might see him this evening. She was resigned now, though, to waiting until tomorrow – it was too late now.

Eventually they reached the end of the pier where they caught up with the other two. Here, anglers sat, their hunched shoulders and long fishing lines etched in silhouette against the red and gold of another glorious sunset. As they turned to walk back, Alice was praying, 'Tomorrow come quickly – *please* come quickly.……'

On his way up to bed, Harry paused at Alice's bedroom door. It took great strength of will not to open it and go softly in but he dare not risk George being awake. Bending, he pushed an envelope through the narrow gap beneath the door and tapped lightly before passing on to his own room at the back of the house.

As he had guessed, Alice had been lying awake, unable to sleep. It was as if she couldn't stop thinking of him. His hands, his body, his face filled all of her mind and she could still hear him telling her that he loved her. Something must have stopped him from seeing her today, it must! If he felt like she did, nothing could have stopped him from making the opportunity.

She had to admit that it was difficult with the house full of visitors. And then, of course, there was Janet. But she mustn't think about Janet until Harry told her what he was going to do about her. Oh, it was no use! She must try to be patient and wait for tomorrow and the sooner she got to sleep, the sooner it would come.

A gentle tapping on the door brought her upright in bed and when she looked, she saw that something white had been pushed through, underneath. In a moment, she was out of bed. There was no danger from George, he had been asleep for hours. Snatching up the envelope, she whipped open the door but the landing was empty. Closing it again, she went to sit at the dressing table, where a lazy night-light flickered. Excitement mounting, she held the envelope beneath the yellow pool of light. Taking out the letter, she read, 'My little love, I haven't been able to see you today but you have been in my thoughts the whole time. Try to meet me at the entrance to the South Pier at two o'clock tomorrow. I love you, Harry.'

Alice raised the notepaper to her lips against the signature. There was no question of merely trying. Nothing would stop her from being at the South Pier tomorrow, if she had to die in the attempt.

Chapter Six

After their mid-day meal, the Boothroyds and the Baileys were relaxing and talking outside number Fourteen. The seating had been augmented by two brightly coloured deck chairs which were occupied by Joe Boothroyd and Tom Bailey. The two women were sitting on the garden seats, Mary with her knitting, and outside in the street, George was kicking a ball about with the two Bailey children. Alice stepped through the front door in a pretty cotton dress, ready to go out. Mary looked up at her in surprise.

"All dressed up and nowhere to go?" she asked, laughing.

Alice came round to join them on the seat. "Oh, I thought I'd go for a walk along the Front to settle my dinner." She avoided her mother's eyes.

"Well, we haven't decided yet what we're doing. We may even stay here this afternoon. It's lovely here sitting in the sun and once you get comfortable, you just don't want to move."

The Baileys murmured in agreement.

"You run along, then," Mary said. "A bit of exercise will do you good. You're a lot younger than us old fogeys."

General laughter greeted this remark and Alice, blushing, stood up to take her leave, promising her mother that she would be back in plenty of time for tea.

"She's a good girl," Mary told Lily Bailey, as Alice swung off in the direction of the promenade. "I've never had a moment's worry over her, you know."

"You're lucky, then," said Lily. "With some of these young girls, you never know what they're going to get up to."

Quickening her pace, Alice sped along the promenade towards the Pier. Her heart was as light as her step, her small feet hardly seeming to touch the ground. It had been so easy! Her heart was bumping painfully and she had a stitch in her side when she spied him, waiting by the pier entrance. He saw her at the same instant, and came hurrying towards her, drawing her close to him before they turned towards the steps leading down from the promenade to the sands below. Today, the tide was far out. Great swathes of dark gold sand stretched away to a creamy line of waves which rolled slowly in over the wet, shining shoreline. Thin bands of glittering water broke up the sand into banks, where one or two figures in waders were shrimping with nets and buckets.

Under the promenade, on the light, dry sand of the beach, the couple picked their way through rows of bathing huts which were full of people changing into swimming costumes. Soon, though, they were trudging through damper sand, past children making sandcastles with buckets and spades. Bare-chested youths were wrestling or playing cricket with rubber balls, before they left behind the crowded beach, walking towards the sea, the sand becoming firmer and wetter as they walked. When they reached a stretch of shallow, shimmering water, they turned and walked along its edge. Here they left the clear imprints on their shoes in the soft, damp sand as they stepped out towards the south and Squires Gate.

They passed along the shore in an enchanted silence. The only sounds were the cries of seabirds as they dipped and swooped over the water and the ever-present muffled roar as the sea rolled towards them in long, shallow waves. Now and again they stopped to kiss and when they resumed their journey there was renewed urgency.

They were heading for the curve of the estuary, where the firm sand gave way to high dunes. The coarse sand had been deposited here by the high tides, and sculpted into hollows and hills by high winds over the years. It was far from the hub of the resort as this part of the coast had not yet been developed. Apart from a gypsy encampment, it appeared deserted. The dunes covered a large area and the Romany settlement occupied only a small space before the sandhills rolled on as far as Lytham, further south.

The Romanies had no caravans, only ramshackle huts which they had cobbled together. Walking past the shacks, Alice glanced timidly at the swarthy occupants as they sat outside on logs or barrels, whittling away at pegs or just staring curiously as they passed. A few healthy-looking, if ragged, children ran about on the beach with their dogs, and the women's washing was stretched out across the scanty grass of the hillocks to dry.

Hurrying now, the couple left behind the camp and picked their way up the sloping sandhills between the clumps of sparse grasses. There were deep troughs between the hillocks and they found a small hollow, away from the shore. There was no one about and Harry helped Alice down into the little valley, spreading his jacket on the sand. They flopped down onto it and the next moment his arms were around her and his lips were covering her mouth, her eyes, her throat. He slid her dress down over her white shoulder, exposing the firm, rounded breast, gently cupping the soft flesh with his hand and caressing the proud nipple, before his mouth came down over it. She twisted towards him, pressing herself against his body. She could feel his erection and her small hand tentatively touched his thigh, bringing her, deep down, a sweet, strong surge of desire. Her deft little fingers found the obstructing buttons and then her cool, soft palm touched his skin.

He moved now, convulsively, his hands sliding down to her groin and, finding no hindrance in her flimsy underwear, he moved his body over hers. In spite of his earlier resolve, the impulse to penetrate her was absolutely overwhelming, and he couldn't stop himself. As he tried to enter her, she cried out a little, and he knew that he had been right about her being a virgin. But he couldn't have stopped himself at this moment if he had tried. Then he felt her arms grasp him around the buttocks, pulling him into her with eager movements of her hips. The next moment, he felt himself deep inside her, and her cries had changed to small gasps of pleasure as he began to move within her. His climax came quickly and powerfully and he knew that it had been too soon for her to have any satisfaction but he had been unable to hold back. Now, they lay in each other's arms, she seeming quite content and he intoxicated by the feeling she had aroused in him.

"I'm sorry, sweetheart, I didn't mean it to happen but I just couldn't stop myself," he whispered. "Is it the first time for you?"

"Oh, yes, Harry. I've never felt like that before with anyone and I didn't want you to stop. I love you so much."

"My little darling! I love you, too – I can't tell you how much. Do you think you could meet me again tomorrow?" He kissed her mouth tenderly "Could you get away?"

She clung to him before answering. "Oh, I must, Harry. I've just got to see you again tomorrow. We mustn't waste a minute of the time we've got left."

And on the following day, Alice was again lucky. After much cajoling, George had persuaded his reluctant mum and dad to take him into the Tower to see the Menagerie and the Aquarium and they were going to make it an afternoon excursion. Alice told her mother, "I'd rather have a bit of fresh air, Mum. I don't feel like being cooped up in a smelly zoo on a nice day like this."

"Alright, love," Mary agreed. "You look much more cheerful today. All this fresh air and walking must be doing you good. We'll see you when we get back at teatime.

Harry was waiting when she reached the pier and, once more, they made their way to the dunes, stopping several times on the way to kiss and hold each other. Eventually, they reached their hideaway and soon they were concealed in the shelter of the sandhills. He folded himself around her, loosening her clothes, kissing and stroking her smooth, white body. He had determined that this time, she, too, would be satisfied. As he entered her, she pulled him closer with small eager hands, lifting her hips to meet his demanding body. By a great effort he managed to hold himself back until he felt her strong pulsating movements suddenly slacken and he heard her cry out, "Harry, oh, Harry!" She collapsed under him and he felt himself released into her in a quick surge of pleasure and joy.

"My little love," he breathed, cradling her dark head with his arms and looking down on her wondering face.

"Oh, Harry, I didn't think... I didn't know, it could be like that!"

"No, love, I know, but it's going to be like that for us whenever we're together. Now we've found each other, we're not going to be apart for long."

"We haven't much time left, have we?" she reminded him. "We've got to go home on Saturday."

"Let's not think about it. Let's just lie here together and forget we've got to part for a while at the weekend." He kissed her trembling mouth before she could answer, stifling any doubts she might have had about what was going to happen when she went home.

She lay with him, savouring the passing moments, telling herself that she shouldn't worry too much about the uncertainties of the future but should make the most of what was happening to her now.

Coming back into number Fourteen separately from Harry, who entered his home by the back way, Alice's luck still held. Her family had not yet returned from their outing when she came into the house. She went straight upstairs to try to compose herself before facing her mother's ever-sharp eyes. She was wondering how she was going to contrive her next meeting with Harry and she was, at the same time, going over every second of the afternoon's idyll. She still found it hard to believe that her body could behave in this abandoned way. She had never felt this way before with anyone. Only Harry had aroused this response, this passionate enjoyment of his kiss, this craving for his body and now this surging fulfilment and the contented joy.

When Mary came into the house soon afterwards, she was pleased to see Alice in the kitchen making herself useful preparing the tea. Her daughter was not an enthusiastic cook and she didn't much care for domestic chores, either. Mary had tried to teach her all she could, knowing that the girl would some day have to run a home of her own. Alice had not yet had a regular young man but Mary knew that such an attractive girl would have no difficulty in finding a husband. Seventeen, though, was far too young, in Mary's opinion, for settling down to a home and family. She wanted her daughter to have a few years of carefree youth before she saw her married to some nice young man with a steady job, like her father.

"Did you enjoy your walk, love?" Mary asked, noticing Alice's radiant face and glowing skin.

Alice's face flushed a bright scarlet, in spite of herself, so she turned quickly round to the dresser, where the cutlery was kept. "Yes, I did, I went as far as Squires Gate." It wasn't really a lie.

Mary bustled round getting out the bread and butter. "I thought we would all go up to Fleetwood tomorrow," she said. "I want to see what they have on the Market there and I'll buy you that material I promised you for your new dress."

Alice dropped the knife she was holding with a clatter. Hastily retrieving it, she said, "Do I have to go? I think I'd rather stay here and just sit around tomorrow. I might go on the beach and put my bathing-costume on – I haven't had it on yet. I'll have a deckchair for the afternoon. You pick some material for me. You know what I like."

Mary looked sharply at her daughter. Normally she was very choosey about the material for her clothes. What had got into her now? "Well, if you don't want to go with us...."

"It's not that, Mum," Alice said, desperately. "I just want to have a rest tomorrow and I haven't been on the beach yet. There's only today and tomorrow left before we go home." The downright lies didn't seem to matter, as long as her mother agreed.

"Alright, if you want to go on the beach, but mind you don't get too much sun. You know what your skin's like. I'll try to get you some nice material on the Market."

"Thanks, Mum."

"But mind," warned Mary, "you're coming with us tomorrow – that's our last day. We're all going out together, no matter where we go."

And with that, Alice had to be satisfied. She knew that this might be her last chance of a rendezvous with him and that they must make the most of it.

This time, Harry took her to the large park at the back of the town. They strolled hand-in-hand down a tree-lined avenue to the ornamental gates, then past hot-houses filled with exotic plants. A path led along the margin of a boating lake, finally winding round beyond the fringes of the park, where an area of woodland lay beyond the environs of the park itself. After the sunlight and colour, the trees of the wood threw a cool shade as the lovers walked, his arm now around her, over mossy carpet. They found a small glade, far from prying eyes, where they made love again, this time with abandon. They explored each other with exquisite pleasure, coming together more than once. They were both in a state of complete detachment from the world, and time and place had lost all meaning for them.

She became aware of the cool dampness of the grass beneath her as she opened her eyes. His head was resting on her breast and his eyes were closed. With a rush of tenderness she noticed the curve of the golden lashes against the tanned skin, the fair, silky hair tumbling over his forehead and his relaxed mouth. Gently she touched his cheek with her finger and his eyes opened and, full of love, they gazed into hers.

"My own little darling," he murmured, kissing her before she could speak.

"Oh, how am I going to be able to leave you now?" Her voice was anguished. "And we won't be able to meet again tomorrow because Mum says I've got to go out with them, and it's our last day!"

"We've been very lucky, you know, so far. We'll try to meet in the evening. I've got to see you again before you go. I couldn't bear this to be our last meeting."

"Neither could I. Oh, I wish we could stay here forever."

"I'm not going to let you go for long," he promised. "We'll work something out, don't worry."

"Oh, I hope so, Harry. I couldn't bear to think I wasn't going to see you again once I get home."

"Hush, don't upset yourself. I promise you we'll meet again soon. Trust me." His lips claimed hers again and then, getting to his feet, he lifted her up and she looped her arms around his neck. They stayed, bodies enfolded, in a lingering embrace. Then, close together, they left the glade to return to the everyday world and to reality.

Although Alice tried very hard, there was no escaping the trip with her family the following day when Joe decided to book a charabanc trip to Fairhaven Lake, at Lytham, that same park to which Janet had taken Harry on their picnic. George had already brought down his wooden sailing-boat and Joe told them he would be hiring a rowing boat to take them all on the water. It sounded to Alice like a dreadful waste of an afternoon, when she could have been somewhere with Harry. But there was no arguing with her father!

As they wandered through the park, Mary noticed that Alice again seemed very quiet and she looked unhappy, too. Of course, it was because they all had to go back home tomorrow. A week soon went by and Alice wouldn't be looking forward to starting work again in the mill. She had never been one to confide in her mother much, hadn't Alice. Perhaps she had brought her up a bit strict, but it was, she knew, very easy for young girls to get into trouble if you didn't keep your eyes on them.

"Come on, love," she called to her daughter, "we'll go and have a lemonade at that place over there, it's so hot."

Around the corner of a brightly painted pavilion, the lake, with its waterfowl, rowing boats and steamer, came into view. Looking at the size of the rowing boats, Mary was glad when Alice told her father petulantly, "I'm not going in one of those."

George, however, was half-way along the planking of a landing-stage, ready to get in a boat and his dad had to call him back sharply.

"If you don't keep with us, lad, we're going home," he threatened.

Looking sulky, George obeyed his father, rejoining his family, who were still hotly debating whether to go on the steamer instead.

"I can't see what you're worrying about," Joe complained. "I can easily manage a rowing boat."

"You three can go without me, then," Alice spoke decisively, turning her back on the whole thing.

"I'd really like to go on the steamer, love." Mary pleaded with her husband. "You know what our George is like. He'll be a lot safer on the steamer than in a small boat."

"Oh, have it your own way, then." Joe capitulated, giving way to his wife and conceding that she had a point about their son.

Before the awful afternoon came to an end, Alice nearly screamed out loud with frustration, especially going back on the charabanc which took the coast road past the sand dunes instead of the inland route by which they had come. The thought that she could have been on the dunes all afternoon with Harry was absolute torture. What a complete waste of a day, when they were going home tomorrow! Only the hope that she might see him in the evening made the trip bearable and when, at last, they arrived back at Nelson Street, she prayed that she would think of some way of meeting him later.

Lady Luck had smiled on Alice all the week and she didn't desert her now. After tea was over, Mary suddenly decided that it would be a good thing to go upstairs to pack the suitcases that evening instead of waiting until the morning. They had to be out of the house by noon and it would give them the whole morning for one last outing, perhaps a quick look round the souvenir shops.

When they had gone upstairs, taking George with them to fetch his clothes out of Alice's room, she went quickly through into the back parlour. She had seen Ellen go next door, where Janet's mother was still poorly – she had heard them discussing it – and she knew that Maud was fully occupied in the scullery.

She found Harry sitting on the sofa in the parlour, staring into the empty fireplace. Looking up swiftly as she came forward, he got to his feet in one quick movement, catching her hands and drawing her to him. "I'm supposed to be packing, but I could get away for a little while," she whispered.

"Thank God! I was beginning to think you wouldn't get the chance to see me alone before you go.

Quick, let's go up to my room. No one will come in there. I'll go up first, then if you follow me to the landing, I'll let you in."

Her parent's door was closed as she slipped upstairs in Harry's wake. She could hear George inside their room, hindering them, as they packed their clothes. There didn't appear to be anyone else about, and then she had reached Harry's landing and he was letting her in at his door. The next moment she was in his arms and his mouth was covering hers. The burning fire ran through her again and she found herself pressing urgently against his insistent body. He drew her towards the bed, lifting her tenderly on to it, where she lay with her head on the pillow. Sitting by her side on the edge of the mattress, he slipped off his own clothes before undoing the buttons of her skirt and sliding it down over her slender hips. Her bare legs under the thin cotton slip shone smooth as satin in the subdued light from the curtained window, and his hand moved up the firm thigh in an exquisitely slow caress as he felt for her drawers. She lifted her slim hips and he slid those off, too, with a deft movement.

She was now quivering with anticipation and his lips, covering her body with lingering, searching kisses, brought her an agony of wanting. With a sudden movement, she pulled him over her and he entered her easily and naturally, she was so ready for him. They were getting to know how to please each other and their climax was mutual and intense. But she dared not stay much longer....

"Harry, oh, love, I'll have to go! Oh, why do we have to keep parting like this? I can't bear to think this is the last time we shall be together. When am I going to see you again?"

"Very soon, my love, trust me. I can't bear to see you go, either. I shall be thinking about you all the time, and it won't be very long before we meet again, I promise."

"But how?" she asked him, in despair.

"I don't know. Just try and be patient for a little while. We will be together, very soon, never fear."

"Oh, we must be, Harry. I couldn't live without you now."

"You won't have to, sweetheart. I couldn't do without you, either."

His lips claimed hers again and the desire rose in warm, swelling waves.

As she quickly stuffed clothes into her suitcase, her mind was in turmoil. Did he mean to come to Yorkshire to see her? But how could he do that while he was engaged to Janet? Perhaps he was going to tell Janet he couldn't marry her, after all? Oh, it was all too much to puzzle over! All she really wanted to do was to go over all that they had done together, to recapture the feeling of being in his arms, to remember everything. From now on, memories were going to be all she had to live on. How could she ever bear it? The hot tears welled up and trickled slowly down her flushed cheeks. Hurriedly, she wiped them away. Her mother would be coming in any minute to see why she had done so little packing. Mary must not for one moment suspect how she was feeling ....

Chapter Seven

Late on Saturday morning, Janet was setting tables in the dining room, ready for high tea, the first meal of the week for the new intake of visitors. Her mother was still in bed and seemed no better. In fact, Dr. Fraser had seemed worried when he had visited her the previous day. Her lungs were congested and she appeared hardly to have the energy to sit up when he wanted to examine her. Although very anxious about her mother's condition, Janet was trying to keep well ahead of the day's schedule. Rose, her sister, had been helping her to change the beds and clean the rooms after the guests had left. Ellen had returned temporarily to her duties next door, where she was saying goodbye to the Baileys and the Boothroyds.

Standing by the window, Janet saw Ellen at the gate, shaking hands with Joe Boothroyd. The daughter looked very glum and she was quite pale. She looked, in fact, as if she had been crying, but then, none of them wanted to go home, back to work for another year. Janet hadn't seen much of Harry this week – she had been so busy looking after her mother. He seemed to have been out a lot during the day and the only time she had caught him in the house one evening, he had seemed preoccupied and she herself hadn't been able to stay very long.

He had not mentioned the wedding and she hadn't bothered him about it because she'd had little time for furthering their plans. Her mother's illness was on her mind the whole time. Sarah didn't seem to be picking up as she should. If it was one of these new strains of influenza that were going about, as Dr. Fraser suspected, it might be weeks before she was back on her feet. Ellen couldn't be expected to help out much longer with Maud beginning to hint that she couldn't manage both the cooking and all the other jobs next door. Robert had suggested getting someone in to help Janet while Sarah was ill and she knew she would have to consider it soon. He was upstairs now with her mother. He had been so worried about Sarah that he hadn't gone in to work again this morning. He had taken drinks up to her but she had told him she couldn't manage any of the food Janet had prepared. While he sat with her, not talking much, just watching her, Janet and Rose got ready for the changeover of visitors.

This was a new experience for Robert. Apart from her two confinements, Sarah had never before had to take to her bed, and the truth was that he was now desperately afraid for her.

Harry, too, saw the Boothroyds leave, from the window of Alice's room. He had slipped in there while his mother and sister were saying their farewells. He knew that Alice had been weeping and his own heart was heavy. Turning abruptly, he went along the landing to the stairs, going down and through the kitchen, leaving the house by the back yard gate. He needed to walk. Turning away from the promenade, he passed the shops, the bakery, the church and rectory without seeing any of them. He knew now that in Alice he had found what he wanted – and she had been taken away from him. Her face and her eyes, filled with love and trust, were before him constantly. How long, then, could he go on deceiving Janet? He must tell her that he couldn't marry her before he was irrevocably committed to the marriage.

But was it fair, just now, while her mother was so ill, to tell her that he couldn't go through with it? There was still nearly a month to go, so perhaps it would be better to wait for a day or two to see if Sarah was any better before telling her. He wouldn't mention Alice, of course. The fact was that his mind had been unsettled before he had even met Alice. She had only confirmed for him that he would be making a big mistake if he went ahead and married his fiancée. When he had sorted all this out, Alice would be there, in Yorkshire, waiting for him. Oh, Lord! What a mess! He felt bereft, too. He hadn't known what it felt like to love someone like he loved Alice and then be parted from them. He had never felt like this about Janet when they had been parted by the War, and yet, here he was, missing Alice with his whole being. How long then, could he go without her?

When Harry returned an hour later, going by the back way into number Fourteen, he found it deserted. This was very unusual because visitors would be arriving during the afternoon and there was always someone on hand to welcome them. He went through the house to the front door and stepped through, seeing the Ford parked by next door's kerb. Dr. Fraser! Quickly, he ran round by the railings and let himself in. Ellen met him at the foot of the stairs, steering him into the back parlour.

"Don't go up until Dr. Fraser's gone," his mother warned him. "Sarah's taken a turn for the worse and Janet's very upset. They think its pneumonia."

"Oh, no!" said Harry, shocked, "Surely not?"

"They're doing everything they can for her but the doctor's warned them she's very poorly. Robert's going to sit with her tonight so that Janet can get a rest. She was with her last night while Robert got some sleep. I'll have to get back next door now. The Kershaws are due in any time and Maud's had to go out shopping."

"I'll wait and have a word with Janet," Harry told his mother.

Janet came downstairs, white-faced, her eyes brimming with tears, closely followed by the doctor. After she had seen Dr. Fraser out, she ran to Harry, flinging herself into his arms and sobbing pitifully. He patted her shoulder, comforting her.

"It may not be as bad as you think, you know. The doctors aren't always right. She'll be alright, you'll see."

"I hope you're right, Harry, but she looks dreadfully ill and her breathing is very laboured. Dr. Fraser says there's nothing else he can give her and we must just wait. He's coming again in the morning. I'd better get back to her now. Dad's with her. He's too upset to do anything but just sit there by her bed."

"If I can do anything at all, you know where I am," he said.

"Thank you, dear, but I don't think you should come in if we can avoid it. It could be infectious, you know."

"Try to get some sleep, then. You look all-in."

"I am tired," she admitted, "but I'm too worried to sleep. I'll just go and lie down for an hour." Kissing him lightly on the cheek, she ran back upstairs.

Slowly, he made his way back round to his own house. It was quite obvious that he couldn't at this moment speak to Janet about stopping the wedding – not with her mother so much worse than he had thought. It would just have to wait. Later, in his own bed, his guilty mind gave him no rest from recriminations. At length, though, he fell asleep.

A loud knocking on the front door brought him sharply awake. He had, it seemed only just drifted off, but a glance at the gold Hunter which had belonged to his father, showed him that it was nearly four o'clock. Jerking himself upright, he swung rapidly out of bed and into his trousers and shirt. On the landing he met his mother, wearing her long dressing gown and they went downstairs, Harry taking the steps two at a time. Janet was standing on the doorstep, her face grey. She swayed against him as he went towards her.

"Come in and sit down." He led her into the parlour while Ellen went to the cupboard for the brandy. "Here, drink this," she insisted.

Janet shivered. It was fiery, but she took another sip. "Dad's gone for Dr. Fraser. I – I think she's going, Harry. She can't, though, can she?" The pathetic question trembled on her lips. She took another sip of the spirit, coughing as she swallowed. Her face looked pinched, even old, Harry thought.

He took her cold hand in his as Ellen slipped through the room and out to the front lobby. A few moments later, she was mounting the stairs of number Sixteen to go to her old friend. Down in the parlour next door, Janet was asking Harry to hold her.

"Oh, Harry, I'm so frightened," she said, as his arm came around her.

He held her to him, trying to comfort her. She sobbed against his shoulder then, the spasm subsiding, she dried her eyes, telling him,

"I must go back to her, Harry."

Helping her to her feet, he said firmly, "I'm coming with you," and reached for her hand.

She didn't argue, but moved towards the door, still holding on to him tightly. They made their way into number Sixteen in silence and climbed the stairs. Sarah lay propped against the pillows, eyes closed, her face calm, even serene. There was little colour in it, but her breathing was now untroubled. It was almost undetectable beneath the embroidered nightgown. She had obviously, to Harry's experienced eyes, sunk into a deep coma and, looking at her, he wondered how long she could last. How often in the Royal Army Medical Corps had he seen men dying, he wondered? It was only a matter of time, he knew. Janet must know it, too and she was desperately trying to come to terms with the fact. He knew that he must stay with her. The only thing he could do now was try to bring her a bit of comfort.

Robert, too, knew that when the doctor came he would not be able to do anything for his wife. Dr. Fraser had been out at a confinement when Robert had hurried into the surgery, but his wife had promised that the doctor would come round as soon as he got back.

Ellen stood in the shadows at the back of the room, tight-lipped and rigidly self-controlled. Sarah had been Ellen's closest friend for many years and she was feeling the helpless frustration of being unable to do anything for her. She just couldn't believe they were all losing Sarah. She knew, too, how Robert must be feeling, sitting there, just as she had sat at her own husband's bedside, all those years ago. Looking at him, Ellen reflected how like her father Janet was. She had inherited Robert's flaming Scots colouring and his sturdy figure. She didn't take after Sarah, at all. It was Arthur, her brother, who took after Sarah, with his dark hair and brown eyes. Ellen's heart went out to them all, particularly to Janet, just preparing for her wedding. It was a cruel blow for them all. She had always believed that these things were in the hands of the Lord, but when they did happen, they were very hard to bear.

Robert was bending over his wife, grasping her limp hand and sobbing openly. What would he do if he lost her? The fact that this could happen had never crossed his mind before.

He had always taken it for granted that he would be the first to go. She was only just gone forty-three years old, so why, oh, why, had this happened to her? Neither Sarah nor himself had been churchgoers like Ellen and her family. They hadn't Ellen's strong faith that matters of life and death are ordained by God.

His wet face touched hers and he whispered, "Oh, lass, don't leave me now. Please don't leave me on my own." Tears streamed down his face. They'd had a good life together. They'd been childhood sweethearts and they'd married as soon as they'd saved enough to get a mortgage on the little house in Marsden Square. He had always been in work at the bakery and Sarah had supplemented their income by taking in summer visitors right from the start. They had eventually been able to leave the little house and put all their money into Nelson Street. It had been a gamble, with the family growing up and making demands on them but Robert had never doubted that Sarah would manage. Oh, God, what was he going to do without her?

He laid his head down on the bed. Janet came to him, putting her arm around his shoulders, her own eyes red and aching. She must try to keep up for his sake. She had accepted now that Sarah wasn't going to recover. It was unthinkable that it should be so but she knew that her mother hadn't long to live. The only comforting thing was that she was no longer in any pain – she was past all that, now. It seemed that with every breath Sarah was drawing further and further away.

The room was very quiet except for the sound of Robert's weeping. The little tableau was stilled, waiting. Before Dr. Fraser could get away from his other case, Sarah sighed gently once and then passed very peacefully from this world to the next.

All through the funeral, Robert Crossley felt that everything which was happening was unreal. Things around him seemed to have a dreamlike quality. He just couldn't believe that it was his beloved Sarah who was being lowered in that shiny coffin into the sandy soil of St. Luke's churchyard. He felt he must wake up, any minute. He was still in a state of shock, he knew that, but he dreaded coming back again to reality. How could he face life without her?

When, at last, it was all over and the funeral party had dispersed from the house, he knew that he had to get outside, out of the house. His sister Hanah, a widow who lived at Lytham, had been staying with him for the few days over the funeral. She was a slight, frail little woman, who suffered from arthritis, and the news of her sister-in-law's death had been a great shock to her. She had made the effort, in spite of considerable pain, to be with her brother until after the funeral, but she was now ready to return to her cottage. In her own home she had everything organised to be handy and within reach, as she found it difficult to get about.

As he helped Hanah into her coat, Robert called to his son, Arthur, "Get your coat son. You can walk with us to the station."

The boy had just this week turned sixteen, but this was no time to be celebrating birthdays. He was clearly bewildered by the sudden death of his mother and was battling to keep the unmanly tears at bay. It had been a cruel blow for a lad like Arthur, sensitive and clever, who was hoping to go on from the grammar school into a local solicitor's office. Now she would never see her son go on into a better job than his father.

Robert vowed that, for her sake, he would see to it that if Arthur got that job as a junior a Peabody and Grundy's, he would do all he could to see that he eventually became a fully-fledged accountant. He hadn't been able to do anything to save Sarah but he could at least look to the children and see that they got as good a chance as he could give them.

They walked slowly towards South Shore station, the train being the main link between Lytham village and Blackpool.

"You're going to have to get someone in to help Janet, you know," Hanah said. "She won't be able to look after you and the children and the visitors as well – a big house like that. It's too much for one body."

"Yes, you're right, Hanah. I did tell her to get someone in when Sarah was ill, before …."

"Now, don't upset yourself again. I think I might be able to help you. If you've no one in mind, I'm thinking about Sam's cousin, Florrie Metcalf. I don't think you've met her, but when Sam was alive, we used to visit them quite a bit. Her husband died last year and she's been helping Mrs. Elton at Church Street, near me in Lytham. Her own cottage is on Fore Street but she wants a full-time, living-in job. Someone has offered her a good rent for her cottage. It's hard for a widow to manage these days."

"Well, I'll have to talk it over with Janet. Thanks for mentioning it. If she's used to the job, she sounds just what we want."

"Well, don't leave it too long thinking about. Janet needs help now."

"I'll let you know what we decided," Robert promised, as the train got ready to leave.

In the back parlour of number Sixteen, Janet sat side by side with her fiancée on the sofa. His arm was around her and she was sobbing as she hadn't been able to do for the past few days. It had been as if she couldn't let go until now. She had shed copious tears, but not these great wracking sobs which seemed to rise from somewhere deep within herself. Of course, it wasn't just her mother she was crying for, she knew that it was for herself, too. Apart from the grief she felt, she had known since her mother died that she would have to postpone the wedding. How could she go on with it now? She was needed by her father and the children, at least until they had sorted themselves out and decided what should be done.

She shrank from telling Harry, now that the wedding arrangements were so well advanced. He would be so disappointed, but she hoped he would understand and wait. If they put it off for just a couple of months, perhaps ....

He was saying, "That's right, let it all out, Janet. It's better to get it off your chest. Don't bottle it all up."

"Oh, Harry, it's not just Mother," she said. "I can't believe that she's really gone, yet – it's us! How can we go on with the wedding now?"

"Of course we can't, Janet. We won't think about it till later on, when you've got over all this." Harry was trying hard not to show his enormous relief.

"You're so understanding, dear, but I don't think I could carry on with the wedding, just yet."

"Of course you couldn't. I wouldn't expect you too, and what's a month or two, anyway? We've waited this long – we can wait a bit longer." He couldn't believe that he had been given this reprieve – this respite.

She lifted her head and he felt the hot tears on his cheek as she kissed him. Seeing her so distressed, he felt desperately sorry for her. He couldn't pile on the agony by letting her think there was anything wrong between them – not just now. The thing he would do was comfort and support her while she needed it. Evidently, she intended postponing the wedding arrangements, which would give him at least a breathing space before he had to tell her. He didn't want to hurt her, but the facts were there, plain and simple – he didn't love Janet, and he did love Alice. The girl had never been out of his thoughts since she had returned home and his nights had been full of wanting her. If only he had felt like this about Janet, he wouldn't now be in this awful situation.

"Would you tell the Vicar that we're putting it off, then?" she whispered. "I'll tell everyone else."

"Of course I will," he said. "Don't worry, it's not for long." What could he say that wouldn't upset her? "Would you like me to stay with you until your Dad gets back?"

"Thanks Harry, no. I think I'll go and have a lie down for a while. I haven't slept much this week. I might feel better afterwards, then Dad and I have a lot to talk about when he comes back."

"I'll get back, then, if you want to rest. Try to get some sleep." Kissing her wet face, he moved towards the door. "I'll see you tomorrow," he said, as he escaped through it.

After he had gone, Janet sat quietly, dabbing at her eyes. She must try to pull herself together and begin the difficult task of cancelling the wedding arrangements. She knew that Harry wasn't showing how he really felt about the postponement of the wedding. He must be as disappointed as she was that the marriage couldn't now go ahead. During these difficult days she must hold on fast to the thought – in another month or two she would be able to go ahead with all the plans that had been tragically shattered.

Later, when Arthur and Rose had gone up to bed, she felt more composed. Sitting with her father over their supper drinks he was very silent, but she knew that when he felt able to, he would talk to her.

"Do you want to carry on here then, lass?" he asked her, at length.

"I've got to, Dad. We've got people booked in all summer. Then there's you and the children – I can't leave you all just now."

"I thought that was the way you'd look at it. You always were a good lass. What does Harry think about it?"

"He's been wonderful, Dad. He understands and he's going to wait."

"I'm sorry you're in this situation, Janet, but if you're going to stay on for a bit, you'll be needing someone to help you. You can't do it all on your own, you know."

"No, I know, Dad. I will need some help with the visitors."

Outlining to her what Hanah had suggested, Robert asked, "Do you want someone living-in?"

"Well, Dad, that would be better than a daily help, if we could find somewhere to put her."

Most of the upper back rooms were occupied by the family and the others were earmarked for visitors. Then the idea struck her. Of course! The attic! It was large and airy. When it had been cleared out and properly furnished it would be as good as any room in the house, bigger than most. The chimney of the parlour fireplace went right through it, too, keeping it always warm. That was why Sarah had used it as a storeroom for all her surplus household goods.

"Alright, Dad, we'll write to Aunt Hanah and invite Florrie to come over right away. We do need someone now. We can't cancel any more visitors. It's been hard enough finding them rooms in other houses as it is and if we're busy it will keep our minds off other things. I'm sure we could make her very comfortable in the attic."

"That's a good idea. Could you write a note to her asking her to come to see us? I'm just not up to it, lass."

"Of course, Dad. I'll do it now and put it in the post when I go out."

Picking up the empty cups, she took them through into the kitchen. As he watched her, Robert thought, with gratitude and pride, how full of good sense she was – just like her mother. Tears welled up again and he got up before she could return and see his distress. His voice was hoarse. You've always been a good lass," he said.

"Don't be silly, Dad. Try to get some sleep. Goodnight."

Listening to his stumbling steps on the stairs, she knew that he was weeping. Her own tears threatened again but this time she managed to check them. She told herself she must remain strong, for all their sakes. She would now have to be a mother to Arthur and Rose as well as a sister. Just now, though, she didn't feel she had the strength to do it.

Chapter Eight

Alice Boothroyd was sitting at home in Bradfield in front of her dressing-table mirror. Powder puff in hand, she was putting the finishing touches to her face before going downstairs for breakfast. The doll which Harry had won for her on the Pleasure Beach held pride of place on it. It was standing by the edge of a small swivel mirror and leaning against the rather rusty hinge.

Although it was well into August and she had been back at work a month, she hadn't settled easily into her old routine at the mill. Fortunately, the work came easily to her but her mind kept harping back to her week on the other side of the Pennines. She couldn't stop going over that wonderful week in Blackpool. Was he missing her as much as she was missing him, she wondered.

After she had got back home, Jimmy Briggs had asked her if she would go out with him again, but she'd found that she couldn't look at him without seeing his pimples and his incipient whiskers. She didn't want to go out with Jimmy

Briggs. He was only a boy, she had realised, whereas Harry was a man. It was Harry she wanted, and nobody else. It had been the same with David Ollerenshaw. She hadn't even answered him when he'd said he'd take her to the pictures, leaving him stammering and confused. She had refused to consider anybody else at all. If her mother wondered why Alice didn't want to go out, she hadn't commented on it.

The only trouble was that Harry hadn't tried to get in touch with her. Of course, she had told him not to write to her home – Mary would want to know who was writing to her from Blackpool. Alice made up her mind to write to Harry herself. No one at Nelson Street would question a letter addressed to him. The only problem was, where was he to send a reply?

Her friend, Ada, at the mill was the obvious answer, but Ada's mother knew Mary, so would she tell her about it? She couldn't risk that. The only other person she could think of was Doris, the most experienced weaver at Foster's, who worked with her on the same floor. Doris was in charge of training the young, raw mill-hands who came to learn to weave. She had taught Alice herself when she had come to the mill part-time as a young girl still going to school in the afternoons. What was more, Doris lived alone. Her husband had died a few years back and she had never remarried.

Doris was tiny and bird-like, yet strong and wiry. She hennaed her hair which gave a fleeting impression of youthfulness. On the other hand, the red colour didn't suit her rather pasty face. She must have been all of fifty years old but she never admitted to it. She had worked in the mill all her life and there wasn't much she didn't know about human nature. Alice decided it had to be Doris. She dare not risk her mother finding anything out through Ada.

Alice waited for Doris at knocking-off time. Today, Doris's hair was looking brighter than usual and Alice had difficulty keeping her eyes off it as they walked together towards the mill gates. "I'm going to write to a friend in Blackpool," she began, as they mingled with the other workers, leaving.

"Oh, yes, a man or a woman?" asked Doris, grinning.

Alice blushed and Doris winked knowingly. "I see you made a conquest while you were away, but you kept very quiet about it. Who is he? A local boy you met there?"

"Yes, but I don't want him writing home and Mum seeing the letter. It might be a bit awkward."

"She doesn't know about it, then?"

"Well, no," admitted Alice. "I met him while I was out alone and they were somewhere else."

"You little minx!" Doris was amused by Alice's nerve.

"Well, I just wondered whether you'd have a letter delivered to your house addressed to me, then Mum won't find out."

"There's nothing wrong, is there?" Doris asked, suspiciously.

"Of course not, it's just that I don't want Mum going on about it to me." She stopped and grasped Doris's arm urgently. "Please, Doris, would you – just this once?"

Doris considered for a moment. She had been young once herself and full of such schemes. "Alright, then, but mind – it's only once."

"Oh, thanks, Doris. You don't know how much this means to me."

"Run off home, then, and mum's the word. If anybody asks me, I don't know anything about any letter – understand?"

They were now passing through the mill gates and they stood for a moment on the narrow pavement, ready to go their separate ways. Doris lived on the other side of the moor. As Doris started off for the tram stop, Alice called after her, "Thanks again, Doris. See you tomorrow."

The four weeks following Alice's return to Bradfield had been fraught with uncertainty and indecision for Harry. He hadn't been thinking any less often about her, in fact his memories of that week with her had been his only consolation as the days went by. The situation in which he found himself seemed to him a hopeless one. He felt as if he was trapped as surely as any fly in a sticky web.

After the respite over the wedding date, he had intended, over and over again, telling his fiancée about his true feelings. Each time, though, he was actually face to face with her, he found his determination crumbling. Her obvious grief over her mother or her references to the future marriage, had defeated him once more. How could he add a final crushing blow to the one from which she was still recovering? Surely it would be kinder to wait until she got over that before he broke off the engagement? That was the least he could do to soften the blow, he reckoned.

Until he broke the engagement, he had no right at all to contact Alice. How could he, an engaged man, go openly to her home to ask for her parents' blessing? Heaven knew, he wanted to do just that, but until he broke off his engagement, it was no use even thinking about it. He couldn't write to Alice secretly, either. She had told him not to write to her home until he had sorted things out. Poor little love! She must be wondering when they were going to see each other again. The trouble was, he was beginning to wonder, too.

He picked up Alice's letter together with the other mail, as he returned from the newsagents with his paper. It was addressed to him in a childish hand and he knew at once who the writer was. Slipping it quickly into his inside pocket, he took the rest of the letters through to his mother in the back parlour. Making a very quick breakfast, he hurried upstairs to read it in private, tearing open the envelope and revealing sloping lines on thin paper.

'Darling Harry,' it read. 'I've been thinking about you the whole of the time and wondering when we shall meet again. You said you'd try and arrange something. You haven't forgotten, have you? I could never forget you, Harry. I love you too much. Write to me at the address I'm sending. Your little love, Alice.'

The simplicity of the message was so evocative of her that he flung himself down on the bed in torment. He was reliving in his mind that moment when they had been together making love on this very bed. The magic of it had never left him but what could he do to change things? He couldn't go to her yet until he had sorted things out here.

As he re-read the letter, he could see her face, smiling, eyes wide. Quickly he folded the paper, replacing it inside its envelope. Unless Fate dealt him some lucky card, he hadn't the right even to answer her letter, not while he was still engaged to Janet.

On the same day that Harry received Alice's letter, Janet was welcoming Florrie Metcalf to number Sixteen. Although a distant cousin by marriage, she and Janet had never met before. She was a pleasant-looking woman of about forty, neatly dressed and well-spoken. Her eyes, a clear light hazel, regarded Janet sympathetically as she spoke a few words of comfort to her. Robert soon left the two together to talk the whole thing over. If Janet liked her, she would do, he thought.

Robert had returned to work to keep all those crowding memories at bay. He thought Florrie looked a good enough sort and she seemed to have a cheerful way with her. Oh, well, it was up to Janet – she was the one who would have to get along with her in the day-to-day running of the place. He took his jacket down from the hook behind the kitchen door and let himself out by the back yard gate.

In the parlour over cups of tea, Janet and Florrie were getting to know each other before they discussed business. It seemed that Florrie had no children. "Of course, I wanted a family when I got married, but it just wasn't to be," she confided to Janet. "It's when you get older, especially when you're a widow, that you're all on your own."

Janet sympathised. She herself had taken it for granted that she would have a family and she found it hard to visualise a childless marriage. "And you want to let your cottage for the rest of the season?" she asked.

"Yes, I've had a very good offer from a businessman who wants to work on the coast for a while. He thinks three months will be long enough. I thought that if I could live-in and work myself for that time it would be a bit of extra income."

"Well, we couldn't afford to pay you a lot, but three months would fit in with our bookings. We're in August now and we're busy until the end of October. After that we won't have anyone else in until Christmas."

"That's good enough for me," Florrie said, smiling and sipping the tea. "It's no good looking too far ahead, anyway."

"Finish your tea, then we'll go upstairs," Janet said, "and I'll show you where I thought we'd put you. It needs a bit of work doing on it and furnishing but I think we could make you very comfortable if you agree."

As they came downstairs after inspecting the attic, Florrie said, "It's much bigger than any of my rooms and I can see it suiting me very well. When would you like me to start?"

"How about this week? I think we should get along together well enough."

It was surprising how quickly Florrie settled into the routine of the house. Now that she was installed and the routine had been re-established, the current bookings could be honoured. In the past, Sarah had done most of the cooking, while Janet had waited on the tables and helped with all the hundred-and-one jobs which needed doing around the place. A similar arrangement was decided upon with Florrie, who liked cooking and baking and who turned out to be an excellent hand in the kitchen.

It was upsetting to see someone else working around the place, but Janet knew that life in the boarding house had to go on. She stifled her feelings and concentrated on getting on with her work. Arthur and Rose, too, were still grieving for their mother but they couldn't help taking to the cheerful Florrie, in spite of themselves.

Seeing her fitting so well into the household, Robert was very relieved. Janet seemed satisfied with her work and the household appeared to be running smoothly once again. Of course, she would never come up to Sarah's standard but he felt that they could have done a lot worse. He must remember to write to Hanah to thank her for her suggestion and tell her that it was working out nicely.

Chapter Nine

Mary Boothroyd slid her feet out of a warm bed without disturbing her husband, her toes meeting the cold lino. Where was that peg rug? Ah, that was better. In the dim morning light, she found her clothes and took them downstairs. She would wash at the kitchen sink down here before starting on the breakfasts. It was a cold September morning, the weather having changed dramatically since their July holiday. A grey, rainy day met her eyes as she drew back the thin flowered curtains. Shivering, she decided that she would light a fire before she did anything else.

The scuttle was full of small coal and sticks of wood, which Joe had chopped the previous evening, and some scrumpled-up old newspapers to fill the bottom of the grate. Soon, she had a good fire going and she dressed herself in comfort before a warm blaze. Brushing her hair in front of the over-mantel mirror, a still-attractive face stared back at her, fair hair unstreaked with grey. Her complexion, too, had remained good, the skin firm and the blue eyes clear and bright. Mary smiled at herself as she ran a comb through her hair. She'd had it cut short like Alice's before the holiday and the cropping had released the curl in it. Not bad for a woman of forty-two, she congratulated herself. If Alice wears as well as I have, she won't do too badly, she thought.

The girl seemed to have something on her mind lately. Mary had caught her once or twice staring into space, as if she was far, far away. Then she had been looking quite peaky this last week or two. She should be looking better, not worse, for her holiday. She hadn't been out much, either, since they had got back from Blackpool. She would tackle her about it when she got back from the mill today. Mary liked to know about anything which was affecting a member of her family!

The porridge was ready and the sausages crisping as Joe came down to breakfast, half-an-hour later. He had to be at work for seven-thirty and he needed a good breakfast, working in the foundry.

"Are you going round to see the old man again?" Joe asked, as he started on his porridge. Mary had been going round to her father's on Ainslie Street for the past week to give him his meals. A widower, he had caught this influenza that was going about and Mary was worried about him. It had weakened him a lot and he didn't seem to be picking up. Of course, he was well over sixty and since her mother had died, he had been finding it hard to cope. It was fortunate that he lived so near, because there was just no room for him to live with them at Moscar Street and his own house was no bigger.

"I thought I'd be off as soon as you've finished. Alice is seeing to George's breakfast this morning before she goes to work. I don't like leaving her to it but I'm worried about Dad – he looked bad again last night.

"He's had a good innings, you know, lass," Joe said. He tucked into a thickly buttered slice of toast and home-made marmalade. "That was bloody good, Mary. Here, give us a kiss before I go."

"Get away with you," laughed Mary, submitting to his strong embrace.

"Here, don't forget your baggins." She passed him his lunch-box, containing a homemade pie, sandwiches and cake, topped off by an apple.

When he had gone, Mary went upstairs to waken Alice before she put on her hat and coat, ready to set off for Ainslie Street.

Alice had been having a nightmare. She had been walking through a wood and the trees were threatening her. They had formed a circle around her and their tapering branches were outstretched towards her. They were advancing on her, their long fingers reaching out. She was just about to scream in terror when she was awakened by someone shaking her.

"No....no...." she moaned, as Mary called her name.

"Whatever's the matter, love?" her mother asked, as Alice's eyes flew open.

"Oh, Mum, thank goodness it's you. I've been having a nightmare – it was awful!"

"Well, you're alright, now, Love. You'll have to get up, though, or you'll be late. Don't forget you're doing George's breakfast this morning. I'm sorry to leave you to it, but I must get off to Grandad. I didn't like the look of him yesterday.

"Oh, yes, Mum, I know. I'll be down in a minute."

"I'll get off, then. See you at tea-time. I'll have some hot-pot for you."

"Thanks, Mum. 'Bye." Alice threw off the covers, trying to push the horrible dream from her mind. She swung her legs out of bed and stood up. Immediately, the room began to spin around her and she sank down again onto the edge of the bed. Whatever was the matter with her, she wondered? She'd had this dizziness once or twice lately but, this time, the whole room had gone round. As everything steadied, she tried standing again, managing to walk over to the wash-stand, a queasy sensation in her stomach.

Mary had fetched up some hot water, and the wash-bowl was steaming. She washed herself before it got cold and put on her working clothes. Emptying the water into a white enamel bucket beside the wash-stand, she added to it the urine from a chamber pot which was kept under the bed. The lavatory was outside in the yard and, on a cold September morning, no one made the trip out there. Hurriedly throwing the covers over the bed, she went across to rouse her brother. He was still lying in deep slumber but, then,George could sleep through anything, specially in the mornings.

"Come on sleeping beauty," she urged him, holding a wet flannel at the ready. "Show a leg, or I'll use this."

George opened his eyes and, seeing the weapon, sat bolt upright, dodging out of bed at the other side.

"I'll put the kettle on and you can come down for some more hot water," she said.

When George came down for the second time, washed and dressed, there was no sign of breakfast on the table and his sister did not appear to be busy in the kitchen, either. He went out through the open back door as far as the lavatory. From within he heard unmistakable sounds of someone being very sick.

"Alice!" he called out, "Are you in there?"

For a moment there was no answer, then Alice's voice came weakly from inside. "Go away. I'll be out in a minute."

"I'm hungry," grumbled her brother. "I want my breakfast. What's the matter with you?"

"Never mind that. I can't make you any breakfast this morning. Put some butter on one of those muffins. That'll do until dinner-time. Go on – Mum'll be back by then. I'll make you a mug of tea."

Shakily, she returned to the kitchen and went over to the stove. A cup of tea might stay down but she knew that nothing else would. She must throw off this nausea which had claimed her since the dizziness passed off. The tea did seem to settle her stomach a little and George, after cramming down another muffin and a large mug of hot tea, rushed off to school – late! She herself was going to be very late for work too, she realised, as she struggled into her outdoor clothes, ready to set off for Foster's.

At dinner-time, Mary stirred the savoury soup she had made from a succulent ham shank, feeling easier in her mind about her father. This morning, to her surprise, she had found him a little better. After lighting his fire and giving him some breakfast, she had tidied up the place and left him comfortable in bed. He had told her he intended getting up later on and she could see that his colour was better and his eyes brighter. She had promised to call on him later before setting off home to prepare the meal.

When she arrived at Moscar Street, she saw that the kitchen had been left uncleared, but then Alice usually took a while getting herself dolled-up even for work, so she had evidently been on the minutes. George soon arrived for his dinner, in a hurry as usual, boots clattering into the kitchen. They were rather on the large side, but Mary was only trying to keep up with his ever-increasing growth rate.

"Go and wash your hands before you sit down," she ordered him, for the umpteenth time. He never seemed to remember.

"Ooo, it hurts," he cried, as he dried his hands on a towel which was hanging behind the back door. He raised his hand, palm upwards, for her inspection. "I got the cane this morning for being late."

"Why were you late?" Mary asked, in some surprise and anger.

"You were up early enough, weren't you? Were you playing about on the way?"

"No, Mum. It wasn't my fault. Our Alice didn't make me any breakfast. I had to wait, and when she didn't come, I had to get some myself."

"Didn't come. Where was she, then? You mean she was still in bed?"

"No, Mum, she was bein' sick in the lavatory," George informed her.

Mary stood completely still for a moment, hand poised over the soup.

"Yes, she was bein' sick for a long time," he said, resentfully.

"Alright, get your soup, then." She must talk to her daughter when she came home. Perhaps Alice was starting with this flu' that her grandad and so many people were going down with? She fervently hoped not, but it sounded a bit like it.

On reaching the mill, Alice went into the weaving sheds to find Doris, to tell her that she wasn't feeling well. "I don't want to stay off," she said, "because Mum will only be mothering me. I feel dizzy and I've been sick."

Doris looked sharply at the girl. Her face was pinched and her eyes heavy.

"If I didn't know different, I'd say you were pregnant," she laughed. Then she stopped, as she saw Alice's stricken expression.

"Look, I didn't mean that – I was only kidding. It could be this flu', you know."

"No, Doris. I think you might be right. About being pregnant, I mean. I've been wondering myself if I am, ever since I set off for work this morning."

"My God! You don't mean…?"

"Yes, I've sent a letter to him, but I didn't even dream about anything like this when I wrote it."

"Well, I haven't had any reply for you. I think you're going to have to write to him again and tell him, that is, if you're sure."

"I've been feeling funny in the mornings for a week or so, but I just thought that something I'd eaten had upset me. You see, I haven't had any period either, and this morning I couldn't stand up properly. Then I was very sick."

"You poor kid. Here, sit down a minute. I've put Sally on your looms." She pulled up a hard chair for Alice while she took off her coat and hat and got into her overalls and cap.

"You're too young to be starting with a family. Whatever will your mother say? She doesn't even know about you meeting him, you said?"

"No, it was someone in the boarding house. He lives there. They didn't know I was going out with him."

"Well I take my hat off to you, Alice, for nerve. You mean you were meeting this lad right under their noses and they didn't find out?"

"Yes, we were lucky. They went somewhere every day and I made excuses."

"Well! Doris was breathless at the audacity of it. "I wouldn't have believed it of you. I thought you were such a quiet little thing. What d'you think he'll say, when he knows?"

"I don't know, he's engaged to someone else."

"Engaged!" Doris couldn't believe her ears. Her voice rose. "You mean he took advantage of you when he was engaged to another girl?"

"No, no, it wasn't like that, really. He doesn't love her, he loves me. He doesn't want to marry her, either, but they all expect him to."

"Oh, yes, he told you that, did he?" Doris asked sceptically, as Alice pulled on her working shoes. "And you believed him, did you?"

"It's true!" retorted Alice, tears springing to her eyes. "He does love me, and I love him."

"Well, then, we'll have to see when he finds out about this little lot whether he does or not, won't we. Now, don't get upset," she said more gently. "I may be wrong about him and the first thing to do is to tell your mother. You can't keep it a secret from her, you know."

"No, but I dread telling Dad. He'll go mad. You know what a temper he's got. I don't know what he'll do when he finds out."

"Are you sure you'll be able to stand here, working all day?" Doris asked the girl, "because you can go home any time you like and I'll cover for you. I'll say you're starting with the flu'."

"Thanks, Doris, I'll see how I go on. I'd rather stick it out here than go home like this and face Mum."

Strangely, by the afternoon, she was feeling a lot better, so much so that she wondered how she could have felt so ill in the morning. She wouldn't tell her mother yet what she suspected. There was plenty of time, she told herself. She wouldn't write again yet to Harry, either. She must wait until she had a reply from him and then, when she was sure, she would write to tell him that she was going to have his baby.

On arriving home, she went through into the kitchen for her meal. Her mother was standing at the table setting a place for her with knife, fork and spoon. She must have made a pudding tonight. It was surprising how her appetite had come back. Mary turned to the stove where two deep plates were warming. She filled them with the steaming hot-pot from the large brown dish, its glaze cracked from frequent use. It was one of Alice's favourites – succulent, tender lamb, with crispy potatoes on the top and juicy onions underneath.

Alice joined her mother at the table and they began to eat.

"How was Grandad?" she asked, savouring the tasty mouthful.

"He seemed a lot better today. I went again this afternoon and he was knocking about."

"Oh, good."

"I believe you weren't so well yourself this morning," Mary said.

Alice swallowed a piece of potato, nearly choking. Mary thumped her on the back as she coughed and spluttered.

"Do you think you're starting with the flu'?" George says you were very sick."

Alice jumped up suddenly from the table and ran quickly upstairs, leaving her mother wondering what on earth was wrong. Mary got up quickly and followed her daughter upstairs. This wasn't like Alice at all. Whatever was the matter with the girl these days? She must have that little talk with her right away. She had been so occupied with Grandad that hadn't found the time.

"Whatever's the matter, love?" Mary asked, as she joined Alice in the bedroom. "You haven't been the same since you came back from Blackpool. Have we done something to upset you, or is it something at work?"

"No," sobbed Alice. "It's nothing to do with you or work. I – I think I'm going to have a baby."

It was Mary's turn to feel the room spinning. She sat down abruptly on the bed beside her daughter. She just couldn't believe what she was hearing. A baby! Alice had no young man in tow, had she? So whose baby could it be? Surely it couldn't be David Ollerenshaw's? Admittedly, he had taken her to the pictures once, but he was so bashful that Mary couldn't believe he had even kissed Alice, never mind seduced her. And she hadn't been out with anyone else since the holidays, Mary was sure.

Something clicked in her mind as the word 'holidays' went through it. Was it, could it be possible, that Alice had met someone in Blackpool, unknown to herself and Joe? The time would be about right. Oh, what a fool she had been to let her daughter go off on her own! But then, she had never had to worry about Alice before. She had been sure that her daughter knew how to behave. She must find out, right away, who the lad was. Was he someone she had met on the Front or the beach. That must be it! She had been led on by some youth who had taken advantage of her and got her pregnant. Mary gasped in horror as she realised that she would have to tell Joe! She daren't even think what he would say when he knew. But at the moment, she must find out who the father was. Putting her arms around Alice's shoulders she urged her, "Come on, love, try to stop crying and tell me all about it."

"I can't stop," sobbed Alice. "Oh, what am I going to do if he marries her?"

"Marries her? Marries who? Who are you talking about?"

"Why, Harry, of course," sobbed Alice, dabbing at her eyes with the edge of the cotton bedcover.

"Harry? Harry who? - You don't mean... Harry Tomlinson?"

"Yes, Mum. I do love him and he loves me. But what about Janet?"

Mary's head reeled again at this piece of news. Harry Tomlinson? Why, he was a grown man and engaged to another girl, at that! Mary asked herself how she could have missed seeing what was going on! He had taken her out a couple of times at the beginning of the week. She remembered the doll, still sitting on Alice's dressing table. Had they met on the sly, then, later on in the week? Her mind flashed back and she could see her daughter, flushed and expectant, going off on her own every day except that last one, when they had all gone to Fairhaven Lake. Why hadn't she seen that there was something going on? Normally she could sense, without really knowing, what was going on in her own family circle, but she had relaxed on that week's holiday and lowered her guard. She'd had no real reason to suspect anything, anyway.

But why had he seduced Alice when he was engaged to be married very soon? Surely Alice hadn't been foolish enough to believe that he loved her? Alice was a very pretty girl and he could have lost his head over her. She couldn't believe, though, that her daughter had encouraged him.

"Hush, hush," she soothed, "You'll only make yourself worse, going on like this. Whatever made you go with Harry, anyway?"

"I've told you, Mother, I love him, and he loves me."

Mary sighed. How many men had told that tale to girls like Alice in the past? She couldn't shatter her daughter's illusions, though, not while she was like this. The first thing to do was to find out the truth from the doctor. It could all be a false alarm. She might not be pregnant, after all. There were other reasons for these symptoms – they didn't always mean pregnancy. Alice had probably jumped to conclusions.

Her mind a little less confused, Mary fished out a clean handkerchief from the chest of drawers and handed it to the woebegone girl. They would say nothing to Joe just yet, until they had seen the doctor. She would make an appointment with Dr. Fitzpatrick in the morning and get to the bottom of this straight away.

"You could be wrong about this, you know," she comforted Alice. "Come on, let's go down and see if we can heat up that hot-pot."

Smiling wanly, Alice got up off the bed. "I don't think I could eat much, but I'll try."

"That's a good girl and you can tell me all about it before your Dad gets in. I want the truth, mind!"

"Yes, Mum," Alice promised, following her mother down the stairs into the warm kitchen.

A glum-faced Alice and an anxious Mary faced Dr. Fitzpatrick across his big oak desk the following day at his Cunningham Street surgery. Middle aged and balding, he surveyed them with a kindly smile over the top of his metal-rimmed glasses. He turned to the apprehensive girl. "Well," he said, "you're very healthy, young lady, and you're six or seven weeks pregnant. The sickness is quite normal and it will wear off in a month or two. I'd like to see you again in four weeks just to keep an eye on you. I don't think you're going to have any trouble, though, carrying this baby." He beamed at Mary, holding out his hand and coming round the desk to her.

"I expect you are delighted with the news of your first grandchild, Mrs. Boothroyd. "I take it that the wedding's going to be very soon?"

"Oh, er, yes," gasped Mary. "Yes, it is, and thank you, doctor. I'll make sure that she comes in again in another month."

The truth was that she was absolutely dumbfounded at this confirmation of Alice's fears. She had managed to convince herself that it was all a lot of fuss about nothing. What were they to do now? She glanced across at Alice, who was gazing miserably down at her own feet.

When they arrived home, Mary went straight through into the kitchen to put the kettle on, Alice trailing forlornly after her. While they both stood in silence, waiting for it to boil, Alice's mind kept going over the same old round. How was she going to tell Harry? How were they going to tell her Dad? What was she to do if Harry couldn't marry her? What if, in fact, he had already married Janet? She pushed that thought firmly from her mind. Harry wouldn't have married Janet – he wouldn't! He didn't love Janet and he did love Alice – and now she was going to have his child!

The tea brewed in the old brown pot, Mary poured out two hot cups, taking them through into the parlour. Huddling together over the fire for mutual support and comfort while they sipped, they were each enfolded in their own thoughts and it was Mary who spoke first.

"I never thought you'd let us down like this, Alice. Whatever possessed you to go with Harry in the first place? You've never been one for going off the rails before."

"It just happened, Mum. There wasn't any thinking about it. I love him and I'm not sorry about it."

"Well, you <u>should</u> be sorry! We've always been able to hold our heads up around here. You don't know whether he's going to marry you or not! He may even have married his girl in Blackpool by now. If I remember they had just fixed the date that week we were there. Have you thought about that? You haven't heard from him, have you?"

"No, Mum, but he wouldn't do that – he doesn't love her."

"You are a silly, foolish girl to be talking like that. He has probably married Janet by now. You're too young to know what men are really like."

"Well, Harry's not like that." Alice defended him hotly. "Oh, it's no use arguing, we'll have to think what we're going to tell Dad."

At the mention of her husband, Mary exclaimed, "Oh, all this trouble's worrying me to death. What he'll say when he finds out, I dread to think."

"Why'm I goin' to Grandad's?" George asked his mother, as she handed him his wooden jig-saw puzzle. She had made him put on his hat and coat telling him that he must behave himself at Grandad's – she would come for him later on. Her father was now nearly over his bout of flu' but it had left him a bit unsteady on his legs and he hadn't been out of the house.

"You'll be a bit of company for him," she told her son, "and you know he likes to help you with your puzzle."

"He keeps puttin' the wrong bits in," George complained, grabbing hold of the box.

"Well, his eyes aren't as good as yours. He's not as young as you are, either."

"And he sometimes goes off to sleep." George continued, ignoring his mother. "He's no good to play with and he snores, like this...." George gave a very good imitation of his grandfather, mouth open, head drooping, emitting at the same time loud grunting noises.

"Yes, well ... never mind about that. And see you behave yourself, "she instructed him, opening the door and steering her son through it, out into the street.

Mary had decided to give her husband his favourite meal of steak and kidney pudding, the meat tender and juicy in its envelope of suet crust, and she went through now into the kitchen to prepare it for the stove in its white rag covering. It would be as good a time as any to tell Joe when he had eaten. No moment in the day would be a good one for telling him, but he had to be told, now that they knew for certain. When the moment arrived, though, it was even harder for Alice than she had anticipated. The sight of her Dad, complacent in his ignorance of the situation, was too much for Alice. She just couldn't face him.

"I'm just going out for a bit of fresh air," she said. "I'll call at Ada's to pick up that knitting pattern her mother promised you."

"Alright, love. You go and I'll have a little talk with your Dad."

"Talk – what about?" asked Joe, as Alice opened the front door and went out. "And where's our George?"

"I've taken him round to Grandad's for a bit. I'll go round for him later."

"Well, what is there to talk about, then?" Joe asked again, tamping down his pipe before lighting it. "Come on, you've got me curious now. You don't take our George round to the old man's for nothing."

"Oh, it's no use, love, you've got to know, sooner or later. It might as well be now."

"What's so important, then?" Joe had caught the serious note in her voice. Placing his pipe down on the table, he felt for the matches in his pocket.

Mary came round to the back of his chair and put her arms around his shoulders, speaking softly and urgently. "Listen love, and don't get angry. What's done is done and we can't change it. It's Alice. No, she's not ill, not in that way," as he moved in his chair. "She – she's going to have a baby. She's pregnant."

For a moment there was a silence so profound that Mary held her breath. Then the meaning of her words got through to Joe.

"What!" he shouted, shaking off Mary's restraining arms and jerking to his feet in one rough movement. "No, no, she can't be! Not Alice! She's too young." It was clear that to Joe, Alice was still his little girl, not a woman with a woman's needs. His voice rose, "Who is it who's done this thing?" he roared, thumping his first down on the table and making the pots rattle.

"Shshsh…" Mary urged him. "Sit down, love, and try not to shout. It won't do any good, you know."

"It'll bloody well do me good!" yelled Joe. "Just wait till I get my hands on him."

"It's not like that, love." Mary spoke quietly, trying to calm him down. "She says they love each other."

"Love! What's love got to do with it?"

"Come on, now, try and settle down a bit and I'll tell you."

"You bloody well will tell me." Joe seized her arm and drew her near him, fixing her with his eyes. They were blazing with anger and hate – not for her but for that unknown who had seduced his daughter.

"Who is it?" He shook her in his rage. "Whoever it is, I'm going round there right now to sort him out."

"You can't, Joe."

"Can't? What d'you mean, can't?" His voice rose again as he gazed at her in fury.

"He lives in Blackpool."

Her husband released her suddenly and sat down abruptly in his chair. This news had knocked the wind out of him. He had been sure that it was some local lad who had taken advantage of his daughter.

"But…" he blustered, "who the devil at Blackpool? D'you mean some lad she picked up there and we didn't know about it?"

"No, no, of course not. It was Harry Tomlinson, at number Fourteen."

Again silence pervaded the sitting-room. It was taking all Joe's efforts to assimilate this latest piece of information on top of everything else.

"You mean Harry Tomlinson seduced her? Let's have this clear."

"Yes, love."

"But… I thought he was engaged to marry someone next door?"

"He is," Mary admitted, reluctantly.

"Bloody hell!" her husband shouted, jumping to his feet again. "I don't believe this! You mean this happened under our noses while we were staying at number Fourteen? But… it couldn't have. It must be someone else."

"Alice says it's him," insisted Mary.

"Well then, engaged or not, if it's him, he's going to marry Alice, seeing he's got her pregnant – and I'm going over there to see that he bloody well does." His normally pale face was suffused with rage and his eyes glared wildly at her.

"Don't go on so, love," his wife pleaded, as Joe paced up and down the threadbare square of carpet. "Perhaps he will marry her when he knows." Mary decided that she couldn't risk telling her husband that Harry might already have married his fiancée. He was furious enough as it was.

"He will, right enough, because I'm taking her over at the weekend to make sure that he bloody well does."

"You can't Joe – not go over there and have a row with him! Not until we know how things stand."

"Oh, can't I? We'll see about that at the weekend!"

When Alice returned an hour later, her father had gone out to the 'Hen and Chickens'. The news about his daughter had shaken him so much that he had felt like strong ale. And he knew that he wouldn't be able to talk to her when she came in without losing his temper again. Mary, too, had been very shaken by the exchange with her husband and when Alice walked cautiously in, her mother was sitting in front of the fire, pale and weeping.

"Oh, Mum, I'm sorry I had to leave you to tell him yourself, but I just couldn't face him. Did you tell him? What did he say?"

"Oh, yes, I told him – and it wasn't good. You're still only a child to him, you know, and he just can't understand how this can have happened to you. He blames Harry, not you, for all this, especially as he's engaged to another girl. He's talking of going over there at the weekend to sort things out with him."

"Oh, no, he can't do that!" Alice cried, echoing her mother's words. "I won't let him."

"You can't stop him, love. You know what your Dad's like once he gets his mind on something."

"He'll spoil everything! I want to tell Harry myself." Her voice rose.

"You want to marry him, don't you? Your Dad's only going to tell him that he should marry you, now that you're having his child."

"I can do it myself," wailed Alice.

"I wouldn't argue with your Dad, he's mad enough as it is. Just take notice of what he says and go with him when he asks you."

"Oh, I'm going upstairs. I just can't think anymore."

"Go on, then, I'll bring you a drink up when you're in bed."

In the morning, Joe had already gone to work when Alice came downstairs. She had taken her time because she was once more feeling sick and in this condition, she just couldn't talk to her Dad. She had had a sleepless night, too. Tea was all she was able to get down at breakfast and she set off for work half-an-hour late. Doris greeted her with a cheerful grin, guessing how she was suffering and told her that she had again put someone on Alice's looms.

"Thanks, Doris, I shalln't forget how good you've been to me."

"I'm sorry for you, love. I wouldn't like to be in your shoes just now."

"I'm thinking of going over to see Harry tomorrow." Alice spoke firmly and calmly as she took down her working overalls from the peg. Doris looked down in astonishment to the bench where Alice was perched, buttoning up her strong working shoes.

"Why on earth should you? Can't you write and tell him?"

"No. It'll be too late by the weekend. Dad knows now and he's threatening to take me over at the weekend to sort things out with Harry. I must go tomorrow and see him myself. Tell him before Dad does."

"Well, you are being the brave one, knowing your Dad. Don't you think you'd be better doing what he says?"

"No, I'm going on my own. I've taken some money out of my Savings box to buy a ticket to Blackpool."

"Well, if you've made your mind up…"

"I'll leave Mum a note to tell her where I've gone. When she finds it, it'll be too late – I'll be on my way."

Mouth agape, Doris gazed at Alice in admiration. "Well, really, when it comes to it, you take the biscuit, I must say… But, if you've made your mind up… Suppose your Dad comes after you?"

"If he does, it won't matter. I shall have seen Harry myself by then and I shalln't care!"

"What d'you think Harry will do when he knows? Doris couldn't help asking her.

"I don't know until I get there," Alice said, suddenly unsure about what she would find on the other side of the Pennines.

Chapter Ten

As Alice alighted from the train at Blackpool, she was even less sure of what her reception would be. Would Harry even be in when she arrived at number Fourteen? No one knew that she was coming, so his mother and his sister would be very surprised when she turned up on their doorstep. Should she tell them that she had come on a day trip, even though she wasn't wearing her best clothes? She hadn't dared put on anything different from her working ones in case Mary noticed and suspected something.

The September sun had brought out the late holidaymakers onto the promenade as she hurried across to the tram. The tide was half-way out and the sea quite calm. A slight breeze was blowing off-shore and little knots of people were dotted on the sands. There even one or two paddling along the edge of the water. The mellow September sunlight glinted on the glassy surface of the water and there wasn't a cloud in the misty blue of the sky. She walked slowly along Nelson Street, past the bay windows, the garden shrubs and the iron gates. The gate of number Fourteen was half-open, so she pushed it against the railings and trailed up the path. There was a tight knot in her stomach and her heart was pounding as she stood on the doorstep, hesitating. It swung open suddenly and a young couple came out, hand-in-hand. They were strangers to Alice, so they must be visitors. They stared at her as they hurried down the path before swinging off in the direction of the promenade.

As she stood on the doorstep, watching the door swing shut, she very nearly turned and followed them out of the gate, but she knew she couldn't. She had to tell him now! She raised her hand to the iron knocker. For a while, no one came to the door but eventually, it opened and Harry's sister, Maud, appeared in the doorway. She had on a flowered overall and in her hand a clean tea-cloth dangled.

She looked at Alice without recognition for a moment before remembering who she was. "Let's see, it's Alice Boothroyd, isn't it?"

"Yes. Please can I come in for a minute?"

"I suppose so." Maud , taken aback, led her into the lobby. "Did you want to see Mother? Are you here on holiday again?"

"Well, no, not really. I'd like to see Harry, if I could."

"Harry?" Maud's supercilious eyebrows rose in surprise. "I don't know whether he's in or not. Is it important? We're busy."

"Yes, it is." Alice was stung to firmness by Maud's haughty manner.

"I'll go up and see if he's in, then," Maud reluctantly agreed. She evidently didn't know what to make of it, at all.

Alice watched the tall, angular figure go upstairs, remembering her own journey up to Harry's room. Her heart gave a painful lurch as she pictured him coming downstairs with his sister, to meet her. Breathing quickly, she waited, but when Maud appeared, she was alone. The disappointment was almost unbearable.

"He must have gone out for some reason. I don't know how long he'll be, though. Do you want to wait?" she asked, no doubt hoping that Alice would now go away.

"Oh, yes, I'll wait," Alice replied, standing her ground in the hall.

"Would you like to go into the front parlour, then? Everybody's gone out and you could watch from the front window. I'll have to get back to the kitchen now. We're just in the middle of making the dinners, so if I can't help you...?"

"Thanks, I'll wait in there," Alice said, crossing the lobby and opening the front parlour door. She walked across the empty, sunlit room to the seat she had occupied on the evening she had waited for Harry to return from Fairhaven Lake with Janet. That had been the evening he had taken her up to the attic – the first time they had been alone together. He had kissed her for the first time that day and told her he loved her. She gazed through the narrow gap in the heavy lace, watching the passers-by, most of them laughing, carefree, as she had been. And now... what was going to happen now?

Maud was waiting for Harry when he stepped into the kitchen. As she had expected when she had put the girl in the front parlour, her brother had come in by the back way and she intended questioning him about his visitor. "Someone to see you," she told him, wasting no time as he stopped by the middle door to hang up his coat and hat on the hooks.

"Oh? Who's that, then?" he asked, unsuspecting.

"Alice Boothroyd," she said, watching him closely.

Maud saw the colour come and go in his face as he heard the name. What could the girl possibly want with her brother, anyway? Harry received the news in silence. His mind was thrown immediately into turmoil. What on earth was she doing here? He strode quickly through, leaving Maud guessing, her mouth a thin line of disapproval.

Alice was sitting by the window, looking out. As he entered the room, she turned towards him and their eyes met. She stood up, to go towards him but as she did so, he watched her sway and fall limply onto the carpet. Striding over to where she was lying, he raised her by the shoulders, cradling her in his arms before lifting her tenderly onto the long sofa by the wall.

"Alice. Alice, love," he called, urgently.

Her eyelids fluttered and she opened her eyes, looking up at him. "Harry, oh, Harry, I just had to come and see you. You didn't write to me and I have something to tell you."

"What is it then, love?" he asked her, gazing directly into her eyes.

"I'm going to have our baby, Harry." It was quite easy, really, because between the two of them there was no need to hold anything back.

He didn't speak, but clasped her to him, brushing her hair with his lips before asking her, "Are you feeling alright now? You fainted, you know."

"I couldn't eat anything this morning, so perhaps that's why but I'm quite alright now I've seen you, Harry. I've missed you so much. Have you missed me, too?"

"Of course I have, love – you don't know how much. I do love you, Alice, and I'd already decided that I couldn't go on with the wedding. It's just that I've never found the right time to tell Janet. Her mother died , you know, soon after you went back home."

"Oh, how awful for her." Alice was genuinely sympathetic. She hadn't given Janet's sick mother another thought after she'd gone home. She shivered as she realised that since she'd last seen and spoken to Sarah on the holiday, she had died and been buried.

Taking her small hand in his, he said, "I didn't want to hurt Janet, after all she's been through, that's the reason I've been waiting to tell her. But you've been in my thoughts day and night. I didn't feel it was fair to write to you until I had everything sorted out here. If you could just trust me a bit longer, I'll tell her very soon."

"As long as you know about the baby, Harry. It does alter things a bit, doesn't it? I don't want to hurt Janet, either, but I know you don't love her and the baby is yours and mine. Are you glad about it?"

"I can't tell you how glad I am – it's not private enough in here! It's just that you've given me a bit of a shock, that's all, coming so unexpectedly, like this."

"I had to, Harry. Dad was going to bring me over at the weekend if I didn't."

"They know, then?" he asked her.

"Oh, yes, I had to tell them. I've been sick in the mornings and Mum told Dad before he found out for himself."

"I'll have to tell Mother – and Maud, as well – but not now. I expect they're wondering at this moment why you've come over to see me. Anyway, you can't go home alone in this condition. I'll go back with you and talk it over with your parents. I want them to know that we're going to be married just as soon as everything's cleared up here. Do you think you could manage some food? You said you'd eaten nothing this morning?"

"No, but now I've seen you and we've talked, I think I could manage something. Now I know you still love me I feel wonderful."

They both laughed and he kissed her tenderly, clasping her hands in his before putting them to his lips. They were small and pink, with well-shaped nails. Soon there would be another pair of tiny hands just like those! Although he hoped that she would have a boy. He had always imagined that one day he would have a son of his own. Looking at Alice, though, so small and dainty, he just couldn't see her giving birth to a bouncing baby boy.

He marvelled at the convoluted workings of Fate. A short while ago he had been feeling caught up in an inescapable situation. Now, suddenly, he had been reprieved! The girl he loved was going to be his wife and the mother of his son – or daughter! He didn't stop at that moment to think about Janet. He wanted a short time to savour to the full the joy of knowing that he now had what he wanted. Just for today, he would enjoy the moment. He would forget all those others whose lives would be affected by this miraculous turn of events.

He stood up, helping her to sit up on the sofa, kissing her again. "I'll go and see Ma. I shalln't tell her anything yet. We'll just have some food and then I'll take you home."

"Will you, Harry? I feel alright, now. Don't leave me too long, though, will you?" She pulled his head down again and her soft lips sought his.

"How could I ever leave you for long again, my little love?" he asked her, as they broke apart."

In the kitchen, Ellen and Maud stood preparing vegetables ready to put on the stove in the black iron pans. Ellen's fine, greying hair was combed back into a tight bun, out of the way, as she worked. Her sleeves were rolled up to the elbows as she delved into a bowl of water, but she glanced up as Harry joined them.

"Alice isn't fit to travel alone, so I'm going back with her," he said, "when she's had something to eat."

His mother's hands paused mid-way up from the bowl. "You're taking her back? Whatever for?"

"She hasn't been feeling too well, so when she's tried to eat something, I'll go back with her."

"Well, I've never heard anything like this. Alice Boothroyd appears out of the blue, and you go running off with her. You've never even mentioned her since she stayed here in the summer."

"No, I know, Ma, and I can't say any more now. Please don't ask me to explain. I'll tell you about it when I get back."

"What if Janet asks where you are?" Maud's acid voice cut in. She banged one of the largest pans down hard on the table.

"Tell her what I've just told you," Harry said curtly, leaving the kitchen to return to Alice.

When her son, together with Alice Boothroyd, had gone to catch the train for Yorkshire, Ellen sat with Maud at the table over a cup of tea before they started on the clearing and washing-up. Ellen's face was drawn and a worried frown appeared between her eyes.

"What do you make of it, then, Maud? I can't understand this at all."

"No," agreed her daughter, "Neither can I, unless she really is ill – although she didn't look it to me. Don't you think she's a bit young to be travelling on her own, anyway?"

"Yes, I do, but I think there's more to it than that. Why should she come here in the first place? What did she say to you when she arrived?"

"Oh, let's see – she insisted on seeing Harry, so I put her in the front room."

Ellen's face grew grave and her eyes bleak. "You don't think there could have been anything between them while she was here, do you? He did take her out a couple of times…"

"Yes, but… Oh, No, Mother, surely not? He was only being kind to her, don't you think?"

"I hope and pray I'm wrong, but it's beginning to look as if there was something going on we didn't know about."

"Surely not, Mother! What about Janet? He wouldn't be bothering with another girl when he's engaged to Janet. Not Harry! How could you think of such a thing?"

"He wasn't too eager to set the wedding date when he came home from France," Ellen considered. "Let me think… I'm sure it was the same week the Boothroyds were here that he finally fixed the date with Janet. I remember that Sarah was in here the day after, talking over plans with me for new clothes…"

"You mean he wanted to fix it up and get it settled so he wouldn't get involved with this girl?" Maud was incredulous.

"It looks like it," Ellen admitted, reluctantly.

"D'you mean – he really doesn't want to marry Janet, then?"

"He's my own son, but he's not been the same lad since he came home from the War. I don't think he feels the same way about Janet now as she does about him. She's the right one for him, though. He needs someone like Janet, not a flibbertigibbet like Alice Boothroyd."

"But, Mother, why hasn't he broken it off, then, if he feels like that about things?"

"He doesn't like hurting her after she's waited all these years, and don't forget, her mother hasn't been gone all that long, either."

"Oh, I don't understand this at all. You think he's lost his head over this mill girl, then?"

Tears welled up in Ellen's tired eyes. "It looks very much like it to me, and if that's true, we're all going to have to suffer for it one way and another."

Chapter Eleven

"Did you put those clean tea-cloths in the linen cupboard when you took them down from the airing-rack?" Janet asked Florrie Metcalf. They were preparing to change round the tables in the front parlour to accommodate fresh guests.

"Oh, didn't I mention it? I've reorganised the whole cupboard and now they're further up, with the napkins and the tea-cloths."

"Well, I wish you'd remembered to tell me. I wasted a lot of time this morning, looking for them."

"Sorry, dear, it just slipped my mind," Florrie apologised, smiling.

Janet recalled that yesterday Florrie had suggested that the menus should be changed. "We've got to keep up with the times," she had said. "All this heavy food isn't good for people on holiday. I think we could cut out some of the puddings and give them something lighter."

She had told Florrie firmly that the substantial meals they provided had kept the same people coming back, year after year, but she knew that it wouldn't be long before the menus were, in fact, altered. It seemed that no matter how much Janet insisted on a thing, somehow Florrie seemed to get her own way in the end. Janet couldn't understand how she managed it. Of course, she should be grateful for all the hard work Florrie put in around the house. Lately, though, Janet had begun to feel that she was beginning to take over. On the other hand, she was always so pleasant and cheerful. There was just no way of really finding fault with her. And anyway, they needed her. When she considered it, Janet knew that they couldn't do without her now.

Sighing, she went into the kitchen to the linen cupboard for the tablecloths. Finding them quite high up in the cupboard, as Florrie had indicated, she made a mental note to put them back again onto their proper place when she had the time.

"We're a cruet short for the window table," Florrie reminded here, as Janet came through with the clean linen. "I lent one to Ellen the other day. Shall I pop round next door and get it back?"

"No, it's alright. You carry on with the tables and I'll go round. I want a word with Harry, anyway."

She hadn't seen much of her fiancée for the last couple of weeks. On the rare occasions they had been together, he had been friendly and affectionate towards her, rather than loving, but it didn't seem the normal attitude for an engaged man to adopt.

Whatever was the matter with her, these days? Here she was, finding fault again with Florrie and now she was beginning to criticise her own fiancée. Could it be she herself who was at fault? She always seemed to be so irritable and tense. Should she have gone ahead with the wedding, in spite of all the difficulties? She would talk it over with Harry tonight and see how he felt about the situation. She must make him understand that all she wanted was to be his wife, even though she had postponed the wedding.

It felt quite chilly outside as she stepped onto the path, although the afternoon sun was warm, the sky cloudless. Another month and the season would be coming to an end and the autumn gales would begin to batter the town. After that, winter would be upon them again and the annual renovation of the boarding houses would begin.

There was no one sitting outside on the bench of number Fourteen as Janet walked past. Shivering a little, she went into Ellen's house through the front door. The guests must all be out or indoors, keeping warm. As she reached the back parlour, she stopped short before tapping on the door. She thought she could hear someone inside, crying softly. If it was Ellen, it was quite unlike her. Should she knock to see if something was wrong? Lifting her hand, she knocked lightly, turning the knob and gently pushing the door open.

Ellen was sitting in her chair, rocking slowly by the fire, tears streaming down her gaunt face as she sobbed quietly. Her work-reddened hands clutched a sodden handkerchief screwed into a tight ball, with which she was dabbing her eyes.

"Ellen, whatever is it?" Janet cried, coming over to her in concern. Ellen had always been one to keep a firm hold on her emotions and Janet had rarely seen her ruffled or upset. It must be something that had touched her deeply to produce this flood of tears.

"Do you want to tell me?" Janet asked gently, "or shall I leave you?"

"No, don't go – I'll be alright now." A flash of Ellen's old determination crept into her voice. She got up as Janet stood hesitating. "Sit down, dear," she said. "I'll make us both a cup of tea. I'm better keeping busy. It stops me from worrying about things."

Janet followed her into the kitchen, offering to help.

"Maud's gone into town shopping, and it just came over me," Ellen explained, filling the kettle from the tap.

"Is there anything I can do?"

"No, dear, take no notice of me – I'm a silly old woman."

"That's the last thing you are! You're one of the most sensible women I've ever met."

To Janet's surprise, tears reappeared in Ellen's eyes, and she turned away again towards the stove.

"Oh, Ellen, I hate to see you like this. Can't you tell me what's upsetting you? Does Harry know about it?"

At the mention of Harry's name, Ellen swung round with a startled expression and again wiped her eyes. She didn't answer. Janet decided that she shouldn't press Ellen to tell her what her problem was. "Come and sit down." She led Ellen by the arm, unprotesting, back into the intimacy of the snug parlour. "Now, you sit there and I'll do the tea. Would you rather I left you alone, Ellen? I don't want to intrude on anything private. I'll come in again, later on. I want to see Harry later, to talk to him."

"He isn't here, Janet." The words were wrenched from Ellen in choking sobs.

"Isn't here? You mean he's gone out?"

"No. He's gone to Yorkshire."

Janet stared at her in bewilderment. "Yorkshire? Whatever for?"

"He's gone with Alice Boothroyd."

"Alice Boothroyd! Who's that?" Janet knew she was echoing Ellen's words but she couldn't stop herself.

"She was here in July."

"I don't remember her. What has she got to do with Harry?"

"She came here today and she was ill and Harry took her back home."

"But why, Ellen?"

"I don't know, but I'm sure there's something between them. Oh, Janet, what if there is and he can't bring himself to tell you? My own son getting himself involved with a bit of a girl like that – no more than a schoolgirl really – and you the one he should be marrying."

For a moment the words sounded alien and obscure to Janet. Then they dropped into place in her mind, like pebbles being slowly dropped into a pond. She stared at Ellen in horror. How could his mother say such things? If Harry had taken this girl anywhere, it was because she was feeling ill. And Ellen herself had said that she wasn't much more than a schoolgirl. What was she doing coming here alone, anyway?

"You shouldn't be getting yourself upset like this about something you're only imagining, Ellen. Whatever made you think this about him? I just don't understand you."

"I only hope I am imagining things, Janet." Ellen's tears subsided but her eyes were sorrowful. "A mother sees things that other people can't... I'm sorry I've upset you, dear. I didn't expect you to come in and find me like this. Maybe I've said more than I should have. Forgive me, Janet, we shouldn't judge him until we know."

"I know, without having to ask him." Janet faced Ellen defiantly, "and I'm surprised at your doubting him for one moment. He would have told me. He wouldn't have gone on with plans for the wedding, and everything...." She paused as a disturbing thought struck her. He had agreed on the date of the ceremony only after she herself had suggested it! He had, in fact, appeared reluctant until then....

Steam from the kettle boiling merrily away in the kitchen drifted in to the suddenly quiet room. In agitation, Janet jumped up, going to take it off the hob. She poured water over the tea in the flowered china teapot, leaving it to brew for a few minutes. Automatically, she covered the pot with the tea-cosy, left handy, staring unseeingly out of the window into the yard. Her mind had gone back to the middle of the season and an image came into her mind of Harry walking up the front path talking animatedly to a very pretty dark-haired girl. She remembered remarking to herself that the girl had managed to engage Harry in lively conversation – a thing she herself had found it hard to do.

Had she been blind, then? Missed something that his mother evidently hadn't? Of course, at the time, her own mother had been very poorly and she had had to spend all her time looking after her. As she recalled that terrible last week of Sarah's illness, a dreadful thought struck her. During that week, when her mother had been so ill, she had seen very little of her fiancée. He had had the opportunity of going around with the girl if he had wanted to. His mother had been occupied, too, next door and Maud fully engaged in number Fourteen.

Oh, no, he wouldn't have done that! Not Harry! She dragged her mind back to the teapot and uncovered it. It felt as heavy as her heart as she lifted it, pouring out a strong cup for Ellen. Taking it through, she handed it to the older woman who accepted it gratefully. They looked at each other and Ellen saw mirrored in Janet's eyes all her own doubts and fears.

Chapter Twelve

As the train pulled up the steep incline to the top of Otterthwaite Fell, Alice and Harry remained locked in each other's arms, secure in an empty compartment. They didn't notice that today, the moors were showing their most alluring aspect. The sombre greens were overlaid with purple and pink heather and an auburn tide rippled across the grasses as the wind caressed their feathery tips. Only when the landscape changed to roads and cottages did they separate. Soon all the dirty clutter of industrial Bradfield closed around them and the train ground to a halt in the gloom of the station.

Alighting onto the platform in a state of mutual bliss, they made their way, hand-in-hand, up Broad Moor on the rackety tram. It could have been taking them up to heaven! Even the sight of Moscar Street and the knowledge that they would have to face Joe and Mary couldn't touch them. Today, they were immured against anything that the world could throw at them, just as long as they were together.

It was Mary who let them in. After reading Alice's hurriedly written note, Mary had guessed that Harry might be bringing her daughter home. They needed to talk things over and it was better this way, just the four of them. Joe wouldn't have helped by going over to Blackpool and making a fuss. He hadn't come in yet from work, and she only hoped he would keep his temper in check when he saw Harry. The fact that Harry was here must mean that he hadn't yet married Janet, so perhaps Alice had been right about him, after all. And he was from a respectable family. She knew that Alice could have done a lot worse for herself.

By the time they were all three sitting having a meal in the parlour, Harry had told her that he and Alice would be married as soon as it could be arranged. Mary was keeping one ear open for the back door latch and when she heard it she got up and went into the kitchen quickly, telling her husband in a whisper, "Harry's here!"

"Harry! What the devil….? Joe started up from his bent position on the chair where he was putting on his slippers.

"He's brought Alice back," Mary hissed.

"Where from?" demanded Joe, removing his overalls.

"Shshsh… Blackpool – she's been over to see him."

"Bloody hell! Why couldn't she have waited and let me do it?" His voice rose.

"It's alright, love. He's going to marry her."

"Has he said so?" Joe didn't lower his voice.

"Shsh… Yes, yes, he has. He's just told me."

"Thank God for that, then. I'm tired, lass. Give me a minute, then I'll come in and see him."

He crossed over to the sink to swill his face and hands under the tap. "Keep that dinner in the oven," he ordered Mary, drying himself on the towel which hung behind the door.

"I've sent our George round to Grandad's. His ears have got a bit too big for comfort just lately."

"Send Harry in here, will you?" Joe decided, suddenly. "I'm better talking man to man."

"Alright, if you think that's better."

Joe lowered himself onto one of the hard wooden chairs by the table, waiting for Harry to come in. Was he getting old, or was it the long, hard day's work he had just put in at the foundry that had made him feel so tired? He had been preparing himself for the weekend when he would go over to Blackpool and tell Harry Tomlinson what he thought about him. Now that his prospective son-in-law was here, though, all the fire seemed to have gone out of him.

"Sit down, lad," he said, as the door opened and Harry stood, hesitating.

Harry spoke first. "I'm sorry it's turned out like this, Mr. Boothroyd, but we're being married as soon as we can. I want to marry Alice. Not just because of the baby, though. We love each other. The only problem is that I've been engaged to the wrong girl, but I'm going to sort all that out when I get back."

"I'm glad you're going to do the right thing by Alice," Joe said, because she's a good girl and she needs someone to look after her. She's always had a good home and I want to know she's in good hands when she leaves us."

"You needn't worry about that, Mr. Boothroyd. I want to look after her more than anything else and she will have a good home at Ma's until we can get a place of our own. I'm going to go and get my old job back as soon as I get home. Then we can start saving up to get our own house when the baby comes. I have a bit put by in the Building Society."

"You seem to have it all worked out," Joe admitted, taking out his pipe and lighting it carefully. "I can't say I'm pleased, though, about the way things have been done, but I can see that you care for my girl."

"Yes, I do, Mr. Boothroyd, more than anything else."

"She's young to be getting married, but as things are, I reckon it's the only thing to be done. You can put that dinner out for me, lass," he told Mary, as she slipped into the kitchen to see how the two men were getting on with their talk.

"You can't go back tonight, Harry, it's too late. We'll put you up on the sofa," Mary said, as she served up Joe's meal. "We can all talk things over after Joe's had his dinner. We've got a lot to talk about now, haven't we?"

Harry travelled back to Blackpool on a late train the following day in a determined state of mind. It had been hard parting again from his love but he knew now, beyond any doubt, that he was doing the right thing. There was no question of his marrying Janet. He would have been doing her a grave injustice marrying her when he didn't love her. Now he had no choice. He must break off the engagement – and without delay! He cursed himself for having become engaged to her in the first place when his feeling for her had been more sisterly than anything. And he had felt that it was, somehow, expected of him. She would be stricken, of course, and so would his mother and Maud, but now he felt a resolve he hadn't had before. Alice was going to have his baby and he meant to speak to Janet as soon as he arrived at Nelson Street.

It was early evening before he opened the front door of his mother's house and walked in. He went straight through to the back parlour, finding his mother and sister there. Ellen was mending linen and Maud going through some accounts. They both paused in what they were doing, looking up sharply as he entered the room.

"I expect you're wondering what it's all about," he began, leaning back against the sideboard and facing them both. A quick glance at his mother's face told him that she suspected the truth. Maud, too, was looking at him accusingly. "We didn't mean this to happen, Ma. We love each other – Alice and me. I can't marry Janet, it wouldn't be fair to her and, well, Alice is going to have a baby – your grandchild," he added.

Maud swung angrily to her feet, scattering papers on the floor and rounding on him furiously. "How could you do this to us, Harry? We all love Janet, and we thought you did, too. What can you possibly see in this bit of a girl? She's nothing but a common mill girl, anyway."

"Sit down, Maud, that sort of thing won't help," Ellen broke in. "If this is how things stand, we've got to face up to it, not start saying things that will make the situation worse. I've had time to think about things since you went off with her yesterday."

"You knew, then, Ma?" Harry asked, ignoring his sister.

"I guessed there must have been something between you. I don't like it any more than Maud, but you're my own son, and what's done is done. We can't change it."

"I just don't believe all this!" Maud said, her face flushed. "And I doubt if Janet will, either, when she hears about it."

"That's just where I'm going now – to tell her. I've left it far too long, already." Straightening up, he paused by his mother's chair, putting a hand on her shoulder. "I'm sorry, Ma, that it couldn't have been different."

Without another glance at his sister, he strode quickly from the room and made for the front door.

After he had gone, silence descended once more on the cosy parlour. Ellen sat perfectly still in her rocking chair, staring at nothing in particular. The rustle of paper as Maud went to retrieve the scattered bills eventually disturbed the quiet, but she didn't speak. She was still recovering from the impact of what her brother had just told them. She would never have believed it of him. This grown man who had just walked out of the room wasn't the same as the young brother who, youthful and innocent, had left them four years ago. This man was a different Harry. Someone she didn't recognise, who cared little for other people's feelings. Her mother had said that the War had changed him, and she had been right. Maud had had little to do with men on a personal basis, so she had no way of knowing whether Harry's actions were typical of them. If this was the way they behaved, she considered herself very lucky not to be involved with any of them.

In number Sixteen, Janet was trying to concentrate on her crochet work. Since yesterday, doubts and fears had haunted her like spectres in the shadows. Her thoughts had swayed this way and that. One moment she was doubting him and the next she was making herself believe that he wouldn't deceive her – he couldn't. She must not give way, she thought, as the ready tears welled up. She must wait until she knew for sure, one way or the other. Surely he wouldn't leave her waiting for long, though, not knowing what he was doing? In restless despair, she got up to put away the delicate stuff. It was no use, she couldn't concentrate on anything until he came to see her. As she closed the drawer, she heard a tapping on the door and, her heart pounding, she called out to him to come in.

All the love and tenderness she felt for him rose up in her and she wanted to run to him to tell him that she loved him with all her heart. But his face had already told her that it wouldn't be any use. Even before he spoke, she knew that she had lost him.

Coming forward into the room, he stood in front of her. Their eyes met and he could see that she was trembling. He put out a tentative hand towards her but she immediately stepped back. "Don't touch me," she cried. "I couldn't bear it."

Dropping his hands, his eyes moved away from hers. White-faced, he asked in a low voice, "What can I say, Janet?"

Her lips quivered and she had to force herself to speak. "Don't say anything. I can guess."

"It's not like that, Janet. I kept telling myself that everything was alright between us, but I knew it wasn't. I should have spoken before. Then Alice came along and I knew I'd behaved very wrongly in asking you to marry me. It's all my fault and I can't tell you how sorry I am." The wretchedness in his eyes was apparent.

"I don't want your pity – I want your love." Anger rose now, preventing the ready tears. "But you evidently haven't got it to give me." Taking off her engagement ring, she placed it carefully on the velvet plush of the tablecover. "Here – give her this – she's taken everything else, so she might as well have this, too." Head held high, she brushed past him, averting her eyes and walked quickly out of the room. He heard her running swiftly up the stairs, across the landing to the back of the house and her bedroom.

Harry stood quite still for a few moments, trying to convince himself that she would soon get over it – that he had saved her from making a terrible mistake. But he knew it wasn't true. He had torn her life apart and she would never forgive him. She would believe, too, that Alice was the reason for his breaking off the engagement. It was too late now, to try to say any more. She would just have to believe what she chose.

Shaken, and suddenly very tired, he made his way back to the lobby and the front door. Florrie must be around somewhere and he didn't want questions from anyone. He had left the ring where she had put it down. She must do with it what she thought fit. From this moment on, he was starting completely afresh. It was only as he was re-entering number Fourteen that he realised he hadn't told Janet that Alice was pregnant....

When she reached her bedroom, Janet flung herself down on the bed, giving way now to the uncontrollable tears which were flooding her. They seemed to come from some deep well and to rise in great waves which turned into gasping sobs, wracking her whole body. How long they went on she didn't know, but they possessed her and she gave herself up completely to their insistent surging. Eventually, they became a steady stream of scalding, angry tears. Lifting her head she saw that the pillow was soaking. Her head felt like lead, but she dragged herself up from the bed in an effort to get a grip on herself.

She was a little calmer now, although her legs felt wobbly and her head muzzy. Why couldn't he have loved her? Why did it have to be this girl? How could he do this to her? A wave of hot anger against them both swept through her. Alice Boothroyd had taken her love from her without a single thought for Janet's feelings. She herself had waited for him all these years through the lonely days and nights of the War and again, since her mother's death. Why, oh why, hadn't she married him instead of postponing the wedding? She should have gone ahead with it, in spite of her commitments to her family. Oh, it was unbearable to lose him now, after all this time.

But then what good would it have been, if he didn't really love her? A fresh upsurge of tears threatened her again and she turned to the wash-stand, pouring water from the jug, cupping her hands into the basin. Lifting them to her red-rimmed eyes, she tried to wash away the anger and bitterness before going downstairs to see if Florrie was getting on with the suppers.

"Oh dear, are you starting with a cold?" Florrie asked her, as she entered the warm kitchen.

"I think I must be," mumbled Janet, avoiding the other woman's eyes. "Florrie, could you manage to serve the suppers on your own tonight? I think I'll go up to bed."

"Of course, dear. You try to get a good night's sleep. It's the best thing if you're feeling under the weather. Would you like me to bring you a drink up soon?"

"No, thanks," Janet whispered. "I'll just have a drink of water and take it up with me."

"Alright then, and if you're not feeling any better in the morning, have a lie-in. I'll do the breakfasts as well."

"Thank you, Florrie, you're very good." Her voice was barely audible.

"Mustn't have you going down ill and worrying that nice young man of yours, must we?" Florrie said cheerfully.

Janet took the glass from her hand, turned and fled from the kitchen.

Well, Florrie thought, I wonder what all that was about?

Chapter Thirteen

Harry Tomlinson and Alice Boothroyd were married in the parish church – St. Peter's, at Broad Moor on a sunny day in early October. Harry would have been satisfied with a civil ceremony but Alice and her mother felt that a proper church wedding was the least they could expect.

For her bridal outfit, Alice had settled on a mulberry skirt and three-quarter coat, both bound with matching satin ribbon, over an oyster-coloured silk high-necked blouse. In choosing the clothes, she had thought that she would be able to wear them during the coming winter if she needed to be dressed up. To go with them she had bought a wide-brimmed mulberry hat in the latest style and, around her shoulders, a soft brown fox fur tippet lent her by Doris, her matron-of-honour.

Harry stood proudly at her side before the altar in his dark grey suit with a white carnation in his lapel. He thought he had never seen her looking more beautiful as she came down the aisle on her father's arm.

At the end of the ceremony, as the vicar told them, "I now pronounce you man and wife," and as Alice lifted a radiant face to his, he felt he wanted to crush her to him. But that would have to wait till later! Kissing her upturned face with propriety, he knew that she, too, was anticipating her wedding night. Holding her arm tight in his and smiling down at her, he escorted her into the vestry to sign the register. Afterwards, they walked out through the arched doorway into the hazy sunshine of the late morning.

Relaxed, and talking easily now, the little group made its way past the terraced houses in the direction of Moscar Street.

George had been left with his granddad in case he misbehaved. He wasn't used to churches and Mary knew that even the awe-inspiring St. Peter's wouldn't have cowed him. This was her daughter's big day and she wanted nothing to spoil it for her.

"I'll go along and fetch our George and Grandad," Joe said, as they approached their own house.

"Alright, love, I'll get everybody settled and give them all a drink while you're gone."

Mary had left everything ready for the party. Samples of her excellent baking and cooking awaited the guests when they came into the parlour. Ellen noted with approval the home-made bread and muffins, the quality of the pastry and the variety of the cakes. A large capon had been carved and also a ham. Ellen wondered whether Alice was as good a cook, but she doubted it. That was something Harry would have to find out for himself!

The bridal couple were returning to Blackpool on the evening train. Harry's room at number Fourteen had been settled on as suitable for them to use while they were living with her. The double bed had fitted in easily, still leaving room for the other furniture. Both she and Maud had been very unhappy about this marriage and Ellen was wondering how things would be once Alice was living with them. It was no use, though, worrying about the future. They must take things as they came and put up with it for the sake of the baby – her first grandchild! Ellen's heart warmed to the prospect, even though its mother wasn't the one she would have chosen for it. And Harry looked so happy now, she thought. All that worry and tension had dropped away from him. She watched him with his bride, staying close to her side as if he wouldn't be parted from her for a moment.

Mary, serving the sherry to Doris, the Matron-of-honour, was thinking how well everything had gone. The weather had been kind to them and although the wedding party at the church had been a small one, the Vicar had given them a beautiful service. He had arranged for a photographer to take pictures outside the church, so Mary hoped they would turn out to be good ones. As she came round the room to Ellen, Mary sensed that underneath that rather haughty exterior, Ellen was just like any other woman – vulnerable in any matter where her children were concerned. This marriage hadn't been easy for her. After all, her son had been engaged to a girl she had known and loved since her birth and, to her, Alice was a stranger.

The door opened suddenly and George, her son, ran in. "C'n I have some lemonade and jelly?" he asked his mother, going straight to the table and looking to see what was on it. "You promised," he reminded her loudly.

"In a minute. Get your coat off, and go and wash your hands – we haven't started yet. Now then, Dad," she said, as her father came in with Joe, "Come and sit here by the fire and I'll get your whisky, then we'll see if we can all get round the table. I think we'll have to pull both leaves out."

Joe seemed to be getting on well with Harry, Mary thought, as they all sat round the extended table for the meal. Now that Alice was married to Harry, Joe seemed to have relaxed and become quite affable, even fatherly, towards him. It looked as if everything was going to turn out for the best, after all. Of course, it would be a wrench for them both, Alice leaving them, but they would be able to visit her at Christmas, Ellen had said as much, or at any other time during the winter. And Alice would be living in a nice clean place – a town by the seaside – with her baby, instead of having to bring it up in dirty Bradfield. She hummed a little tune to herself as she served tea in the best china teacups and saucers. It looked as if they were all going to be happy, today, no matter what tomorrow brought.

Later in the day, Ellen, with the bride and groom, alighted from the late train at Blackpool, flushed with the wine and the wedding breakfast and all the excitement of the day. They had dozed a little on the journey, Alice with her head on her husband's shoulder. Ellen had caught herself thinking resentfully that it should be Janet sitting there beside her son. She had rebuked herself sharply, telling herself that from now on, Alice was his wife, for good or for ill. That was how she must be regarded and treated. But would Maud see it that way?

In the softness of a mild, windless evening, they made their way towards the promenade and boarded a tram. Soon, they were entering number Sixteen and, after such a hectic day, they were glad to take off their clothes and relax. Alice's new hat had survived the day well, and she had taken care not to crease her dress while she was sitting on the train. She still looked fresh and rosy but then, thought Ellen, I'm nearly three times her age, so it's no wonder I feel jaded.

Leaving the newly-weds sitting close together on the sofa in the back parlour, Ellen went through into the kitchen to see if Maud could produce cups of tea and supper. The time was now half-past ten, so Maud would already have served the visitors their suppers. Her daughter looked up from the sink, pushing back a stray wisp of mousy-fair hair, without asking how the wedding had gone.

"I think you might have come into the parlour to welcome them back, Maud."

"I haven't had the time. I've been too busy with the suppers." There was a defiant note in Maud's voice which Ellen recognised only too well. It was no use arguing with her when she was in this mood.

"How about some tea, then? If you're too busy, I'll do it."

"No, it's alright, Mother, I'll put the kettle on again. I'll do it this once, but I must make it perfectly clear that I'm not going to run around waiting on them."

"Of course not, Maud, but we've had a very full day today, and we're tired. We're ready for a drink and a bite and then we can all go up to bed."

Leaving her daughter to clear up the kitchen, Ellen took the tea into the parlour. If she wanted to be awkward and behave in this truculent manner it was best to leave her to come round in her own good time. Eventually, the bags were taken up and Alice's clothes put away in the big wardrobe which now had it's two halves filled. The time was well after midnight. Maud had gone up to bed without coming to congratulate her brother. Alice noted her absence but she didn't comment on it. She wasn't going to let anything spoil her day, which had been a wonderful one from start to finish. Starry-eyed still, she sat on the edge of the double bed – their bed – while Harry undressed at the other side. It seemed strange to be sitting here as man and wife. No need now to snatch an hour here or there to be with him. Now they could take all the time they wanted and no-one would be able to stop them ....

Slowly, she unfastened the buttons at the front of her dress, before lifting it carefully over her head. Then she rose and went over to the wardrobe, opened it and placed the dress on one of the padded hangers. The dressing table was next to it and, standing in front of the long mirror, she let her lacy petticoat drop to the floor. Placing one small foot on a chair, she slowly rolled down one of her stockings, then the other. Through the mirror, she could see Harry lying on the bed in his nightshirt, watching her.

Smiling, she moved over to him, perching on the bed at his side. "Loosen me up, love," she said softly. His hands came up to undo the hooks between her breasts. For a moment, he fumbled, but the next, she was free of her corselet and the rest of her underwear slid on to the floor. There was plenty of time now, but for him there was urgency as he gazed in wonder at the soft whiteness of her naked body, like marble in the dim glow of the gaslight. He touched the satin skin and them, compulsively, he slid his arm around her waist, pulling her over him to straddle his hips. It was as if they had always been together like this, and the feeling now was deeper. She was his wife and she was carrying his child. Tenderly, he caressed her as she responded to his every movement. He knew she wanted to please him in every way she could and he knew, too, that she was delighting in their love-making as much as he was.

Much later, very early in the morning, he awoke with his arm over her breast and the moment he moved, she opened her eyes. Gently kissing her uncovered breast, he laughed softly,

"We never even turned out the lamp." She didn't answer but both her arms slid down to his buttocks, pulling him close and again, they made love. It was as if they couldn't get enough of each other.

"Oh, Harry, I never thought I could be so happy," she whispered, as they lay together in an ecstasy of fulfilment.

"Neither did I," he murmured, kissing her mouth tenderly, then again, passionately.

Chapter Fourteen

On the eleventh of November, a month after the wedding, the War officially came to an end with the declaration of the Armistice. Bunting flew from all the hotels along the promenade and a huge Union Jack was hoisted high above the Town Hall. The rejoicing was tempered with sadness, though, as people remembered the losses suffered by many families throughout the town.

In Harry's church the following Sunday, thanksgiving was offered up for his safe return, and for those others who had survived the horrors of the conflict. Alice, sitting with her new family in their regular pew, wasn't yet used to the order of the service. She was following her mother-in-law's example the whole of the time. Occasionally, out of the corner of her eye, she caught sight of Maud, on Ellen's other side, watching her. When she made a mistake, she saw Maud's supercilious smile. Alice hadn't been used to going to church. Neither her mother nor her father had been church goers, but Sunday attendance at church had always been a part of the Tomlinson's lives. Harry had come to church on this particular Sunday to give thanks for his own deliverance and to remember all those friends who had not come back. Sitting close to Alice's side, Harry couldn't hold her hand, but he shared his hymn book with her, fingers touching.

At the end of the service, as they walked out into a cold November day, little was said between the family. The emotional atmosphere inside the church had affected them all and it was a quiet party which gathered for their meal later in the back parlour. The holiday season now being over, there was no longer a rush to serve anyone before they ate.

"I'll clear the pots," Alice offered, after the meal was finished.

"No, don't trouble yourself, I'll do it. I wouldn't like you to tire yourself." The sarcasm in Maud's voice was obvious.

"It's no trouble. I'm not an invalid. I can still do jobs around the house, you know."

"Let Maud do it," Harry said. "You've got to look after yourself, you know."

"Alright, Harry, if you say so," Alice gave in gracefully. "But I don't seem to be doing much around the place at all."

Maud jumped up, sweeping the cups onto a tray and hurrying into the kitchen with it, banging the door behind her. There was an embarrassed silence as the door closed on her.

"I'll go and give her a hand," Ellen declared, following her daughter out and into the back. Carefully shutting the door, she told Maud roundly, "You should have let Alice do this, you know." She removed a tea-towel from the airing rack overhead and started drying a cup.

"Oh, no, Mother, *I'm* the drudge around here. She does precious little else but carry a few pots in now and again."

"Well, you can't expect her to do much as she is. She does dust their room and keep it tidy."

"Oh? does she? And how much of it does Harry do? I've never seen her dirtying her hands and she never has a hair out of place." There was pure venom in Maud's voice. "And we do all their washing with ours – and all the cooking." Her sharp nose took on a pinched look as the anger spilled over.

"It isn't going to be forever, Maud. It's only for a short time. Harry's seeing about going back to work again after Christmas. They need to start saving for a home of their own, like any newly-wed couple, especially when the baby comes."

The crockery was in grave danger as Maud banged down a cup and saucer onto the wooden draining board.

"Well, all I can say is, the sooner the better."

"I wish you'd try to get on with her a bit better, Maud."

"I can't help it, Mother. When I think what a poor thing she is compared with Janet. And think about this, Mother, if he'd married Janet, he wouldn't have to be thinking about getting back to work, would he? Is he *fit* to be going back?"

Ellen was silent for a moment. She herself had been wondering that same thing when he had told her of his intention.

"Perhaps he isn't completely well," she said, at last. "What else can he do, with a wife and a child on the way? Perhaps he would have been better waiting until next summer, as the doctors advised, but now, really, he has no choice."

Changing the subject quickly, Ellen reminded her daughter that next week they must start on preparations for Christmas. They usually had a couple of families staying over the short holiday season from Christmas Eve until after New Year. The Christmas puddings and cakes would be made first, ready for storing to mature for a couple of months. Shortcakes and mince pies would be made much later on – just before the start of the holiday. They discussed the ingredients they would need,

Maud making a list ready for the shopping. Then, sighing, she told her mother,"I'm not looking forward to Christmas this time. It just won't be the same, at all."

Early preparations for Christmas were also underway next door. Florrie Metcalf was still in residence there because her Lytham tenant had asked for an extension of his lease until after the New Year.

She had come to an arrangement with Janet about staying on with them. They would be fully booked over the festive season and she would be needed then, after the lull in business during November and December. While they were empty of visitors, Janet intended cleaning and clearing all the cupboards and storage areas, so Florries's help would cut down her own work a lot. The re-decoration of one or two rooms would be left until after New Year before the new spring holiday season started.

Over the past weeks, the two women had come to an unspoken understanding. Janet never spoke of Harry and, although Florrie knew of the changed circumstances between the couple, she sensibly kept quiet about it. After that evening when he had broken off the engagement, Janet had determined to shut him out of her life forever. The only salvation lay in hard work and so, after the Christmas cakes and puddings had been made and stored, she and Florrie got down to the cleaning and clearing.

One evening, on Florrie's half-day off, as Janet sat over tea with her father, he commented, "I don't know what we would have done without Florrie these last few months."

"No," Janet had to agree. "At first I had misgivings about her. I thought she wanted to take over from me, but she's settled down well now and we know where we stand with each other."

"So you're quite happy about her staying on here, then?"

"Oh, yes, I don't think we could have got anybody better," she admitted.

"Pleasant sort of woman," Robert commented. "She doesn't look anything like her age, either. She must be as old as me, but she looks ten years younger," he added, appreciatively.

Janet's green eyes widened. She herself hadn't really considered Florrie as a man might look at her. Surely she was mistaken in thinking her father meant anything more than polite comment? His grief over her mother's death was still too fresh, anyway. Brushing away these thoughts as unworthy, she got up to clear the pots ready for washing up.

In the kitchen, her thoughts strayed next door, in spite of herself. Harry and his bride were still living there, and she felt that things would be a lot better for her when they found a home of their own and went right away. She couldn't help seeing Harry occasionally, at a distance, as he and his wife came and went from next door.

She hated Alice uncompromisingly, but she found she couldn't hate Harry. The feeling she'd had for him over all those years had been too deep for that. He had destroyed her world that night when he had walked in and told her he didn't love her. Now and then, thought, she couldn't stop herself from thinking what might have been if Alice hadn't come along, or if her mother hadn't so tragically died. But those things had happened and Alice was now Harry's wife. Until they got a place of their own, Janet knew she would have to avoid meeting them at all costs.

She did bump into Harry, though, one morning as she came round the corner at the back of the bakery, carrying some bread and cakes. As she put her hand on the latch of the high gate to open it, he came out of number Fourteen. She hadn't seen him come down the yard to the gate because of the height of the walls. As he stepped through, he stopped for a moment, staring at her and she thought he was going to speak. Quickly, she pushed open her own gate, going through it and banging it shut.

She was breathing hard as she put the basket down on the kitchen table. She knew that she couldn't have spoken to him for the world – she just couldn't! Closing her eyes, she prayed that some lucky chance would take them both right away from here – out of her sight forever.

As it turned out, Christmas was very mild that year. Both houses were fully booked and a great deal of preparing and serving of food was going on in both. Sprigs of holly and mistletoe placed strategically decorated the interiors and in number Fourteen, Harry had placed a large Christmas tree which reached almost to the ceiling. The firs were grown inland on the Moss, a large tract of agricultural land on the edge of the town. They were hawked around the town by horse and wagon at the festive season. Harry had knocked together a wooden tub big enough to hold the thick, solid trunk and it stood now, in a corner of the parlour, covered with shiny baubles of every colour. To the topmost branch was attached a celluloid fairy, complete with tiny wand.

Underneath the tree, on Christmas Eve, nestled one or two brightly-wrapped parcels. In the kitchen, hanging from separate hooks whilst maturing inside white muslin cloths, were half-a-dozen Christmas puddings. The air was fragrant with the aroma of a ham Ellen was cooking, together with a large piece of Scotch beef. On the top of the hob stood a row of fluffy mince pies, dusted with icing sugar. They were warming up ready for consumption by the family when they had their drinks in the back parlour.

Alice's mother and father had been invited to stay over the two days of Christmas and they had already arrived. With a bad grace, Maud had been persuaded to give up her room and move in with her mother so that Mary and Joe could be accommodated. Ellen had put her foot down firmly when Maud had proved argumentative about it.

Mary and Joe were now sitting on the sofa in the back parlour in front of a glowing fire which was heating the fireside oven. From it came a delicious smell of baking cakes and in the centre of the fire-grate, standing on sturdy steel bars, stood a large iron kettle, heating up water slowly over the fire. Underneath on the hearthstone, with its metal kerb, stood a shiny poker of steel, next to it a pair of fire-tongs and a long-handled toasting-fork, all ready for use.

Ellen came into the cosy heat and the glowing brightness of the room carrying a tray with glasses. "We're not going to wait any longer for Maud," she said, lips compressed with irritation. "Harry and Alice are just coming down with their presents for under the tree."

"Where is Maud, then?" Mary asked.

"Oh, she's gone next door to give Janet her Christmas present, in spite of everything. She's been gone an hour already – on Christmas Eve when she knows we're busy."

"Don't worry, Ellen. If you need help with anything, I'm only too willing to do it."

"If she doesn't come back in time for the suppers, I'd appreciate a hand," Ellen accepted gratefully. "Anyway, here they are," as Alice and Harry joined the family circle. "Let's all drink a toast – a happy Christmas to all of us and in the New Year, our first grandchild."

As the Tomlinsons were raising toasts in number Fourteen, Robert Crossley was out on the promenade with Florrie Metcalf. He had suggested that they go to have a look at the multi-coloured fairy lights which were strung along there this year. Soon, it was said, all the old gas lamps were being replaced by the new electricity supply and cables were being laid all over the town. There were more houses than ever being connected to the new power. Walking into Talbot Square, guiding Florrie by the arm, he asked her, "Well, what d'you think of that, then?"

"It's wonderful, Robert," she said, gazing in admiration at the strings of coloured bulbs which criss-crossed the square, and at the façade of the Town Hall itself, ablaze with coloured lights.

"Aye, it's not so bad," he admitted knowing full well that Lytham could not boast such a spectacle. He glanced across the square, where the Wine Lodge doors stood open, emitting subdued light and the sounds of music and laughter. "Would you care for a drink in the Lodge, Florrie?" he asked her. "This year has been a bad one for me, but maybe the next will be better. It couldn't be worse, anyway."

"It does get a bit better as time goes on." Florrie's kind face creased into a sympathetic smile. "Come on – we'll both drown our sorrows. Christmas only comes once a year, after all. It's a sad time when you've lost someone as I well know," she said, as they strolled into the welcoming warmth of the Lodge.

In the back parlour of number Sixteen, Janet sat with Maud after supper, all the other Crossleys being out for the evening. Maud didn't seem in any hurry to return next door and Janet was finding it hard to keep the conversation away from touching on Harry and his bride. She knew she was being uncharitable to Maud, but how she wished she would leave her and return to her own home. Maud was lingering over her third glass of sherry. She didn't see why she should rush back next door when there were Mary and Alice there to help with the work. Leaning towards Janet, she said, "I can't tell you how angry I feel about the way Harry's treated you, Janet."

"I don't want to talk about it, Maud," Janet said, through tight lips.

"Alright, then, I'm sorry I spoke, but I don't know how long I can stand it there, especially with her in that condition."

Janet looked up quickly, interest aroused, her green eyes questioning. "You mean... she's pregnant now?"

"Didn't he tell you? She was pregnant when he married her," Maud said, surprised that Janet wasn't aware of this fact. "I'm sorry, Janet if I've upset you, but I couldn't help saying something. I've been wanting to talk to you about it for a long time."

"Oh, no," breathed Janet. "Pregnant! No, he didn't tell me."

"We thought you knew, Janet. We thought he'd told you. We haven't said anything to anybody else because the baby's due in April and they were only married in October. Time enough when it's born for people to be reckoning up. I'd say the only reason he married her was because she's having his baby. I can't see any other reason. He must have lost his head over her, that's all I can say. I can't understand what he was thinking about, when he had you. Well, I promised Mother I wouldn't be long. I couldn't face all evening with them but I'd better be getting back. The sooner this Christmas is over the better, as far as I'm concerned."

Mechanically, Janet saw Maud out at the door. She really hadn't heard a word Maud had said since her remark about Alice being pregnant when she had married Harry. She was realising that Alice couldn't have met Harry again after her holiday until that day when she came over to see him. Of course! That was what she had come to tell him – that she was going to have his baby. That was why he had gone back with her to Bradfield so suddenly. So.... It must have happened while Alice was staying next door, even while Harry was fixing the date for the wedding, he must have been seeing the girl. Oh, it was unbearable! It was far too humiliating for tears. She felt a numbness creeping over her and her brain seemed to have ceased functioning.

Walking upstairs like an automaton, she went into her bedroom and opened the top drawer of her dressing table.

Underneath a pile of handkerchiefs she found the small box and, taking it out, she opened it. The engagement ring winked up at her and she swiftly snapped the box shut, holding it for a moment before running downstairs to get her outdoor coat. Putting it on, she lipped the box into one of the pockets and let herself out by the front door.

Soon, she had reached the promenade. The tide was fully in, heaving against the sea wall. She stood looking out over its fearful darkness for a long time, over the black troughs which surged through the railings, tearing at the frail, man-made structures, asserting their enormous power. In the dark, standing by the parapet, their fascination was awesome and the temptation to jump almost irresistible.

But she knew she couldn't do it. She was needed by her father and the children. No, that wasn't the answer. Taking the box from her pocket, she flung it as far as she could into the heaving waves. In the blackness she couldn't see it disappear, but she knew that it had now gone forever, together with any love or respect she had for him. From now on, he just didn't exist as far as she was concerned.

On this resolve, she turned and ran all the way back until she reached the house. Her father and Florrie were still out and Arthur and Rose still not back from the Sunday School play when she came in. By a supreme effort of will, she went upstairs to bring down the children's Christmas presents. She let her mind slip back to last year when she and her mother had stayed up late to fill the pillowslips. Even though Arthur was nearly ready for leaving school and Rose was now twelve years old, Sarah had kept up the old practice of hanging up presents in pillowcases by the sides of the fireplace. She felt she just couldn't do it this year. They would have to go under the tree with the rest. She would be going up to her bedroom, too, just as soon as everyone arrived home. She couldn't face another hour of forced gaiety, even for their sakes. What was she doing, anyway, all on her own on Christmas Eve, like some veritable Cinderella? Large tears formed on her eyelids, rolling down onto her pale cheeks.

Dashing them away in anger, she turned and laid the packages under the tree. The only thing her father would have to do now was to stop Arthur and Rose opening them before the morning.

Chapter Fifteen

After the festivity of the Christmas season, during which the weather had remained mild, January brought cold, north-westerly winds with flurries of snow. In number Fourteen, a kind of uneasy truce existed between Maud and Alice. Harry's sister had made it very clear that she didn't like Alice and the feeling was mutual.

Although Ellen tried to keep the peace between them, there were difficult moments when one or the other flared up or flounced upstairs to sulk. Harry tried not to get involved, but it soon became obvious to him that things couldn't go on like this for much longer. He and his wife needed a home of their own. Alice often complained of Maud's attitude and he knew that her grievance was justified. He had realised, too, after that encounter at the gate, how his ex-fiancée must be feeling.

Meeting Janet suddenly, like that at the back gate and seeing how distressed she was, had upset him more than he had expected. He had made up his mind that neither his wife nor his old love should suffer much longer. The first thing, then, was for him to see about getting back to work. He wasn't coughing nearly as much now, and he felt stronger than when he had come home.

As he entered the carpentry shop, all the old familiar smells of new wood, glue, varnish and linseed oil met him. He walked from the doorway down the corridor that led to the small wood and glass office where Sid Greenwood kept his books. Sid owned the shop, but he did a full day's work in it, like all the men he employed.

"Harry! It's good to see you back. I hear you had a bad time of it out there, before you were invalided out."

"Not so good," admitted Harry, "but a lot of them fared worse."

"Aye, and that's a fact," agreed Sidney. "I believe you've got yourself a wife since you came home. I suppose it's that nice girl from next door?"

"Well, no," Harry appeared embarrassed, "she's a Yorkshire girl. Her name's Alice, and I'm going to be a father as well." He knew, as he looked around that this was where he belonged. He realised how much he'd missed not being here.

"Congratulations," Sid was saying. "You'll be wanting to start back here soon, then, if you're going to have a family. How're you feeling now?"

"Oh, a lot better, and the sooner I start work, the sooner we can think about moving into our own place. We're living with Ma at the moment."

"Well, we've plenty of work in just now, so you could start on Monday, if you like."

Harry glanced around at the workbenches full of saws, planes and chisels. All the tools of the trade had been left there while the men ate their dinners in the back room.

"Come and have a look at the stuff we've got ready," Sid offered, leading the way into the shop. One or two pieces of furniture in the process of being assembled stood at one end of the room, while several completed items waited at the other, ready to go on the delivery van.

"Nice sideboard over here for Councillor Jackson. And a table and six chairs to go with it. Best mahogany, as you can see."

Harry admired the craftsmanship. The quality was unmistakable. Had he really been away for four years? It seemed like only four weeks as the old atmosphere invaded his senses, wrapping around him again as if the six years of his apprenticeship had finished only yesterday.

When he reported for work, he was surprised to find that he hadn't the strength for continuous planing or sawing. His old skills hadn't left him but he was very slow at all the jobs. He even began to wonder if he would ever be in shape for the work again. After a week or two, though, his muscles began to readjust to the exertion, his speed increased and he began to enjoy the job again. He loved the feel of the quality wood under his hands – the way it responded to the tools he was using. It had always been like this for him. The wood seemed to be his natural medium and a finished piece of furniture gave him as much pleasure as it did the customer who had ordered it.

The only trouble was that the sawdust didn't seem to be doing his chest much good. He found that he was coughing more again, but he ignored it and got on with his work. As a tradesman, the wages were good, too, and every week he added to his account at the bank. At this rate, they might soon be able to put down a deposit on a house of their own, he thought, as he ran the plane expertly over the piece of oak he was shaping into a table leg.

Working around the house in number Sixteen, Janet had expected that she would be tackling the clearing for the decorators alone. Florrie should have returned to her house at Lytham by now, but her tenant was still in residence there, having become involved in further business on the coast. She had told Janet, 'You'll need help with the cleaning-up too, when the men have finished.' Which was true enough. Last year, Janet and her mother had tackled it all between them and found it hard work for the two of them. So it had been agreed that Florrie would stay on right through the spring until the summer season began again and the bookings started to get heavy. She told Janet that when her tenant finally moved out, she would advertise her house locally, for rent. It looked as if Florrie was becoming a permanent fixture at number Sixteen, but then, no one was complaining about that.

Alice's baby, a healthy seven-and-a-half pound girl, was born on a bright morning at the beginning of April in the double bed at Nelson Street. Dr. Fraser hadn't anticipated any complications and there were none but the birth was long-drawn out and it was a wan and exhausted Alice who greeted her husband when he came into the room, just before noon.

The hours following the onset of labour had been an agony of waiting for Harry. There had been a continual coming and going of people to and fro from the bedroom, but he had been quickly dismissed as of no use at all in this particular situation. He had been sent off to pass the time as best he could while the women did their work. Finally, the doctor had arrived and stayed with Alice for so long that he had felt he couldn't stand the waiting a moment longer. Then, quite suddenly, Ellen had come down the stairs, smiling, to tell him that he now had a beautiful daughter.

When he tiptoed up to the bed, he saw that his wife was almost buried in the pillows, his daughter wrapped in a soft shawl, cradled on her arm. He saw that Alice's face was much paler than usual and the deep blue eyes were heavy, with shadows beneath them. By the bed Ellen was sitting, and as Harry approached his wife, she lifted the baby into her own arms. The next moment he was kissing Alice tenderly. As he lifted her up from the bed into his arms, he noticed how frail she looked now that she had been delivered. Had she been as small and dainty as this before? He had become so used to seeing her swollen and heavy these past months, he had forgotten how petite she normally was. No wonder she'd had a long, hard labour. His heart reached out to her as he held her to him for a moment before laying her gently back against the pillows.

"How are you feeling, love?" he asked her softly.

"I'm alright now, Harry. Oh, I'm so glad it's all over! I don't think I could go through that again. She's like me, Harry, dark, but your mother says she could change in the next few weeks. Go and have a look at her."

For some reason, Harry felt that he had to continue tiptoeing round the bed to his mother's side. Holding out his daughter proudly for him to see, Ellen pulled back the edge of the shawl. A pink, wrinkled face peered up at him through half-closed lids. He noticed the dark hair, already luxuriant on the small head. He put a finger near to one of the tiny hands and a small fist closed over it. His heart thumped painfully as the full realisation hit him that he now had a child as well as a wife to look after.

"Alice needs to rest now," his mother said. "We've sent for her mother to come over for a day or two. With the labour coming on so suddenly there hasn't been any way we could tell them beforehand. She needs to be left alone now to sleep."

"She's beautiful, love," Harry told his wife proudly, going up to the bed again to kiss Alice before he and Ellen took the child downstairs to let Alice have a good, long sleep. "I'll come up again love, when you waken up." Holding his daughter reverently, he carried her down the stairs, Ellen following.

"I should let Alice sleep as long as she can," his mother advised, as he handed the baby to her. The new perambulator was standing in the parlour and Ellen intended putting the child to sleep in it while Alice rested. She herself would attend to her until her mother was ready to feed her, she thought happily. "Alice has had a hard time, you know," she said, "but the baby's perfect – very healthy, the doctor said. Alice is quite alright, too. Just a couple of stitches, he said, so you've nothing to worry about at all. The only thing is, I don't think she's got much milk, but we'll have to wait until she tries to feed her. We may have to give her the bottle."

It was eight o'clock in the evening when Alice stirred. The doctor's sedative had helped to give her a long, unbroken sleep. As soon as Harry heard her call, he ran up the stairs and up to the bed to hold her again.

"My own darling," he said, kissing her tenderly. "How are you feeling now?"

"A lot better," she said, yawning and snuggling down again into the bed.

"Ma's getting a tray ready for you. D'you feel you could eat something now?"

"I think so, Harry. Where is she? The baby?"

"Ma's put her in her pram downstairs until you're ready to feed her. She'll bring her up after you've had something to eat."

"Alright, then," Alice agreed, sitting up and reaching for a bed-jacket. "But I thought I'd give her a bottle instead. It's much better," she added quickly.

Harry gazed at his wife, hesitating before he spoke. "Don't you think you should try first, love?"

"No, I don't want to bother with that. I don't think I've got much milk, anyway. Dr. Fraser told me cow's milk is alright if you heat it and put something with it."

Nonplussed, Harry told his wife that he would bring up her tray. He intended asking his mother what she thought about Alice's ideas on the subject of feeding. She would know what to do.

"Don't worry," Ellen said, as he rejoined her in the parlour. "She'll change her mind when I take the baby up to her."

Things were a bit different, though, when Ellen handed over the child to her mother.

"I don't want to try," Alice said, stubbornly.

"Well," Ellen urged, "I think it's wise to put her to the breast to let her suck, for a start."

"It won't be any use. I don't think I've got enough milk."

"Perhaps not, but if you have any milk at all she'll bring it. Mother's milk is always best, you know, and you've got to think of your baby. You want the best for her, don't you?"

"Alright," Alice capitulated, slipping her nightdress down and putting the baby to her breast. She knew she hadn't much milk. There had been no fullness and no leaking. She would show Ellen that it was no use. What was all the fuss about, anyway, when the doctor had told her that she could give the child a bottle? She would try once, and that was going to be all, she determined, as the tiny mouth closed over the nipple and the baby began to suck. She felt the pull of the milk but very soon she knew that she was drained. The baby was getting no more. Taking her away, she held her on her arm. The child immediately began to wail.

"It's no good," Alice said. "I told you so. I haven't got enough. You'll have to give her a bottle to make up."

Holding the child out to Ellen, she lay back, feeling the tightness of the binder around her stomach gripping her. "I'm not going to bother trying any more. The doctor left a recipe for something to put in the milk, so Harry can go to the surgery to get it."

Defeated, Ellen got up, taking her grand-daughter from Alice, to carry out her wishes. Most mothers would have persevered, she reckoned, for the sake of the baby, but it looked as if Alice had already made up her mind that she wasn't even going to try to feed her. Sighing, Ellen took the crying child back to the parlour to give Harry his instructions.

That night Harry joined his wife in their double bed. He held her tenderly, not passionately – it was too soon for that. Their baby slumbered peacefully yet in the wooden cradle Harry had made for her.

"Are you pleased, Harry, that it's a girl?" Alice whispered.

"Of course I am, love. Anyway, there's plenty of time for one of each."

"Don't say things like that, Harry. I don't want to think about it."

"You'll soon forget all that, love," he assured her.

"That's easy for you to say. You didn't have to have her."

"No, I didn't," said Harry, taken aback by the determined note in her voice, "but I thought that women took these things in their stride."

"I didn't expect it to be like that, and I don't want another." Her eyes filled with tears as she turned her head away from him.

"Alice, love, whatever's the matter? Nobody's expecting you to have another baby yet. I only meant that we've got a long time ahead of us. I didn't mean to upset you, love."

"Alright, Harry, as long as you know I don't want another baby soon." The words trembled on her lips as the ready tears threatened.

"Of course I understand, love. Here, wipe your eyes. We mustn't be arguing over such a thing. Come on, give me a kiss and we'll forget all about it. You'll feel different in the morning."

"Harry, I'm so frightened. How am I going to look after her?"

"You poor little darling," Harry soothed. "Your mother will be here tomorrow and she'll stay as long as you need her." He smiled to himself. She really was only a child yet herself, he thought, as she cuddled up to him for comfort. He wondered, suddenly, what sort of a father he himself would turn out to be.

Florrie Metcalf rapped on the door of number Fourteen and walked into the hall. Her apple cheeks were rosy with exertion and she was wearing a brightly-flowered, sleeveless overall which covered her dress completely. Her sleeves were rolled up and on her head, covering her thick golden-brown hair, was a blue and white mob cap. "Anyone at home?" she sang out in her cheerful voice.

"Come through." Ellen's deep tones reached her ears as she turned the door knob, letting herself in to the back parlour.

"I'm sorry to trouble you, Ellen," she began, stopping as her eyes took in the picture of Harry's mother with a baby on her lap.

Smiling at her, Ellen told Florrie to come in and sit down for a minute.

"I thought I saw Dr. Fraser's car outside yesterday!" Florrie cried delightedly. "And I wondered – but as things are next door, I couldn't say anything to Janet."

"No," agreed Ellen, "I haven't spoken to her about it, either. Maud's the only one who goes in, these days, but I don't think she would be foolish enough to tell Janet. I've felt very sorry for Janet, but what can I do? I've known her since she was a child and her mother was a very good friend to me. My one comfort is that Sarah isn't here to see how things have turned out. It would have broken her heart. But God moves in mysterious ways, as I've always believed. I know how Janet must be feeling and I know that my son's to blame. But I try to face up to things as they are. We've just got to think about this little one now."

"Is it a boy or a girl?" asked Florrie, coming nearer to take a look.

"A little girl. She's asleep now and so is her mother. I've told Alice to get all the rest she can for a day or two. She had a long labour, you see. Alice's mother is due here this afternoon, so that should make her feel better. I think she's worried to death about looking after the baby."

"I never had any myself," Florrie said, "and it's been a great disappointment to me. Can I hold her for a moment?"

"Of course you can."

Florrie took the baby eagerly, cooing over the sleeping child, reluctant to give her back to her grandmother.

"Did you want me for something?" Ellen asked her, at length.

"Goodness, yes, I'd quite forgotten! She's beautiful, isn't she? Have you got a spare ceiling mop I could borrow? We're doing the bedrooms and Janet's using ours. We shall have to get another one next time we order from the hardware store."

"We're not using ours at the moment – we're too busy with mother and baby," Ellen said happily. "I'll just go and get it from the broom cupboard."

When Ellen returned with the mop she found that Florrie had seated herself on the sofa with the baby, still sleeping, on her lap. Florrie reluctantly exchanged the child for the mop, standing, ready to get back to work.

"You're staying on next door, then?" Ellen asked her, resuming her seat by the fire, the baby on her lap.

"Yes, my tenant has been in the house since last summer but he's finally leaving at the end of this month. His business here has taken him a lot longer than he expected. Anyway, he's definitely given me notice now. He's handing me back the keys at the end of this month."

Ellen looked up with sudden interest. "You mean – you want a new tenant, then?"

"Well, yes. I might as well be getting some rent as leave the house empty. Janet needs me next door and if I'm living here, I've no travelling. D'you know someone who…. Oh! You mean your son and his wife?"

"Yes. They need to be on their own, especially now that the baby's arrived. I shall be sorry to see them go, but things haven't been easy for them up to now. Maud resents her sister-in-law and I've thought more than once that it isn't fair for them to be living right under Janet's nose, after the way Harry behaved. It would be better all round if they moved away from here. Lytham would be just far enough so that we could visit each other. They are saving hard for a mortgage and this would give them a bit more time to get a deposit together. Whereabouts in Lytham is it, Florrie?"

"Just behind the front, Fore Street."

"Well then, I'll tell Harry when he comes back from work and perhaps you'll come in again to discuss terms with him – that is, if you agree to them having it."

"Of course I agree. I'm only too glad it's someone I know. You never know what sort of tenant you get when you advertise. I've been lucky up to now. The gentleman who's there now was recommended to me by a friend. He has looked after the house very well, but he's had someone to come in to clean for him."

Ellen's face lit up with one of her rare smiles. "Thank you, Florrie. You've taken a load off my mind. I'm sure this will be the answer to our problems. Don't worry about bringing that mop back. It will do any time."

"Thanks, Ellen, and tell Harry I'll pop in again to have a chat with him about it. Better for me to come in here. It wouldn't do for him to come next door, would it? As things are?"

Chapter Sixteen

On a cold, bright day at the beginning of May, Harry Tomlinson, as the new tenant, moved into number Twenty, Fore Street, at Lytham. Key in hand, he led the way up the garden path, Alice following closely, carrying the baby. Harry's mother brought up the rear, loaded with bulging parcels and bags. She shut the low gate with a click, as the others reached the front porch.

In spite of Alice's protests, Ellen had insisted on accompanying the family into their new home. She had made up her mind to stay with them for a day or two until they got settled in, feeling that Alice was going to be fully occupied looking after her child. Alice's mother had now returned to Bradfield after staying with her daughter for a week at Nelson Street. She couldn't leave her husband to manage on his own for longer, and her father needed her, too.

Although Mary had been a great help showing Alice how to cope with the baby, Ellen had a suspicion that her daughter-in-law was going to find it hard looking after a house, and a husband as well. There were two bedrooms at Fore Street, so Ellen determined to make use of the spare one at the back. She could be spared just now, before the start of the season proper, and Maud would be glad to see the back of her sister-in-law, as she had so often told Ellen. She would make no difficulties about it.

As she turned and walked up the path to join her little family at the door, Ellen thought that this house of Florrie's should suit the couple very well. Slightly set back from the main road through the village, its diamond paned front windows looked over a small garden filled with low shrubs and rose bushes. A green-painted porch erected over the front door offered protection from the weather and later, in summer, wisteria would cover its arched top and sides. At the back, a door led directly from the scullery into a long, enclosed yard, with the usual outbuildings of lavatory and coal-house. The bottom of the garden had been dug over as a vegetable plot. Alongside, a narrow path led down to the high gate in the wall, which cut off the yard from the back street beyond. Hanging on the house wall, on a large iron hook, was a galvanised bath, large enough for an adult and standing underneath and a little to one side, was a large mangle with wooden rollers.

All Florrie's furniture had been left in the house during the previous tenancy and the same arrangement had been agreed upon for the Tomlinsons. Their own few nick-nacks and clothes, together with the cot and perambulator had been delivered earlier and now awaited the couple in the house.

As Harry placed the key inside the lock and turned it, Alice stepped up to join him on the threshold. Their eyes met in anticipation and excitement as the door swung slowly open.

I should carry you over, you know," Harry laughed, "but I can't manage the two of you."

Ellen put down the bags on the path. "Give her to me for a minute, if you like." She received the small bundle in the lacy shawl eagerly, forgetting her son and his wife in her absorption with her grandchild. The pink face was smoother now and the already abundant hair lighter in colour. The eyes were a deep blue, like her mother's but it looked as if she was going to be fairer when her colour changed completely.

Laughing happily, Harry had by now lifted his bride over the doorstep and deposited her, giggling, in the parlour. Holding hands, they glanced around at the comfortable room, with its chintz covers and flowered curtains, so different from the formal velvets and brocades of Nelson Street. The furniture wasn't as heavy, either, the wood being walnut, Harry observed. The whole effect was one of light and warmth.

Ellen, following them in and noting the cosy atmosphere of the place, felt that there was nothing here to dim the happiness of the couple who were to occupy it. Handing back the baby to her mother, Ellen passed through into the scullery to survey the facilities there and, finding everything to hand, she filled the kettle, putting it on the gas stove to boil. She had gathered together a selection of goods from her own kitchen cupboards to start the couple off in their new home. These were waiting, too, in the kitchen, ready to be put away in the cupboards. It would be up to Alice to replenish the items as they were used but at least she would have a well-stocked kitchen to start with.

"We'll all have a cup of tea before we start putting everything away," she called to the couple, who were opening drawers in a chest they thought suitable. Meanwhile, Alice had laid the baby in her pram. She slept for long hours as yet, awakening only for her feeds or to be changed. Later, under Ellen's expert guidance, the cupboards were filled in both the kitchen and the parlour. Alice insisted that she herself would prepare the first meal to be eaten in the house. There was a piece of tender, cold brisket in the larder which Ellen had cooked previous to the journey. Alice said she would serve this with a green salad. She fetched out an embroidered tablecloth – one of her wedding presents – from a drawer she had just filled, placing it over the polished table. Setting places for the three of them, she retired to the scullery to begin on the meal.

It was quite a long time before she reappeared, rather flushed, with a large plate of bread and butter, cut thickly, and a teapot. Before she could place the pot down on the table, Ellen jumped in time to snatch the tea-pot stand from the sideboard, and get it under the pot.

"We mustn't spoil Florrie's good table, must we?" she said. "D'you need any help in there?"

"No," Alice replied shortly. "I've done the salad. I've only got to bring it in." Turning abruptly, she disappeared into the kitchen.

Ellen glanced at her son, who was watching his wife indulgently, wondering how he was going to fare in the future. But perhaps Alice would learn in time. She fervently hoped so, but as Alice served the thickly sliced beef and the undressed salad, she began to despair for her son.

"Sshsh, love, she's going home soon," Harry assured his wife as Alice sobbed in his arms a couple of nights later, lying in their new bed. "She's only trying to help you, you know."

"How can I do things right with her watching me all the time?" Alice moaned. "She's always telling me what to do."

"It's a big thing for you having the house and the baby and me to look after, love, and it's only for a bit longer now – then we'll be on our own."

"Oh, I hope so, Harry. I want to see to everything myself. I want to cook and clean and look after you and the baby all on my own, not be watched all the time as if I can't do it myself."

"You will soon," Harry promised, "and you're doing very well already."

This wasn't strictly true, but he couldn't bear to listen to her sobbing. Changing the subject quickly, he asked her, "Have you decided which of those names we're going to call her?"

Alice's tears subsided as she considered the question. "I think it's going to be Jenny," she gulped. "What do you think?"

"If you like it, then that's what we'll call her," he agreed quickly. "We'll have to be fixing up the christening soon, now we've decided."

Her soft arms stole around his neck and she snuggled into him. "I can do it, Harry. I know I can. Say you think I can," she pleaded.

"Of course you can, love." He kissed her quivering mouth. "Don't upset yourself so. Everything's going to be alright, you'll see."

As the Tomlinsons moved into Fore Street, redecoration was nearing completion at number Sixteen, Nelson Street. March and April, two very cold months, had given way to May, but there had been no respite from the strong winds and the low temperatures. It looked as if spring was going to be very late this year. The summer itself seemed far away, even though the first sprinkling of visitors would soon be arriving.

Looking much more relaxed now that Harry and his wife were gone from next door, Janet was placing dust covers over the front parlour furniture before the decorators started in there – the last room to be re-painted. Janet had to admit that Florrie had worked like a Trojan helping her to clear the rooms, always cheerful and uncomplaining as they moved the furniture about together. The two of them were getting along better, too. It was difficult not to like Florrie. She had a way of getting past any reserve one might have and, since Harry's departure, Janet had lowered her defences in the presence of the other woman.

"Is it getting any better, then?" Florrie asked her one day, as they were putting the furniture back into place in the front parlour, the decorators having finally moved out.

Janet took her time before answering. Florrie had never before spoken about the break-up between Janet and Harry but, somehow, it now seemed natural for her to ask. "Since they moved out, yes, it is," she admitted.

"I don't suppose you'll ever forget him, but it does get better as time goes on." Florrie remembered saying something similar to Janet's father at Christmas. "I don't want to meddle, but don't you ever feel like a bit of a change? Going out a bit more, for instance? You're always in here, slaving away."

"Where would I go to, Florrie? I've never been one for gallivanting. Working in here has been the one thing that's kept me sane this last six months." It was good to be able to talk to someone about things after her long, self-imposed silence on the subject. The sympathy in Florrie's eyes was apparent and words came flooding out of Janet. "Why did he have to meet her and leave me, Florrie? We could have been so happy together, I know we could." The long-suppressed tears flowed freely as Florrie came round a chair to place her plump, comforting arms around Janet's shoulders.

"It just wasn't to be love," she said. "Believe me, time will show that. We can't understand these things – we wonder why they have to happen – but later on, we find there was a good reason for them. Come on, dry those tears. You're made of stronger stuff than this and you'll go on to better things, believe me."

"Do you really believe that, Florrie?" Janet's voice broke again as fresh tears surfaced.

"Of course I do, love. Come on, we'll have cup of tea before we tackle these curtains. I'll just go and put the kettle on."

As Florrie went through the door, Janet let the hot tears fall unheeded. With them seemed to be flowing out the last of the bitterness she had felt towards Harry and his wife. When eventually Florrie returned with the welcome tea, she had finally dried her eyes and got hold of herself. She felt drained, but somehow freer than she had been for a long time.

"Feeling better?" Florrie asked, as they drank the hot, sweet tea.

"Yes, I am, much better, Florrie, and I don't think I shall ever shed any more tears over him again. This is the last time."

"Good for you!" Florrie picked up one of the rich drapes, preparing to mount the ladder which was propped against the edge of the bay window. Janet got up and took hold of the bottom of the curtain to release the weight while Florrie threaded the rings onto the pole. She glanced up at the other woman, managing to smile. Florrie really did understand how she had been feeling – and she cared, too.

"That's more like it," Florrie called down. "Why don't you go into town tomorrow and buy yourself a new dress?"

"I might just do that," Janet told her, letting the curtain fall into place as Florrie finished putting on the last ring.

As Janet and Florrie were having their heart-to-heart talk, Robert Crossley sat in the private office of Mr. Jonas Peabody, of Peabody and Grundy, Accountants, in the centre of the town.

Robert, in his best clothes, sat stiffly on the other side of a large mahogany desk, while Mr. Peabody addressed him.

"I think we can take your son, Arthur, into the General Office as our new junior," he said, sitting back in his green leather chair, placing his finger-tips together and surveying Robert through pince-nez. "He seems a bright lad. We'll see how he goes on for the next six months."

This was very good news for Robert. Mr. Peabody had been impressed by Arthur's school-leaving report and had interviewed the boy himself the previous week after having a word with his headmaster.

"Tell Arthur to report to the General Office on Monday, at eight-thirty sharp."

"Thank you, Mr. Peabody," Robert replied. "I'm sure you won't regret it."

"I hope not, Mr. Crossley." Mr. Peabody rose, dismissing Robert with a gracious inclination of the head. "Good-day to you."

Walking back towards the promenade and the tram, Robert thought how proud Sarah would have been of her son. He, too, felt great pride as he realised just how well his son had done in getting this coveted job. As he entered the house, Florrie met him with a cheerful greeting.

"You look pleased with yourself. Is it good news, then, about Arthur?"

"Aye it is, Florrie – he's got the job – starts next Monday," he said, almost dancing into the kitchen.

"I've sent Janet to look round the shops. She doesn't get out enough Robert. She'll cheer up, though, when she hears about Arthur. Would you like a slice of ham and those scones with cream and jam for your tea?"

"Anything you like, Florrie. I wouldn't complain today if you gave me jam and bread!"

Florrie laughed happily. "It's good to see you looking so cheerful. It's a long time since you've done much smiling."

"Aye it is, Florrie, but Sarah would be proud to see this day, wouldn't she?"

"Yes, she would, Robert. We're all proud of Arthur and I know he's going to do well in this job. You've got a smart boy there, you know. I couldn't be more pleased if he were my own son," she said, as she began preparing the tea. "I'll do a few extra scones," she decided, "those two will be ravenous when they come in from school, especially your son, when he hears the good news."

"You do seem to understand things, Florrie," he said happily, as he waited for Arthur to come in, eager to tell him all about the interview.

In number Fourteen, too, redecorating was in full swing. Since her visit to the house at Lytham to help install her son and his family, Ellen had been fully occupied. Several of the rooms were being re-papered and painted, Maud doing her full share of the work it entailed and seeming less irritable since her brother's departure. Ellen had been tempted to return to Lytham to see how the couple were going on, but each time some new problem in the house had kept her busy and prevented her from going.

The atmosphere between herself and her daughter had improved appreciably since the couple had left, but Ellen still had to be careful to avoid remarks about her son and his family. The couple had been over to see her once, bringing the baby who was to be christened after Whitsuntide, at the Parish Church at Lytham. They had both looked well, Alice as pretty as ever and Harry, in spite of a persistent cough, had seemed reasonably fit. The baby, now two months old, had looked a picture in her pink matinee jacket. Mary's mother, a prolific knitter, had sent it, together with a bonnet to match. Ellen had been upset when Maud had refused, point blank, to act as the baby's godmother.

"It's no use, Mother," she had told Ellen afterwards, "I just couldn't bring myself to stand there and promise. I would be a hypocrite if I had. Anyway, she says she's going to write to her friend Doris, at Bradfield, to ask her if she'll do it. And good luck to her if she does, that's all I can say."

Really, Maud was becoming more bitter than ever, these days. Ellen started clearing up the decorator's litter as her mind went back again to that day. Maud had barely looked at her niece during the course of the visit and had spoken little to either her brother or his wife after refusing their request. Maud could be extremely rude when she chose to be. She might at least have shown some interest in the child. It didn't look as if Maud was ever going to have any children of her own, and Alice's was such a beautiful baby! Ellen's eyes misted over as she pictured her grand daughter. She loved her dearly already and longed to hold her again. Maud didn't realise what she was missing by behaving in this foolish fashion, Ellen reckoned, as she moved a pair of steps which had been left in the wrong place by the decorators.

Chapter Seventeen

From the moment she wakened, the day didn't go well for Alice. When she looked at the small clock by the bedside, she saw that it was now nine o'clock! Goodness, she must have overslept again! Harry must have been gone for ages and made his own breakfast. Why was it that she could waken at six o'clock, decide to get up, and then go straight back to sleep again? Perhaps it was because she was always so tired? It seemed as if she had been on the go ever since Ellen had finally left, a month earlier. Frequently, since then, Alice had actually wished that Ellen was back – there was so much to do! As soon as she had finished one job there was another one waiting. Then the baby seemed to be crying more and it took ages to settle her. Before she had realised, it was time for getting the evening meal ready for Harry and after that there was the clearing and washing up. It was just one endless round of work, work, work. Running six looms at the mill had been easy compared with what she had to do now.

She remembered with shame that last night Jenny had been crying in the middle of the night. She had turned over in bed, covering her ears. Too exhausted to get up to see to her, she had pretended to be asleep and eventually Harry had got up and made her a bottle. How could she have done such a thing? Harry had to be up again early to get to work by eight o'clock. He must have been tired, too, and yet he had let her stay in bed and lie on without waking her. He knew how hard she was trying and he was making allowances for her all the time.

She must remember to check the cupboards today to see what needed replacing. There had seemed an awful lot of gaps in the shelves yesterday when she had looked for some flour for the Yorkshire puddings. That was one of the things she did well, having had some practice at home. But you couldn't have Yorkshire puddings every day and she was rapidly running out of ideas for what to give Harry when he came home. He had told her he didn't care what she gave him but she had noticed that he often played with his food and he didn't always finish up what she cooked. Oh, well, he couldn't expect her to be an expert cook like his mother. He hadn't married her for her cooking, anyway!

A sharp wail from the cot roused her as she began to drift off again and she sat up in bed – too suddenly! Immediately, the dizziness hit her and she dropped her head onto her knees. Then the thought struck her. Oh, no, no, she told herself in horror, as she remembered last time. No, it couldn't be! She had told Harry she didn't want another baby for a long time yet. He couldn't do this to her while she had Jenny to cope with and the house to see to and all the washing and cooking. It was too awful even to think about.

As she swung her legs out of bed, the room steadied. Perhaps she was imagining things? She had been too busy, lately, about keeping track of her monthly cycle, but now that she considered, it did seem a long time since the last one. Please, please, she prayed, let me not be pregnant again, suspecting that she was.

Well, whether she felt giddy or not, she would have to go and make the child's bottle and then go and get the washing done while Jenny slept. Eventually, the child finally settled, she went into the scullery to wash the clothes in the big, galvanised tub. She wasn't going to go to the trouble today of boiling them as well in the copper boiler. The long-handled posser was kept hanging on a hook on the wall, near the back door and she lifted it down, ready to start. It was hard work, alternately lifting up and pushing down the posser inside the tub, but it was easier than washing them all by hand. Even so, it was a couple of hours before they were all put through the wooden rollers of the wringer outside in the yard and pegged out on the line.

By the time she had finished she was ready for a rest, and once again, she was behind schedule. She was hungry, too, because she'd had no breakfast, she hadn't the time, except for a cup of tea. I'll make myself a sandwich, she decided, flopping down onto the sofa and pulling up her legs. As she made the snack she couldn't help thinking of that carefree time when she had first met Harry. Their love had been so wonderful then. Nothing had intruded on it. There had been just the two of them in a golden bubble of delight. That was how she had foolishly thought it was always going to be. The months, though, at Nelson Street had been full of arguments with Maud and once she'd had the baby and got her own home, she had been caught up all the time in domestic chores. It hadn't been at all what she had expected. Even her relationship with Harry hadn't been the same, lately.

Her mind skipped back to that holiday week in Blackpool. Even their lovemaking wasn't like that any more. They were both so physically weary that there didn't seem much joy in their union now – at least as far as she was concerned, there wasn't. Harry satisfied himself always, but now he didn't bother with the preliminary stroking and caressing of their early days. He didn't even bother to kiss her like he used to do. She had the feeling that all he wanted to do was get the act over quickly, then he could get off to sleep. She found she couldn't tell him that often she was left unsatisfied. Sometimes she was so tired herself that she actually pretended that she had climaxed. It was easier than trying to let him know how she felt about things .

As she looked back to those golden days of her holiday, a picture of a brown, wrinkled face came into her mind and she heard a voice saying, 'You'll only have brief happiness…' Of course! It was the old gypsy on the Pleasure Beach, when he had taken her there that morning! Well, she had been right – her happiness had been only brief! What else had she said? She couldn't remember clearly, but she thought it was something about 'paying later'. Well, if she herself was right about being pregnant again, she was going to have to pay dearly for her folly. Sighing bitterly, Alice carried the tray into the parlour, which she noticed needed a good clearing-up.

In the late afternoon, she remembered that she had the shopping to do. There were several things she required. Two of the items she needed before she could start on Harry's tea. Wheeling Jenny in the direction of the grocer's, breathing in the cold, fresh air, she groaned with dismay as Jenny started crying. The long, wailing cries told her that she needed changing. Alice decided that she wasn't going back again, not when they were approaching the shop. They wouldn't be long, anyway, but when they reached the shop, two women were already inside, waiting to be served.

Both of them stared at Alice as she opened the door, pushing the pram through with the child crying lustily. After a few minutes, she had to lift Jenny out and, as she felt her mother's arms around her, the baby's wails abated.

"I won't be long Mrs. Tomlinson," Alfred Simpkins said, as he attended to his first customer. It seemed hours before he had served them both, though. "I'm sorry you have had to wait," he apologised, after they had finally both departed.

"I'll try putting her down," Alice said, placing the child in the pram. As soon as her harassed mother let go of her, the cries began again. In despair Alice said, "I'll take the flour and lard with me but would you please send everything else round to the house with the errand boy? I shall have to get back home to put Harry's tea on."

"Of course, my dear. I'll send round the rest of your order later on this afternoon. You've got your hands full there, I can see." He handed her the two items, which she placed in the pram.

Alfred Simpkins' pale, rather featureless face behind the thick spectacles was creased into a knowing smile. Skirting a couple of boxes of oranges and apples, he approached Alice, who handed him her list.

"Thank you, Mr. Simpkins," she said, making for the door.

He came forward to open it for her, wishing her 'Good afternoon," and nodding benevolently at the child. "You can have your order sent round every week, you know," he suggested, kindly.

"Yes, thanks, Mr. Simpkins." She pushed the pram quickly away from the shop.

As she hurried home, the awful thought struck again at her heart. However would she manage if she was having another baby? She was finding it hard enough to cope with one. Two large tears trickled down her cheeks and she got home in a panic, she had to change Jenny before she could start on Harry's tea.

He came in before it was ready and sat with the child on his knee, waiting patiently, thinking that his poor, darling Alice was trying so hard to cope with it all. Her flushed, harassed face flitted in and out of the kitchen, smiling anxiously at him each time she reappeared in the parlour. She really had no idea how to run a house, let alone manage a husband and a baby. He knew she was looking after the child properly, but she was always behind with her work, forever trying to catch up with the jobs. He had realised how tired she was, so he had let her sleep on in the mornings and seen himself off to work.

He was finding the work easier at Greenwood's, but he was very glad when he knocked-off at the end of the day. The sawing, especially, took it out of him, and it was mostly hardwood they were working with. Not that he was complaining. He had always loved working with wood, it was just that these days he didn't seem to have the same energy. When he got home, all he wanted to do after he had eaten was to doze off for an hour, and then it was time for bed. He wasn't blaming anybody, he was just facing up to the fact that his health had been undermined by the War. He wasn't alone in this, of course. There were thousands of others just like him, and some a lot worse.

"I'm sorry, love, it's so late," she apologised, putting the beef pie in front of him. "I've had such a lot to do today and I had to wait ages in the grocers." She lifted Jenny from his knee and placed her back in the pram.

"Don't worry about it. I can't expect it to always be on the table when I come in," he said, as she joined him.

He tackled the unappetising plateful with determination. The crust of the pie was heavy and the meat underdone. She would get used to cooking in time, he reckoned. It was a lot to expect from a young girl who had never done any domestic work except help her mother occasionally in the kitchen. A spasm of coughing seized him as he tried to swallow one of the tough pieces of beef and he had to jump up from the table to retire to the kitchen to get rid of it. It took some minutes to get his breath back and return to the meal. After a while, he gave up the effort of eating, leaving half the food on the plate.

A sudden vision of his mother's appetising, beautifully cooked meals flashed into his mind, and with it a memory of Janet. He tried to push both pictures from his mind as he sat staring down at his place. An insistent inner voice told him that Janet was as capable as his mother and that if he had married her he wouldn't be sitting here now with a half-cooked meal in front of him. Quickly smothering these treacherous thoughts, he waited patiently for his harassed wife to come in again from the kitchen. Bless her, she really was trying very hard, he told himself, finally pushing the plate to one side.

"Aren't you finishing that?" she asked him, as she brought in the rice pudding.

"I just don't feel hungry tonight," he said, wondering whether the pudding would be as disastrous. Fortunately, it had been cooking slowly in the oven for some hours so, although it was thick and rather stodgy, it was thoroughly baked. He filled up with that before leaving the table to sit on the sofa before the fire. She would get it right, given time, he thought, as he took off his shoes, put on his slippers and stretched out his legs. His eyes slowly closed and he drifted into a light slumber, as he usually did, these days.

The baby was christened Jenifer Mary in the lovely old parish church at Lytham. June was now well advanced and much better weather prevailed.. At the end of May it had seemed that the unseasonable cold winds would last forever, but now a gentle breeze blew off the land. With it came a warm hint of summer to come.

Doris had arrived early in the afternoon from Bradfield, still perky, hair aflame. She had agreed without hesitation to be the baby's godmother. Having been the first person to know about Alice's pregnancy and her confidante in the affair, she felt that it was appropriate that Alice should have asked her. She had no children of her own so she meant to take a special interest in this one.

Alice went to meet her friend at the station, Jenny asleep in the pram. Harry would join them at Fore Street with his mother, who was coming later, Maud having declined the invitation. As she had pointed out, *someone* had to be on duty at Nelson Street. Harry had made the effort of travelling to his mother's, hoping to persuade his sister to come to the christening, but it was no use – it seemed she was adamant about it. He had to resign himself to the fact that Maud had never accepted his wife as part of the family, and it looked as if she never would.

"Let's have a look, then, at the star performer, my godchild," Doris said, bending over the pram where Jenny was still sleeping peacefully. "Oh, she's beautiful Alice," exclaimed Doris, gently pulling back the covers to look at the child. Doris wasn't exaggerating, either. Jenny's thick, curly hair had lightened to a rich, golden nut brown, the long, matching lashes resting on the rounded cheeks like miniature fans. The small pursed mouth promised shapely lines and, although they were at the moment closed, she guessed they were blue, like Alice's.

Doris exclaimed again over the cottage, as Alice showed her over the rooms. She had already remarked on the pretty garden and porch as they had approached the house and she now enthused over the interior. After she had finished admiring everything, Doris remarked, "I'm sorry your mother couldn't come over with me, but your grandad's bad again and she couldn't leave him."

"Yes, I'm so disappointed. I'd have liked her to have seen Jenny christened," Alice said, as they returned to the disorderly parlour.

"Harry says that we'll have a trip over there and we'll stay for the weekend. He says a change will do me good."

"Yes," agreed Doris, having noted the general untidiness of the rooms and Alice's own wan appearance, "I think it would."

"Doris," Alice confided suddenly, "I think I'm pregnant again. I seem to have to tell you first each time."

"Good grief, girl, not so soon, surely?"

"Yes, I'm sure now. I hoped at first it was a false alarm, but I've been sick again and I know I haven't had any periods," Alice said flatly.

"You poor girl," Doris sympathised. "I thought there was something. Have you told Harry yet?"

"No, I thought I'd wait until I was sure, after I've seen the doctor this week."

"I can see how you feel about it. It looks as if you've got your hands full enough already," Doris said, looking round.

"Yes," Alice said bitterly, "I told Harry I didn't want another baby for a long time yet. He wants one, though. He wants a boy. He told me so when I had Jenny."

"Yes, but I don't suppose he meant straight away."

"Well, then, why did he give me another one so soon?"

"My dear girl, didn't you tell him to be careful?" Doris spoke in some surprise.

"Oh, no, Harry wouldn't talk to me about it. I've never talked to anyone about it. I don't know whether he believes in doing anything or not. I've just left it to him."

"Well, I think you should talk to him and tell him how you feel. If he doesn't want to try to prevent any more babies, you could do it yourself, you know."

"Could I, Doris? Mum's never said anything to me about it."

"No, perhaps not, but the doctor would advise you, seeing you're going to have two young ones so close together. It's too late now, but I should think about it after you've had this one."

"Oh, I don't know whether I could do that or not. I don't know whether Harry would like it or not."

"Goodness, child, if Harry won't do anything and you don't, you'll have a roomful in no time at all. Think about it, anyway, and have a talk to Harry. Come on, let's get this little one into her christening gown ready for her big day and then we'll see about clearing up a bit before Ellen and Harry arrive."

Somehow, after Doris's arrival, thinks started to go like clockwork. When Ellen came through the parlour door, dressed in her best grey, together with Harry, who was wearing his good suit, the house was looking unusually shipshape. Harry's mother had brought with her a home-cooked ham and muffins for later on and the party settled down to general chit-chat until it was time to leave for the service.

Entering the cool quiet of the church, they ranged themselves around the font, an expectant silence coming over the party as Alice held Jenny, Harry close by her side. Jenny was wearing Alice's own long, cream silk gown, which Mary had put away for just such an occasion. She behaved beautifully during the service, even when she was sprinkled with holy water. It was a much more relaxed and happy mother who received her back from the vicar afterwards.

Later, over Ellen's ham muffins and the cakes which Alice had bought specially from the local bakery, there was family fussing over Jenny before Ellen had to depart for Nelson Street.

Harry took his mother to the station before rejoining his wife and Jenny's godmother in the parlour. Doris was staying the night – it was too late to travel back – so Harry went out to the local public house for a large jug of beer to 'wet the baby's head.' Alice didn't care much for the taste of beer but as her husband and Doris seemed to be enjoying it, she accepted a glassful. Soon there was much laughter as they all toasted the child. Alice even forgot for a time that she might be christening another baby not long after the year was out.

Chapter Eighteen

Small flecks of sunlight speckled Miss Walker's carpet through the lace of the sitting room window. Janet stood before a cheval mirror trying on one of her new dresses. She had taken Florrie's advice and ordered some new clothes. This was her first order for the dressmaker since the cancellation of the wedding. In choosing the materials for two new dresses and a jacket, she had carefully avoided the subject of Harry, concentrating on discussing the cut and the length of the clothes.

The cornflower blue dress she had on was quite slim on the hips and it finished well above the ankle, where it flared out slightly. Two bands of matching satin ribbons decorated the hemline, echoed on the bodice and decoration. Janet wondered, as she gazed into the mirror, whether it was too short, but Miss Walker had predicted that clothes would go even shorter next season. The other dress, in her favourite shade of deep jade green, with a jacket to match, was hanging under its cloth cover ready to be fitted.

"That seems a nice fit, Janet." Miss Walker seemed satisfied, having inspected every inch of her work, as Janet turned herself round for inspection. "And the colour suits you very well, don't you think?"

"Yes I do. I feel comfortable in it even though I don't usually wear this shade."

"Well, I suppose the green is your colour, but this will be a nice change for you. Shall we try the other one on now?"

As Janet slipped off the blue and slid the green dress over her head, her mind went back to the day she'd tried on the amethyst wedding dress. She could see herself in this same room, standing there while Miss Walker pinned and fussed over it. She remembered how happy and full of joy she had been as she'd seen it taking shape under the dressmaker's skilful hands. Who was wearing that dress now, she wondered? She had told Miss Walker to give it to someone – anyone – just as long as she never saw it again. She would never wear that colour again – never!

Miss Walker's voice cut into her reverie. "Could you just put the jacket on over it, dear?" I'm not quite sure about the length. I think it may need to be slightly shorter because the hem of the dress is up a bit. Yes, I though so. An inch would do it. How are your father and the children at the moment?

As the conversation turned to family matters, Janet tried to let the intrusive memories slip back where they belonged – into the past. When she arrived home, she found there were two letters waiting for her in the morning post. Slipping off her outdoor clothes, she sat at the table to open them, paper-knife in hand. The postmark on the first one told her that it was from Wales. It could only be from Aunt Ruth, her mother's sister. After enquiring about her father and the children, Ruth suggested that Arthur and Rose might like to go down to Llandudno to stay with them for a week before they went back to school. Janet realised that she hadn't let Aunt Ruth know that Arthur had left school and now started work. She had been so caught up in her own problems that she had quite forgotten. She recalled now that Joan and William, their cousins, would be off school on holiday. The children had stayed before with their cousins and had always come back with enthusiastic reports about the good times they'd had. Janet decided that if Mr. Peabody, Arthur's employer, stretched a point about his holiday, she would advise her father to let the children go.

From all accounts, Arthur had proved an exemplary employee at Peabody and Grundy's. He had told his father that Mr. Peabody himself had commended him for his conscientiousness. She determined to speak to her father about the visit as soon as he came home from work.

Turning to her other letter, she wondered who could be writing to her from Preston. Then she recognised the handwriting. Ann Ferguson! Her old school friend, Ann, had written once before to Janet – it would be a couple of years ago – to tell her that she was living in Preston after becoming a war widow. The letter had told her that after qualifying as a nurse, Ann had left for France, where she had met and married an Army officer who had been subsequently killed in action. She had invited Janet to visit her in Preston – a short trip by train – but Janet had been too busy at the time to accept. After that, Ann had dropped out of sight again. Now, here she was, writing once more, right out of the blue, but that was typical of Ann! Janet smiled to herself as she slit open the envelope.

Opening the letter, she saw that it was quite short and breezy. 'Dear Janet, I haven't been in touch with you for a while and when I last wrote, you said you were too busy to visit me. Surely you aren't busy all the time? Can't you just have one week off from the place to come and stay with me?

We could have lovely chats about old times and I'll take you to Ellswick, out in the country here, where I'm thinking of accepting a place on the staff as a nurse. It's convalescent home, mainly for hospital cases, but they get some war-wounded as well. So you see, I shalln't be available for that much longer. Do say you'll come and stay and we can catch up on all our news. Your old friend, Ann."

Janet's smile broadened as she finished reading the letter. That was the effect Ann always had on Janet – a lightening of the heart and a feeling that life wasn't, perhaps, as serious as all that, after all.

Ann always seemed to have the ability to skim over life's surface like some colourful dragonfly over a pond. Then the smile slowly faded. She herself was still in the same position as she had been when she had received Ann's last invitation. She was tied to this place by an invisible chain. She couldn't leave Florrie here to manage on her own, just as she couldn't have left her mother, before. For the first time, Janet realised fully how restricted her life was here. She couldn't even contemplate taking a week off to go to visit a friend!

It was ironic that they looked after holidaymakers most of the year and yet none of them ever thought about having a holiday themselves. Oh, it was so unfair that she wasn't free to write and tell Ann that she would love to go over to see her. But, it was no use, she couldn't! Not while the family all needed her. Sighing heavily, she put the letter back in its envelope. She couldn't see any way she could go to Preston for a week in the foreseeable future.

And by the time September came in, with mellow warmth and hazy sunshine, Janet had resigned herself to the fact that she wasn't going to get away. She had written to Ann to tell her how impossible it was for her to leave everything just now and wishing her good luck in her new job. Once Ann started working, she, too, would be tied up and it was very unlikely that the two of them would get together again in the future.

A reply from Ann informed her that she wasn't starting her job until the beginning of October and that if Janet found that she could, after all, visit her before then, she would be delighted to see her. Putting this second letter firmly away, Janet put the question of the visit out of her mind completely. It was out of the question, and that was all there was to it, she decided.

"Come and see which of these dresses you want to take," Janet called to Rose, a fortnight later. She was packing the girl's suitcase ready for her departure for Wales. It had been arranged for Rose and Arthur to travel down to Wales by train at the end of September, Mr. Peabody having graciously allowed Arthur to take his holiday slightly earlier than officially decreed. Rose danced over to the wardrobe, dragging out her best Sunday muslin and handed it over to Janet.

"Arthur's got his clothes packed already," she said. "He's been doing it all week and we're not going till tomorrow."

"Well, if you'd been as tidy, yours would be packed as well," Janet pointed out. "As it is, I'm having to put everything in at the last moment. It will be your own fault if anything's missing. I did ask you to get the things sorted out. I can't do everything around here, you know."

There was an edge to her sister's voice which took Rose by surprise. Janet didn't usually speak to her like this, even if she did deserve it. Unlike Arthur, Rose was habitually untidy and her wardrobe and drawers were continually in need of sorting out.

"Don't be cross, Janet. I really did mean to do it, but I've been trying to finish those compositions Miss Mason set for us for the holidays. I shall be going straight back to school when we come home from Wales and I shalln't be able to do any while we're on holiday."

"Alright, I'm sorry I snapped at you. I expect it's just because I'm tired. You do help me a lot around the house, dear. I'll just go and fetch the straps to go around the cases, then we'll fasten them both up."

As Janet opened the store cupboard door and reached for the straps she heard Florrie coming up the stairs.

"Hello, dear. Can I do anything to help?"

"No, thanks, Florrie, they're all packed up and ready to go. We shall seem quiet next week without them, shan't we?"

"Yes, and we've only got one family booked in – the Ackroyds – four of them, that's all."

"Well, I shall be glad of a quiet week. It's been a busy season. How about you, Florrie? Don't you want some time off?"

"Me? Oh, no, I don't think so. I thrive on hard work. It's you who needs a break. Didn't you mention that a friend of yours had asked you to visit her if you could manage it?"

"Yes, I did, Florrie, but I've put it right out of my mind. I couldn't think of going as things are."

"Why not? Why not go this weekend? It would be the perfect time, with Arthur and Rose away and only one family in here. I could manage perfectly well for a week on my own, and see to your father's meals as well."

It took Janet a few minutes to take in what Florrie was saying, but, slowly, her eyes brightened as she considered Florrie's proposal. "Could you really manage on your own? Oh, Florrie, do you really think I could go?"

"Of course you could, with such a light week here. Now, you get straight off to the post office and send your friend a telegram to let her know you're coming. It's too late for a letter. Go on, dear, don't stand there wondering. I shall be perfectly alright."

"Oh, Florrie, thank you! I have been feeling a bit down lately, and if I could get away for a week it would be a wonderful change for me."

"Of course it would. It's what you need. Give me those straps for the cases and I'll go and fasten them up while you go round to the post office. You'll be needing to do some packing yourself when you come back, I reckon." Smiling happily at the outcome, Florrie went into Rose's bedroom while Janet went downstairs, her head in a whirl. On her way to the post office, Janet decided that she would travel tomorrow afternoon, after Arthur and Rose had left for Wales. She would be with her friend within the hour after leaving Blackpool by train.

A tiny thrill of anticipation, even excitement, quickened her steps. Tomorrow she would be free. Free from all the chores of the boarding house. She would be free to go where she liked with her friend, free to think about herself for the first time since her mother's death. And it was Florrie who had released her from her responsibilities for one whole, glorious week. She hoped she would be able to repay her in some way in the future. Her heart warmed towards the woman who had, to all intents and purposes, taken her mother's place.

As Janet was sending her telegram to Ann Ferguson, Alice Tomlinson, now nearly four months pregnant, was sitting alone on a promenade bench at Lytham. The seat was positioned on the narrow walk which edged the broad lawns all along the front from Fairhaven Lake to Lytham. To her left stood the old white windmill, unused now, except as a boat-house, but still supporting its four slatted sails. Beside it stood the lifeboat station, a very necessary institution in these treacherous waters, where the swift tide sculpted deep channels and hid large sandbanks.

Today the estuary was showing its most benevolent face. There was little wind and the hazy sun was reflected in silvery sheets along the edges of the shallows. Above her, sea-gulls curved and dipped, their rowdy squabbling filling the air. To her right, the river flowed out in its main channel through the sandbanks, finally spreading out to embrace the wide expanse of the Irish Sea, with its cool, blue horizon.

Straight in front of her, she could make out the buildings on the opposite shore at Southport. On a clearer day, they would stand out, sharp and clean, like cardboard cut-outs silhouetted against the blue back-drop of the sky. Today, the sun was shining through a misty veil and the air was beautifully warm. It didn't touch her heart, though, even if it warmed her skin.

Jenny, now nearly five months old, sat happily in her pram by Alice's side, oblivious to her mother's state of mind. All her concentration was focussed on a rag doll, which occasionally she threw over the side and which her mother had to retrieve. The child had that rare combination – sweetness of temperament combined with unusual beauty. Everyone passing by stopped to admire her rosy cheeks, her chestnut curls and the laughing eyes above the rosebud mouth. They didn't tend to look at Alice in quite the way they used to, though. She just couldn't be bothered, these days, to get herself dressed up. If she did, Jenny soon messed her up and now she was getting bigger, nothing fitted except the old maternity dresses she had worn before. It was all Harry's fault, she thought resentfully, that she was pregnant again. When she had told him she was going to have another baby, he had reached for her, his face lighting with joy.

"That's wonderful, love," he'd said. "Perhaps it will be a boy this time. Come here and give me a kiss." He had caught her to him, sitting her on his knee and fondling her. All the time she had been screaming inside, You don't understand – I don't want another baby. You knew that and yet you didn't take any notice.

Somehow, she hadn't been able to actually say it to him. Some strange barrier had risen up between them and she had found she couldn't talk to him like she used to. When this baby was born, though, there would be no more. She was quite determined on that. He would have to agree, or she wouldn't let him touch her again.

Getting up from the bench, she put her hand to the pram's handle and walked slowly back towards Fore Street to tidy up the house a bit and start on the tea. Harry had begun to mention lately that he would like more variety in his meals so she would have to make him something different tonight. Sighing, she pushed on, Jenny laughing merrily as a large dog on a lead passed them by. At least her child was happy, Alice thought, as she crossed the main road towards the house and the next unwelcome chore.

On the Saturday morning of Janet's departure for Preston, a telegram arrived at number sixteen Nelson Street. It was from the family of four people who should have been arriving that afternoon, the Ackroyds, cancelling their booking due to a sudden bereavement. This meant that, for once, the house would be empty and that Janet could go away with an easy mind.

"I might try to get out a bit myself while everyone's away," Florrie said, as Janet prepared to leave for Preston. "Don't worry about your father's meals. We'll have them together, to suit him. Have a good time now, and forget everything here. Enjoy yourself."

"I'll try, Florrie," Janet promised, taking her hand before stepping into the waiting taxi cab which was to take her to the station. "See you next week, then, and thanks again."

The house seemed very quiet as Florrie closed the front door after the cab had disappeared round the corner of the street. Robert was due in any time now for his dinner, so she went into the kitchen to see how it was going on. For the first time the thought struck her that the two of them would be in the house alone together. She wondered if the same thought would strike Robert. If she was honest, she had to admit that the prospect wasn't unwelcome. Robert was still in his prime. He had not allowed himself to become overweight and he had been fortunate in having good health. His thick red hair and moustache were as luxuriant as ever, like those of a much younger man. Florrie smiled to herself. The way I'm going on, she thought, you might almost think I was a bit soft on Robert. Blushing like any schoolgirl, she told herself not to be such a fool and to get on with her work instead of thinking all these daft things.

Shrugging off the very idea of fancying Robert, she opened the oven door, revealing the golden crust of the steak and kidney pie which he liked so much, and, lower down, the baked custard, firm and smooth under a nutmeg dusting. She was beginning to feel hungry herself. She had made enough for the two of them, intending to join him in this first meal. It would save her having to cook for herself later on. She had to admit it now. She was looking forward to this tete-a-tete opportunity, but on no account must Robert guess as much.

"Would you like to go somewhere tomorrow, Florrie?" Robert asked, after they had eaten and were chatting over a cup of strong tea. "There's nobody in and tomorrow's Sunday. I could do with a bit of fresh air after working in that place all day." He inclined his head towards the bakery. "D'you fancy a ride on the horse bus to the Cherry Tree Gardens?"

"Why, Robert, that would be nice," Florrie said, surprised and pleased that he had thought of it. She had intended going out herself somewhere anyway, and Robert's company would be very welcome. "Shall we have an early dinner tomorrow, then, and have our tea in the Gardens?"

"Aye, that's a good idea," agreed Robert. "I can't remember when I last had a meal outside the house."

"It won't do either of us any harm. Everybody else is on holiday, so why shouldn't we have one as well?" Florrie laughed, pouring him out another cup of tea.

For September, the weather really was keeping fine and warm, Florrie thought, as she sat with Robert on the wooden seat of the horse wagonette. They had mounted the steps behind the wagon onto the deck, which was full of people taking advantage of the weather on this glorious afternoon. The bus was pulled by two immense shire horses, both a-jingle with brasses and adorned with bobs and bows. They plodded the route slowly, giving the passengers time to enjoy the scenery along the way. The route started at the Pleasure Beach, then ran inland, past the dykes and cultivated fields of the Moss to the village of Marton. Here stood the Cherry Tree Inn amongst extensive gardens. It took an hour to make the trip, but no one was worrying about that on a day like this. They were all out to enjoy themselves – not rush about at twenty miles an hour in motor cars as some people seemed to be doing these days.

Florrie had taken a good deal of care over her clothes and her toilette. Robert, sitting quite close to her, occasionally caught the scent of the fresh cologne she used for special occasions. He considered that she was looking very handsome in her lavender dress with the creamy organdie collar and cuffs. As she turned to make some remark, he noticed the burnished lights in her upswept hair and the sparkle in her hazel eyes.

In the gardens of the Inn, long tables and benches had been placed under the old oaks and amongst the apple and pear trees, which were laden with fruit. Here, the horse wagonette deposited its passengers, the horses were changed and a few people boarded it to make the return journey back to the Pleasure Beach.

"How about stretching our legs a bit before we have our tea?" Robert suggested as he handed her down from the bus step. "We could stroll along the lane and pick a few blackberries, if you like. If there's anything I'm partial to, it's a nice blackberry pie. They don't taste the same, somehow, made in the bakehouse."

"I'll ask for a basin at the Inn, then," Florrie said, smiling. "I noticed how thick the blackberries were in the hedgerows as we came into Marton."

They strolled along the lane in the sunshine, filling a large basin provided by the landlady as they went. Taking their time over the picking, they soon had it full of the ripest fruit. Robert had to rescue Florrie's dress from the prickly branches at times, so his hand brushed her thigh once or twice, but it was all good-humoured. Flushed with laughter and effort, they returned to the Inn, happy and satisfied with the afternoon's work and each other's company.

"What will it be, then? D'you fancy boiled beef and pickled onions? I think that's what I'll have, with apple pie and cream to follow."

"So will I, then," said Florrie. "It will be nice to be waited on, for a change."

Tea finally over, they relaxed, sitting on outside in the Gardens with the heavy branches of the oaks dappling the tablecloth and throwing longer shadows across the mown grass. The air was heavy with the scents of phlox and roses. Energetic wasps buzzed around the sticky morsels which were all that remained of the delicious meal. In vain, Robert attempted to wave them away.

"Leave them be, Robert," Florrie begged him. "They're not doing any harm and today I just don't want to hurt anything."

"Alright, but don't blame me, my girl, if you get stung."

Was she really blushing again? Hurriedly, Florrie took out her handkerchief to hide her flaming cheeks. But he hadn't noticed. He was just about to go in to the Inn for a glass of their excellent ale and he intended bringing Florrie a glass of port to put the finishing touches to the meal.

It was quite late when they got back to Nelson Street. It had been such a beautiful evening that they had stayed on longer at the Cherry Tree, letting two wagonettes go before they decided to return. Robert had been enjoying, too, the quality of the ale and he had seen to it that Florrie had had what she wanted in the way of port wine. When, finally, they boarded the horse-bus, blackberries transferred to a waxed paper bag given them by the landlady, they had been quite merry. Some of that euphoria remained now, as they sat together on the sofa in the back parlour.

"Have you enjoyed it then, lass?" Robert asked her, as his hand settled on her knee. She didn't move it as she told him that it had been a wonderful day – the best she could remember for a long time.

"Aye, I've enjoyed it, too," he said, removing his hand but staying close at her side. "Florrie, d'you think you could care for me a bit?" he asked her suddenly, head bent, avoiding her eyes. "I didn't think I could look at another woman after Sarah but, well, this last few months I've begun to think about you a lot, and you've made me feel like a young lad again today."

Florrie placed her plump hand under his chin, tilting it up so that their eyes met. "Robert Crossley, I've fancied you for a long time," she said. "What do you suggest we do about it?"

"Well," Robert replied, replacing his hand on her thigh and squeezing it, "it's a long way up to the attic, so how about only going as far as my room tonight?"

At four o'clock the following morning, Robert, whistling a little tune, let himself out of the house by the back way and walked across the street, only needing to turn the corner to reach the bakery. It was situated inland from the promenade and it boasted a stable for the carthorse and a shed for the delivery wagon. The bread had to be kneaded and baked early so that it could be put on the wagon ready for delivery when the shops opened. He was so used to this early rising that it was no effort to him. On this morning, especially, he had jumped out of bed like a two-year-old. And no wonder! Florrie was a fine woman, he had discovered, with her full, rounded breasts and her soft, yielding thighs. When you came down to it, there was nothing like a woman to make you feel on top of the world, he thought, as he pushed open the bakery door. He reminded himself that it was only Monday and no one would be back at the house until the weekend.

He hadn't forgotten Sarah. He never would. She held a place in his heart that no one else could ever supplant, but there was no reason now, after twelve months, for abstinence. As for marriage, well – they weren't children, and Florrie would have her own ideas on the subject. They would have to see how things worked out before taking a big step like that.

What would Janet say, if she knew, he wondered? Recently, she had seemed to be on much friendlier terms with Florrie, so perhaps she would not be as shocked as he supposed. Oh, well, sufficient unto the day, he told himself, as the smells of the bakery enveloped him and his mind went forward to anticipate the other nights to come before the weeks was over.

Chapter Nineteen

Janet sat opposite Ann Ferguson in the Sugar Bowl, one of Preston's fancier tea-shops. It was patronised mainly by women, but occasionally they took their lovers inside, to sit at secluded tables within its further corners. The two friends had secured a table for two near the window, not needing privacy. From here they could watch the comings and goings of other customers as well as the passers-by. After eating creamy meringues and drinking Indian tea, they were lingering at their table, being in no hurry to leave.

She had been with Ann at Fulwell Road for three days and already Nelson Street and its problems seemed far away. The two friends had had plenty of time to catch up on all their news while they toured the shops or walked in the park or just sat in Ann's comfortable sitting-room. Janet has soon learned from Ann all about her tragic marriage to Tony Warren, an Artillery Officer whom she had married in France when she was only eighteen. They had been very much in love and both had accepted that their marriage could be short. Tony had been returned to the Front soon after the brief ceremony at the dressing-station, and he had never come back. Ann had kept on hoping but eventually she had received news that he had been killed in action. She had been completely devastated and had returned to Preston to be with Tony's mother. It hadn't been long before Mrs. Warren, a widow, in deep shock at her son's death, had fallen ill and finally died. The house had been left to her son and, as Tony's widow, Ann had inherited it. "Tony would have wanted me to come and live here," Ann explained, "and now Mother and Dad have moved back to Edinburgh, I've no family left here. Dad always said that when he was getting near to retirement he would move back home to Scotland." Mr. Ferguson, Ann's father, was a partner in a firm of solicitors which had branches both in Scotland and the North of England. He had moved down from Edinburgh early on in his career, Ann being brought up and educated in Blackpool at the same school as Janet.

Janet hadn't needed to say much about her own disastrous relationship with Harry. Ann seemed to understand the situation without having to go into the whole sorry story. It appeared to Janet that Ann was very familiar with life's large and small tragedies and that she'd had experiences she herself couldn't even guess at. It made her feel as if she had been living in some small backwater, out of the mainstream of life. Tucked away on the coast in Blackpool, she had been going on from day to day in the same old way for as long as she could remember. How ordinary her life appeared to her now, compared with Ann's exploits as a nurse, both here and in France.

"Would you like a trip to Ellswick tomorrow, to see the Home?" Ann asked her, lifting the teapot to se if there was another cup remaining in it. "It's in the country just outside the town – there's a small station there. We could go on the train and then walk. It's not far."

"Yes, of course," said Janet, "I'd like that. Are you looking forward to working again?"

"Oh, yes, I get bored with myself. Nothing to do but housework doesn't suit me. I can travel on the train, I won't have to live-in, although I could do if I wanted to."

"You make me feel my life's very dull, you know," Janet said. "I don't suppose anything exciting is ever going to happen to me again. That's how I feel, anyway."

"You've got to *make* it happen, dear. Start thinking of making changes in your life right away, if you want to get out of a rut."

"That's a lot easier said than done," Janet argued. "I can't see any way I can make a change at the moment."

"The thing is, you've got to grasp at any opportunity that comes along, that's the secret, or you'll stay forever in the same old situation. You have to take the plunge or life passes you by."

"I'll remember that when my big chance comes along," Janet laughed. "Have you managed to squeeze another cup of tea from that pot, or shall we order another?"

"Not unless you want some, Jan."

"Right, shall we pay our bill, then, and let someone else have this table?"

"Alright, and how about us having an early night tonight? I could do with washing my hair. How about you? Then we'll get off early in the morning to Ellswick."

"That suits me," Janet said. I'm looking forward to seeing the place where you'll be working next month."

As Janet sat on the train the following day, en route for the convalescent home, she reflected that she and her friend were quite unlike both in temperament and in appearance. Ann, with her short, dark hair curling around her delicate features above the slender figure, had a Peter Pan quality about her. She would still look the same, Janet was sure, another twenty years on, when she was forty. Ann had such vitality too – the kind that took one through life on a tidal wave of enthusiasm which swept everyone else along with it. Yet they got on very well together. Perhaps it was true that opposites attract. She glanced at her friend, who was busy chattering away to a tweed-suited woman sitting opposite them in the carriage. That was another difference between them. Ann always talked freely to anyone who was willing to listen, whereas she herself shrank from conversation with strangers.

"Our stop, I think," Ann said, turning to Janet. "I think it's going to be a nice day after all."

The sky had lightened during the last half-hour, after a doubtful start to the morning, when lowering clouds had threatened. Now they had lifted and bright blue patches were beginning to appear here and there, promising sunshine later on. They alighted from the train in a tiny station where only a small waiting room and a ticket gate separated the line from a country lane outside. As they walked, they passed one or two scattered houses, most of them set back from the road amidst cultivated gardens and allotments. The convalescent home was a few minutes walk from the station and its surrounding stone wall soon came into view. The Home had originally been a large country mansion, built for one of the local cotton barons, now long since deceased. It was large enough for its present use, even if it was rather ugly in appearance. Set in its own grounds, it faced a semi-circular carriageway and drive which led down to the main gateway, which they were now approaching.

"Mrs. Stokes, the housekeeper, has offered to give us lunch," Ann told Janet. "We'll make for her office first and see if she is free."

"I should think that's quite a job – seeing to all the stores for a place like this," Janet said, as they came up the front steps and entered the lobby where the front desk was situated.

Mrs. Stokes turned out to be a mature, well-rounded woman, dressed in a green overall over a spotless white blouse. Janet guessed that she was in her late fifties and that she was very efficient at her job. The three of them sat in the housekeeper's small office, chatting for a while, once introductions were over.

"I've arranged for us to have lunch in the staff room, so we'll go in if you're ready." Mrs. Stokes led the way along a corridor into a room where one or two of the nurses were already being served at a hatch which opened onto the kitchens at the back.

"How about sitting over there and I'll bring your trays across?" the housekeeper offered. "Would you like beef or ham?"

Over the meal, the conversation turned to personal matters, Mrs. Stokes showing both women her engagement ring. A widow, she had just become engaged to a long-standing friend. Mrs. Stokes enthused over her husband-to-be. "Charles is talking of us getting married at Christmas. Although I think it's a bit soon myself. Mind you, there's nothing stopping us. We could live in either his house or mine. He's a bit lonely on his own, you know."

"I'm very happy for you, Mrs. Stokes," Ann said, "and I hope it all goes well for you."

"Thank you, dear. It's the thought of leaving this place that's bothering me but we're none of us getting any younger and we've got to think of retiring some time, I suppose."

On the return journey to Preston in the afternoon, Janet was rather quiet, but Ann presumed she was feeling tired. They'd had quite a busy week already – out every day somewhere – so maybe they would relax tomorrow. Janet was actually thinking that Mrs. Stokes had hit a raw nerve when she had said that none of them were getting any younger. It was looking as if she herself could quite easily end up as an old maid, if she didn't do something about it soon. It was time to be thinking of striking out on her own. She had done her duty by her family. Now it was time to be thinking about herself. The question was, thought, would she be able to bring herself to do it?

On the night before the family were due back, Robert and Florrie lay in bed in his bedroom, easy and comfortable with each other after a week of intimacy. In the afternoons and evenings Robert had been at home and, after his early afternoon nap, he had taken Florrie out for a walk or a drink and once to the Music Hall at the Palace Theatre, a place he hadn't been in for years. After the first night it had seemed quite natural for them to sleep all the week in Robert's room. They had both appreciated having a partner again and enjoying to the full the physical pleasures which had been denied them, to Florrie longer than to Robert.

"It won't be easy when Janet comes back tomorrow," Florrie said, "and the house is full again. Do you want to carry on with this, then?"

"You know I do. What about you, lass?"

"Do you need to ask me? The question is, Robert Crossley, "what are your intentions?" she asked him, laughing.

"That I don't know, Florrie, believe me," he answered, suddenly serious. "I only know I'm comfortable with you and I think you feel the same. It's been good, lass, hasn't it?"

"Very good, Robert, but what am I going to do when everyone comes back? Sneak into your room like a thief in the night?"

It was Robert's turn to laugh. "Oh, I don't think so, Florrie. It shouldn't be all that hard to manage. I think I've just about got enough energy left to climb up to the attic to visit you for a change!"

As Florrie worked around the house the following week, she found she was avoiding Janet's eyes, but since her return from

Preston, Janet seemed to have been caught up in her own thoughts much of the time. Neither Florrie nor Robert wanted to tell Janet of their new relationship until they were sure of themselves. It wouldn't do to force the issue, anyway, especially with Janet. Things must take their own course, they had decided.

"You seem a bit preoccupied, Janet," Florrie said, as they stripped the beds and took out clean linen from the bedding chest. "Didn't you enjoy your visit with your friend?"

"Oh, yes, I did, very much, but, well – I think it has unsettled me a bit. I've begun to realise that other people live far more exciting lives than I do."

"If it's excitement you're after, I don't suppose there is much to be had round here at the moment – for you, anyway," Florrie added, flushing and turning away to pick up the linen she had taken out.

"No, it really looks as if I shall go on here forever, working in this house, waiting on people and washing up dishes. What sort of a life is that, Florrie? – I'm twenty-two years old. Most women of my age are married and – have children. What is there here for me in the future? Nothing that I can see."

"Have you anything else in mind?"

"Well, Ann thinks there may be a vacancy at Christmas at the convalescent home in Ellswick where she's going back to nursing next month. She suggested that I should apply for it. I'd be living-in, of course, but how could I, Florrie? I've Dad and the children to think about. I told her it was out of the question."

"What sort of a job? Not nursing, surely?"

"Oh, no. It would be for a housekeeper to run the domestic side of the Home. Someone is leaving at Christmas to be married."

"Why, Janet! That would suit you down to the ground," Florrie cried. "You would make a wonderful job of it, and you would be near your friend."

"I think I could do it, Florrie, but what's the use? I just couldn't entertain the idea."

"Sit down a minute, dear. I've got something to tell you. I didn't mean to say anything yet, but it seems you need to know. It could make a big difference to your situation."

"Need to know? How d'you mean, Florrie? You're not thinking of leaving us, are you? Oh, don't say that!"

"Far from it, dear. In fact, I'm thinking of staying on here permanently."

"Permanently?" Janet gazed at Florrie with puzzled eyes. "Has Dad asked you to stay on here permanently, then, while I was away?"

"You could say that he has," Florrie chuckled. "Can't you guess, Janet, dear?" Your Dad and I are thinking of getting married."

Janet's bewildered expression turned to one of intense surprise. She stared blankly at the other woman before speaking. "Well, I can't say you haven't given me a shock, Florrie," she said, at last. "I should have guessed that Dad might come to care for you. We all have, and it's over a year now, since mother died. He is quite free to ask you to be his wife and I think you'll make him happy. I've never seen you other than cheerful and I think you'll be good for him."

"What about Arthur and Rose, Janet? Do you think they'll accept me as their stepmother?"

"They already think of you as something like a favourite aunt and I think the changeover will be very easy for them to make."

"Yes, I feel myself that it's right for us all," Florrie agreed.

"Oh, Florrie, I was forgetting <u>you</u>. I was only thinking about us. How do <u>you</u> feel about it, Florrie?"

"Me? I'm over the moon about things," Florrie laughed happily. "And as for the children, well, I've never had any as you know, and I already think of them as my own."

"Goodness! You have given me something to think about, haven't you? This does change things for me, doesn't it?"

"Yes, it does, and that's the only reason I've told you about how things stand between your Dad and me. It's up to you now to think again whether you want to make a change. It looks as if you're going to be free to go anywhere you want to, quite soon. We should have to think about getting some help in, of course, but that's a minor detail."

During October, Harry Tomlinson came to visit his mother straight from work one Saturday dinner time when he had finished at Greenwood's. Alice hadn't felt up to making an official visit to her mother-in-law, and Harry had been feeling that he was neglecting his mother. Ellen had managed to make a visit to Fore Street, on her own as usual, to see Jenny and to enquire how Alice was keeping during her second pregnancy. She hadn't been impressed by what she had seen of the house or at Alice's obvious displeasure over her present condition. She had refrained from commenting, but if Maud had been with her, she knew that her daughter would not have been so charitable.

Harry arrived at Nelson Street for his dinner tired and ready to sit down. A delicious smell of roasting lamb greeted him as he took off his overalls before sinking into an easy chair.

"It won't be long," his mother said. "Would you like a glass of ginger ale?"

"Thanks, Ma." Harry accepted a foaming glassful poured from the stone bottle. Drinking it gratefully, he reflected that his throat seemed to be perpetually dry these days.

"How are things, then?" Ellen asked, while they were alone together. Maud was out shopping at the market.

"Oh, not so bad, Ma," he said, not committing himself.

"Jenny's coming on, isn't she? She's beautiful and I'm sure you're proud of her."

"Yes, I am, Ma. I only hope my son's as healthy when he's born."

"Now, Harry, you mustn't bank on this baby being a boy, you know. She could have another girl, quite easily."

"No, Ma. I'm sure that this time it's going to be a boy."

"Well, if you're so set on it, I hope you're right," Ellen said, going into the kitchen to serve up the food. "You look as if you need this." She placed the savoury plateful of lamb with mint sauce and vegetables in front of him. "Have you lost some weight lately? You look all bones to me."

"I don't think so, Ma. I'm eating alright." He tried to fend off her next enquiry.

"And that cough of yours isn't getting any better," she persisted, as he tucked into the meal with pleasure. For the first time in months – in fact since they had last visited Alice's mother and father at Whitsuntide – he realised how much he was enjoying the food. In spite of his hopes, his wife's cooking had not improved. She seemed to have no enthusiasm or imagination for cooking although, bless her, she tried hard enough. He still wouldn't find fault with her, although he knew, now, that she would never make a good housewife. But, as she had pointed out to him, he hadn't married her for her domestic merits. He still loved her dearly. She was the mother of his lovely daughter and she would soon be the mother of the son he had always imagined he would have some day. The thought cheered him as he tucked into the beautifully cooked meal, while his mother watched him speculatively across the table.

Chapter Twenty

Robert Crossley and Florrie Metcalf were married in the Central Register Office in Blackpool at the beginning of November. This was as early as they could arrange it and, as Florrie said, it gave them all time to get used to the idea that the two would soon be husband and wife. As Janet had supposed, both Arthur and Rose, with the natural resilience of youth, had accepted the fact that they were to have a step-mother. Florrie was someone they already liked and trusted, so it was in her hands whether they eventually came to love her.

Although the ceremony didn't have quite the solemnity of one performed in the Church, it had dignity and sincerity. Janet was Florrie's witness and Robert's brother James, a Fleetwood fisherman, acted as witness for Robert, bringing his wife, Aunt Dorothy, with him. Arthur and Rose were also present at the ceremony, on Florrie's insistence.

Robert's sister, Hannah, wasn't going to the Register Office because of her difficulty in getting about. She was coming on later from Lytham to number Sixteen for the wedding breakfast and the evening festivities, and would stay overnight.

Ellen and Maud had offered to prepare the wedding breakfast and have it ready for the guests when they returned from the ceremony. Since the departure of Harry and Alice, the two families had managed to get back to a normal friendly relationship. As neighbours, it would have been difficult to let resentments come between them. Neither family spoke of the affair in the presence of the other, so it was possible to carry on almost as before. They would both join the party in number Sixteen for the evening. By now, neither house had any visitors, the season being well and truly over so the wedding breakfast would be set out in the front parlour.

"I feel like Royalty, Robert," Florrie said, as she stepped down from the shiny black car outside the house on their return. "I bet everyone in the street is watching us from behind the curtains."

"Let them watch," Robert said cheerfully. "They're only envious because we're doing it in style."

Inside the parlour, they found the tables set with the best white damask linen cloths, each one adorned with its centrepiece of arranged flowers and flickering candlestick. Silver cutlery glinted everywhere and a two-tiered wedding-cake, topped with a large horseshoe, stood in pride of place on the mahogany sideboard, together with a large selection of Ellen's finest cooked meats and savouries. On two silver trays, wine glasses stood ready, besides those placed on the tables for toasts after the meal. As a gesture to Janet's family, Ellen had done them proud!

There were cries of, "Oh, it's beautiful," or "Oh, what a lovely cake," as the guests took their places and the meal got under way. Afterwards there were several toasts raised to the bride and groom, Florrie asking for Arthur and Rose to be given a small glass of light wine with the grown-ups.

As a child, Maud had been taught to play the piano and she still played occasionally, so she was persuaded to open up the piano and see what was in the music stool. Settled with their after-dinner drinks, the guests were encouraged to join in such wartime favourites as "Pack up your Troubles," and "It's a long way to Tipperary".

"How about giving us a solo," Ellen suggested to Rose, during a lull while the drinks were being replenished.

At first, Rose refused, shyly, but she was eventually persuaded to sing "Oh for the Wings of a Dove," a song she had sung at a recent school concert. She stood by the piano, her light auburn hair nearly as long as Janet's, the two heavy plaits hanging almost to her waist. They were tied at the ends with green velvet ribbon, to match her dress. Her voice was pure and clear and the small fidgeting sounds in the room died away as the soaring melody climbed to new heights of sound. There was complete silence when she had finished singing, then loud clapping and congratulations when she told them that she had been chosen for the school choir which was a finalist in the Musical Festival at the Winter Gardens next month.

"Rose has done her party piece. It's time for someone else. What about you, Arthur?"

"He knows some poems." Rose didn't intend Robert getting out of doing his recitations.

"No, I don't." He blushed furiously, under the dark hair.

"Oh, yes, you do. You did them at the Sunday School – at the Anniversary," Rose argued.

"Please, Arthur, we would really like to hear a poem, and I'm sure you'll do it beautifully," Florrie appealed, and the reluctant lad got to his feet. At fourteen, he was growing fast and already he stood as tall as Janet. In his colouring he took after his mother, but he had his father's strong facial bones and long, slender hands and feet. He stood, awkward and hesitant, before he burst out,

"I'm not all that good but I'll have a try. I'll do 'Sea Fever' – that's short." Arthur, like Rose, had a clear, light voice. He began with the famous lines, 'I must go down to the sea again, to the lonely sea and the sky….," gaining confidence with every line. The room was hushed. The sea was an ever-present entity to all the people in the room. They knew it well. Its alluring yet savage fascination was familiar to them all. Embarrassment forgotten, Arthur put real meaning into the words. There wasn't a rustle as the poem came to an end, applause breaking out as he sat down again.

"Well done, lad," said Uncle James. "Couldn't have done it better myself."

There was general laughter. It was well-known by the company that James, a trawler man, had never read a poem in his life, never mind interpreted one, as Arthur had just done.

"How about a game?" Robert suggested. "Who fancies hide the Thimble?" Robert himself was thrust out of the room, protesting, because he had been the one to suggest it. But he was still searching, in spite of helpful prompts by the others, when the next round of drinks came along and he eventually gave up in disgust.

After this the party settled down to general chatter and soon Robert suggested that Arthur and Rose say goodnight to the company. Hanah, too, said she was ready for bed and after another hour, the party began to break up.

"Why don't you all get off to bed, now?" Ellen suggested. "Janet and I will do the clearing. The washing-up can be left till morning for once."

"I think I'm ready for a bit of shut-eye," James said. "How about you, Dol?"

"I'm ready when you are," she said. "It's been a lovely evening – the best we've had for a long time."

Laughing and joking the couple, closely followed by the newly-weds, made their way upstairs, leaving the three women to clear up the room and stack the dishes by the sink ready for morning. Maud departed for next door to see about putting in the hot water bottles, leaving Janet alone with Ellen in the firelit parlour.

It was Janet who broke the silence, "I know what you want to say, Ellen. Things haven't worked out right for us, have they? But that's all in the past now and I've decided to make a new start. I've applied for a job as housekeeper at a convalescent home near Preston. I go for an interview at the end of the week. If I get it I shall be living in and starting work in January, after the New Year."

"I told you how I felt about the engagement being broken off at the time, dear, and I don't know what to say to you now, but I can understand you wanting to make a new life for yourself. Now that Robert has married again, I can see that this is the time to do it."

"Yes, Ellen. Florrie knows I've had this chance and she has encouraged me to take it if I want to. I expect she will get some help in here if I get the job."

"I'm sorry it's had to come to this, Janet – that you feel you have to go away from us all."

"It isn't just that, Ellen. I feel that there's nothing left here to stay for now, and I shall be near Ann Ferguson. D'you remember her?"

"You mean the little dark-haired one with the dolls she was always bandaging up? Didn't she go in for nursing, later on?"

"Yes. She's a widow now, you know. I went to visit her recently – perhaps Florrie told you? She's got a nursing job at the Home where I'm applying, so I think we could pick up our friendship where we left off at school."

"Well, I'll be sorry to see you go, dear," Ellen said. "I can't forget that you should have been my daughter-in-law, you know".

"I haven't got the job yet, Ellen," Janet pointed out, "but I shall be sorry, too, to leave you all, if I do get it."

"You'll be coming home to visit, won't you, so we won't be losing you altogether?"

"Oh, yes, of course I will. I shall come and see you all as often as I can."

"I hope you find it's what you want, Janet. You deserve to be happy, if anyone does. Let me know, won't you, if you get the job and come to see me before you go?"

"Of course I will, Ellen. I'm glad we've had this little chat. You don't need to worry about me, you know. I shall be alright."

"Well, good luck to you, dear. I'd better be saying goodnight now and getting round next door to let Maud lock up for the night."

When she was finally left alone with her thoughts before she turned out the last lamp, Janet wondered, was she really ready for making such a drastic change? Was she really doing the right thing?

When the day of the interview came she presented herself, smart in one of her new dresses, her hair coiled and pinned up under a new hat, wondering what she was doing in this strange place, sitting before the Board of Governors. The questions came thick and fast from the panel – half a dozen portly gentlemen and one hawk-faced matron in a large hat. One red-faced man, in particular, asked her some questions which she found personal and difficult to answer. In the end, though, they thanked her, dismissing her and telling her that they would notify her when they had made their decision.

She called at Ann's house on the way home, tired and unnerved by the whole experience. Her friend had arranged to be off work to receive her. Full of optimism – Ann was never pessimistic about anything – she rushed to meet Janet at the door as soon as she heard her knock. After she had insisted firstly on Janet telling her in the hallway about the interview, she led her into the sitting-room, assuring Janet that she would get the job, in spite of her misgivings.

"Don't worry," Ann said. "They're always like that. They have to make a performance of it, you see – going through the motions, I mean. I had it from Matron herself that you're at the top of the short list. You'll get it, alright. Come on, into the sitting-room, I've got the tea all ready. I'm sure you're dying for a cup after that little lot."

And sure enough, a week later, an official looking envelope arrived on the mat at Nelson Street, offering Janet the position and asking her to begin work at the home as housekeeper on the first Monday after the New Year.

Chapter Twenty-One

Alice's baby, another girl, was born in Bradfield during February the following year, 1920, while the couple were staying with her family. As healthy as Jenny, the new infant, while longer-limbed, promised to be as bonny as her sister. Mary had known that, so near her time, Alice would have found housekeeping even more of a struggle. With the delivery imminent, she had invited the family to come over to spend the laying-in time at her old home. Harry had arranged with Sid Greenwood to have his holiday in Yorkshire, hoping that Alice would be delivered to her term.

The new baby arrived almost to the day predicted by the doctor and without the same amount of effort on Alice's part.

"For a small girl," Dr. Fitzpatrick told Alice, "you seem to be able to produce some bouncing babies. Nearly eight pounds! Am I going to have the privilege of bringing the next one into the world, then?" he asked her conversationally, as Harry opened the bedroom door for him when he was ready to leave.

"No, you're not. I'm not having any more." Alice spoke forcefully. Dr. Fitzpatrick laughed. "They all say that when they've just been delivered. They change their minds again when they've forgotten all about it."

"I shalln't change *my* mind," Alice said fiercely.

Harry looked sharply at his wife. Alice's eyes were burning with some emotion which he could only think was anger. Surely she was a bit feverish?

"I've given her a strong sedative," Dr. Fitzpatrick told him as he preceded Harry downstairs. "It should settle her down. Some women do seem a bit emotionally disturbed after they've given birth. I shouldn't worry about it. She will come round. The only difficulty I can see is that she hasn't got enough milk of her own, but I understand that this was the case with the first one?"

"Yes," said Harry. "Dr. Fraser at Blackpool told us to give Jenny the bottle."

"I suggest you do the same with this little one, then. Your other child seems to have come on splendidly. She's a strong, healthy little girl, by the looks of it."

"Jenny's never been sickly," Harry assured the doctor.

"I can't see any reason why this one shouldn't be exactly the same."

"Thank you, doctor." Harry let the doctor out by the front door.

"Don't thank me, young man. Your wife has done all the hard work. I've only come in at the very end of the story. I delivered Alice myself when she was born, so I know a thing or two about her, you know. Let her rest for a bit before she starts doing much work when you get back home."

"I will, doctor," he promised, as Dr. Fitzpatrick's brisk steps took him towards the gate. For an elderly man, thought Harry, Dr. Fitzpatrick still looked remarkably fit and active. Better than I am, he couldn't help adding to himself, as he closed the door.

Upstairs, Mary cradled the baby against her soft, comfortable bosom. It felt good to be holding a little one again, so tiny and helpless. Alice had sunk back into the pillows, closing her eyes. The sedative was beginning to take effect. Mary was puzzled as she cuddled her grand-daughter. It almost seemed that her daughter wasn't interested in her child.

Shocked by this thought, Mary gazed down at the small, puckered face, wondering what could have brought on this change in Alice. She had been happy enough over Jenny, even though that had been a long, hard labour, but this was something different. Mary had not missed the grim determination in Alice's eyes as she had spoken to the doctor. Was it just the birth itself that had affected Alice? She had seemed depressed when she had arrived at Moscar Street, listless and indifferent to her parents' anticipation of the coming birth. Harry had seemed quieter, too. In fact, now that she considered it, there hadn't been much conversation between husband and wife since they had arrived.

Jenny, of course, an active child, had kept the family fully occupied during the visit, when Alice hadn't the energy to see to her. Mary asked herself just what was wrong. This second baby had come very quickly after the first – Jenny was only ten months old – but she herself would have been happy about that. If it hadn't been for her own miscarriages, she would have had a much larger family. Alice, though, evidently felt differently about things and she was blaming Harry for her situation. She hasn't really grown up, Mary thought. She had married Harry in a kind of romantic dream and she'd had motherhood thrust upon her before she was ready for it. Now she was having to waken up to real life – and it wasn't suiting her!

Sighing, she placed her grand-daughter tenderly in the cot she had borrowed from one of the neighbours. It stood by the side of the bed but it wasn't likely that Alice would waken for some time, once the drug took hold… She went downstairs to see how Harry was faring. His eyes had looked worried, she had noticed, his tall, thin frame seeming to bend under some invisible weight. And he seemed to be coughing a lot. A little dart of fear sped into Mary's heart. Was Harry as well as he thought? He hadn't been convulsed by coughing spasms like this when the family had visited them at Christmas. Perhaps it was just the bitterly cold weather that was affecting him? It had turned very cold this last week, with strong north winds and a promise of snow to come.

She reached the warm parlour where her son, George, and her grand-daughter, Jenny, were playing on the floor. Joe was sitting in his favourite chair, waiting impatiently for his wife, his pipe clamped in his mouth.

"Well?" her husband demanded, removing his pipe, as she came into the room.

"She's quite alright, love, but she's got to sleep for a bit now."

"Where's my new grand-daughter, then," Joe asked, seeing that his wife had come downstairs without her.

"I've put her in her cot for a minute while I see to the dinner. Let them both rest for a bit. Harry has gone out, then? He does seem to have a lot on his mind."

"No wonder," Joe said, "with two babies so close to each other. He said he was going out for a walk."

"I'll get him to bring the baby down when he comes back, then. Alice is going to have her hands full, right enough, when she gets home to Lytham. I'll just go and see how the dinner's going on. Keep your eyes on those two," indicating the children, "while I'm in the kitchen."

As she passed behind the sofa, she saw that George had lifted Jenny on to it. "I told you not to put Jenny up there," she said irritably. "I can't take my eyes off you for a second. She'll fall off – I told you before."

"She doesn't want to play. She's too little," George complained, as Mary picked up the child, placing her safely on the floor.

"She would, if you weren't so rough with her. You *will* lift her up and pull her about. I wish you would do as I tell you."

As his mother turned her back on him to go into the kitchen, her son made a rude face at her, which, fortunately, his father didn't see.

Walking against the biting wind in the direction of the moor, his overcoat closed tightly at the throat, Harry didn't notice its wintry aspect as he clutched at his collar. The low hills rose, bleak and sullen under swathes of grey cloud, their tops hidden under thick veils. The heather had turned a rusty-brown and only the swirls of coarse grasses showed any colour in this sombre landscape. A few stunted, skeletal trees stood out here and there, the only survivors of previous bitter winters when nothing else had lived in this desolate spot.

His wife had not given him the son he had hoped for. She had presented him with another baby girl who promised to be every bit as bonny and as healthy as his dearly loved Jenny. Why, then, did he feel so empty of joy at this birth? Was it because Alice herself seemed so indifferent to the child? Surely, as the doctor had said, she would soon get over the birth and turn to the baby, like any normal mother?

But then, he asked himself, was Alice normal in this respect? She hadn't wanted this baby, that was plain enough and she was still saying that she didn't want any more. She had even hinted that, afterwards, she would expect him to make sure that she didn't have any more children. How could he give that promise when they still hadn't got the son he so wanted? Of course, Alice needed a rest now from confinements, but afterwards, he couldn't promise that they would never have any more children. That was too much to ask of any man, but that was what she seemed to be suggesting.

When he had married her, he had automatically assumed that she wanted more than one child. They had never even discussed it. Most women loved babies and she had seemed happy enough with the first one. She had been harassed looking after her, though, he admitted that. He supposed that there were those women who just weren't very maternal. Could it be that Alice was one of these? Her reaction to this pregnancy strongly suggested it, and if it were true, the future was going to be difficult for both of them, he thought, bitterly.

The walking had tired him and as he turned to make the return journey, he paused to get back his breath. He found that he was getting breathless lately, after any exertion. He pictured his new daughter, lying there in her snug cot, and his heart suddenly warmed to her. She was his child, daughter or not, and that was all that mattered. He would see to it that she got the same kind of love that he had lavished on Jenny. As for the future, well, that was in the lap of the Gods. Eventually, he let himself in, shivering, to the warm little house.

A week after the baby was born, Alice was still lying in bed, listless, refusing to attend to her child. She had held her for only short periods before surrendering her again to Mary. While Mary was feeding and changing her, she was wondering whether this was some illness her daughter had picked up through the pregnancy. She decided to call in Dr. Fitzpatrick for his opinion, and after he examined Alice, the doctor spoke to Mary at the foot of the stairs, before leaving.

"It isn't unusual, Mrs. Boothroyd, for a mother to behave in this way. She isn't really ill. It's a kind of nervous disorder which sometimes affects mothers after they have been delivered. With patience and gentleness, she will get over it," he promised her. "Don't force the baby on her. Let her take her own time with her. It might take a few days or a few weeks, so you'll need to be patient. She will come round in the end, I promise you."

So Harry had to return to the coast alone, to start work again after his holiday. He had arranged to stay with his mother until Alice was fit to come home with the baby. He hadn't liked the idea of leaving her with Jenny, in Bradfield, but he really had little choice. They were very busy at the joinery shop and he didn't want to lose any money by being off work now that he had an enlarged family to support.

"Is Alice any better? Have you heard anything from them this week?" Ellen asked Harry, as they sat over their evening meal during the second week of his stay at Nelson Street.

"Yes, I've had a letter from Mary – it came this morning. I didn't see you to tell you this morning."

"No, you were off before I came down, but I've been trying to get a bit of extra rest. The decorators are in again next week and I've been feeling a bit tired, lately."

"I don't blame you, Ma. You sometimes forget that you're not getting any younger. You're doing just as much as you ever did."

"If I did let up now, I should probably stop altogether." She gave him one of her rare smiles. It was good to see him back again, sitting at her table, and she knew he was enjoying the meals she prepared for him. Poor lad, he probably hadn't had anything like them since he had moved to Lytham. But he had made his bed, and he must lie on it, she thought, getting up to re-fill the teapot.

"What do they say about Alice, then?" she asked.

"She's up and about, now, but she's still not well enough to come home. She seems to have no interest in anything, according to her mother. I've decided to go over at the weekend to see how things are. I'm finding I can't work properly thinking and worrying about it all."

"The baby's alright, isn't she?" Ellen asked, quickly.

"Oh, yes, Mary's looking after her until Alice feels up to it. She's enjoying that, by the sounds of it. I can't understand why Alice hasn't picked up again after this baby. She was well enough when Jenny was born. She was back on her feet in no time at all."

"Yes, but every birth's different," Ellen said. "Are you sure she really wanted this one?" She wondered if she had spoken out of turn, but she felt she had to ask him. "It's a bit soon after Jenny, you know."

He didn't answer her, but carried on eating, not looking up from his plate. "No, I don't think she did, Ma," he admitted, at last, in a low voice.

"Didn't you talk it over before you decided to have another one?" Ellen pressed on, although she knew she was on dangerous ground.

"We really didn't think about it, Ma. It just happened."

"Don't you think you <u>should</u> have talked about it, first?" She hadn't been able to talk to him like this for a long time – not since he had left for the War. Perhaps that was half the trouble. He hadn't had advice from anyone. If only his father had been alive, he might have given Harry some good advice before he married. But it was too late for what might have been…..

"You think I've made a mistake, don't you, Ma?" he said, putting down his knife and fork on the plate before rising from the table. "Well, you're wrong. I love Alice and she loves me. We'll make a go of this without anybody else telling us what we should do."

Turning from her, he walked out of the parlour, picking up his coat and hat on the way out. "I'm going out for a bit. I'll be back before supper."

As Ellen cleared the table, tears pricking her eyes, she determined that, in future, she would keep her mouth firmly shut where the couple were concerned. She reflected that it was only an old fool like herself who would try to interfere between a man and his wife.

It wasn't until the end of March that Alice was able to travel back to the coast with her baby. They had agreed to leave Jenny with her grand-parents in Bradfield until Alice was fit enough to look after both children. Harry had travelled to Yorkshire most weekends, but now he was bringing his wife and their new baby back with him on the train to Blackpool. He carried the baby himself, Alice still seeming weak and listless but her colour was better, he thought.

"A bit of sea air will do you good," he said, as they set off from Moscar Street for the station in one of the new taxi cabs. There was a rank of them there now, outside the station. Harry had wondered whether it was wise to take his wife to stay at Nelson Street but he felt that she still wasn't up to looking after her baby and seeing to his food and the house in Lytham, as well. It was only right, too, that his mother should have a chance of seeing her grand-daughter. Ellen had offered to look after them all for a few days until Alice felt ready to go back to Fore Street.

It was the news that Maud would be away which decided Harry on staying with his mother. Ellen had persuaded Maud to have her holiday now, before the season started and she would be staying with Agnes Ridley, a distant relative who ran a boarding house in Southport, across the estuary from Lytham. She called herself a hotelier, but she was in reality just a landlady, like Ellen, although she considered herself a cut above the Blackpool landladies. Maud she found congenial, with her snobbish ideas.

Ellen welcomed the little family at Nelson Street, tears in her eyes. "Come on in and take your things off," she said. "It's chilly out there." She was sniffing audibly. "Don't worry about all this stuff. The decorators are moving out tomorrow. Give her to me a minute, Harry," taking the baby while he helped his wife off with her coat. Alice didn't speak.

"Oh, she's lovely," Ellen exclaimed, as the cherubic little face was exposed inside the woollen shawl. "She's a lot fairer than Jenny, isn't she? She takes after Harry. His hair was nearly white when he was born." Ellen was so taken up with the baby that she didn't notice Alice's silence.

As Ellen held the baby, crooning over her, Alice suddenly said, "Give her to me."

Very much taken aback, Ellen stared at her daughter-in-law, then, slowly, she handed the baby over to her mother. "I'm sorry, dear I was only admiring my grand-child."

Harry broke in quickly, "We'll take our bags upstairs, Ma, and get settled in. You can have another look at her when we come down."

Carrying her baby for the first time, Alice made for the doorway, closely followed by her husband, with the suitcases. When they reached their room Harry asked his wife if she couldn't have been more polite to his mother but Alice only shrugged her shoulders. At least, he thought, she has asked for the baby. Alice now appeared to be clinging to her like a limpet.

"Put her down on the bed for a minute," he suggested, "while we sort these bags out."

"No," she answered shortly, "I want to hold her."

It was the same story the whole of their stay with Ellen. Alice stubbornly refused to be parted from her child, except at nights, when the baby slept beside their bed in a spare cot. It was almost as if she didn't want Ellen to have the pleasure of doing anything for the child, or so Harry began to think. She hadn't been like this at her mother's. At home, she had let Mary do everything for her, while she herself had mooned around the place. Now it looked as if she had accepted her daughter and was prepared to look after her. She still spoke very little, answering in monosyllables when spoken to, but she seemed physically more active and she was looking better every day.

At the end of the week she suddenly told Harry that she was ready to go back to Fore Street and that she felt she could do all the work and look after the baby as well. As Maud was due back home, Harry told his mother that they would be leaving before she returned. He knew it would upset Ellen to see them go again, but the fact that Alice had improved so much during their stay would help to compensate for that.

There was only one thing now worrying him. Alice had stubbornly refused him any sexual intercourse at all since she'd had the baby. She had turned away from him, night after night, without any explanation of her rejection of him. Of course, she didn't need to explain. He knew why. She was afraid of conceiving, yet again. He hoped that now they were going back to Fore Street, she would change her attitude and that they would take up again their old life, as man and wife.

On the first night of their return to Fore Street, he watched her undress and then slip quickly into bed, turning her face to the wall and closing her eyes before he had removed all his own clothing. His heart sank. Already, he could feel an erection beginning. He didn't want to be demanding but his body was forcing him to approach her once more. Easing himself into bed on his own side, he turned to her, putting his arms around her, cradling her limp body. He was quite aware that she was awake. She could feel him, hard and urgent, against her back. "Aren't you going to turn over, love," he pleaded in her ear. She didn't answer, but lay quietly, ignoring him. He couldn't stop himself from futilely trying to drive into her but she suddenly moved sharply out of the way, leaving him maddened with desire and frustration. In desperation, he reached for her, pulling her towards him. She gasped, "No, no," as his insistent body tried to claim hers.

"I can't go on like this," he moaned, as she managed to roll away from him again and he lay, swollen and humiliated in the darkness of the bed. Flinging the bedclothes aside, he swung himself out in an angry movement. He would leave her to her self-imposed chastity and go and lie down in the spare room bed. He wouldn't sleep, he knew that. Hadn't he spent countless other nights, sleepless, trying to figure out, in vain, what to do?

They had been home a week and he was still sleeping in the back bedroom when, one evening after he had finished his tea, he burst out in anguish, "Alice, I just can't stand this any more. Talk to me, love. Tell me you want me to come back into our bed again. I'm only sleeping in the back because I can't bear to lie beside you night after night like a stranger."

"Alright, then," she said, "come back to me, but you've got to promise that there won't be any more babies."

"How can I promise that, Alice? The only thing I can say is that I'll be careful in the future but I can't promise that you'll never be pregnant again. No man could promise that, love."

"Well, then, if you can't promise me, I'll have to do something about it myself."

"You can't do that," he protested, horrified. "It isn't right for a woman to be thinking of taking precautions, that's up to me."

"Well, you can't promise, so I shall have to see to it." With that, she walked out of the room with the used dishes, leaving him with his mind in torment.

She was true to her word, too. The following day, when he came home from work, she told him she had been to see Dr. Brown, here in Lytham. He'd had a little talk with her and, considering that she'd had two babies very close together, he had advised her what to do.

"You shouldn't have done that, Alice," Harry complained bitterly. "You want to come back into our bed again, don't you? And make love?" She looked up at him with big, dark eyes.

"You know I do. I've been going mad, sleeping on my own, knowing you were lying there, on the other side of the wall. But it won't be the same if I know you're taking precautions."

"Well, it's up to me now, so we won't argue any more about it."

And with that, he had to be content. He rejoined her the same night in their double bed in the front bedroom and this time there was no reluctance on her part. She took him straight into her arms and he didn't yet consider her needs, he was so urgent with his own. It had been three months now since they had made love together. She had been parted from him for weeks after the baby's birth, and afterwards he had been rejected by her – until now. During all that time, his sexual energy had been pent-up and now he knew that in a little while he would be able to satisfy her as well.

She seemed to sense it, because she started caressing his body, kissing and fondling him until he felt himself beginning to harden again. When he knew he was ready, he put both arms around her, pulling her over him, entering her as he did so. She lay on him, light and quivering. Soon her body moved with his, in strong rhythmic thrusts. He forced himself to respond slowly and after a little while she gasped out, "Harry, oh, Harry!" and lay slack over him while he expended himself inside her again.

He felt absolutely drained, but gloriously happy. It had almost been like those few months when they had first been married. She rolled off him and put her head on his shoulder, snuggling up to him as she used to do and he drifted off to sleep almost at once. He hadn't even heard her get up to feed the baby, he had slept so soundly. He even dared to hope, after last night's reunion, that they were going to get back to something like normality.

Chapter Twenty-Two

Janet started work at Ellswick just before Christmas. Her friend, Ann, was now a member of the nursing staff, and the present housekeeper, Mrs. Stokes, was due to leave in a week's time, to be married. Officially, Janet was not on the payroll until the beginning of the New Year, but she had arranged to come in a week early to give herself a little time to learn exactly what her duties were. She understood that she would be expected to order and maintain all the supplies for the Home except those for the dispensary. Mrs. Stokes had offered her, first, a tour of the hospital wing, with its men's and women's wards, afterward showing her the big lounges for convalescents. Then they had taken the lift up to the bedrooms, some with as many as four beds in them. Her own room was up there too, at the back of the house, overlooking the orchard and the vegetable gardens. Mrs. Stokes seemed pleased that she was handing over to a friend of Ann's, whom she felt would be caring as well as capable.

"It isn't just the job, you know, dear," she said, as they arrived, finally, at Janet's bedroom door. "You really have to care for the patients, too. There are some sad cases brought in here and we all try to help them as much as we can."

After Mrs. Stokes had left her, Janet looked around at the furnishings. It was adequate, even comfortable, with its single bed, its small dressing-table, long mirror and chest of drawers, completed by a large wardrobe which filled the whole of the space in the alcove. Before she had left her, Mrs. Stokes had suggested that Janet settle in before she showed her the kitchens and the utility rooms. The laundry, she had said, was sent out. Mrs. Stokes had arranged to meet her later over a cup of tea, when they could go over the work for the day. Apparently, Mrs. Stokes had an office next to the dining room, which of course, would be Janet's daytime domain when she took over the job.

Janet retired to her bedroom at the end of the day, brushing her long, glossy hair in front of the mirror before retiring for the night. At this moment, she felt that she would never, ever be able to cope with it all! Most things had to be ordered by the gross, or at least, the dozen and some of the supplies were quite unfamiliar to her. But Matron had promised to give her all the information and help she could after Mrs. Stokes left. Mrs. Stokes had assured her that by the end of the week, she would have sufficient grasp of the work to carry on alone. Janet fervently hoped she was right, as she pulled up the covers and got into bed. At this minute, she felt that she was completely out of her depth with it all.

By the end of May, Janet was beginning to get on top of the work at Ellswick. So far, she hadn't made any glaring mistakes, except for now and again omitting to order some item which had later been needed. But then, Matron had said that allowances would be made during her period of setting in to the job.

Her friendship with Ann Ferguson had flourished again. She often called at Ann's house in the evenings when she had finished for the day and the two of them sometimes went together for tea in Preston at the Sugar Bowl. At the weekends, if they happened to be off work together, they would go by train to Lancaster, or over to the coast to look round the shops in Southport, or call on Janet's family in Blackpool. There was now little chance of running into Harry and his wife. Ellen had passed on the information to Florrie that Alice had been unwell after the second birth. The couple now visited Nelson Street very infrequently, Florrie had told Janet on a recent visit.

Janet rarely thought about Harry, these days, filling her mind with her work. In her spare evenings she often wrote letters for those tragic young soldiers who had been blinded in the War, or read their mail for them. It all helped to fill her time and keep her busy. When she looked at others who had lost limbs and were struggling to come to terms with their disabilities, she felt it was a small price to pay, fetching and carrying for them.

She had missed her family dreadfully, at first. She had been happy, though, to see how well her father was looking and how happy he seemed. The children, too, were obviously fond of their stepmother, who seemed to be running the house as well as ever, with the help of a Mrs. Brooks, recommended by Ellen. But every time she returned to Ellswick, it felt more and more as if she belonged. The place was beginning to feel like home. The staff were very helpful and it was a happy place to work in, in spite of the sad cases they treated. Some patients were recovering after serious operations. Others were suffering from chronic disorders, mainly caused by the War. They had many chest cases and there was always the wracking sound of coughing and wheezing from the men's sitting rooms and the wards. Poor souls! Some of them had been badly gassed and they were never really going to recover. A vivid picture of Harry would flash through her mind as she toured the sitting rooms but it was instantly dismissed. Harry had been one of the lucky ones. These patients here were the ones who deserved all her sympathy and support.

Janet and Ann had arranged between themselves to share their summer holiday if they could both be off work at the same time. Ann had suggested that they should go to stay in the Lake District for a week. On their weekend outings they had often met parties of hikers who were going up to the Lakes. They were always lyrical in their descriptions of the area.

Ann, who knew it well, assured Janet that what they said was true. She had an aunt who lived in Windermere – Aunt Jessie, a widow, her father's sister. She lived in a stone house behind the main street and she had offered them a room if they wanted to stay with her. She occasionally took in paying guests, but she would make the room available to the two friends if they let her know when they were coming. It would truly be a complete change, Janet thought, from the flat, monotonous landscape of the Fylde. The holiday was finally arranged for July with Matron and as the time drew near for their departure, Janet began to feel a small twinge of excitement. Would this trip into unknown territory be as wonderful as Ann had predicted?

Harry Tomlinson was sitting on the train on his way home from work at the end of a beautifully warm June day. He felt desperately tired. In spite of the glorious weather, he was coughing incessantly and his hunched shoulders gave him a defeated look. He was finding it a hard physical struggle to keep up with his work and at the same time, fulfil all his obligations at home. He wondered what new domestic crisis would await him when he reached Fore Street. There was always something he had to sort out for his wife before he could relax and sit down to his meal.

With two children now to cope with, Alice was even further behind with the housework and sometimes he had to serve up his own dinner. Once or twice he had even had to cook it himself when she'd had a particularly bad day. He had begun to anticipate her complaining tone the moment he entered the house, and today was no exception.

"Harry, would you mind taking the potatoes off the gas for me? I've just had to change the baby – she's been sick – as if I haven't enough to do. And I think Jenny's starting with a cold, this weather!" she moaned.

"Alright, love, I'll see to them. I can see you've got your hands full."

"Yes, and whose fault is that?" she replied swiftly, while he hurried into the kitchen to escape her barbed thrusts. It was no good. He was far too weary to engage in this kind of exchange.

Taking the potatoes off the ring and turning out the gas, he returned to the sitting room, where Alice had laid the baby in her pram. She was now attending to her other child, encouraging her to blow into a rather soiled-looking handkerchief.

"Come on, Jenny, a good, big blow. I can't stay here all day wiping your nose." Her mother's sharp tone, combined with the misery of a stuffed-up nose, started the tears rolling down the child's face as she nearly choked.

"Here, give her to me," Harry offered, taking Jenny in him arms. "You go and finish off in the kitchen." Patiently soothing the distressed little girl, he gently wiped away the tears with the handkerchief and cleaned her face before sitting her in her high chair ready for her tea. Putting on her bib and tying it carefully around her neck, he kissed her and told her she was a big girl now. Jenny banged down her spoon on the wooden tray in front of her, good temper restored, ready for her meal. "We're going to have it soon," he told her, retiring to the easy chair and hoping that was true.

Later, as he lay in bed with his wife and he realised that she was already asleep, he knew that he was too exhausted himself for making love. This had been a regular pattern, lately. How long was it since they had last made love? In spite of that short period of the re-union, when he had returned to their bed, he had been unable to keep up that virility. He just hadn't the energy and Alice seemed to have lost interest again in their love-making.

All the same, he knew that she was still using contraceptives of some sort. He was far from happy about the reversal of roles she had forced upon him, but he couldn't see how he could change things without upsetting her again. In the end, he had had to accept the fact that she had gained the whip hand over him in this matter – and it rankled!

Chapter Twenty-Three

It was on a warm, sunfilled afternoon in July that Janet and Ann travelled up to Windermere on the train. All the way up from Lancaster Janet had been admiring the scenery, as the train left the Pennines behind, turning west, towards the southern end of the Lake District. The magnificence of the panorama which began to unfold now took her completely by surprise. Then, finally, she glimpsed a vista of cool, blue water, nestling under rugged peaks before the train slowed and pulled up in Windermere station.

The two women stepped down from the carriage into the tranquillity and peace that only a country station possesses. Scents of roses and mown grass wafted in on a warm breeze as they made their way outside into brilliant sunshine, where a single taxi cab stood, waiting after the train's arrival.

"It's not far, but these bags are heavy. I think we'll ride," Ann said. "You can't see the Lake from here. You have to go down to Bowness."

"Is that far?" asked Janet, as they climbed into the cab.

Ann directed the driver to take them to Oak Street before replying.

"No, it's only about a mile. After tea we'll have a walk down there, if you like. It's been a lovely day so it should be good viewing later. We'll be able to see the mountains as clear as a bell right down the Lake."

The taxi turned off by a small general shop in the middle of the town. It was really only a village, with its two short streets which converged on a few shops in the centre. From here, a single road ran down to Bowness, which boasted a few shops and the Lake itself. Oak Street turned out to be a short terrace of stone houses, each with a ground-floor bay window, like Nelson Street in Blackpool, had discreet notices in the window, advertising 'Bed and Breakfast,' or 'Vacancies', but the houses were quite small, in comparison.

Aunt Jessie turned out to be a fresh-faced woman with a clear, enviable skin and the sort of fair, sandy hair which never goes completely grey. She met them at the door, welcoming them with true Scots hospitality before taking them up to their room. It overlooked similar houses on the other side of the road and, as Janet went over to open the window, she noticed that the house walls were nearly two feet thick and that they appeared to be dry-stone built, no mortar being visible on the outside.

She commented on this fact to her friend, who laughed. "They can't be too thick up here, you know. It's alright on a day like this, but the weather up here can be wet and cold, even in summer. Come on, I'm starving. Just wait till you sample Aunt Jessie's cooking. You won't be able to move, once you've had your tea."

Sure enough, after an enormous meal, they found themselves sitting around in the comfortable sitting room, chatting, with no inclination to move. Happy to see her niece again and to have company, the older woman plied her guests with questions about their lives and their work. Janet concentrated on talking mainly about her work, managing to parry awkward questions about whether she was involved with any particular young man.

Soon, the evening almost gone, they decided to leave the walk down to the Lake until the morning. By the time they had said goodnight to their hostess, they were both ready for bed. Janet chose the bed nearest the window and before drawing the curtains across, she glanced casually down into the street. Two young men in flannels, sporting open-necked shirts, were just pushing open the gate of the house next door. One of them looked up at the lighted window and, seeing Janet framed against the light, he smiled up at her. Quickly, she whisked the curtains together.

"What was all that about?" Ann asked her, as Janet stood with the curtains clutched tightly together in her hands.

"Oh, it was just a couple of fellows coming in next door. I think they saw me at the window."

"Well, you haven't got undressed yet, so what are you worrying about? Here, let me see." Ann rushed over to the window, peeping through the curtains at the side. "They've gone in. Too bad. We'll have to look out for them tomorrow."

"I didn't think you had come up here to flirt with strange young men," Janet said primly.

"I'm not interested in them myself – it's you I'm thinking about. It's about time you had a beau again."

"Don't you dare try doing anything about it for me, that's all I ask."

"Oh, come on," Ann smiled. "Don't be so stuffy. We're supposed to be here on holiday. Just relax a bit. You never seem to let up at all. A bit of fun wouldn't do you any harm."

"Fun?" said Janet, "I don't know the meaning of the word."

236 / Sally Redmayne

"No, that's just the trouble," Ann agreed, getting into bed with a bound. "I'm going to sleep and sleep and sleep, and make up for all those extra nights I worked before we came away. Goodnight, dear. Sweet dreams of your new young man, next door," she added laughing.

In reply, Janet shied a pillow at her, sending Ann sprawling back on the bed. They were both beginning to unwind!

"Come on, lazybones, I thought you wanted to see Windermere," Ann's voice in her ear the following morning told her she had slept like a log!

"I don't think I moved, after my head touched the pillow," Janet said.

"This place is doing you good already. Everything's much slower up here, you know. We'll never want to start work again when we've been up here a week."

Between the lavender-scented sheets, Janet was luxuriating in the thought that today – the whole week – could be spent just drifting along, forgetting memos and lists and stores. "Don't even mention work to me," she said, smelling the delicious aroma of frying bacon already wafting up from the kitchen.

"I'm going to put a stone on at this rate," Janet laughed, as they attacked the large breakfast put before them by Aunt Jessie.

"Don't worry, they'll soon work it off us once we get back to Ellswick." Ann grimaced at the prospect.

"Shall I pack you up a few sandwiches, then you could stay down in Bowness as long as you like?" Aunt Jessie asked, after they had eaten. "I'll have a good meal waiting for you when you get back at tea-time."

"That will be fine," Ann said. "It looks as if it's going to be another good day. It changes very quickly up here, but the weather really looks settled. We've been very lucky, so far, choosing this week."

As the two of them, in light summer dresses, set off for Bowness and the Pierhead, Janet saw that the road ran downhill gently at first. One or two fine houses stood along it, most of them large, residential properties in their own grounds. Then they reached the brow of a hill and the street fell sharply down and round a couple of curves. Here the Lake came partially into view, obscured by another bend in the road.

"Oh," gasped Janet, "it's beautiful!"

"Wait till we get to the bottom, then we'll have a full view. You can't see it all from here."

Walking quickly now down the steep street, they soon rounded the last bend, between a couple of Inns and a few shops. The view opened out before them and the Lake appeared in full prospect, with its tremendous backdrop of rugged peaks. Today, the water was still and glassy, sunlight rippling along every tiny wavelet produced by one or two small boats as they crept in and out of their moorings.

"What do you think, then?" Ann asked. "It is beautiful, isn't it?"

Janet had been silent because she couldn't find words to describe the splendour of the sight before her eyes. The mountains along the bank of the Lake rose, tier upon tier, growing ever paler as they receded into the cloudless azure of the sky. The water was deepest cobalt, stretching away into the distance. Just off-shore, a small island introduced a splash of green into the seemingly limitless blue, and this was echoed all along the shore line in the woods which came down to the water's edge on the further side.

They were standing on a small promenade on the near-side of the Lake where quite a few people were strolling, mostly dressed, as they were, in summer clothes. There were groups, too, of serious walkers wearing khaki shorts and humping rucksacks on their shoulders, huge boots on their feet.

"Come on, we'll walk round past the jetty," Ann said.

Janet followed her friend past the wooden piers where the steamer came in, round to the furthest margin of the Lake, where green lawns sloped down almost to the water. A few snowy swans waddled in and out from the shallow water, quacking loudly or taking wing and flying off with a load creaking of wings. From here, the view was even better.

"It's absolutely wonderful, Ann," Janet said, at last. "It's so much better than I ever imagined. Look! Is that the steamer coming in now?" as a large boat came into view from behind the island.

"Yes, it is. Shall we get on it? We won't have a better day than this. It's coming from Ambleside, so it will be going the other way, down to Lakeside. It's the quietest part of the Lake but there's a small railway that goes up into the fells. The station's just behind the landing-stage."

"Anything you like," Janet agreed happily. "It's all so wonderful that it doesn't matter in which direction we go."

A small flock of sea-gulls followed the steamer as it left the pierhead for the southernmost end of the Lake. The two women walked along the deck, out in the warm sunshine, where they settled on the wooden seating admiring the changing scenery as the boat progressed towards Lakeside.

"I wonder what they are all doing in Ward Two at this moment?" laughed Ann.

"I thought we were going to forget all that this week?"

"Oh, I am, but I'm just telling myself that this week I'm as free as air, while they're all working away back there. Poor things! Look over there. Lakeside's coming into view." She pointed to where the landing-stage could just be seen in the distance, another steamer drawn up by its side, ready to depart.

As their own boat neared its destination, the other steamer set off. All the passengers rushed to the opposite side to wave as the boats passed each other with a great blowing of whistles on both sides. The magic of the day continued as they stepped ashore at the landing-stage. Behind it, a cloud of steam from the immaculate little engine told them that the train was ready to leave. It was only a short journey up the pretty valley to its head at Haverthwaite, above the Lake, so they got into a carriage. Soon, they were travelling through wooded banks where sunlight flickered in and out of leafy screens as the train chugged slowly upwards. Then they were among the high fells, looking down on the Lake, and they pulled up at a small station in the high, clean air.

"Let's have our picnic up here," Ann suggested. "We can get a later train back to the boat."

Walking the short distance before they came out onto a flat, green plateau of grass, they laid a rug down and ate their meal while bees, heavy with honey, buzzed around them amongst the clover. Lying on their backs amid the scented clover, the two girls gazed up into the cloudless vault above them, watching the sparrow-hawks as they wheeled above.

Later, they made their way back to Bowness, revelling in the unbroken sunshine and the beauty all around them. By the time they got back to the house at teatime, Janet felt quite overwhelmed by it all and she told her hostess as much.

"Och, yes, I used to think that there was nowhere like the Highlands," Jessie admitted, "but since I've lived here, I've had to change my mind."

After the fresh air of the day and another of Aunt Jessie's generous meals, the two of them sat around in the evening. Jessie had gone out to meet a friend, and they were debating whether or not to go out themselves for a short walk. As they idly watched by the front window, two young men walked past the house, deep in conversation. Ann, sitting nearest to the window, asked, "Are they the fellows from next door?"

"Yes, I noticed one was fair and the other's the dark one."

"Is the dark one yours, then?" Ann asked, impishly.

"Neither of them are! But the one who smiled at me had dark hair."

"Alright then, I'll have the fair one," Ann laughed merrily. "Perhaps he'll fancy a brown-haired beauty like me." Her dark eyes twinkling she jumped up, telling Janet that she had decided they should, after all, go out. "We'll walk up the street, past the Wellington," she said. "A stroll up there will do us good. We'll walk down all that food."

Protesting, Janet was led out of the house and onto the now empty street. "I hope you don't think I'm going chasing after those two," she said, firmly.

"Of course not – we're just going out for a nice, quiet stroll. Oh, come on, Janet, don't be a spoil-sport. They looked quite respectable to me. What harm can it do if we speak to them?"

"I can't see them now, anyway. They've probably gone off somewhere for the evening." Janet was very relieved as they reached the main street.

"Do you fancy a glass of cider at the Wellington?" See – people are sitting outside, it's so warm."

"Yes, if you like. It's much too nice to be inside."

"We'll get a seat over there, then." Ann said, keeping an interested eye on the doorway of the inn whilst seating herself on a bench.

"You're up to something, aren't you?"

"You'll see in a minute," Ann promised. "Ah, here they come." She nodded her head as the two young men emerged from the inn, glasses of ale in their hands. Looking casually around they sat down quite close to the two women.

Just wait till we get back – I'll deal with you then. Did you know they were in there?"

"No, of course not. It was just an inspired guess." Ann giggled and the men glanced across. She smiled at them and the fair young man raised his glass, the dark one looking on with interest. Janet, her face crimson, kept her eyes down.

"Oops, they're coming over," Ann whispered. "Now do try to be nice and talk to them. They're not going to bite us, you know."

"Are we right in thinking you are staying next door?" a pleasant Northern voice enquired of Janet, as the two men appeared in front of them.

"Yes, you are," she replied, looking up into dark eyes in a tanned, healthy-looking face. The hair, too, was very dark and the intelligent eyes were sober and steady as they gazed down at her.

"We are staying with my friend's aunt. I think I saw you last night as you came back to the house."

"Yes," he said, showing very good white teeth. "We've been here a week and that was the first time we'd seen a light in that room, so I thought somebody must have just arrived. Can I get you ladies a drink?" Both girls having decided on cider, he went back into the inn for two glasses and his friend seated himself beside Ann.

"Are you staying another week, then?" Ann asked, as Peter returned with the cider and then seated himself alongside Janet.

"Yes. We schoolmasters have long holidays to compensate for everything else," he said, laughing. "I'll introduce myself – I'm Peter and my friend is Donald."

"Right," said Ann, "I'll do the honours for us. This is Janet and I'm Ann."

"Where do you both live, then?" Donald asked.

Soon, they were all swapping information about their various jobs and activities. Even Janet joined in the general exchange. It appeared that the two men were grammar school teachers from the Lancashire mill town of Bolton, on a hiking holiday based at Windermere. They hadn't been able to go out for the last couple of days because Donald was having trouble with his feet. They weren't hardened enough for the heavy boots and he'd had some blisters.

"Although I should be alright now, with a nurse on hand to tend my wounds," he said lightly, glancing at Ann hopefully.

"Come on, now. We're supposed to be on holiday." She protested. "Plenty of surgical spirit's the thing to get those feet hardened up."

Groaning, he told her, "You have no heart, nurse. I expect you're one of those nurses who go around the wards jabbing everybody and not batting an eyelid."

"Naturally, what else?" Ann lifted her eyebrows in mock surprise.

"Would you like some more cider?" Peter asked. "I'll go in and get us all another."

"I'll help you carry them." Donald followed his friend into the inn.

"Well, what do you think?" Ann asked, as the two men disappeared inside.

"They seem alright," Janet had to admit.

"I think Donald's rather nice," Ann said, "and I think Peter likes you."

"He doesn't know me," Janet pointed out.

"Well then, he likes what he sees of you."

"It's no good trying any matchmaking schemes on me, you know."

Ann grinned, confident that, in spite of her protests, Janet and Peter were going to get on well together.

There was quite a bit of further talk when the men returned with the drinks. The evening finished with a general decision that all four of them would walk as far as the station and the Ambleside Road to stretch their legs. The party finally finished up at the gates of the two houses in Oak Street.

"Don't overdo the walking tomorrow, and put plenty of plaster on those feet," Ann advised Donald.

"You wouldn't like to come at the crack of dawn and do it for me, would you? I thought not! Ah, well, it was just a beautiful idea."

On this bantering note, the two men walked up to their own door. "Perhaps we'll see you again during the week?" Peter said, as they prepared to go inside.

"We're going up to Ambleside tomorrow," Ann said, "but we could see you in the evening, if you like. Come round after your meal."

"Fair enough. Have a good day, then."

"Thanks. You too." Upon this agreement Janet and Ann walked inside the house and through to the parlour.

"Had a nice walk?" asked Aunt Jessie. "I've only just got back myself."

Ann smiled mischievously at her. "Oh, yes, and we had some company, too – male!"

Aunt Jessie's eyebrows lifted slightly. "Anyone I know?"

"I should think you've seen those two from next door, Auntie. They are decent enough – grammar school teachers from Bolton. We all got on quite well."

"Yes, I've noticed them going past in their hiking clothes once or twice. I'm glad you've made some nice friends. It gives a bit more interest to your holiday."

"That's what I thought." Ann grinned at Janet, who knew that she herself wouldn't have gone out of her way to meet them, as Ann had done. After a supper drink and preparations for bed, the two girls lay awake. The day's events had given them a lot to think about.

"It has been a good day, don't you think?" Ann said. "Be honest Jan. I know you enjoyed the Lake, but did you enjoy the evening?"

"Yes, I suppose I did. They were quite good company."

"What do you think about Peter, then?"

"Oh, Ann don't ask me yet. I can't say until I know him better. After all, I've only just met him."

"Well, I like Donald," Ann admitted, "and I think I like him without even knowing him." After this involved bit of reasoning, she turned over and promptly went to sleep.

Janet lay awake for quite a while. Ann was always so enthusiastic about her activities. She seemed to have about twice as much energy as anybody else. Janet wished she could throw herself into things like her friend did, but as far as men were concerned, she had carefully avoided them since Harry had deserted her. How could she even think of trusting any one of them, after the way she had been used?

She awakened the following morning to sunlight beating against the curtains, lighting the room with warm promise. Quickly, she stepped out of bed, pulling back the curtains, letting in a flood of glorious light. It was going to be another beautiful day! By the time she finished her toilette, Ann had awakened, too, and seeing the bright promise of the day, she hurried and was in time to join Janet at the breakfast table.

"Are you going up the Lake today?" Aunt Jessie asked, eyes bright as buttons as she brought more hot toast.

"Yes, we thought we'd go to Ambleside."

"Well, it's going to be hot again, mark my words," Aunt Jessie said. "There are some nice shops in Ambleside, if you're intending taking any souvenirs home."

"Don't bother with sandwiches, Auntie, dear. You are doing enough for us as it is. We'll get a light lunch in one of the cafes."

"Och, I enjoy cooking for you. Now, if you've finished breakfast, off with you both and I'll clear these things. Don't be wasting a minute while the weather's like this."

On the steamer going up the Lake to its northerly head, the views became more and more spectacular as they sailed by some of the most majestic and renowned peaks in the Lakes. Ambleside itself, set against a backdrop of mountains which seemed to have their heads permanently in the clouds, was a bustling little town. As they wandered around its hilly streets they were tempted this way and that by the shops selling all kinds of local craftwork. They had lunch in one of the small cafes which seemed to be open all day serving tea or coffee. Then, at Ann's suggestion, they set off to walk up to a local beauty spot just above the town which boasted a spectacular waterfall. It proved to be a longer trip than they had expected but, when they had arrived, the falls and the view made up for all the effort. It was so cool and refreshing up there, that they stayed for the rest of the afternoon, only just managing, after the long walk back, to catch the last steamer of the day.

As they walked up the iron ladder onto the upper deck into the cool air of the Lake, the figures of two hikers came into view. They were sitting on the long bench in the centre of the planking. Donald and Peter were wearing Khaki shorts and they had on heavy boots over thick stockings. As the girls appeared, bit by bit, up the companionway, they looked up in surprise and with obvious pleasure.

"We thought you would have gone back long since. Surely you are very late for tea?" Donald said.

"Yes, we are, but it took us much longer than we thought to get up to the falls. Aunt Jessie won't mind – she'll keep it warm for us. How far have you been, then? Ann asked.

"We've rambled around a bit on the other side of the Lake, up behind Hawkshead," Peter told her.

"How are the feet, then?" Ann asked Donald.

"Much better today. They've stood up quite well. We've taken your advice and not done too much."

"I can see you're enjoying it up here," Peter said, dark eyes on Janet. "You said you haven't been up here before, then?"

"This is the first time, but I know I shall come again, it's so beautiful everywhere." She found herself talking quite animatedly to Peter about Ambleside. He, in turn, told her about his own love of the area and about his trips here in the past.

The boat journey passed swiftly and they found they were all very hungry as they prepared to go inside their respective lodgings, in the early evening.

"Why don't you come round after you've eaten, for a glass of Aunt Jessie's elderberry wine? It's better, any day, than all that beer you men drink," Ann offered.

"Well, if you're sure she won't mind, that sounds like a good idea." Donald took up her suggestion quickly. "See you later, then."

"Are you sure your Aunt will want them to come in?" Janet asked, as the two of them went through into the parlour.

"We've asked the two lads from next door to come in for a glass of your elderberry, later, Aunty. Sorry we're so late coming back."

"That's alright, dear. I've kept your tea hot in the oven. Have you had a good day in Ambleside?" Unperturbed by Ann's invitation to the two men, she bustled into the kitchen to serve up the meal, which didn't seem to have suffered at all by their lateness.

"They seem a couple of nice young men," was Aunt Jessie's opinion when Donald and Peter finally left after a convivial evening over the elderberry wine.

"Glad you approve, Aunty. They've asked us to go walking with them tomorrow. Donald is going out in his soft shoes to give his blisters a chance to heal. We're going across on the ferry and then we'll walk up into Hawkshead. It's all along roads – no rough tracks or anything like that."

"I hope this weather keeps up for you, then," Aunt Jessie said, carrying off the empty glasses before either of them could forestall her. "Off to bed, then. You'll be wanting to be up early in the morning."

The four of them set off, as arranged, with the sun on their backs, for the ferry. It would take them across the Lake to the further shore, where the water was edged thickly by forest land. The one large village of Hawkshead, at its centre, was becoming a thriving little tourist spot. It boasted one or two good shops which sold quality woollen articles and Janet intended buying a new skirt to replace her old serge.

The two men, much stronger walkers than the women led the way as the foursome took the road from the ferry towards the village. There was quite a bit of laughter and chatter as they walked steadily, not pushing the pace.

When eventually, the first of the two village inns came into view, the girls were ready to collapse onto a bench outside.

"We'll go in and get some cool drinks," Donald said, preceding Peter into the interior. When they emerged with long, cold glasses, the women saw that the landlord had provided hunks of bread and a large bowl of yellow butter and fresh cheese. To complete the meal, Donald went over to buy apples from a small shop and the feast was taken over to in inviting patch of grass where they sprawled in the sun at their ease, munching the food with relish.

"I was ready for that," Ann said, licking her lips and feeling in her pocket for a handkerchief to wipe her hands.

"Allow me." Donald whipped out a large white square from his shirt pocket. "Clean this morning," he assured her, with a grin.

"Thank you, kind sir." Ann accepted the handkerchief with an intimate smile.

Donald didn't miss the warmth of it and a flush of pleasure came into his fresh-looking face. He was the kind of light-haired, light-skinned young man who, in later years, would carry his age well. Although the same age at Peter, he appeared the younger of the two, ready laughter lurking in his blue eyes. Ann found him boyish and appealing, whereas Peter seemed mature by comparison. Sitting next to Janet, Peter was peeling apples and asking her whether she felt up to the walk back to the ferry.

"Oh, yes, I think so. I enjoyed walking up here. We may not be experienced hikers, but I think we're reasonably fit."

"Shall we go and have a look in the woollen shop?" Ann, asked her friend, tearing her eyes away from Donald's. "We'll leave these two here."

The two girls got up, to walk the short distance and entered the shaded interior of the shop. Janet chose a flecked wool skirt in dark green which would go well with most of her other clothes. Having had the garment wrapped, they rejoined the men, Peter immediately taking charge of the parcel. After they had walked around the village, they started slowly back in the direction of the ferry. Strolling along in pairs, Janet and Peter in front, Ann and Donald bringing up the rear, Janet glanced back once or twice and it looked as if Donald had his arm around Ann's waist. Oh, well, it was her own affair, she thought, as she turned politely to answer one of Peter's questions.

On the evening before they were all due to leave for home, the four of them were sitting on the grass in a small clearing by the edge of the Lake. They were surrounded by woods and the air was sweet with the scents of fir and pine. The smoke of a wood fire in an isolated cottage garden drifted across the tops of the trees and the silence was only disturbed by the flutterings of birds.

Ann and Donald sat close together, his arm now familiarly around her. Janet, a little apart from Peter, was leaning back against a tree trunk, talking about the prospect of returning to their different jobs the following week. The other two, involved in their own private conversation, only glanced up as Peter suggested that Janet might like to stroll along the narrow path that led into the woods, leaving the other two to be alone. Ann and Donald hardly noticed their departure as the two set off into the trees.

"I can see that those two want to be alone," Janet said, as she joined Peter along the track. "After all, this is the last evening before we go home."

They walked along in silence for a while before Peter spoke. "Can I say something, Janet?" I'd like to get to know you better, but I feel you have barriers up all the time."

Janet answered him slowly, choosing her words carefully, "I'm sorry, Peter, but I've never been one for casual relationships and I find it difficult responding to people."

"Yes, I can see that. Have you known someone in the past who has hurt you?"

"Whatever makes you think that?" flashed Janet, stung by this sudden insight on Peter's part.

"I'm sorry, Janet, I can see I've upset you. It's true, then?"

She walked along in dogged silence before Peter spoke again. "Alright, We'll change the subject. Would you object to Don and I visiting you when we get home?"

"If you like." Janet appeared indifferent. "I'm sure Ann wouldn't object."

"That's what Don thinks but I don't want to force my company on you if you don't want it."

"Oh, I'm sorry, Peter." Janet was suddenly contrite. "I like you very much, it's just that I'm not a romantic girl any more. I'd like you for a friend, that's all."

"Fair enough," Peter agreed. "It's not all that far for us to pop over to Preston, especially if we get that second-hand Ford I mentioned. We're thinking of buying it between us. We'd be able to take you out at the weekends or when you're off duty."

"That would be nice." She smiled suddenly. "My family would be surprised if I turned up with a presentable young man in tow!"

Harry Tomlinson had been forced to come home from work in the middle of the day, he had felt so ill. He had now been lying in bed for a week, recovering from a bout of pleurisy. The doctor had ordered him to have at least a fortnight off work and Sid Greenwood had told him not to rush back. "Take your time, lad," he'd said, "and get yourself properly right before you come back. It's no use killing yourself for the sake of a week or two." Sid knew that Harry always put in a good day's work for his money and that if he came back too soon, he would be trying to do too much.

Harry didn't like lying in bed and he intended getting up as soon as he felt stronger. Alice had gone out, taking the children with her. As she had pointed out to him, "You need to rest, and you can't do that with the children bothering you with their noise." She seemed to have been out a very long time and, in the end, he got up to make himself a hot drink. He was shivering and coughing as he got back into the warm bed.

He didn't know where she had gone, and he hadn't had the strength to ask her, in case she snapped back at him. As he felt at this moment, he just couldn't cope with any arguments. The children though, it seemed, were getting out into the fresh air and the sun. They were both looking bonny and healthy and they would be christening the baby as soon as he was well enough to go to the ceremony. They had decided to call her Susan. That was one thing they had found to talk about between themselves. They didn't do much talking, these days. Alice seemed to have withdrawn into herself in some strange way. It was rather as if she were going through the motions – living an apparently normal life with him but, underneath, he suspected, she was feeling differently. Heaven knew he had tried to get near to her, but each time he had thought they were coming closer, she had slipped away again. And it was the same in bed. When they did make love – and it was far less frequently – he often felt that she was far away and not with him at all.

Turning restlessly in the bed, he waited for her to return. He had not felt up to eating earlier but now he was beginning to feel weak and empty. It was another hour before he heard her come in at the front door and then she had to see to the children before coming up to ask what he wanted for his tea. "Do you fancy some of that hot-pot I've got in the oven?" she asked him.

"Yes, alright," he said. "Don't go to any more trouble for me."

By the time it arrived, though, he felt he didn't want the greasy dish but he forced it down rather than upset her. He determined to get up tomorrow and be back at work by the end of the week. Staying at home was no good for a man. He was better back at Greenwood's, where there were no aggravations, even though the work took it out of him.

It was a full three weeks, though, before he could start work again. When he did return to the joinery shop, he found he couldn't do anything like his usual stint. It was weeks before he got back to his regular output and by then the summer was nearly over. As the autumn days began to blow colder, raking the estuary, they seemed to strike right through him, making him gasp for breath.

They would all be going to Bradfield again for Christmas. Alice had already arranged it, even though it was still three months away. These days she always seemed happier when she returned to her family. The baby, now christened in Lytham Parish church since Harry's return to work would be nearly a year old at Christmas , and Jenny two, at the turn of the year. It would be 1921 next year, he realised, with a shock. Had he been out of the Army for nearly three years? Sometimes he couldn't believe he had a beautiful wife and two lovely children. Alice had started taking care again over her appearance and when she walked out, all dressed up, she was once again turning heads as she passed by. He should be very proud of his little family, and he was. He still loved his wife dearly, in spite of her deficiencies as a housewife. The question he was beginning to ask himself, though was, did she still love him, too? And he dare not speculate on the answer.

During the months following Janet's visit to the Lakes, Donald and Peter came over often to visit the two girls in Preston. The Ford had been duly purchased by the two men and the black, shiny machine, an open tourer with a retractable hood, was either parked outside Ann's house or on the forecourt at Ellswick. At the weekends, the four of them would go off for a day at the coast, sometimes to Morecambe, or Southport or to visit Janet's family in Blackpool.

It was quite evident that Donald and Ann were becoming serious about each other. Janet was happy to see her friend falling in love again although she herself didn't feel anything other than regard for Peter. She suspected that he felt something more for her, but he did not try to force the issue. He seemed content to remain as a companion and friend and as long as this situation continued, Janet was quite happy to go along with it. She wasn't ready yet to trust herself to any man, even the pleasant, reliable Peter.

One beautiful Sunday morning in September, the Ford appeared unexpectedly at the front of the Home. Looking out of her small office window, Janet could see that Peter was sitting in it alone. He came into the office to tell her that Donald was involved in some activity at school and that the car was at his disposal for the day. "How about running over to Blackpool?" he suggested. "I thought you might like to visit your family."

"Oh, yes, I would," she said delightedly. "I'm just doing a couple of things here, then I'm free. Ann's gone home this weekend, to visit her parents."

"Yes, Don told me she would be away. They keep in touch all the time, you know."

"She is always telling me so," Janet smiled, as she pictured her friend's rapturous face whenever she had heard from Donald.

An hour later, they were on their way through the centre of Preston and then out onto the country road which went straight out to the coast.

"They will be so pleased to see us," she said, as she visualised their surprise.

"Glad I came over, now?" he asked her, glancing across at her quizzically, but with an earnest note in his voice.

"Yes, of course I am," she said, deliberately misunderstanding him. "I'm looking forward to seeing them all."

When the car drew up outside number Sixteen and they got out, Janet said, "We'll not knock, we'll go straight in and give them a surprise."

In the hall Janet came upon a large navy pram which she presumed belonged to one of the visitors. There would still be a few people in at this time of the year. Goodness, she thought, fancy bringing this sort of thing away with them! Pushing past the bassinette, she went through to the back parlour. The door was slightly ajar. She turned to Peter, putting her finger to her lips as she slowly pushed it open. Walking through, she called out, "Guess who?" Florrie, with a young child on her lap, looked up in complete astonishment as the two figures came through the door.

"Janet!" she cried. "What on earth? Why didn't you let us know you were coming. It's so good to see you – and Peter, as well. Come in and take off your coats. I'll sit Susie in her pram for a moment while I take them."

"It's alright, Florrie. I know where they go. And are you baby-minding, then?" Janet retreated to the lobby, where the clothes closet stood.

Florrie sat the child in her pram, where she started playing with the coloured beads strung across on elastic. Then she followed Janet out into the lobby, as Peter took a seat in the parlour. Florrie's face appeared embarrassed, as if she had been expecting a question she didn't quite know how to answer. "It's a shame you've come over on this particular day," she managed, at last, "because Harry and Alice are next door, visiting Ellen. Harry came in earlier with Susie. He knows I'm fond of the children. He wanted to talk to me about some repairs to the roof of my house at Lytham. I asked him to leave her with me for a bit, and come back later. He's due to come in any time now to see me and fetch her back."

"Oh, no!" breathed Janet, in dismay. "We won't stay, then, if that's the case. I don't want to see him again – ever!"

"Nonsense! Florrie spoke firmly. "Can I be frank, dear? You've got to face him sometime and now is as good a time as any. The past is dead and buried, as I see it, and you've nothing to be ashamed of. I'm glad you've got your young man with you. Let's go back into the parlour and you just carry on with your visit as usual. If Harry comes in talk to him just like you would to anybody else. I'm sure it's better to see him now and get it over with, because you'll bump into him sometime in the future, mark my words. Come on, we'll join Peter in the parlour. He'll be wondering what we're chattering about – and don't you worry! It will be alright."

"I only hope you're right, Florrie." Reluctantly, Janet returned slowly to the parlour with her stepmother, who apologised to Peter for keeping him waiting.

"Would you like a drink of ale, or would you prefer tea?"

"Tea, please, Mrs. Crossley."

"Yes, that would be very welcome, Florrie," Janet agreed, her troubled eyes on Susie, who was still playing happily with the coloured beads. Occasionally the child looked up, staring at the visitors. She was tuning into a pretty child, with blonde curls and large grey eyes that were wide and solemn. She had a way of looking at you as if she were weighing you up, Janet thought. The likeness to Harry in the pale, serious face, the baby-fine hair and the light eyes, was remarkable. What a calamity to have come on this, of all days, but they could hardly leave now without offending her father or Florrie. Robert appeared to be out at the moment but they would have to wait for him to come back, wherever he was.

As if in answer to her thoughts, Florrie reappeared from the kitchen to tell them that he had gone across the street to the Grapes for a gill, and that he wouldn't be long. "He'll be very disappointed if he doesn't see you," she said. "D'you feel you can wait for him?"

"Of course we'll wait," Janet said, as a brief knock sounded on the front door and familiar footsteps came along the lobby towards them.

Harry opened the parlour door wide, stopping short when he realised who the visitors were. "Why, Janet!" he exclaimed in some embarrassment, his gaze moving to Peter. "I saw the car, but I didn't connect it with you. Florrie didn't say you were coming."

"I didn't know. They only decided this morning."

Gazing at Harry in dismay, Janet saw at once that this was a very different Harry from the one she had known and loved. He was so much thinner, almost stooped, his face haggard. "How are you, Harry?" The polite, meaningless words were wrenched from her as they assessed each other.

He saw that she was looking well – even blooming – and that the young man she had brought with her was regarding her with admiration, and no wonder! Janet had developed into a fine woman. As a child and into her teens, she had been rather a plain girl, except for her wonderful red hair. Now he saw that she had gained in looks and poise since the time they had been engaged, and he, if anyone, knew what her other qualities were. Whoever he was, this young man was very lucky to be her companion – or was he more than that? Harry felt an unexpected surge of envy, which was entirely irrational. Janet was quite free to make what friends she liked and he had no right to be even talking to her.

"I'm alright," he said awkwardly. "What d'you think of Susie, our youngest?"

"She's very like you, Harry. This is Peter, a friend from Bolton. We met in the summer when we were on holiday in the Lakes." It was very difficult, but she managed the introduction, forcing herself to speak normally.

"Glad to know you." Harry shook hands as Peter got up. "I'll come back, Florrie, next time we come, to talk about the roof." Going over to the pram, he prepared to wheel the child next door.

"Yes, you do that, Harry. Robert will be in soon and we shall all want to catch up on our news." She held the door open for him to wheel the pram through.

"Perhaps I'll see you again, some time," Harry said hesitantly, pausing in the doorway, ill at ease.

"Maybe – if we come over again," Janet replied brusquely, as he left.

"Now then, Janet, you mustn't stop coming to see us, you know, just because that happened," Florrie begged her, as she came back from seeing Harry out.

"Of course not, Florrie. I shall come to see you whenever I like. Nobody's going to stop me from coming to see my own family."

As she spoke, the door re-opened and Robert walked jauntily in, crossing to his daughter and embracing her. "My, it's good to see you, lass. I recognised the car as I walked up."

Janet's eyes misted over as he kissed her warmly, his rough beard brushing her cheek. "Dad! It's good to be back." Some of the tension left her, as her father welcomed Peter, and the family launched itself into a discussion of current events on both sides. She tried to push the encounter with Harry to one side, but his grey, haunted face remained until, in the early evening, she and Peter said their goodbyes at the door.

On the way back in the car, she was rather quiet, but then Janet had never talked a lot, Peter thought. One thing he had learned, though, from this outing, was that Janet's former love had been Harry Tomlinson. He had been certain that someone in her past had hurt her but she had never admitted to it or hinted at who the man might be. It explained why she was wary of men and this afforded him some satisfaction. Her aloofness, then, wasn't because she didn't care for him personally. She evidently mistrusted men in general. He determined never to give her cause to doubt him. He meant to ask her to be his wife, but he intuitively knew that the only way to win her was to wait.

Fortunately, he wasn't an impetuous man. He had always been able to set up a goal in his mind and work steadily towards realising that objective, no matter how difficult or how long it took. Perhaps he was a bit of a plodder, unlike Don, who seemed to have a capacity for breezing through life with very little effort. But Janet was worth waiting for and he meant to muster all the patience he possessed, until she was ready to accept him as a lover, as well as a friend.

During the winter, they couldn't go about as much in the car, especially after Christmas, when the roads became treacherous. There were times, after the New Year, when a week or two went by before the car appeared, not quite as immaculate in the bad weather, in front of the Home. Janet knew that Ann's romance with Donald was blossoming and she could always tell when her friend had received a letter from him. She would rush through the rooms in a state of joy, oblivious to the trials of the day, wrapped in her own little cocoon of happiness. Janet was expecting her friend to tell her any day that Donald has asked her to marry him.

When he finally did so, it was summer again, and he came over alone in the car, taking Ann back up to the Lakes to her Aunt's. From there, he intended going on up to Edinburgh, where Ann's parents lived, to tell them what he proposed. Janet was very happy to know that her friend had found another man she could love. If only she herself could have felt the same way about Peter. Ann's wedding was fixed for October and Janet was to be her bridesmaid. Peter, of course, would be the best man. At work, Ann's forthcoming marriage was the main topic of conversation amongst the staff, everybody wanting to share in her excitement and happiness. Ann's first marriage had, of necessity, been a hasty, War-time ceremony and this time she meant to do everything properly. She and Janet talked for hours about clothes and flowers and all the other essentials for the kind of wedding that she visualised. Janet knew that her friend was finding it hard to keep her mind fully on her work, but she was naturally so full of energy that she got through her work in a kind of efficient euphoria.

Sitting in her office, pen in hand, Janet tried to concentrate on what she was doing. The wedding seemed to have invaded all her privacy lately. She was trying to compose a letter for one of the patients, a blind boy, Reggie Knowles, who had been blinded, as well as gassed, in the War. She had written so many for other ex-soldiers that it should have been easy, but this one was giving her difficulty. It was to Reggie's elder brother, who had a house in Devon. Janet had already written to Reggie's parents, at his request. They lived abroad, but they had a house near Preston, to which Reggie would return after his convalescence. His father and mother were due to return to England in another month, when they would be staying permanently and would be able to look after their younger son in their own home.

It had been hard enough writing to a man and woman she had never met, but to an elder bother, what could one say? She visualised an older version of Reggie, heavily jowled and stout, with a large moustache. Sighing, she ploughed on, struggling to make it interesting enough to read out to Reggie before she posted it. Why, oh why, had she ever started doing these kind of jobs in the first place? Peter would probably be coming over next weekend, so they might run over to Blackpool in the car, while Ann and Donald made plans – something to look forward to.

They had only been over once since that surprise trip, when she had met Harry and been forced to speak to him again. She hadn't wanted her father and Florrie to think that she was deliberately staying away to avoid seeing him. On the other hand, she hadn't wanted to run the risk. That meeting had unsettled her more than she liked to admit, not because she still loved Harry. She knew now that her feelings had changed. But when she had seen Susie, sitting there in the pram, so like her father, she hadn't been able to stop herself from thinking that the child could have been hers.

Of course, both Florrie and her father expected something to come of her relationship with Peter. Florrie had winked at her that last time, as Peter, with a touch of proprietorship, had helped her into the car. Robert, too, liked her young man, as they insisted on calling him. Janet liked Peter, too, but she didn't love him, that was the problem.

Sighing again, Janet concentrated on putting the finishing lines to Captain Edward Knowles' letter, finally writing the address, Forest Lea, Babbacombe, Torquay, South Devon, on the envelope. She had done her best and it would just have to do. Getting up, she took the letter through into the sitting room to read it through to Reggie before taking it to the posting box.

Chapter Twenty-Four

Alice Tomlinson was sitting on the sofa in her friend, Betty's house, lower down Fore Street. It was now her regular calling-place but she hadn't said much to Harry about Betty Furlong. He would probably think she was rather common, with her untidy hair and her down-at-heel shoes. Alice had only become acquainted with Betty quite recently. They had been sitting on the same promenade seat and their children had started playing together. Betty had a boy, Stevie, who was about the same age as Jenny. As they had chatted, Alice had discovered that Betty lived on the same street, having moved in during the past month. Alice often called at Betty's house now. It was good to be able to talk to another woman who seemed to understand how she felt about things. Betty, too, was a reluctant housewife who preferred to go out with her son, rather than stay indoors, doing chores.

On this particular afternoon, Alice had arranged to call at Betty's before they went onto the promenade with the children. She had on a pretty pink dress which she had just bought from one of the small shops in Lytham. It had the new longer bodice and raised hemline and it showed off her calves to perfection. She drew her legs up, lounging full length on Betty's dingy moquette sofa. Susie was still asleep in the bedroom and Jenny was playing on the floor with Stevie. The child was now nearly three years old – a healthy, lively girl, whose beauty had grown with her. It looked as if she was going to be as slim as her mother and she was quite fair now, with her dark-blonde ringlets and apple-blossom skin. But her eyes were Alice's, deep and intense.

Betty was at present occupied with trying to make the 'Cat's Whisker' wireless set work. As she attached a wire to the set, a crackling, overlaid with the strains of music, issued from the ear-piece.

"Is it dance music?" Alice cried eagerly. "I love dance music."

"I'll try to get it louder," Betty said, as she twiddled with the wire. "Here, come and have a listen," as Alice came across the rug towards her.

Holding the earpiece to her ear, she could just make out the announcer's polished voice over the interference. "I wish Harry would buy one of these," she grumbled. "He won't buy anything like this."

"Bert didn't buy it. He made it from bits and pieces he got from someone who sells the parts. He's very good at putting things together."

The music suddenly came through louder, although the crackling continued as a low background hiss.

"It's a waltz," Alice said gleefully, handing over the earpiece to Betty and dancing round the room. "Oh, I wish we could go dancing. I'd love to go to a dance."

"I shouldn't think Harry would be one for dancing."

"Harry? No, he isn't." Suddenly, Alice stopped twirling, turning round to her friend. "He would never think of taking me to one of the tea-dances they have at the Lowther Pavilion here," she said, resentfully.

"No, neither would Bert. They seem to think that all we want is housework and babies. It's not my idea of fun."

"Mine, neither. Tell you what. How about one of us going some time to a tea-dance and the other one looking after the children?"

"Oh, I don't think so, Alice. We couldn't do it in Lytham, anyway. Someone would be sure to see us. I suppose we could go into Blackpool. Alice! Would you dare do it?"

"I'm so bored!" Alice complained. "I think I'd do anything for a bit of excitement."

"Alright, then, I'll do the baby-minding if you want to go one afternoon."

Betty wasn't as pretty as Alice or as stylish and she couldn't afford a new dress like the one Alice had on. Her husband was only a lowly labourer, whereas Harry got tradesman's pay. She hadn't had her mousy hair cut yet, either, in the new short style like her friend's. It seemed that Alice was always abreast of the fashions and secretly Betty was envious of her trim figure and her elegant appearance.

"Would you really, while I go?" Alice asked her. "Don't you mind looking after them all?"

"Oh, no, they'll be alright with me. Susie always sleeps in the afternoons and the other two play well enough together. Where would you go, then?"

"The Tower Ballroom, I expect." Alice collapsed once more onto the sofa. "I've heard they have dances there in the afternoons in the season, and then there's the Children's Ballet, afterwards."

"Are you sure about? I mean…. Suppose Harry finds out? He'd go mad."

"Well, he won't find out, if you don't tell him, will he? How about leaving all the children with your mother, then you can come with me? I'm not keen on going on my own, really."

"Well, I could ask her, but I'm not sure I want to risk going myself."

"Oh, well, I'll have to go on my own, then. You'll wish you'd come with me, though, when I tell you what a good time I've had."

"Anyway, Bert would kill me if he knew."

"He's not likely to know, is he? No one we know goes to the Tower. There's so many visitors we'll never be noticed."

"Where am I going to tell Mum we're going, then?"

"You could say you're coming with me to visit someone in Blackpool. Not Harry's mother, though, that's too risky."

"I'll see what she says, then, but mind, it's only for once!"

Betty, too, was weary of the daily round of cleaning and cooking, so the prospect of a glamorous afternoon in the Tower, all dressed-up in the best frock she had was very tempting. Alice didn't seem to have any reservations about going, so why should she? After all, as Alice had pointed out, who would find out, anyway? Could she persuade her mother to have the children for an afternoon? She had offered to have her own grandchild any time and she had once or twice looked after all three children for an hour while she and Alice had gone shopping. But a whole afternoon? That was a bit different.

Nothing more was said on the subject until Alice called round again on her friend. The children were with her, Susan in her pram. Jenny running along, swinging a black golliwog by one leg, making it dance.

"Have you thought any more about going to the Tower?" Alice asked, as the two of them settled down to cups of tea in a cluttered sitting-room.

"Well, I have mentioned it to Mum that we'd like an afternoon out. I said we wanted to go to the pictures in Blackpool. It's my birthday next week, so I said she could treat me instead of buying me a birthday present. She's going to get Bert's tea ready as well. What about Harry? Will he get his own?

"Oh, I'll leave him something. It won't be the first time," Alice said indifferently.

In spite of her interest in clothes, Alice could only afford to have one or two dresses in her wardrobe, the children often having to come first when Harry gave her money. Each of her outfits, though, had been chosen carefully to enhance her naturally dramatic colouring. She knew that the soft pastel shades she wore accentuated the blackness of her hair and the blueness of her eyes. Harry liked her to look nice and when he could afford it, he gave her money to buy what she wanted. She was well aware that the new soft pink dress was the colour which suited her best of all. She had worn it at Betty's to get her friend's opinion of it and had seen that Betty was impressed and envious. Betty would never have been able to wear anything like it – she was too plump! Alice decided to wear the new dress for the Tower and, as the two women met ready for the journey, she noticed that Betty had on a flowered silk which couldn't match her own outfit for either styling or quality.

They both boarded the train giggling like two schoolgirls, congratulating themselves that they were on their way to the ballroom, as the train pulled out of Lytham station. It took less than half-an-hour to make the journey and soon the two women were pushing their way through the brass turnstiles which led into the ground floor of the Tower building. To reach the ballroom, they had to pass through the dimly lit aquarium with its glowing green tanks. Hurrying past staring, fishy eyes, they soon reached a flight of shallow, wide steps which led up to the dance floor. Their pace quickening, they ran lightly up, their feet cushioned by red velvet carpeting.

The next moment, the ballroom opened up before them in a blaze of golden light. The floor was full of people dancing – a kaleidoscope of ever-changing patterns.

"Isn't it wonderful?" gasped Alice. "I'd forgotten what it was really like. I didn't come in here the last time we stayed at Nelson Street." Of course she hadn't. She had been too busy seeing Harry! How long ago that idyllic week seemed now! Almost as if it was in some other lifetime! Dismissing the past, Alice followed Betty around the edge of the floor, past marble pillars which supported the double tiers of gilded balconies, they came to a halt at the furthest end of the room, near to the stage, where the dance orchestra was playing. Seating themselves on one of the red velvet sofas, they watched the band as it played against a backdrop of potted palms and pastoral scenery. The whole of the upper part of the stage was fronted with a carved and gilded framework, at the sides of which hung heavy velvet drapes, each tied back with a massive golden rope.

"I wouldn't mind some of this carpet on my floor," Betty said, gazing with awe at the enormous expanse of medallion-strewn Wilton laid down all around the walking area.

"D'you think anyone will ask us to dance?" Alice asked, gazing up at the magnificent crystal chandeliers glittering above the heads of the dancers as they swayed and swirled to the music. Just behind them two young men, wearing the new baggy trousers, were lounging against the wall and it wasn't long before Alice's question was answered. They came over to where the two girls were sitting.

"How about a dance?" one of them asked Alice, while the other grabbed Betty's hand, taking her with him onto the floor. Alice's feet moved rhythmically to the music and she followed her partner quite easily. Betty, on the other hand, seemed to be having some difficulty coping with hers, and when the dance had finished, the two girls wandered off, further round the dance floor.

"I'm not keen on them," Betty said, as they left the young men behind.

"You did seem to be having trouble," Alice said. "Did he have two left feet?"

"Yes, he did, and he couldn't keep his hands to himself, either."

They were both asked again to dance, their partners a mix of callow youths and older men. Flushed from the exercise and the enjoyment of this newly-found pleasure, they decided to go and reclaim their original seats by the bandstand. Their first partners had disappeared and, laughing at the success of the venture, they watched an organist rise slowly from a pit below. It looked as if the band had gone off for an interval while the organist played for the dancers.

Alice sat, crossing her slender legs gracefully, one foot tapping the floor to the music. She noticed a young man dressed in a white jacket and smart black trousers, his black patent shoes matching his shiny, slicked-back hair. He was walking round the edge of the floor in their direction and, as he approached, she could see the expert cut of the jacket and the knife-edge crease in the trousers. Then it struck her – of course! He was a member of the band which had just left the stage. The next moment he was standing in front of her, asking her to dance. She was too surprised to speak and she didn't move until Betty gave her a little push to get her to her feet. Holding out one white, elegant hand, showing the gold cuff-link at his wrist, he escorted her onto the floor.

"I saw you dancing," he told her. "You're a good little mover, aren't you? What's your name?" And when she had told him that it was Alice, he said that his own name was Jack Fenton.

He had obviously had dancing lessons and plenty of practice, she could tell, as he led her expertly through the other couples out onto the fringes of the floor. She felt as light as thistledown as she tried to match his steps. None of the others she had danced with had attempted these intricate little movements. As the dancers slowed down at the end of the music, he asked her, "D'you go dancing often?"

"Oh, yes," she lied, taking this as a compliment, and drifting back into his arms as the organist started to play a dreamy waltz. It was heavenly, floating along, in perfect harmony with Jack, as the melody swelled and they swayed, bodies close together, oblivious to all else but the moment.

"I've got to get backstage soon," he said, as the dance came to an end. "I have to have a drink before we play again. Blowing a sax dries you up, you know. 'Bye, kid, it's been nice dancing with you."

"Bye," Alice said weakly, as he deposited her back at her seat, Betty watching goggle-eyed as she sat down.

"My, he's a good dancer," she said enviously, as Alice's eyes followed his progress round to the back of the stage.

"Yes, isn't he?" Alice nodded dreamily, as she watched the organist descend into the subterranean pit.

"I'll bet he's married, too!" Betty laughed.

"He's not the only one, is he? But I haven't felt as free as this for ages. I haven't felt as if I was married at all this afternoon! I can't remember when I enjoyed myself as much, and there's another hour to go yet."

Each time Alice went round the floor with a partner, she tried to steer him as near the stage as she could. Sometimes, as she danced past, she managed to catch Jack Fenton's eye as he sat on the stage, playing his saxophone, and he had grinned at her in return.

Eventually, when they left the ballroom as late as they dared, the dancers of the Children's Ballet had taken the stage for the first part of the evening's programme. This was always a popular show with the visitors and locals alike, but Alice and Betty dare not stop to watch it. It was time for the two Cinderellas to leave the ball and return to the real world.

A few weeks later, Alice asked her friend, as they were shopping in Lytham, "Are you going to the Tower again, then?"

"I suppose you want to dance with that saxophone player again," Betty said, grinning. "It was a good idea, wasn't it? When he came to ask you to dance, I nearly died. The only thing is, I don't think I could ask Mum again so soon. She only did it for my birthday, you know. What could I tell her this time? And Bert wasn't too pleased, either, about her not being in when he came home. It's alright for you, Harry hasn't got a temper like Bert. Bert wouldn't think twice about going for me if he thought I was up to something. Not that I didn't enjoy it," she added, smiling fondly at the remembrance of the afternoon's pleasure. "If you want to go, I think you're going to have to go on your own, next time. I don't mind having the children for you, though."

"Thanks, Betty, but it won't be the same on my own." Pushing open the door of Simpkins' grocery shop, Alice added, "Well, if you don't want to risk going, I'll have to think about it myself, if you don't mind having the children."

"Of course I'll have them, but if you do go, for goodness sake be careful. I don't want to be dragged into it. If anyone finds out, especially Harry or Bert, I don't know anything about where you've gone."

"Don't worry," Alice said, as they approached the counter, "No one will find out. They didn't last time, did they?"

Once again the ballroom was full of swaying, happy couples, dancing away the afternoon, as Alice, dressed in the same pretty pink dress, made her way round to the seat near the bandstand. She felt a bit self-conscious, sitting there on her own, but she didn't have long to wait before a young man came up to ask her to dance. After that, she hardly sat down and it was the interval before she had realised it. She found herself looking along the floor for Jack Fenton. She had seen him up on the bandstand, of course, and he had smiled, but she didn't really expect him to come again and ask her to dance. There were dozens of other girls he could ask. Why should he pick on her? The next moment, there he was, holding out his beautifully manicured hand to her. She stepped down from the seat and they floated off into the crowd.

"Where's your friend this afternoon?" he asked her, as they negotiated a bend at the corner.

"Oh, she couldn't come. She had something else on."

"I haven't had as good a partner since you came before," he said, holding her closer as the quick tempo changed to a slow foxtrot.

"Go on – I'll bet you tell that to all the girls." She could feel his body, lean and flexible, against hers. "I'll bet you're married, if the truth were known."

"How did you guess?" He grinned at her. "Are you married, too, then?"

"Yes, and I've got two children," she admitted, "but I get so bored at home all day. This place is wonderful. It makes me feel as if there's something else going on in the world besides housework and looking after children."

"Oh! So that's the way the wind blows, is it? What about your husband? Does he know you come here?"

"Of course not – don't be silly. He would go mad, if he knew. Does your wife know you dance with all the girls, then?"

"I should think so, but she works, too, and we have no children. She's out all day and I work late at nights, so it works very well. We don't see enough of each other to be falling out all the time."

"It doesn't sound much of a marriage to me," Alice said doubtfully. Doesn't she want any children, then?"

"Oh, yes, but she can't have any. The doctor's told us that she'll never be able to have any."

"Isn't that funny? I don't want any more, but I seem to get them, and there's your wife, really wanting them, and she can't have any."

"That's life," said Jack, philosophically. "Shall we waltz, then?"

Holding her close to him, placing his smoothly-shaved cheek to hers, he whispered, "You're a great kid. We could have some good times together."

She could smell the sweet scent of the hair oil he used, and a sudden surge of excitement ran through her. Did he mean that he wanted to meet her away from the Tower? The daring thought increased the tingle of pleasure and she found herself pressing closer to his lithe body.

On her way back to Betty's her mind full of the afternoon's enjoyment, Alice was walking on air. It had been so easy! No one she knew had seen her. It wasn't likely that they would All her acquaintances were over the Pennines in Bradfield. She hadn't had any social contacts here on the coast except for Betty – her life had been so dull! Having collected the children from Betty's, she made her way quickly in the direction of number Twenty. When she arrived, Harry was already in the house, warming up the stew she had left for him.

"Sorry I'm a bit late," she apologised, skipping over and kissing him, "but I stayed at Betty's longer than I should have."

She seems so happy and bright tonight, Harry thought, as they settled down to their meal. He listened to her chattering as they ate, seeming not to have a care in the world. How her moods seemed to swing from depression to this happy euphoria! His mood lightened to match hers, and they spent a pleasant evening with the children before Alice started getting them ready for bed.

Seeing him relaxed and cheerful, Alice thought it a good time to renew her request about having a radio set, like Betty's. The last time she had mentioned it, he hadn't seemed at all keen on the idea. He had pointed out that, soon, better models would be produced. "Harry," she began, "why don't we have a wireless set now? It's ever so interesting. You can get the news on it and all sorts of things."

"Would you really like one, love?" he asked her, his resolve wavering. Wirelesses were still very much in the experimental stage and he felt that in another couple of years some better model would be produced but, if she really wanted one.... "Alright, love, I'll see Bert about it. He seems to know all about them. He might offer to put us a wireless set together."

"Oh, that would be lovely, Harry." She put her shapely arms around his neck. "Shall we go up to bed soon, tonight?"

But as he made love to her, she found her mind wandering. In her imagination, it wasn't Harry she was with – it was Jack Fenton. She could almost smell his brilliantine and feel his elegant white hands around her body. In her mind, she floated off somewhere with Jack, clasped in his arms. But when she came back to earth, it was only Harry she was with, and he was already turning over, ready for sleep.

She lay awake for a while, reliving in her mind the excitements of the afternoon in the Tower and anticipating what Jack's remarks about 'having a good time' might mean. If he suggested taking her out, or meeting her somewhere, would she go? That question trembled on the edge of sleep, as she, eventually, drifted off....

Chapter Twenty-Five

Ann Ferguson's wedding took place on a cool but sunny day in late October. There had been an overnight frost but, after a misty start, the day brightened and by early afternoon, the sun had come out. It was shining through a pearly mist as the guests gathered in Ellswick's small Parish church. The couple had decided to hold the ceremony there so that colleagues and friends could attend, and Ann's Scottish relatives were staying locally as guests or at local hotels.

Donald seemed to have as many guests as his bride. Besides his own relatives there were colleagues and friends from the grammar school who would be returning to the Bolton area later in the day. So the small church was quite full when the bridal party arrived. Janet had already seen how beautiful Ann looked in the soft, creamy satin dress, lavishly embellished with lace, which had taken so long to be decided upon. The filmy half-veil, thrown back over her dark, curly head and held in place by the tiara of pearls and yellow tea roses, complemented the dress perfectly. The veil now over her face, she walked confidently down the aisle on the arm of her father, Angus Ferguson, very correct and elegant in dark grey.

Mr. Ferguson, an Edinburgh solicitor, had presented the couple with a second-hand Ford car as a wedding present. It was similar to the one jointly owned by the two friends, and he had also offered them the use of his summer lodge up in the highlands, for the honeymoon. Donald, waiting nervously at the altar, looked up as his bride reached him and Janet could almost hear him catch his breath as he saw Ann in the wonderful wedding dress. At his side, Peter, too, seemed slightly bemused as Janet took her place near the altar, dressed in palest blue lace. She smiled briefly at him, but her eyes avoided his.

During the wedding breakfast at a local hotel and afterwards at the reception, Peter stayed by Janet's side. Once or twice, she wondered if people were imagining that the two of them would be the next couple to walk down the aisle together. He hadn't actually asked her yet, but he had suggested that she might visit his mother, a widow, in Bolton. She lived on the northern edge of the town, quite close to the main Preston Road so it would be a short journey by car. She had apparently been questioning her son about how long she would have to wait to meet his lady friend. Janet had stalled him about the visit, not wanting to give the impression that she was anxious to meet his mother. She had wondered whether Ann's departure from the Home to live near her husband's school would make any difference to her friendship with Peter. One weekend, though, shortly after the wedding, Peter called at Ellswick to see if she would like to go over to visit the newly-weds.

"Oh, yes, I'd love to," she said. "I'm missing Ann so much."

"She asked me to bring you over as soon as I could. They've settled in very quickly. It's a nice old house and not too far from the school. Anyway, you'll see," he said, as she got in to the car, eager to see Ann again and hear all her news.

Ann was bubbling over with plans for the house as she showed them around. It had been chosen by the couple for its position, being situated on the main road into Bolton, quite close to the school buildings. Ann had far-reaching ideas about what should be done in her new home and it was fortunate that Donald listened to it all indulgently.

"Where's the money to do all this coming from on a schoolmaster's pay?" he asked her, with a teasing smile.

"Oh, we'll find it from somewhere." She kissed him en route to the kitchen.

Janet knew that her friend had a small income of her own which she intended using to further her schemes. It was good to see that they were getting on so well and that they were quite obviously very much in love.

It seemed to Janet that this trip to Bolton in what was now Peter's car was going to be the first of many and she was proved right. He came to pick her up a couple of weeks later, taking her over to the coast to see her family. They were welcomed rapturously by her father and Florrie, who seemed to take it for granted that Peter should be bringing her to visit them. She wondered if they were expecting her to announce her engagement to Peter quite soon. She herself felt that he was on the verge of asking her to marry him, but she knew that she had no answer for him.

After the Blackpool trip, Peter took her, on a cool but sunny day, inland, towards Yorkshire, going up into the Pennines. It was a formidable climb for the old Ford, but they climbed steadily up over the moors towards the village of Ripponden. Here, magnificent views could be had over the western slopes and further across on the other side, into Yorkshire. It wasn't perhaps, quite as spectacular as the Lakes but the moorland scenery had a bleak charm all of its own.

The wind was quite cold up here on the high plateau of the moor so, after a brisk walk up to the reservoir, they got back into the car, picnicking inside. As they ate, they talked about everything except their feelings for one another and then, before they set off on the journey home, Peter tried to kiss her.

Janet managed to avoid his embrace, saying quickly, "I'm sorry Peter – I'm just not ready for anything but friendship yet. Please bear with me a little longer."

"Forgive me, Janet – please! I don't want to spoil our friendship. I was hoping that – perhaps – you wouldn't object. Goodness knows I've wanted to kiss you so many times. But if you want it this way...."

"Oh, Peter, it's my fault. I find it so hard to respond. I do like you very much so maybe I'll feel differently very soon. Please give me time before we try to change things."

"I shouldn't have tried to force the issue. Let's start again, shall we?" Smiling at her, he took both her hands into his. His hands were long and slender, with sell-shaped moons to the nails. "And when you're ready," he said, "just let me know."

He was so kind and understanding, Janet told herself. Why, oh why couldn't she love him?

Alice Tomlinson, in the middle of a rainy afternoon in late Autumn was dancing round the Tower ballroom in the arms of Jack Fenton. They were dancing as close as they dared, his cheek against hers. The familiar pulsing excitement ran through her as she felt his warm, white fingers squeezing hers, his pliant body pressing against her as he held her in his arms. She knew that what she was doing was wrong, even dangerous, but somewhere inside her a little devil drove her on.

"Look, Alice," he said, "how about coming out in the old jalopy for a ride after I've finished here this afternoon?"

Alice thought quickly. It would make her very late home, but she could always find some excuse for Betty and afterwards, for Harry.

"Well, perhaps I could manage half-an-hour, but no longer. I've got to pick up the children and then see to Harry's tea."

"We'll go into the country," he said, "out onto Preston Road."

An hour later it had stopped raining as Alice went round to the back of the Tower where he had said he would pick her up. When the car arrived it wasn't a new one, but it was big and roomy and it set off at a cracking speed. Soon they were driving out of the town between fields and hedges and then he turned up a narrow lane with a wood on one side and deserted fields on the other. There wasn't a soul in sight.

Stopping the car, he smiled at her before sliding a hand under her coat, caressing her breast with expert ease and bending to cover her mouth completely with warm, eager lips. She opened her mouth to him and his tongue began a slow exploration. She was seized with raging anticipation. It had been a long time since she had felt like this with Harry. Responding feverishly, she unbuttoned his trousers until she felt him harden against her.

"How about transferring into the back?" he suggested, "there's more room in there."

Half-undressed she opened the passenger door and got into the rear bench seat. A moment later he joined her, stripping off his trousers while she took off her dress and unfastened her corselette at her breasts.

"You're a great girl," he told her, as they lay on the long bench seat, her head cushioned on the arm, her body trembling with arousal. He ran his hands with practised ease along the full length of her slim legs, finally bending and kissing the soft skin just above her stocking-line with butterfly-soft lips, then again on her inner thigh, as her knees parted and his fingers sought her groin. As he found the sensitive spot, his lips came up to fasten on her nipple and she pushed her hips forward, crying out, "Hurry, Jack, oh, please hurry!"

Ignoring her, he took his time, entering her with exquisite slowness so that she clutched at him to pull him closer.

"Don't be so impatient, sweetheart," he whispered. "It's better this way."

Taking his time, he extended the pleasure for as long as possible – much longer than she had expected or had been used to with Harry. The long, slow movements gradually heightened the mounting pleasure, sustaining and raising it. At last, a deep, swelling orgasm spread in fiery, gratifying waves over her loins. By the time it was over all she wanted to do was to lie there, revelling in the warm, radiating satisfaction of it.

"Did you enjoy that, sweetheart?" he whispered, knowing perfectly well that she had.

"Oh, it was wonderful, Jack," she breathed. "I didn't know it could be as good as that."

As he got up to straighten himself and get back into his clothes, she released a foot from where it had been jammed up against the upholstery of the car. She had only just realised that it was hurting her, she had been oblivious to everything else until this moment.

"Like to come out again, another day?" he asked her, as they drove through the lush water-meadows back onto the metalled road that led to the town.

"Oh, yes, Jack," she said eagerly.

"That's what they all say!" Then, seeing the look on her face, he added, "Only joking!" There was no point, after all, in upsetting her. She was a good kid, pretty as a picture, light on her feet, and no prude, either. He congratulated himself on picking her up. He could see that they were going to have some good times together in the future – until he got tired of her, of course!

It wasn't until the summer that Peter asked Janet to marry him. She had finally let him kiss her once or twice while they had been parked in the dusky lanes or by the sea-shore, but it had gone no further than that. She hadn't felt a lot of pleasure in the embraces, but, on the other hand she hadn't found them repugnant. She had also been to visit his mother at Chorley for the first time, and had got on well with her.

Mrs. Hargreaves, a widow for some ten years, had been speculating for some time about her son's involvement with Janet. Her son hadn't had many lady friends, he had been too caught up in his work. Peter had always put his career first. He wasn't a frivolous-minded young man. He had done well at school and he'd always known that he would finally go into teaching. It was a job which occupied most of his time, both in school and out of it.

In Janet, Mrs. Hargreaves could see the perfect wife for her son. She felt that he needed to be settling down to a home of his own and a family before he became too set in bachelor ways. After Janet had visited her, she began to hope that if her son proposed, she would accept Peter soon. And what could be more desirable than the couple living near to her and the school and in the same district as their friends, Ann and Donald?

Janet, too, had been thinking lately that there seemed no real reason why she shouldn't say 'yes'. Peter had a good post and there was every reason to think that he would go, eventually, into a head-master's job. She, too, realised the advantages of living near to Ann and her husband. She had missed Ann's friendship so much since her marriage, and Ann had taken care to point out each time Janet visited the house, that they could be a companionable foursome again, if Janet married Peter. The two women would be able to pick up their friendship again where it had left off.

Janet still hesitated, though, in spite of the advantages. It seemed fair to ask herself, as a test of her feelings for Peter, whether or not she would be able to live without him if their relationship ended – and she knew with certainty that she would. She told him that she would give him her answer as soon as she was able to, and he had agreed to wait.

They were returning from Bolton, after visiting their friends, and as they entered the outskirts of Preston, she asked Peter to drop her off in the town as she had one or two things she wanted to pick up in the shops. "I'll catch the train back," she told him, waving him goodbye and watching the car being caught up in a line of traffic on the main road. Motor cars seemed to be getting more numerous every day, and in the narrow streets of the town, the exhaust fumes were choking to pedestrians. Her mind slipped back again to the big question of the proposal, as she made her way to the street where the main post office was situated. She needed more stamps for letters, both for herself and for people in the home.

There were one or two people at the counter, waiting to be served. Joining them, she took out a purse from her bag, at the same time dragging out a piece of paper which fluttered to the floor. A voice behind her, low and courteous, asked,

"This is yours, I think?"

The Army Officer, standing behind her, raised his hat as he spoke, revealing tow coloured hair, immaculately brushed back from the long, sensitive face. The light, amber-green eyes stared into hers for a moment's scrutiny, assessing and measuring, before he let go of the piece of paper.

"Yes, how silly of me," she exclaimed, "it's my shopping list. I should have taken it out and put it into my pocket."

"My pleasure," he said, and for some reason, she stood there, staring into his eyes.

"Your turn, I believe," he reminded her, as the people in front moved away after being served.

"Goodness, yes, I hadn't noticed." She moved up to the counter to get the stamps feeling very foolish.

As she passed by him before moving on to the doorway, he smiled at her. At greater range, as she stood by the entrance putting away the stamps, she became aware of his tall, erect carriage and of the perfectly fitted uniform over the disciplined figure. The face, too, tanned and strong-jawed, matched the rest of the man, who looked to be in his late twenties or early thirties. You couldn't tell with these Army men, she thought. The uniform made them look older.

What's the matter with me, she asked herself? Here I am, speculating on a perfect stranger. Even so, she turned once at the door, to look back. He didn't see her because he now had his back turned to her and his face to the grille at the counter. She slipped quickly through the door before he could turn around, walking swiftly in the direction of the shops. She would put the vexed question of the engagement to the back of her mind. She wasn't going to think about it any longer today, she decided.

During the winter, Harry Tomlinson was off work for two months at once. He had caught a chest infection and he couldn't seem to shake it off. The doctor gave Alice strict instructions about poulticing his chest and back with hot fomentations. She had never done anything of the sort before but she tried to do as the doctor had instructed. She had to heat up the grey, thick kaolin in a can placed in a panful of hot water on the stove, afterwards plastering the paste onto rags, ready to apply. Then she had to bandage it on and leave it until the paste had cooled, before making another application. It was an irksome task to her on top of all the other jobs she had to do. Her little outings to the Tower had been discontinued while Harry was ill, so she was having to muster great patience.

By Easter, though, the weather improved and he seemed better. At the end of April, he went back to work. He was thinner than ever, gaunt and hollow in the face. His illness had weakened him again and when he came home at night and had eaten his meal, he invariably went straight off to sleep on the sofa. In bed, too, he had no energy for lovemaking, but, by now, Alice didn't care. Her one thought was to get back to the Tower – to her lover there.

She managed to get out a couple of weeks after Harry had gone back to work. The minute she set foot in the Tower, all her worries and frustrations fell away and she ran up to the ballroom, the exhilaration was so great. This particular afternoon she had so many partners that Jack Fenton had to cut in at the interval. She flew into his arms as to a magnet.

Where have you been, all this time?" he asked her as they drifted close together down the room. "I've missed you like hell."

"Oh, I'm quite sure you've had plenty of other girls after you," she teased him, as they swayed, clasped tightly together, to the music.

"None like you! Are you coming for a ride afterwards?"

Smiling, she snuggled closer. "Of course I am. I've been waiting weeks to see you again."

The truth was, he thought, that he hadn't had such a good thing since he had last seen her, when they had again made love in the back of the car. Anticipation flooded him and he felt an erection beginning. She knew it and she pressed as close to him as she dared out here on the dance floor, but he knew that it was a promise for later on.

She was beginning to learn a few things, too, he realised, as they lay together on the back seat. He had shown her what he liked from a woman and she had made no bones about obliging. In return he had extended the foreplay and prolonged the intercourse as long as he could and he knew that she had appreciated it to the full.

"It's no good, I've got to get back." Her urgent whisper roused him as he lightly dozed, lying over her limp body.

"Alright, sweetheart, we'll make tracks." He got up off her and quickly dressed himself.

"Happy?" he asked, as they climbed into the front seats.

"You know very well I am," she said, as the car set off at high speed for the town.

"Satisfaction guaranteed, every time," he grinned. They laughed together and she told him she would see him again just as soon as ever she could.

As Alice was dancing in the arms of Jack Fenton, Ellen Tomlinson had decided to pay a visit to Lytham. Her daughter-in-law hadn't been to see her at Blackpool for some time and she had received a letter from Harry telling her that he had been off work with chest trouble. She had decided to see for herself how he was. When she reached Fore Street and knocked on the door, there was no answer. She turned the knob and tried to push it open, but it wouldn't budge. It was the same at the back – everything appeared to be locked. Harry must have gone back to work and Alice must be out with the children. After all, she had given Alice no prior warning that she intended to visit, so she couldn't be blamed.

Ellen remembered that Alice had a friend lower down the street, so she turned her steps in that direction. Her knock on Betty's door brought a surprise. The door was opened by Alice's friend, who was closely accompanied by Ellen's own grandchild, Jenny. When she was asked into the house and they sat in the untidy parlour, there sat Susan on the floor, playing with a boy she took to be Stevie, Betty's son. There was no sign at all of Alice and Betty appeared taken aback at Ellen's presence.

"She's – gone out," mumbled Betty, "to – to Blackpool, for something in the town." Betty seemed to be searching for the right words.

"Well, then I'll just have an hour with my grandchildren, if I've come on the wrong day. They are both looking well."

"Oh, yes," Betty was quick to tell Ellen, "Alice looks after them alright."

"I should hope so," said Ellen stiffly. In fact, the children, although healthy-looking enough, appeared grubby. Ellen put that down to the effects of their playing on Betty's carpet. This looked to Ellen's expert eyes, to be in need of a good cleaning. Neither Jenny nor Susan saw their Grannie very often so they made the most of this visit, vying with each other for her attention. Susan's face was sticky with some kind of toffee and before she left, Ellen took the child and washed her face and hands at the kitchen sink. As she stood by the slopstone, she reflected that she had thought Alice untidy, but this was far worse. She couldn't help noticing the pile of dirty dishes by the sink and the washing lying in a tumbled heap in the corner. The rubbish bin, too was piled high with scraps and left uncovered. She determined to have a word with Harry about it when she saw him. It wasn't right for her grandchildren to be playing in a house like this which, Ellen could see, hadn't been tidied up for some time, never mind bottomed. There was no telling what the girls might pick up! It really was too bad of Alice to leave them there, like this.

Curtly taking her leave, Ellen gave the children some coppers for their money boxes and made her way thoughtfully back to the station. The trip had disconcerted her but she didn't intend telling Maud what she had found at Lytham. Harry, though, would surely hear of it when next she saw him, she was determined on that. The only question was, when was that likely to be?

Chapter Twenty-Six

March had come in, and Janet was sitting with Peter in the same sheltered spot above Lake Windermere which they had shared nearly two years ago. The wind blowing off the Lake was cool but a waxing sun tempered its edge. Peter had felt that a reminder of the holiday which had brought them together might draw Janet closer to him. He loved her and he wanted her for his wife, not just as a friend and companion, which was all she seemed to want from the relationship. And in his job he had to be practical about things. The qualities in a teacher's wife were very important when it came to promotion and he couldn't have wished for anyone better in this role. In every way, she was everything he could have wanted. The only thing wrong was that he knew she didn't love him in return.

Was that so very necessary to a successful marriage, though? He had seen lots of far more prosaic matches come off brilliantly, and they had lasted for many years. Surely, once they were married, she would come to love him, given time? He watched speculatively as she twisted daisy chains in her strong, capable fingers.

Looking up suddenly, she spoke, "I wouldn't be honest if I said I loved you, Peter, not as you deserve to be loved. I'm very fond of you and we do get on well together, don't we? I think we have a lot in common and I think we have a lot to give each other. I can't see why we shouldn't be married. I'm saying 'yes', Peter."

"Janet!" He reached for her hands, scattering the flowers. "You're quite sure about this?"

"Oh, yes, quite sure," she said, as she lay in his arms, unresisting. He kissed her tenderly, knowing that it was too soon for passion. Janet, accepting his kiss, felt wanted and needed and that knowledge was warming.

If she married him now, she would come to love him in time, she was sure. He had proved his own love for her over and over by waiting for so long, and when the time came, she would show him that she could love him, too. Smiling up at him, she asked, "Shall we call at Blackpool on the way back and tell them the news? They have been expecting this for a long time and I want them to be the first to know."

"Of course, darling," he agreed quickly, "and so has Mother. She has guessed that I've asked you to marry me. She very much wants you for a daughter-in-law."

"You've been very patient with me, Peter, but you must have realised that Harry and I were once going to be married, and then he met someone else. He broke off our engagement and it took me ages to get over it. The wedding was all fixed, you know. But that's all a long time ago and it's the future I'm looking forward to now."

"I guessed that someone had let you down, but it wasn't until I saw you and Harry together that day at Nelson Street that I knew for sure. Come on, darling, we'll get back to the car and have a quick trip to the coast as you suggest."

His arm around her waist, he led her down the grassy bank to the car below, kissing her again as he handed her in. Comfortably at ease with each other, they drove down through the Lakeland hills onto the Fylde plain, heading for Blackpool.

"That's wonderful news," Florrie said, kissing her stepdaughter and shaking Peter's hand warmly. "Robert will be tickled to death when he comes in. Not that he'll be surprised, mind. We've both seen this coming a mile off," she laughed. "When's it to be, then?"

"We haven't got that far yet, Florrie. You're the first person to know. I expect it will be quite soon.

"Well, give us fair warning, then, because I like a good excuse to go out and buy myself some new clothes."

"You won't need to do that, Florrie. It won't be a big affair, will it, Peter?"

"Not if you don't want it," he said. "As long as Janet marries me, Mrs. Crossley, I don't mind what kind of wedding we have, and don't worry, as soon as we fix the date, you'll be the first to know."

Robert was overjoyed at the news, when later he came in from work. He turned to Florrie. "Get that whisky bottle out, lass. This calls for a toast. When Janet brought you here for the first time, I thought what a good lad you were, and I know my lass will never let you down. It hasn't been easy for her this last few years and she deserves a bit of happiness. Let's drink to that," he suggested, as Florrie brought out the glasses.

The wedding was fixed for the end of June, at Peter's own parish church in Bolton. There was no reason to wait any longer, yet it left time for both families to make arrangements for the ceremony. Janet couldn't consider St. Luke's after what had happened in the past and to have been married in Ellswick parish church would have made it difficult for both lots of relatives. Mrs. Hargreaves, Peter's mother, had invited Robert and Florrie to stay with her over the wedding period, and Peter's sister, who lived in Cheshire, would also be coming to stay overnight at the house on Chorley Road.

As soon as they had made their plans, they called on Ann and Donald to tell them that they had decided to be married.

"And about time, too," Donald said. "I've been waiting for a long time to do the honours for you as best man. I thought you were never going to ask me." He shook Peter's hand and clapped him heartily on the shoulder.

"I'm so thrilled for you both," Ann cried, eyes dancing.

"You'll be one of my bridesmaids, won't you? I thought, perhaps, you and my sister, Rose?"

"Don't you mean Matron-of-honour? I'm well past the maiden stage now, especially as I've just found out I'm a mum-to-be."

"Oh, Ann, how wonderful! I'm so happy for you both. Isn't everything turning out beautifully for us all?"

"Yes, it is dear, and if we're going to be living quite close to each other, we'll have some good times together, just like it used to be when we were at Ellswick. I've missed you very much, you know."

"I've missed you, too. We're staying with Peter's mother after the wedding until we decide on a house. We shall start looking round as soon as we get back from our honeymoon. We're going up to the Lakes."

"There is plenty of good property in this area," Donald said. "Solidly built like this one, of Accrington brick. It lasts a lifetime."

"Yes, it would be nice, living in this neighbourhood. If we could get a house like this, we'd be happy. I see your wife has managed to get one or two of her little alterations done already." She glanced around at the bright room, with its chintz covers and matching curtains.

"I don't know how the little witch does it," Donald said, grinning at his wife, "but if she sets her mind on a thing, it's not long before it materialises."

"Do you really think of me as a witch?" Ann went over to sit on his knee, putting her arms around his neck.

"Oh, yes, definitely a sorceress of the first water."

It was quite evident to Janet that the two were as much in love now as they had been before their marriage. A twinge of envy passed through her. She and Peter were starting off life together on quite a different footing from their friends, but she determined to work hard at making her husband-to-be happy.

The weekend before they were to be married, Peter took Janet over to Blackpool for a final visit. The next time they all met would be in Bolton for the ceremony. Florrie eagerly showed Janet the new clothes she had bought specially for the occasion and her father reported that his new suit was nearly ready.

"I didn't have a new suit for my own wedding," he complained. "The poor old bridegroom counts for nothing, so I'm having one for my daughter's."

"I expect you're only having a new suit because you're finding it difficult to get into the old one," she teased him, noticing that lately he had put on a bit of weight.

"What's this? My own daughter stabbing me in the back? There's no respect of their elders in children, these days."

And it had been a merry party over tea. Rose was to be Janet's younger bridesmaid, and her cheeks were pink now with excitement because her pretty blue dress hung on a padded hanger up in her bedroom. She had only just taken it off after parading for them all in it, and she couldn't wait to run upstairs to have another look at it.

Peter drove Janet home from the coast in the late evening, both of them still savouring the happiness of the day they had enjoyed with her family. The fine, hot day had ended in a pearly-pink sunset and the afterglow still lingered in the western sky behind them, as the car, with the roof taken back, headed inland for Preston. As Peter deposited Janet at Ellswick, they stood in the front porch of the Home. He whispered, "Only three more days, darling, then you'll be leaving here for good."

Her replacement, a Preston girl, had already been working in the Home for the past week, getting used to her duties. Janet was to stay with Ann, at Bolton, until they left for the ceremony on her wedding day.

"Yes, I can't really believe it. I've almost come to look on it as my home."

"Well, you'll be looking for another one, just as soon as we return from the Lakes. We'll start house hunting as soon as we get back."

She had told him she wasn't worried about having a honeymoon but he had insisted and when he had suggested Windermere, she had agreed. They were to stay at a hotel they had noted on their previous visits.

"Goodnight, darling. I'll be with you on Friday, to take you to Ann's. She's so excited about the whole thing. It will soon be Saturday, Janet…." Taking her in his arms, his head came down to kiss her and she returned the kiss with more warmth than she had intended or expected. I really do care for him, she thought, in surprise and joy, as he let her go, turned, waved and was gone to the car.

As Peter drove onto the country lane which joined the main road, he was thinking what a lucky man he was to be marrying a girl like Janet. He had realised that he was in love with her at Donald's wedding. He had watched her coming down the aisle in her hyacinth blue dress, her wonderful red hair falling over her shoulders under the circlet of pale flowers.

She had looked very beautiful. He had wanted to tell her then that he loved her, but he had known instinctively that he must wait. Now, that waiting had been rewarded with her promise to be his wife.

Of course, he hadn't attempted to make love to her yet, but he couldn't help anticipating their union, as he had many times before. Would she be passive or would she respond to him? She hadn't yet shown much passion in the kisses they had exchanged, but tonight he imagined that she'd been warmer when he had kissed her goodnight at the door of the Home. He pictured himself arousing her with his own ardour, his impatient hands travelling over her unresistant body – that body he hadn't yet seen. He could picture it, though, from the curve of her clothes – the full, rounded breasts and the generous hips, the plump arms and the shapely legs. He visualised himself making love to her, considerately, not with rough passion. His love for her would prevent him from treating her selfishly. She hadn't told him whether she and Harry had been lovers, but he wanted to think that she was a virgin.

As he rounded a bend in the road, he saw the ewe standing in the middle of the road. He had no time to think. Instinctively he jammed his foot on the brake, at the same time screwing the wheel round to the verge in a desperate attempt to avoid her. The road wasn't wide enough! As the car veered sharply left, it hit the edge of the ditch, the front wheel going over. The car seemed to stay poised for a second before it tipped over on to its side, its wheels still revolving slowly before eventually coming to rest. The moment the car toppled over, Peter was thrown out of the open top towards the back of the ditch and its looming bank. He felt his head make violent contact with something very hard before blackness finally enveloped him.

Janet was checking up on supplies for the laundry the following morning when a policeman from the Preston force came into the front lobby, asking to see her.

"A policeman? Whatever can he want?" She made her way along the corridor, her thoughts flying to the coast. Surely no one was ill at Blackpool? She had only just come back from there and all had been well.

"Can I have a word with you in private, Miss Crossley?" he asked her, as the girl looked on curiously.

"Come into my office," she offered.

A terrible sense of foreboding gripped her as she opened the door to let the officer in. "Is it my father?" Her heart was hammering painfully. Robert's own father had died very suddenly from a heart complaint, she remembered.

"No, Miss Crossley, it isn't your father. In fact, it isn't anyone in your family. Won't you sit down?"

"Please tell me what you have to say," she begged him, remaining on her feet, her hands clenched.

"I'm very sorry, but there's been an accident. It's Mr. Hargreaves, your fiancée. His car went off the road. I'm afraid it's bad news, Miss Crossley. I have to tell you that he was killed."

"Oh, no, no, not Peter! He couldn't be!" She sank down into the chair without volition on her own part. "You mean – after he left me last night?"

"I'm afraid so. The car registration number is his and he had papers on him which confirm it."

"But why…. How….?" It was quite unbelievable. Peter couldn't be dead.

"We don't know exactly what happened, but the car was undamaged, on its side in the ditch. There was apparently no collision. Your fiancée was thrown out and he struck his head on an overhanging tree. It knocked him unconscious. The farmer found him there this morning."

"Do you mean…. He wasn't killed outright?" She had to know….

"This is very difficult, Miss Crossley. No, he wasn't killed outright. I'm afraid he was drowned."

"Drowned? But that's impossible! How could he be? The shock was beginning to affect her voice. It sounded hoarse and inaudible in her own ears and she had started to tremble violently.

"We think that perhaps, a sheep got onto the road. The farmer says that one or two were in the wrong meadow this morning. It's not uncommon on these country lanes. He mustn't have seen it until it was too late. He was probably unconscious when he rolled down into the ditch after knocking his head on a tree. I'm sorry, Miss Crossley, but the farmer found him face down in what bit of water there was in there, in the morning."

"Oh, no," Janet gasped. "You mean he might have been saved?"

"I don't think so, Miss Crossley. He must have died within a few minutes and he wouldn't have known anything about it," the officer finished kindly. "Let me go for one of the nurses. I think you could do with a drop of brandy – it's been a big shock for you. I have to tell you that Mrs. Hargreaves and her daughter have both been informed and that her daughter is travelling from Cheshire to be with her."

"Thank you," Janet murmured weakly, as the big man went in search of one of the staff.

She couldn't have got up if she'd tried. He had just knocked from under her feet the flimsy foundations upon which she had been building for a new life with Peter. He must have died, then, soon after he had left her, while she had been so happy to think that she was beginning to care for him, at last. Now he was dead, lying in some cold, lonely mortuary. Shivering uncontrollably, she waited for the footsteps to return down the corridor and when they eventually came, she gulped down the brandy as if it might anaesthetise her against all the anguish which must follow.

The same day, she travelled home to her father – the only one she wanted to be with, until the funeral.

Chapter Twenty-Seven

Early one June morning, Alice Tomlinson was consulting a calendar she had hanging in her kitchen at Lytham. Goodness, how the years went by, she thought, realising that nineteen-twenty-three was now nearly half over. She had made herself a cup of tea before getting the girls ready to take them out. Jenny, now aged four, and almost ready for school, was hopping about, trying to fasten her shoes.

"Wait a minute, I'll do those," she called, as Jenny fiddled with the buttons, trying to push them through the shiny straps of the black patent leather.

Then she gazed again at the calendar, aghast. No! It couldn't be! Anyway, she hadn't had any sickness or dizziness, so she must be wrong about the dates. In any case, she had stuck to the contraceptive method the doctor had suggested. A shiver ran through her as she remembered his warning about 'any method not being a hundred per cent safe, yet.' She had been alright for three years now, since she had been to see him and he had advised her. Oh, no! She must be getting mixed up with the dates, she decided, finishing fastening Jennie's shoes and getting both girls into their outdoor clothes.

"I'm just taking them out for an hour," she called up to Harry. He was in bed again with the usual chest trouble, but this time she had been really worried about him. The doctor had told her that it could easily turn to pneumonia and he had given her orders to call him at once if Harry appeared to be any worse. She would go up to him as soon as she got back from the promenade, and poultice him again. He had everything he needed while she was out and she wouldn't be long. He hadn't answered her, so he must have gone back to sleep again. Locking the front door behind her, she walked towards the promenade, holding on to Susan's hand while Jenny skipped along in front. Although they were now in June, the wind on the Front penetrated their thin coats and they had to stay on the move to keep warm. It looked as if summer was going to be late this year.

When she returned a while later, she went straight upstairs, leaving the children in the parlour to get out of their outdoor things. Quickly opening the bedroom door, she called, "Do you want a drink, Harry?" There was no answer. She saw he was lying in bed, breathing erratically, his face like putty, his eyes closed. Alice flew to him, giving him a little shake, but he didn't move or waken up. Blind panic struck at her heart and she ran downstairs again, flying out of the house, along to Betty's. She would have to risk leaving the girls for a few minutes. Her friend opened the door and, seeing Alice's wild eyes and breathless haste, she asked no questions, but let Alice into the house.

"Can you come for a minute, while I go and fetch the doctor?"

Alice's frightened face urged Betty to immediate action. She was already taking Stevie by the hand, ready to follow her friend back into the street.

"You get along to the doctor's. I'll go and stay with him until you get back."

"Thanks, Betty." Alice set off at a run, as Betty followed more slowly with her son hanging on to her. Alice stopped to get her breath before she rounded the corner, where Dr. Brown had his surgery. Dashing into the waiting room, she gasped out her story to the white-coated pharmacist who assisted the doctor.

"Alright now, calm down Mrs. Tomlinson. Dr. Brown will be along right away. You go home and wait with your husband. You said his breathing was irregular?"

"Yes," cried Alice. "He was gasping and he won't wake up."

"Alright, Mrs. Tomlinson, Dr. Brown will be along almost as soon as you arrive yourself."

Alice ran back to Fore Street, her heart pounding. She was panting when she reached the door. Surprisingly, Betty's mother let her in.

"I saw you both rushing in here when I was coming back from the baker's, so I knew something was wrong. Is there anything I can do?"

"Thanks, the doctor's coming any minute. Please can you keep an eye on the children downstairs while Betty and I stay with Harry in the bedroom?"

He looked dreadfully ill, she thought, as she rejoined Betty upstairs. He hadn't moved, Betty told her and she saw that, although his face was grey, a fine sweat glistened on his forehead, and his breathing was jerky and fast. A knocking on the door brought her downstairs again, to let the doctor in.

"How long has be been like this?" Dr. Brown asked, as he examined her husband.

"About an hour," she said, breathlessly.

"An hour? Why didn't you call me sooner, then? I told you to call me right away if he seemed any worse." His voice was sharp.

"I didn't know he was like this – I mean – I thought he was asleep. I – I've been out with the children," Alice finished miserably.

"Very well, I'm not accusing you of anything." Dr. Brown's voice was curt. "We're going to have to get your husband into hospital, I'm afraid. I'll go back to the surgery and send for an ambulance. Wait here with him until I get back."

In his day, he was thinking, a wife had stayed day and night with a husband as sick as Harry Tomlinson, not gone off with the children, leaving him alone.

Later the same day, Alice took the children on the train to Blackpool to see Ellen. Harry had been admitted to the small hospital at Lytham. They had told her he was going to recover but that it would be very slow. Her object was to tell Ellen her own version of the story before she heard it from anyone else. Harry, it seemed, had no recollection of being unconscious, as she had found out at the hospital. It was obvious to her that he had no idea of how long he had lain there alone in that condition and no one had told him. But the doctor had warned her strongly that in future she would have to be much more watchful when he was eventually sent home. He had indicated, too, that it would be a long time before Harry would be well enough to go to work.

Ellen's tired eyes brightened as she opened the door and saw who her visitors were. Jenny ran straight into the house, making for the back parlour. She knew that in one of the long dresser drawers, her Grannie kept a selection of toys and games which she allowed the children to play with. Susan, too, toddled after her on fast little legs. They both loved 'rooting' as Grannie called it, finding all the familiar treasures which Grannie had told them had belonged to Daddy and Auntie Maud when they were small children.

"How nice to see you, Alice." Ellen gave her daughter-in-law one or her rare smiles as they followed the girls into the parlour.

"Wait a minute, now," said Grannie, "let's have your coats off before we start getting any toys out."

"Would you like some tea, dear?" Ellen asked.

"Yes, please."

"Alright, I'll open the drawer first for you, Jenny, but don't get everything out at once. You know you'll only have to put them all back again afterwards."

Jenny took out a picture book made of thick, rigid card on which all kinds of fascinating pictures were painted. Soon, she was quite absorbed looking through the familiar pages, one by one.

"Well, how are you, then?" Ellen asked as she poured the tea. She meant to question Alice about the children being left with that slovenly woman, Betty, on Fore Street, but there would be time for that before the family went home.

"I'm alright, thanks. It's Harry I've come to see you about."

Ellen put down the teapot sharply. "He's not ill again, is he?"

"Yes, I'm afraid he is," Alice told her.

"He's in bed again, then?"

"No, he's in the hospital at Lytham. They took him in this morning. Please don't get upset," Alice begged. "He's going to be alright. They say he's going to get better, but it will be very slow. He may not be able to get back to work for a long time."

In the silence that followed, Jenny got up and put back the picture book into the drawer. She took out two coloured wooden tops. They were pear-shaped and they had thin, leather whips to make them go. She couldn't manage them properly yet, but she loved trying. Susan had claimed the doll with the china face and was systematically taking off its clothes, right down to its lace-trimmed drawers.

"Take those tops into the yard," Ellen told Jenny. "You'll have more room out there than in the kitchen. Now then, Alice, what exactly did the doctor say about Harry?"

"Well, they say it's a touch of pneumonia, but it hasn't got any worse and they've got him round again."

"Round again? Was he unconscious, then?" Ellen came straight to the point, as usual.

"Yes – he – I found him in bed and I couldn't rouse him."

"Found him? Where were you then?"

"I was out with the children but I'd only gone onto the Front for a bit and they got him to the hospital straight away."

"Alright, I'm not trying to blame you, Alice. It's just been a bit of a shock, that's all. Naturally, I'm very worried."

"I knew you would want to go to see him, that's why I've come, to let you know."

"Yes, thank you, Alice, I'll go tomorrow if you'll tell me the visiting times."

"Oh, you can go in and see him any time," Alice said.

Ellen's heart sank. Alice was a very naïve girl, to say the least. Didn't she know that a patient had to be very ill to be allowed unlimited visiting? And if Alice was to visit Harry often, she would probably have no alternative but to leave the children with that slatternly Betty. Now wasn't the time, perhaps, to reprimand her about it.

"Are you alright for money?" she asked Alice, instead.

"Yes, I've got some housekeeping money in the house, but if Harry has to stay in the hospital, I shall need some more, soon."

"Well, we'll see how it goes on and if he does have to stay in for some time, we'll work something out between us. Don't worry about it, I'll see that you don't go short."

"Thank you, Ellen." Alice was genuinely grateful to Harry's mother. She had been wondering how she was going to ask Harry for more housekeeping money. It wouldn't do to worry him while he was so poorly. If he was off work he didn't get any wages but she knew that he had some money put away in the bank which he intended using as a deposit on a house of their own, so they wouldn't starve. She supposed that they would just have to draw some of this money for their day-to-day living expenses until he could manage to get back to his job again.

Alice drained her cup, saying, "I think I'd better get back, now. If you are going to see Harry in the morning, I'll go in the afternoon. Betty will look after the children. Say goodbye to Grannie, now. Give her a nice, big kiss."

Jenny ran up to Grannie's chair, planting a big kiss on her cheek, Susan following more slowly in her wake. After struggling into their coats, the small family left, leaving Ellen worried and depressed. She had to face the fact squarely now that her son was never going to be really well and that there was even some doubt about his going back to work. What would his small family live on, then, when his savings were used up?

Maud would have to be told about Harry when she came in. She couldn't be denied the chance of going to see him, no matter what remarks she might make about Alice being the whole cause of it. Pulling herself together, Ellen took the tea things into the kitchen and washed up, afterwards going upstairs to sort out some linen. When Maud came back from the shops, she would tell her that she herself was going to visit Harry in the morning, no matter how busy they were. Maud would decide whether she wanted to visit her brother during the week. Ellen suddenly felt very old and weary. Sometimes life seemed one long, continuous struggle against overwhelming odds, she thought, as she came downstairs again to re-set the teacups and saucers on the table ready for Maud's return.

When Alice's mother received her daughter's letter a couple of days later, she decided to go over to Blackpool to stay for at least a week, until they knew how Harry was progressing. Alice would then be free to visit her husband whenever she chose.

As she stood with Joe on the platform before the train set off, he commented, "I didn't think Harry was looking so good at Christmas. Our lass has had her work cut out this last couple of years. He wasn't as good as they thought when he was invalided out of the Army, I reckon."

"No," Mary said, "he mustn't have been. Alice has had her work cut out, right enough. All we can do is help her, that's why I'm going. Are you sure you'll be alright? Don't forget that Mrs. Rushworth is seeing to your meals after work, so see that you and George have a good breakfast every day. She said she'd put you some baggins up as well."

"Of course I'll get us a good breakfast – stop worrying, but it won't be the same on my own. I shall miss you, lass." He kissed her soundly as she prepared to get into the carriage.

"Look after yourself, love," she said, leaning out of the window as the train began to move. "It won't be long before I'm back."

"Give my love to Alice," he called after her.

She remained with her head out of the window, waving to him, as the train pulled out of the station. Not until it had moved out of sight did he leave the platform to return to Moscar Street and a lonely week on his own. Except for his son, of course, and he'd better behave himself while his mother was away or he'd cop it!

After her mother's arrival, Alice found things much easier. She was free to visit Harry every day and watch him improving. Mary visited him after Alice had returned and they both agreed that he was looking better.

Propped up on pillows, he was still not allowed out of bed, but they could stay longer with him every time. It was hard finding things to talk about, but he seemed happy just to have her there. She told him what the children were doing each day, but there was no indication, when she left the ward, that he would be coming home.

One day during the week, Alice called at Mr. Simpkins' corner shop for her grocery order. For once, she was alone in the store, and as she gave him her list and he surveyed her across the counter, he thought what a pretty little thing she was. She had a certain air of helplessness and yet she had two beautiful children and an ailing husband to look after. It was a pity that such a frail little thing should be burdened with all that responsibility. He reflected that Edna, his late wife, hadn't had the worry of looking after a family like Alice had. Alice reminded him quite a bit of Edna. Of course, he and Edna had had no children and she had become an invalid in the later years of their marriage. He had looked after her himself in between serving in the shop and he'd tried to give her everything she had wanted to make up for his failings in other respects.

"I'll get the boy to bring these round, Mrs. Tomlinson. They're too heavy for you to carry." His rather short-sighted, watered-down blue eyes behind the thick spectacles regarded her sympathetically as he went round the corner to open the door for her. "How is your husband going on? I believe he's still in the hospital?"

"Yes, Mr. Simpkins, I'm afraid he is. He seemed a bit better today but he's still poorly. My mother has come over for a week to help me."

"I'm glad to hear that. You need someone to look after you, my dear. We can't have you going down as well, can we?"

How nice of him to enquire about Harry – to be so understanding, but then Mr. Simpkins had always been kind to her when she had been in the shop. For the first time, she noticed that he wasn't really old, as she had imagined. The enveloping brown overall and the smooth, rather featureless face under the mousy hair had given her the impression that he was a much older man. Now that she had looked at him properly, she decided that he was only in his late thirties.

Smiling in return and thanking him for his kind enquiry, Alice made her way back along the main street with a lighter step, to rejoin her mother and children. Later, when the boy delivered her order, she discovered that Mr. Simpkins had put in a small bunch of flowers for her to take up to the hospital later. What a kind man he was!

She wondered again how long Harry was going to be kept in the hospital. She knew she couldn't resume her visits to the Tower while her mother was here and Harry was so ill. She even wondered whether she would ever be able to go there again if he was going to be at home a long time. Then when he did come home, how was she going to cope if he was ill all the time and look after the children, as well? It wasn't fair that she should be having to do all this. If, as she suspected, she was pregnant again, she would have another child to look after in the new year.

As the full realisation of her situation hit her, a sentence surfaced in her mind, 'You'll only have brief happiness'. She had never really believed in gypsies before, but somehow, Madame Rosalie had known what was going to happen if she married Harry. Alice had ignored that warning, to her cost. Now she was going to have to pay for her folly, just as the old gypsy had predicted!

Chapter Twenty-Eight

Janet returned to her position at Ellswick soon after Peter's funeral. Her erstwhile successor had not, after all, stayed on in her old job and the Matron had written to Janet begging her to consider returning to the post. She had been back at work for nearly two months, but today, she was to serve on a white elephant stall. The charity fair was held annually in the grounds of the Home and the proceeds were this year to be used to provide wireless sets in each of the sitting rooms.

The weather hadn't provided a particularly good start to the day. It was still very changeable and cool for the time of the year but, although cloudy, it wasn't actually raining. The stalls had all been erected and the men were putting finishing touches to the tea tent. Janet stood behind one of the long tables, where it looked as if they were going to have a busy afternoon selling bric-a-brac, judging by the numbers of people who had already gathered for the official opening by the Mayor.

Janet liked keeping busy all the time, these days. Since Ann's marriage she'd no close friend amongst the staff. Devastated by Peter's death as she was, she hadn't any inclination to make new friends, and every visit to Ann at Bolton reminded her of Peter and upset Donald.

The clouds were looking higher now and there was a hint of brightness over in the west. Half-an-hour later, she was surrounded by people picking through the various articles piled on the stall. Soon, her cash box was filling up nicely and the items on the table were diminishing. Someone came with fresh boxes filled with replacement items and after these had been added there was a fresh rush around her stall.

She looked up, to find someone staring at her. She recognised him immediately. It was the Army Officer she had met in the Post Office at Preston! He obviously recognised her, too.

"I see you are on the other side of the counter today," he said.

"Yes. It's surprising what people want to buy. I've been wondering where they put some of the things I've sold."

"This, for instance?" he lifted up a particularly hideous vase.

"Exactly," she agreed. "Believe it or not, I've sold dozens of other things far worse than that, today."

"I do believe you, but let's be charitable and say that they are contributing to the wireless fund, shall we? How did you get mixed up in this affair, in the first place?"

"Oh, I work here."

"You're a nurse, then?"

"Oh, no, nothing as dedicated as that, I'm afraid. My job's much more prosaic. I'm the housekeeper."

"Well, the quartermaster is a very important part of the organisation," he said. "Are you a very efficient housekeeper?"

"When I keep dropping lists all over the place?" she asked, laughing – for the first time in weeks, she realised.

"I don't think that was a true indication of your character! How much will you take for this pretty thing?"

"You don't mean you're going to buy that vase!"

"Certainly! I must do my bit for the Home. I'd like it wrapping up though, please. I wouldn't like anyone to see it and imagine that my artistic taste was quite so bad."

Smiling, she took the vase from him, wrapping it up completely in brown paper and in return he gave her some silver.

"That's far too much," she said, accepting the generous donation.

"You're not a good saleslady, are you? Put it in your little tin box before I change my mind, there's a good girl."

"Thank you, then."

"My pleasure, I've got good reason to be grateful for the work you all do here. Anyway, I can see there are people waiting for you to serve them, so I'll push off now and give someone else a chance."

She had the feeling of having been put at a disadvantage, although she couldn't have said why. She watched the tall, broad figure, erect and assured in the beautifully tailored uniform, striding away towards the second-hand book stall. He did look round once, and he caught her staring after him. He lifted a hand to her – the one holding the parcel – and then he was lost to sight as people blocked out her view at the front of the stall.

She didn't see him again that day but afterwards, she found that parts of their conversation would drift into her mind at the most unexpected times. It was most disconcerting and she had no idea why this should be the case. She didn't even know the man. Then a thought struck her. He had found out who she was. It was as if he had cut the ground away from under her feet in some strange way, leaving her vulnerable and unsure. But how could a perfect stranger have this effect on her? Her mind seemed to be working the thing out of its own accord. Was she actually hoping that he would contact her again, now that he knew where she worked? She decided, eventually, that she was.

Harry Tomlinson was sitting up in bed in the hospital at Lytham, bedclothes tidied by the nurses. He was waiting for the doctor's round of the wards. Sister had hinted yesterday that he might be moved from the hospital soon. He was still not walking far on his own. He had managed to get through the ward doors to the lavatory, just beyond, but only slowly. Each time he had been exhausted on his return, his heart hammering painfully.

He watched the doors eagerly as the doctor pushed them open and entered the ward, followed by Sister and one of the nurses. Stopping by every bed to read each patient's chart, then giving the staff their instructions, he eventually reached Harry.

"Well, Mr. Tomlinson, how are you feeling today?"

"A lot better, doctor, but I'm still a bit unsteady on my legs. The least bit of walking tires me."

"Yes, it will for quite some time yet. I don't see that we can let you go home at the moment. I think we might send you convalescent somewhere. See how you go on, before we send you home."

Disappointment flooded Harry. He had been so looking forward to tell Alice on her visit today that he would be coming home soon. To have his hopes dashed was galling.

"It's for your own good, Mr. Tomlinson," the doctor was saying. "We want to get you back on your feet before you go home, and they will be able to do that at the Home. Our job here is to get you through your illness. I suggest Ellswick, Sister. Will you arrange it, as soon as they can accommodate him?"

"Yes, doctor." Sister made a note as they passed on to the next bed.

His first day at Ellswick was better than he had expected. He was in a wheelchair most of the time and at intervals he was walked slowly by the nurses either to the lavatory or to the dining room and up and down the men's sitting room. They had promised him that very soon he would get back the strength in his legs and that he would be walking out of here on his own. He had realised, as he sat in the wheelchair, that it wouldn't have been fair to Alice for him to be at home, like this. She had the children to look after and she couldn't have pushed the chair about, as the nurses did here.

Alice had promised to come and see him as soon as she could. He was missing her visits, but the journey to Preston wasn't easy for her. She would have to leave the children with someone for quite long periods and travel herself on the train. Seeing her again was the only thing he was looking forward to and he expected her every day. Then a letter arrived, telling him that she would be coming over at the weekend – Sunday – and his anticipation mounted. He made up his mind that, by the weekend, he would walk unaided along the corridor outside the sitting room to say goodbye to her when she left.

In the long corridor outside the men's sitting room that same day, Janet nearly bumped into a man being taken into the room in a wheelchair. She had just stepped out of her office and the chair had gone past her before she had turned, to look again. Inconspicuous in her new white uniform, similar to the nurses', her hair pinned up under a white cap, she dodged quickly back again into the security of her office, sinking down into a chair. She found she was breathing fast. Could it really have been Harry? If it was, she had hardly recognised him. The man in the chair had been painfully gaunt and thin, but all her instincts told her that it had been her former love. What a terrible toll his illness had taken, if it was! The only thing to do was enquire from the almoner if he was on her roll of patients. She determined to go and find out, right away. The almoner, Molly, would make no objection to Janet's seeing the admissions list – the patients names weren't confidential, only their medical records.

The corridor was clear as she slipped quickly along to Molly's office. The almoner looked at her rather closely, but produced the book without comment. Yes, there it was, admitted today, Harry Tomlinson, 20, Fore Street, Lytham. A tremor ran through her, the colour draining from her face.

"Good heavens! You look as if you'd seen a ghost," the almoner said. "You evidently know this man. Is he a friend of yours?"

"He was, once," Janet admitted. "It has been a shock, seeing him here, that's all. The last time I saw him, he wasn't well, but now he looks dreadfully ill."

"Does he know you work here?"

"No, he doesn't. I don't want him to know, either. He didn't see me, I'm sure. Please don't mention this, Molly. I shall have to try to keep out of his way, that's all."

"Very well, dear, if that's what you want, but it won't be easy."

"I'll manage it somehow, for the time being. Thanks, Molly."

Walking quickly, she avoided the passage that led into the sitting room. Her mind was in a turmoil. There was one thing certain, though. Harry was very ill indeed. Working in the Home had taught her to recognise the serious cases. She recognised, too, that what she was feeling for him now was pity, not love. But what should she do? It had been difficult enough speaking to him when she had met him in Nelson Street and now, here he was again, crossing her path in this unlooked for way.

Surely, too, he would be having visitors soon – his wife – oh, no! She couldn't meet Alice, that was too much to ask – and his mother and Maud! For the time being, she must avoid meeting Harry, at all costs, until she decided what was the best course to take. She herself was not on duty in either the wards or the sitting rooms. She was quite private in her own office or her bedroom, and she ate with the rest of the staff.

Yes, she decided, she could do it, if she was very careful. She felt better for making the decision and a moment later, the almoner came in with a cup of tea.

"I thought I saw you come in here," Molly said. "You looked as if you could do with a strong cup, so here it is. I've just had one. It's nearly time for you to go off duty, isn't it?"

"Yes, another half-hour, but there's always someone wanting something at the last minute. I'll wait, just in case."

"You know best, but I can see you've had a bit of a shock."

"Thanks, Molly, I'm quite alright now, and thanks for the tea," she added, sipping the hot liquid gratefully.

"Think nothing of it. There's nothing like a cup of tea to settle jittery nerves. I'd better get back now or I'll have Matron on my tracks."

"You're very good, Molly."

"What are friends for?" the almoner asked, as she retreated in the direction of her own office.

Alice had been told of the doctor's decision to send Harry convalescent and she had accepted it with some relief. She was now on her own again with the children, her mother having returned to Bradfield. She was now quite sure that she was pregnant again, but she hadn't told anybody. It was strange that, this time, she didn't feel resentful about it, as she had with the last one. To begin with, she'd had none of the distressing symptoms that had accompanied both her previous pregnancies. In fact, she felt very well, and she was eating heartily. But there was one big question that she was constantly asking herself. Was the baby Harry's? After weighing up all the circumstances she thought, most likely not! And if it wasn't, there was no way she could tell Jack Fenton, or expect him to stand by her or acknowledge the baby as his. For all she knew, he could have fathered other children on other women, in the past. She wasn't silly enough to think she had been the only one, or that he felt anything special for her. They had both gone into it with their eyes wide open. They'd had some good times and she had thought she was safe enough, but something had gone wrong, somewhere.

Of course, it was just possible that the baby was her husband's, but there had been very little sexual activity between them this last few months. Harry had been too ill and tired. No, she was sure it was Jack's. But then a thought struck her. Harry did want another child. She was sure, too, that this time it would be a boy. If she told him about it when she visited him at Ellswick, it would give him something to get better for. If it was a boy, he would accept it without question, he was so set on having a son.

Jenny, the lively one, would be going to school soon and Susan, a quiet child, was much easier to cope with. It was no use crying, anyway, over spilt milk. She must make the best of things and hope that no one ever found out who the father really was. After all, no one knew about her meetings in the country with Jack Fenton. Even Betty didn't know she had been out with him in the car, so how could anyone find out?

That kind Mr. Simpkins had offered to take her over to Ellswick in his motor car at the weekend. He was visiting a friend in Preston, he had said and he had insisted that she shouldn't be travelling alone on the train. Ellen had offered to have the children for the day while she went to visit Harry, so she was quite looking forward to riding in a car all the way. It would be much more comfortable than sitting in a dirty train and having to walk all the way from the station at the other end.

When he arrived at her gate, the Ford looking immaculate at the Kerb, the children rushed out to see who could climb in first. Alice restrained them while Mr. Simpkins, scrubbed and polished like his vehicle, opened the door to let them in. He looked different today, she thought, out of his brown overall. Instead, he had on a dark blue suit, a stiff white shirt with little wings at the neck and a hard hat. The whole gave him an air of extreme respectability and she very nearly giggled when he handed her in, like royalty, after putting the two girls into the back.

She knew she was looking her best in her favourite pink dress under a light grey coat, with a small hat to match and she knew that the baby wasn't beginning to show, yet. They dropped off the children at Nelson Street and Mr. Simpkins turned the car in the direction of the Preston Road. It was only half-an-hour's drive and as they moved sedately along, Alice's mind flashed back to her drives out here, at high speed, with her lover. She wondered, for a brief moment, who he was dancing with now? But it was no use, she must put all thoughts of Jack Fenton from her mind. She turned to Alfred, chatting to him about Harry and the children. He, in his turn, told her about the shop, mentioning that he was occasionally lonely. He told her that he lived over and at the back of the store and said that there were now far too many rooms for a widower. She appeared sympathetic to his plight, being lucky enough to have a family to look after.

Outside the Home, the car parked in the driveway, he handed her out, saying gallantly, "I hope you find your husband much better." Lifting his bowler hat, he made his way down the steps and into the car, driving off carefully through the gates.

How nice it was to be treated like a lady, Alice thought. She was looking forward to being driven home by Mr. Simpkins in his comfortable motor.

After he had left Alice at the Home, Alfred turned his car in the direction of Preston itself. Coronation Park was on the other side of the town and he had arranged to meet Norman by the clock tower, which overlooked the tennis courts. They had decided not to meet at the house in Preston today, as a mark of respect for Norman's mother. Since the funeral, the place had been upside-down anyway, full of boxes and cartons, as well as furniture, ready for removal to Blackpool, to Norman's own place on Southgate Drive.

Alfred had quite understood when, two years ago, Norman had gone to live with his widowed mother. She had been too ill to look after herself and Norman was an only child. Alfred knew from experience that Norman was as capable as any woman. Oh, yes, Alfred understood Norman's obligations. He himself had looked after his own mother and later, Edna, under similar circumstances. The only problem had been that the two men hadn't found it easy to meet while Norman had been living with his mother and it hadn't been wise, as the law stood, to bring Norman to the shop too often. Lytham was a small community and people made it their business to know what was going on.

Now that Norman's mother had passed on, though, they would be able to get back onto the old footing once more. They had always been able to meet in Norman's house in comparative safety. While he had been staying with his mother in Preston, Norman had let out his Blackpool property, and his tenants had just moved out, so the next time the two men met would be in the comfort of the Southgate house. Smiling at the thought, Alfred stopped the car by the entrance to the park, locked it and started on the walk to the tower. As he quickened his steps he could see Norman already waiting....

Inside the men's sitting room at Ellswick, Harry Tomlinson moved about restlessly in his chair, waiting for his wife to arrive. Today, he had walked the length of the corridor and he wanted to tell her he had managed it. If he kept this up, he would be going home soon. One or two of the other patients who were ready to be discharged were out in the grounds, or on the veranda, with their families. He had been told not to overdo things and to stay indoors for a few more days.

Why wasn't she here? It was gone two o'clock and most of the other visitors had already arrived. He told himself to be patient. She had to see to the children before she set off to travel from the coast. He supposed she would be coming by train and the afternoon one got in by one-thirty at the station. It only took a short time to walk from there so why was she so late?

It was another quarter of an hour before Alice walked into the room, coming towards him, arms outstretched, looking fresh and cool. She had taken off her coat and all the other men in the room looked up as she came in – and no wonder! She looked positively radiant, he thought. Catching her hands in his, he drew her close to kiss her, a delicate flush in her creamy skin, her shapely body sleek in the figure-hugging crepe. As she sat down gracefully on the chair next to his, he noticed that, always abreast of fashion, Alice had shortened her skirt again. He could see part of a shapely calf and ankle, set off with pointed-toe pumps. Her black hair, under the small grey hat, was as beautifully waved as ever and her eyes seemed to have darkened in intensity since he had last looked into them. She smiled at him, asking him how he was.

"I'm much better. I walked the length of the corridor today, so I'll be coming home soon."

"Oh, I'm so glad, Harry."

"You're looking well, love."

"Yes, and I think you'll understand why when you hear the news I've got to tell you."

"How d'you mean, love?" he asked her, puzzled and interested.

"Can't you guess?"

"No – you tell me."

"Well, I'm going to have another baby," she said, blushing and keeping her eyes down.

He was absolutely dumbfounded. He had been quite sure that she was avoiding getting pregnant again. She must have changed her mind without telling him. He wondered how it was possible to ever really understand women. They said one thing and meant another. They changed their minds without telling you, just like that! He couldn't assimilate it until she assured him that she was quite sure about it and that she didn't mind one bit.

"Perhaps it will be a boy, this time, Harry," she said, smiling and saying she hoped it would be this time, for his sake.

"You've made me very happy, Alice love, and I shalln't mind whether it's a boy or a girl." Reaching out for her hand, he pressed it in his. He wanted to get up and take her in his arms and kiss her properly, but he could hardly do that in the day-room with several pairs of eyes watching curiously from chairs scattered about the room. It was such a wonderful and unexpected piece of news that it dominated his thoughts as she talked about the children and he answered her. Now, perhaps, he thought, as she chattered on, he was going to have the son he had always longed for. It was strange, but she seemed to be pleased that she was pregnant again. Were things going to improve, then, once he got home? Now that she had changed her mind about having another child, he felt that he couldn't get home soon enough. He would show the doctors here that he could be on his feet much sooner than they expected.

At five o'clock, Mr. Simpkins came to pick up Alice at the Home, to take her back to Lytham. She kissed her husband goodbye in the corridor, telling him not to come right out to the front lobby. He returned the kiss very tenderly and told her again how happy he was with the good news she had brought him. Alice smiled and said how glad she was, too, and with that, she went off to join Mr. Simpkins at the front door.

When she had told Harry about the ride with the grocer, he hadn't liked the idea. However, as Alice had pointed out, Mr. Simpkins had an appointment in Preston, so why shouldn't she have a comfortable ride in his car instead of having to travel by train? To which, of course, he had no answer. She had promised to come to see him again the following weekend, but Harry had made up his mind. He was going to be out of here before then, especially now he knew she was pregnant. She needed him to be with her. He remembered the distress she had suffered over the last child. This time, though, she had said she was feeling very well.

As he slowly returned to the sitting room, mulling over all she had said, he thought he saw someone with auburn hair disappearing into a doorway further up the corridor. Probably a new nurse, he thought. Strange, how that colour of hair could whisk him back to earlier times and former loves, he reflected. For one brief moment, he wondered where Janet was now and whether she had married the young man who had been with her when she had visited Blackpool last year.

The tea bell interrupted his thoughts with its clamour. He made his deliberate way into the dining room, thinking that he had enough on his mind now, without going back into the past and raking up old memories. Afterwards, he made his way back into the sitting room to look at the evening papers. A son, he thought – how wonderful that would be! He didn't let himself hope too much, though. He had done that before, and it hadn't happened. Sitting back in the comfortable armchair, he found himself dozing a little, the paper unopened by his side on a low table.

He surfaced suddenly as a sharp pain stabbed him in the chest. Straightening up, he found that it eventually eased, although he felt very tired. He didn't want to read his newspaper, after all. Perhaps he would take it up to his bedroom and read it there, after his supper drink. It had been quite an exhausting day, one way and another. A shooting pain bent him over and he put his had to his chest – an involuntary gesture. That, too, gradually eased off, as he signalled to one of the nurses. "Could you help me to the lift? He asked. "I think I'll go up to bed, now. I've done enough walking today, and I've got a touch of indigestion."

"Alright, Mr. Tomlinson, I'll take you up first in the chair and get you into bed, then I'll bring you something up for the indigestion."

"Thank you, nurse," Harry said, as she brought the wheelchair to his side, before wheeling him to the lift. As soon as he had got into bed and his head sank into the pillow, he drifted into sleep at once, before she could return with the medicine. It seemed he had only been asleep for a short time, when he awakened from a muddled dream. In it, he had been with Taffy Evans, his old Army pal, who had been killed in action. His father, who had been dead for many years, was also in it somewhere, too. A soft night-light was burning and the nurse had come in earlier with the medicine and a drink, which had long since gone cold. But by the hands of the wall clock, he saw that it was nearly four a.m.!

His body felt as heavy as lead and yet his head felt light and free. He was sweating, but he couldn't feel his feet – they were completely numb. There was a bell by the side of the bed to summon the nurse, and he knew with certainty that he must press it. It took an enormous effort to lift an arm and push back the bedclothes. Then he had to concentrate hard to control the arm and the hand and point them in the direction of the button. At first, he couldn't locate it and when he did, the finger refused to stay in place. In the end, though, he thought he had managed to press it once, but he never really knew whether or not it rang because the next moment a tearing, squeezing agony seized his chest – and he knew no more.

There was an urgent tapping on Janet's bedroom door. It eventually penetrated her sleep and she opened her eyes. Surely, it was too early yet, to get up? She glanced at the little bedside clock. Four-thirty! What on earth was the matter? Quickly slipping on her dressing gown and slippers, she went to the door, opening it slightly.

"Can you come a minute, Janet?" It was Nurse Gordon. "We didn't know whether or not to get you up, but Molly told me that you know Harry Tomlinson." She whispered. So – they had been gossiping about her, Janet thought. "It's just that he's had some kind of heart failure – they don't know whether he's going to live or not. He's rambling, but he has spoken your name a few times. Do you want to see him, Janet?"

"Yes, I'll come down." After the first flutter of shock, she felt no panic, no fear. In fact she felt calmer than she had felt for a long time. It was as if she had been waiting for this moment ever since she had seen him wheeled into the sitting rooms.

They walked downstairs into the ward, between the beds with their sleeping occupants, who were unaware of the drama taking place behind the curtains of the end bed. Sister O'Brien's face peered out and she lifted the curtain.

"There you are! I believe you know this man, my dear?"

"Yes, Sister," Janet said, looking down on Harry's ravaged face.

322 / Sally Redmayne

"I'm afraid Dr. Marshall has just been and he says there's nothing else he can do for him. He doesn't know how long he'll last. If you want to stay with him for a minute or two, we'll wait just beyond the curtain." They withdrew, leaving her alone with him.

Taking the cold hands in hers, she willed him to open his eyes. The eyelids were fluttering wildly and he was muttering incoherently. Miraculously, they suddenly opened, and he saw her. "Why, Janet," he whispered weakly, but quite lucidly, "I've been gassed, you know. That's why they brought me here. I'm coming home soon and then we'll be married."

He smiled up at her with that old heart-warming smile that had kept her loving him for so long in the past. It was quite obvious to her that his mind had slipped back into the past to that year when they had been engaged and he had been in the convalescent home. He thought he was there now, she realised. She had heard the nurses here say that some patients suffered confusion, especially where time was concerned.

"Yes, Harry, of course we will." She humoured him, tears of compassion streaming down her face. "Just rest now. There's no need to worry any more."

"Why are you crying? I want you to smile. D'you know, I've seen Taffy Evans and my Dad just now," he said, conversationally.

"Did you, Harry?" It took all her willpower to force a smile as he had asked her to do.

"I think I'll have a little sleep now...." His voice trailed off, his eyes closed and he began to gasp for breath.

Janet twitched back the curtains and called urgently to the two nurses. As they came round the bed, she stepped back into the ward, waiting. After a while, they joined her, Sister O'Brien shaking her head sympathetically. "I'm afraid he's gone, dear," she consoled Janet softly. "It's always upsetting. I'm sorry we had to get you out of bed but we knew he couldn't last long. Did he manage to talk, then?"

"Yes, and thank you for sending for me, Sister."

"Molly told me you knew him." Sister led the way out of the ward, leaving Nurse Gordon in charge. "It happened too suddenly to send for his wife and he had no one else on our list as next-of-kin, so I decided to send Dorothy up for you. We did hear him saying your name, you know, once or twice."

"He thought he was back in the Army convalescent Home, I think. It was a few years back – at the end of the War."

"That does often happen," Sister said. "They often hallucinate, or get confused about where they are. Come on, we'll go along to the kitchen and brew a large pot of tea. I could do with one and I'm sure you could. It's going to be a shock for his wife," she continued as they entered the kitchen. "She was only in here yesterday, and there was no chance at all of contacting her tonight. We shall have to get on to the police at Lytham, now. They will send someone round to tell her, I expect."

Janet felt drained and exhausted. All she wanted to do was to go back to bed to curl up and try to find oblivion in sleep. She had wondered many times why Fate had sent Harry to Ellswick, the very place where she was working. Now she knew. It was so that she could make her peace with him before he died.

As soon as she heard about Harry's death, Mary Boothroyd came over to stay with her daughter at Fore Street and Joe arrived the following day. Today, the day of the committal, Alice sat on the settee, close to her mother, dressed in her navy-blue coat and a newly bought hat to match. She was crying softly into a clean handkerchief. She'd had to go out and buy the hat because she very rarely wore dark colours and she meant to be as correct as her mother-in-law. She knew that Ellen, and Maud, too, would be dressed from head to toe in black out of respect for Harry.

Mary had made do with her navy, too. It was so dark that it could be taken for black, anyway. Joe, in his best dark-grey suit, was perched on the very edge of the chair, fiddling with his black tie. He desperately needed a smoke but he didn't want to risk offending the ladies by lighting up his pipe. Perhaps he would manage it when they got outside.

Ellen and Maud had come from Blackpool in a taxi cab. They were, as Alice had guessed, dressed in deepest black. They were now on their feet by the door, waiting for the hearse and the big funeral car to arrive. Harry's mother and sister were obviously keeping themselves rigidly under control and it was plain that they had both been weeping. Ellen had expected that Harry would be buried in St. Luke's churchyard, like all his family, but Alice had said she wasn't up to going to Blackpool. Knowing now of Alice's condition, Ellen had felt that she couldn't insist and she'd had to give way. He was to be interred at Lytham Parish Church – the church where both his daughters had been christened.

Sydney Greenwood, representing the joinery shop, with Betty Furlong and her mother, were to meet them at the church. Mr. Simpkins had told them he would be there to pay his last respects.

He had called round to offer his condolences to Alice as soon as the news of Harry's death had reached him, considering it his Christian duty. After all, he himself had had the privilege of taking Alice to visit her husband just before his death. He had told Alice and her mother that he would be glad, as a churchwarden at the Parish church, to help them in any way with the service. Of course, he told them, the Vicar, Mr. Fairchild, would be visiting her himself, but if she needed any help in choosing the hymns he would be most happy to oblige.

"Isn't he a kind man?" Alice asked her mother, afterwards.

"Yes, I suppose he is," Mary had to agree, "but he seems a bit namby-pamby to me. You said he was a widower?"

"Yes, and from what he's told me, he looked after his wife and she never had to worry about anything before she died. I think he's kind."

"You may be right, love. Perhaps I'm misjudging him." One thing she did know, which she didn't tell Alice – Joe wouldn't be impressed by Alfred Simpkins at all. He was what Joe would call a cissie. Her husband liked men to be real men, not pansies, which was his other descriptive word for rather effeminate looking men like Alfred Simpkins.

The service inside the church was plain but moving and by the end of it, there was audible sniffing and some blowing into handkerchiefs amongst the party. The Vicar's eulogy contained references to Harry's service to his King and country, and to his qualities as a loving husband and father. Mary, staying close to Alice, supported her daughter, as they walked slowly back to the church entrance before going on to the graveside.

After the committal, where Alice appeared quite overcome, they finally prepared to return to the cars. Mr. Simpkins raised his hat as the two women passed him, Alice inclining her head towards him in mute acknowledgement.

"Was that little man with the hard hat the one who brought Alice over with the children?" Ellen asked later, as they sat down to tea at Fore Street.

"Yes, he's the grocer from the corner shop," Mary said, as she handed Harry's mother one of her daughter's best cups. "He's been very kind to Alice. He felt he ought to come to the funeral to pay his respects."

"I thought I recognised him. He didn't come in to the house when she brought the children in. He stayed in the car. Did you say he was a churchwarden?"

"Yes, he's always at the church, according to Alice. I thought she could bring the children over to me for a week or two, when we go back. She's not up to doing any sorting out yet and she needs an eye keeping on her, especially now she's carrying again."

"That's for the best, I think. It's a weary business sorting out papers, but she's welcome to our help, when she gets back. I want you to tell her that."

"I will, Ellen. She's going to need all the help she can get, in her position."

"As far as the money's concerned," Ellen said, "she'll be alright for a while. Harry has some savings, but they won't last forever. We'll do our best to help them all we can. I've got a bit put by and I'll not see any of my son's family going short."

"Thank you, Ellen, you're very good. Joe and me haven't much, but if they need it, we'll try to help."

"Well, it's no use looking too far ahead," Ellen said, as she prepared to leave. "If Alice let's me know when she gets back from Bradfield, I'll come to see her."

"She'll do that, Ellen, and I just want to say how much I feel for you over Harry. It's a terrible thing for a mother to lose her only son, especially a good son, like Harry."

Ellen took a moment before answering. "Yes," she said, "it's been very hard, Mary. I've had to face the fact during the War, that he could be killed – four years of wondering and waiting. Then he comes home safely and you can't believe that there's anything radically wrong with him. This must have happened to hundreds of families – their men come back, only to go to early graves because their health has been undermined by the conditions they were fighting in. I feel sorry for Alice, too, left with two children and another on the way. It's the last thing Harry would have wanted for her. That's why I shall give her all the help I can, to try to make up for what he can't do for her."

This was such a long speech for Ellen to make that Mary stared in some surprise at the older woman, while Alice came across to join them.

"Take care of yourself, Alice," Ellen said, putting her arms around Alice and giving her an awkward hug.

Alice gulped, nodding her head at her mother-in-law, who patted her hand as she went out. Maud, hard on her heels, passed Alice by with stony eyes. She had felt that she should attend her brother's funeral, but she had no intention of speaking false words of comfort to her sister-in-law. Who else but Alice was ultimately responsible for Harry's death?

It had been obvious to her for a long time that Alice was quite incapable of looking after her brother, or any other man, for that matter. She had said as much, many times, to her mother, but her opinions on the subject hadn't been welcomed. Now she felt that she had been proved right! She would never be able to forgive Alice for what she had done to Harry – never!

Following her mother out to the taxi cab, she vowed that in the future she would have nothing more to do with her sister-in-law, if she could help it.

Ellen was wondering, as she sat in the back of the taxi cab with her grim-faced daughter, whether this time Alice might have a son. If she did, he would probably be just like Harry. It was a crumb of comfort in a desolate world, and she badly needed something to cling on to. Harry's daughters would eventually get married and change their names, but a boy would be a Tomlinson all his life and he would carry on the family name.

Ellen sighed, choking back the tears, looking out of the cab window and noticing that it had started raining. This life was truly a vale of tears, she thought, watching the relentless drops of rain slashing against the glass as the vehicle carried them back to Nelson Street, to grieve.

Chapter Twenty-Nine

Janet was finding it hard keeping up with her work at Ellswick. She had only just begun to feel that she was getting on her feet again after Peter's death, when Harry had been brought into the Home. All the people who worked with her had been very sympathetic and supportive in the weeks following the loss of her fiancée, when she had decided on returning to her job. Harry had been brought in here very soon after the trauma of Peter's death and that last conversation with him kept intruding into her thoughts. Her only feeling for him then had been pity, but she had loved him once and the memory of that love lingered like the echo of a familiar tune, long gone.

She even considered giving up her job and returning to Blackpool and her family, but something inside her – some stubborn streak – drove her on. She noticed, as she went about her regular jobs, that some of the familiar faces she had been so used to seeing, were now gone. The blind boy, Reggie Knowles, for instance, had been discharged recently. He had been allowed to go home to his parents now living in Leyland, quite near to Preston. She wondered how he was coping with having to re-orientate himself to different surroundings. But if Reggie had gone home, there were plenty of others who needed her help, although just now she found it hard to concentrate on anything for too long.

By the end of the summer, she had managed to throw off some of the melancholy. She had made an effort, when the weather was good, to get out into the countryside, into the sunshine and fresh air. One golden afternoon at the end of August, she was told that someone was asking for her at the desk in the front lobby.

"For me? Are you sure? Did they ask for me by name?"

"Well, no, he asked for the housekeeper."

"Oh, I expect it's about the laundry. We've been having trouble with it and I've complained."

"I don't think so," Dorothy said, smiling mysteriously. "He told me to say that it was Captain Edward Knowles, Reggie's brother."

"Captain Edward….? Oh, yes, I wrote a letter to him for Reggie. But Captain Knowles lives in Torquay. What is he doing up here? Anyway, I don't really know him," she said, picturing the elderly gentleman with the bristling moustache and the balding head she had seen in her mind's eye when she had written the letter. What on earth did he want?"

"Alright, Dorothy, I'll come and see him."

"Well, I wouldn't be long about it," Dorothy said impishly, "or someone else might snap him up."

Whatever did she mean? Janet strode briskly towards the front entrance to sort it out, opening the door from the corridor. He had his back to her, but she knew the figure in the uniform straight away. He was leaning on the front desk, waiting, and as the door opened and Janet came forward, he straightened, turning to face her.

"Thank goodness it's you," he said. "I was beginning to think you'd left and I should have to account to some elderly lady in a flowered overall."

"It's you!" She gasped. "But you – you aren't Reggie's brother – you can't be! You're not a bit like him – and you're not old enough."

"I take it that's a compliment to me, not an insult to my brother?"

"Oh, I didn't mean…." Here he was again, laughing at her and making her feel foolish.

"My dear Miss Crossley, don't be embarrassed. Your observations are, in fact, correct. Reggie is only my half-brother. I'm staying with my step-mother for a couple of weeks in Leyland while I'm on leave. The Regiment goes out to Gibraltar in a couple of months, before Christmas."

"Did you want to see me for some reason?" Janet managed, at last, to ask.

"I wanted to thank you for sending those letters to me and to Reggie's parents. He has only just told me who wrote them for him. He said it was one of the staff and presumed, wrongly, that it was one of the nurses. When you told me you were the housekeeper, it never occurred to me that it might have been you."

"Why not? Because I appeared so uneducated?" she asked, scoring a point, at last.

"No, of course not. Look, we can't stand around here like this. How about driving to Preston with me to Kendals' when you finish here. I'd like to treat you to afternoon tea…. To show my appreciation."

"Oh, but I don't know what time I shall finish. I have several lists yet to check."

"Would you like me to come in and ask Matron to allow you to leave earlier, then? I think I might be able to persuade her."

"No, no!" she cried. "I think I can get through them in time."

"That's better. Right, then, I'll call for you at four o'clock. Until then, Miss Crossley, don't overdo it!" He took his leave, smiling, leaving her pink and confused. How dare he presume in that high-handed way that she would want to go out with him to tea? Cheeks burning, she hurried back into the corridor where she bumped straight into Dorothy, the probationer.

"Well," asked the girl, eyes dancing. "What did Captain Knowles have to say? Has he asked you out with him?"

"Never mind about that, Dorothy. I've got a lot of work to do. Have you been listening at the door?"

"Of course I have. You don't have visitors like that every day," Dorothy admitted, unashamed, accompanying Janet as far as her office door.

"Well, yes, he did ask me to have tea with him at Kendals."

"Kendals! You must have made an impression."

"I'll never get there if I don't get on with these lists," Janet pointed out, opening the door and walking inside. Dorothy, hovering in the passageway outside, didn't seem anxious to move. Hoping to fend off any more questions, Janet asked the girl, "Haven't you got any work to do, Dorothy?"

"Point taken," said the girl, grinning. "Enjoy your rendezvous and if you change your mind, just send for me. I'll accompany Captain Edward Knowles to Kendals, any day!"

In spite of her protests, Janet finished the lists in plenty of time, afterwards going upstairs and dressing carefully in one of her new blue dresses, with the slightly shorter skirt. She still had her thick hair up, but she had been considering having it cut, like some of the nurses. It was so much easier to manage, they said, and her hair had a natural wave in it, so it should shape up nicely, she thought.

A flutter of excitement ran through her, in spite of her doubts about the invitation. Then she told herself that he had merely been carrying out a courtesy visit on behalf of his brother. She shouldn't read too much into it. As he followed her through the elegant little café, she knew that other women, sipping tea, or eating toasted muffins or cakes, glanced curiously or enviously at her. She chose a table near the wall, away from prying eyes. Edward settled her in a chair, seating himself opposite to her. He seemed quite at ease while she sat, self-consciously gazing at the menu he had presented for her inspection. She noticed that it had a pink bow painted above the order list and that the ribbons of the bow extended down from the top of the card, along each side in a twisted spiral, almost to the bottom. She glanced over it warily, meeting his eyes and she felt they were laughing at her again, as he asked her, smiling,

"Is it to be tea, then, or would you like something else?"

"No, just tea, thank you."

"Very well, Miss Crossley, so be it. Now I suggest we introduce ourselves properly. You know my name. It has never been abbreviated by anyone except Dad, who calls me Ted, but the choice is yours. It's the only Christian name I've got. Now then, how about you?"

"I'm usually called Janet, but my friend, at Bolton, Ann, calls me Jan. You can take your pick, as well."

"Alright, Janet it is, then. And have you any family, Janet?"

"Oh, yes," she said, but at that moment a waitress arrived to take their order and her next words were cut short. Afterwards, she began to tell him about the boarding-house, and about her mother dying. Then she went on to tell him about her father remarrying, and about Arthur, her brother, going to work at Peabody and Grundy's office. "And I have a younger sister, Rose, who is almost ready for leaving school," she finished, breathlessly. It had all seemed to come out in a rush and he had listened as if he was interested in everything she had told him.

"Look, Janet," he said, "I don't know whether you have anything arranged for the weekend, but if you would like to come to dinner tomorrow evening with the family here at Leyland, I'd be pleased. I told Reggie I was going to ask you. We'd very much like you to come, and so would Isobel, my stepmother. We're all grateful for what you did."

"Oh, it was nothing, really." Janet sipped tea to give herself time to decide whether or not to accept the invitation. "How is he, then?"

"He's doing very well. Glad to be living at home, of course. Dad doesn't think he will be going abroad again. His firm are expanding now in England and they are concentrating on opening a branch here in the North. Dad has been made Managing Director up here. The house I have in Torquay belonged to my own mother – she left it to me. I stay there sometimes when I'm on leave, but it's a bit lonely down there on my own."

"I'm glad for Reggie. His case was one of the saddest – blinded so young. His chest trouble has improved, then?"

"Seems to have, yes, and he's had a lot of help from the Braille people. He's learning the language, you know."

"Oh, that's wonderful!" Janet said. "Can I pour you another cup of tea?" She took the cup, emptying the dregs and putting in a small amount of milk from the delicate china cream jug, before filling it in front of him. "You'll come, then, this weekend?"

"Yes, I will, and thank you for asking me." It would be nice to see Reggie again and talk to him about the progress he was making, after the desperately hard time he'd had convalescing at Ellswick.

"Good girl. I'll pick you up then, tomorrow evening about seven."

In the middle of a warm, humid August afternoon, as Alice Tomlinson waited for Mr. Simpkins to come through from the back room into the shop, she felt suddenly faint. Gripping the counter with her hands, she bent her head, closing her eyes.

"Can I help you, Mrs. Tomlinson?" Mr. Simpkins' solicitous voice reached her ears and she raised her head. He lifted the flap of wood which was hinged to give him access to the other side of the counter. Seeing the colour of her face, he told her, "Come in here for a moment." He placed a hand under her arm and led her gently into his sitting room, which was reached through the shop.

"Now then, sit there, while I get some water."

"Thank you," Alice whispered, sitting down on the rich plum velvet settee.

"Now, don't move, I'll be back." He left her to go into the kitchen returning with a gleaming crystal glass, half-full of water.

As she sipped it slowly, the attack gradually wore off and some colour returned to her face.

"That's better," he said. "Pardon me for asking, Mrs. Tomlinson, but are you eating properly? It's very important not to miss your own meals, you know, when you are seeing to the children."

"It's not really that, Mr. Simpkins," she said, blushing now. He looked at her more closely. "I'm going to have another baby."

"Oh, I see." He seemed not at all embarrassed. "Another child is going to be hard for you to face up to, on top of a bereavement."

"Yes, it isn't easy. I'm keeping up, for the children's sake."

"I do admire you, Mrs. Tomlinson. You've put such a brave face on things since the funeral. It will take some effort to go through with this and look after your other children, as well."

"I'm trying very hard," she said, as she glanced around the room noting the expensive furniture and the thick carpet, the pictures on the walls and the good china scattered about on the surfaces. Mr. Simpkins' sitting room had come as a pleasant surprise to Alice. It spoke of money and good taste. His business had evidently given him a good standard of living as she could see, from the red velvet of the sofa on which she was sitting to the thickness and softness of the carpet under her feet. There was no tapestry upholstery or needlecord floor covering here.

"Have you been alone for long?" she asked him, sipping the water slowly.

"Nearly four years. The house is really too big now. When Mother was alive, we occupied more of it. Edna and I had no children, so, since she died, I've been here on my own."

"Yes, it's a shame," said Alice, thoughtfully. "This is a lovely room."

"I like to be comfortable, and I like beautiful things."

"I like nice things," Alice agreed, "but I've never been able to afford them."

"I've been very lucky. The Lord has been good to me. Are you feeling any better, now?" he asked, taking the glass from her.

"Yes, thanks, much better. You've been very kind."

"Glad to have been able to help you, my dear. I consider it my Christian duty. I'll see that your order is delivered right away."

A week later, Alfred Simpkins looked once more at the girl in front of his counter. He felt sympathetic towards Alice. It was now a couple of months since her husband's death and they were nearing the end of August, the weather staying warm and sticky. So – Harry's widow had been left pregnant, as well as having to look after two young children and cope with a house into the bargain. He thought she was looking most attractive. Sometimes pregnancy had that effect upon a woman, he had noticed. He'd had enough women in his shop in his time to know a thing or two about them and their intimate affairs. He understood them – who better? They never stopped talking about their own personal business in the shop, just as if he wasn't there, sometimes.

"I'm alright, thank you," she said, in answer to his query. "Susan's had a bit of a cold, but she's better now. Jenny's missing her dad. It's only natural, and Susan can't really understand where he's gone."

"And when do you expect – er – the new baby, then?"

Alice blushed – delightfully, he thought – and told him that it would be before Christmas.

"Your friend, Mrs. Furlong doesn't mind having the children occasionally, I see. You ought to try to get out more. It isn't good to be tied up with the house and the children all the time. You could get morbid, you know, a young woman like you."

"It's difficult getting out far," she said. "I've been on the train to my mother-in-law's with the children, but I won't be able to go when I'm further on."

"No, indeed, you mustn't struggle like that. Next time you want to visit her, just let me know and I'll run you over in the car with the children any evening or at weekends."

"Oh, Mr. Simpkins, that's really good of you," Alice cried happily. "I've still got a few things to settle – Harry's affairs, you know – and it isn't easy getting about with the children in the train and I can't always be leaving them with Betty I could really do with going over to see Harry's mother again as soon as I can, to talk over one or two things with her. It's so hard for her to come here in the middle of the season, when they are busy. Could you – could we go over next Sunday, do you think, Mr. Simpkins? It's quite alright if you're busy, but it would help me a lot if you could take me."

"Of course, my dear, I'd be delighted. I could drop you all of at your mother-in-law's, then call on of a friend of mine in the town and bring you back later in the day."

"Thank you, Mr. Simpkins," she said, with a pleased smile, "You're very kind."

"Nonsense, I consider it my Christian duty to help you. I'll call round one evening in the week to make the arrangements." He went round the counter to open the door for her. "I'll send the boy round with your groceries. Take care of yourself, my dear."

"I will, Mr. Simpkins," she assured him, smiling warmly at him as she left the shop.

The following Sunday, Mr. Simpkins helped Jenny and Susan into the back of the Ford, afterwards handing Alice carefully into the front seat beside him. As they set off in the direction of the Blackpool road, Mr. Simpkins asked Alice if she would like to call him Alfred. It was much better than addressing him as Mr. Simpkins all the time.

"Why, yes, of course, and you must call me Alice. It doesn't sound as stuffy, at all."

He gave her a satisfied smile, patting her hands as she sat primly with them on her lap. "Are you comfortable on that seat? I have some cushions in the back?"

"I'm quite alright Alfred. It's so nice to be driven in a car instead of having to wait around for trains. I'm glad I have a friend like you. It's not easy for me to see to all the things I have to do. "I'm not used to signing papers and sorting things out, like I've had to do since Harry died."

"Yes, it's a trying time, as well I know."

"Of course, I was forgetting – you've been through it all yourself. You know all about it."

"Indeed I do, Alice. I know just what you're going through. You must let me take you out again. Any time you want a spin, just let me know and I'll be glad to oblige."

On their arrival at Nelson Street, Alice insisted that Alfred should come into the house to be introduced to Ellen and Maud. She hoped the latter would be out and in this, she was lucky. She knew only too well that her sister-in-law might upset Alfred, but it was Ellen who met them at the front door. She was inclined to stare at Alfred as she let them in, but once in the parlour, she asked him, "Have you any plans for this afternoon, then?"

"Yes, I have a very good friend on Southgate Drive, up by the park. I thought I'd pay him a little visit while Alice and the children are with you."

"Well, if you'd care to come back here for tea, you're very welcome, then you could take Alice home afterwards."

"Thank you, Mrs. Tomlinson, that's very kind of you. I should be happy to come back here to have tea with you all." Replacing his bowler hat, Alfred took his leave.

"Well, Alice, how are you keeping?" Ellen asked her, as the girls went straight to the fascinating toy drawer and she opened it for them.

After he had reached the end of Nelson Street, Alfred Simpkins turned his car in the direction of the park. He eventually turned down a tree-lined avenue which led down to the environs of the park itself – that same park which had once been Alice and Harry's trysting place. He didn't stop in front of Norman's house, but left the car near the end of the avenue. There were no boarding houses in this area, only private homes, each one indicating the degree of affluence of its owner. Alfred knew that Norman had no money worries now, since his mother's death. He'd had a comfortable income before, from his father, but now his mother's estate had come to him in full, as her only child.

Going through the gate and up the path through the beautifully kept lawn and flower-beds, Alfred glanced around before lifting the door knocker. There was no one in sight on either side of the road, but you never knew who was watching. The door was opened by an elegant young man wearing pale grey flannels and a very white shirt, open at the neck. His golden hair had been waved expertly back from the high, wide brow. The hand that he extended to Alfred had polished nails. Norman stepped back, as Alfred went forward into the hallway, then carefully closed the door and locked it.

The two men embraced in the big hallway before going into the back sitting room. The large front lounge wasn't private enough! At the back of the house, French windows gave onto a paved area, with plants in tubs which fronted the back lawn, surrounded by perennial borders. A high wall enclosed the garden at the bottom end, upon which evergreen plants were climbing. The upper windows of a similar house were visible some distance away, over the top of the wall, the garden of which came up to Norman's, the wall dividing the two.

Alfred was sensitive to Norman's moods and he could see at once that something was troubling him. "You seem a bit edgy today, love," he said, taking a seat on the expensive flowered velvet settee.

"Oh, I am, Alfred," Norman said, going to the window and swishing the heavy brocade drapes across, but not quite closing them. There were thick net curtains underneath, but Norman was taking no chances.

"You see the house over there?" He indicated the house over the wall. "Well, Mrs. Slater, next door, told me this morning that a policeman had bought it. They moved in yesterday. What are we going to do about it, Alfred?" Norman stood nervously, twisting his hands together.

"Are you sure it's a policeman?" People often get hold of the wrong end of the stick, you know."

"Oh, yes, a detective inspector, I think she said. He's in plain clothes, anyway."

"Good heavens!" Alfred's voice rose in pitch. "So they're buying houses round here now, are they? We shall feel soon that we can't move anywhere without being spied on. Of course, they can't arrest us without proof, but it means we shall have to be extra careful." Alfred's fastidious soul shrank away in horror from the thought of a prison cell.

"I've been worried to death about it, Alfred, since I found out this morning." Norman was saying, as he took out two slender wine glasses from the rosewood cabinet in the corner.

"Well, it's no use us getting into a tizzy about this. We shall have to think very carefully about what we should do. The trouble is that wherever we both live we're going to have this problem. I shall have to give it some serious thought. I've got another couple of hours before I'm due back, so let's not worry about it while I'm here."

Later, when he returned to Nelson Street and they were all sitting together at Ellen's table for tea, Alfred next to her, Maud asked the grocer, "So, you've been in business for a long time, Mr. Simpkins?"

"Oh, yes, the shop belonged to Mother. I helped her in it right from the start when I left school. She was a widow by then and I used to do all the delivering on my bicycle. I didn't get the car until much later, of course. Then, when I married Edna, we had one of the spare bedrooms over the shop and shared the sitting room with Mother. Not long after that, the Lord took her – she had been ailing for some time – and then

Edna, too, became ill. A permanent invalid she was, in her later years, so I had to take on the boy to help with the shop and do the delivering."

"You haven't had an easy time of it, then" Ellen said. "Like us all, you've had to work hard for what you've got."

"Indeed, yes, Mrs. Tomlinson, but I consider the Lord's been good to me. I've never wanted and I've always had a bit over and to spare."

"It's not everyone who can afford to run a car," said Maud, sourly.

"I bought the car so that I could take Edna out more easily. It isn't good for an invalid to be lying about all day so I used to take her out in it on nice summer evenings or at the weekends when I'd shut the shop." He didn't add that he'd also had his own little outings in it.

"I like riding in the car," Alice said. "It's so much nicer than trains."

Alfred told them that it would be his pleasure to give Alice a ride any time she liked and by the time they left, they were on very friendly terms. As he handed her out at Fore Street, he asked, "May I call in again to see if you need the car for anything?"

"Yes, please, Alfred, that would be lovely. Tell Mr. Simpkins 'Thank you' girls."

"Thank you, Mr. Simpkins," they chorused, as they ran up to the door. As the car drew away, Alice let herself into the house, deciding that it had been a very successful day. Smiling speculatively, she went inside to give the girls their supper and get them ready for bed.

Putting the car away in the garage opposite the shop, Alfred Simpkins was thinking very carefully about his own and Norman's present positions. Locking the garage doors, he walked across the road, round the side of the shop and let himself in at the house entrance. In the hall he removed his hat, placing in on the top shelf beside others, before easing his coat onto a padded hanger. His slippers were standing ready on the bottom ledge and, taking these up, he walked into the sitting room and settled himself on one of the velvet easies. You could never be sure where the police were going to move in next, he thought. Of course, it was probably quite co-incidental in Norman's case, and the new neighbour knew nothing of Norman's proclivities. The house was, after all, a very desirable property, in a good residential area. But it wouldn't be very long before the policeman did familiarise himself with all his neighbours. The police were trained to do just that. Would it now be possible to visit Norman at the house on a regular basis, he wondered, without attracting attention – and suspicion? It might even mean poor Norman moving house, he reflected, picking up the church magazine from a low table at his hand.

Was he himself as safe as he might be, living alone, without a wife? If he had a wife again, he would be above suspicion, as he had been with Edna. A picture of Alice Tomlinson came into his mind. She reminded him in many ways of his late wife. She, too, had been very pretty when she was young. Alice needed a husband – a husband who was a good provider, with her two children and another one on the way. If that unborn child should turn out to be a boy, now ….

Alfred had always regretted that because of his way of life he was never going to have a son who would, eventually, take over his business. It wasn't just he himself who had built it up. It had been in his family for three generations. His grandfather had been the first Simpkins in the original corner shop, small as it was in those days. Then his mother had taken it over and extended the shop as it still was today, with its ample living and bedroom space. He knew that his mother had been bitterly disappointed at his failure to produce the grandchildren she had wanted. The name of Simpkins had always been over the shop and he wanted to think that it always would be.

He would be able to visit Norman quite safely if he were a married man, but what was Norman going to think about that idea? It wouldn't affect their relationship in any way, of course. It would be just a matter of acquiring a ready-made family to protect them both from prosecution by the law – but would Norman appreciate that? They had been safe enough when Edna had been alive, so why not another Mrs. Simpkins, especially one with a family? They would have to discuss it very seriously, he decided, picking up the church magazine. He thumbed it through, but found he couldn't concentrate on the Vicar's 'Thought for Today – Judge not that ye be not Judged'. He would make his mug of cocoa, get into bed and sleep on his idea.

On the day following her trip in Alfred's car, Alice sat gazing out of her front window at Fore Street, seeing nothing of the passers-by. Her mind was occupied with the problem which had haunted her ever since Harry's death. What was she going to do when Harry's capital ran out? She reckoned that the money would last until after she'd had the baby, but she knew she must do something before that happened.

Ellen had offered her a home at Nelson Street, but she couldn't consider living again under the same roof as her sister-in-law. It wouldn't work for either of them, she knew. She couldn't go back to Bradfield, either. There wasn't room at Moscar Street, and Grandad's was no different. What she needed was some income, so she didn't have to keep taking money out of Harry's savings. Yet, she couldn't go out to work, with the children to look after and another one coming.

If only Harry had lived! How many times had she said that to herself? He would have accepted Jack Fenton's baby as his own. He had been over the moon about it when she had told him that last day at the Home. They could have gone on without Harry ever knowing that the boy wasn't his. By now, she was certain that it was going to be a boy. She just knew it was, this time.

Oh, it was so unfair! Here she was, going to have a child that would have to be looked after for years, and there was Jack Fenton, getting off scot free! She was the one who was going to have to pay – just like the old gypsy had predicted. But then a thought struck her. Why shouldn't she go and see Jack at the Tower and tell him that the baby was his – explain to him how she was placed? He had a steady job, and his wife worked, as well. They had no children to burden them, so why shouldn't he contribute to the upkeep of the child? Once the money she had was gone, the only help would be the Parish. The first thing she must do, then, was to make the journey to Blackpool to see Jack Fenton. She must tell him she was pregnant and that the child was his.

As she entered the Tower, she was trying to compose herself for the confrontation. How would she tell him about the baby? What should she say? Before she had reached her usual seat, she saw him up there on the bandstand, slick and smooth as ever, his hair gleaming under the bright lights. She didn't think he had seen her yet, and if he had he hadn't acknowledged her. Once or twice, she was asked to dance, but each time she shook her head in refusal. She hadn't come to dance today – she had come on business.

When the interval came, and the band left the rostrum, the familiar figure didn't appear, although she reckoned he must have seen her, now. She waited, but there was no sign of him. Then, all at once, she spotted him, dancing with a very attractive fair girl in a figure hugging dress. He was holding her close and she was clinging to him so that their bodies pressed intimately together.

I used to dance with him just like that, she thought bitterly. As they waltzed past, she caught his eye, but he deliberately ignored her, steering his new partner away and along the dance floor, out of her view.

Tears of humiliation shone in Alice's eyes as she stood up, turned away from the dancing, happy crowd and ran from the ballroom. No doubt the girl would be meeting Jack after his final session of playing and then she would be going for a run in his fast car. After what she had seen, she couldn't bring herself to confront him now. She had naively imagined that he would ask her to dance, as he had before, and that once they were on the dance floor she would tell him about the baby. What a silly little fool she had been to think that she could appeal to a man like Jack Fenton! He wouldn't have helped her if she had asked him, she realised, as she hurried outside into the soft rain.

Pulling a small scarf over her head, she crossed the promenade, the tears glistening on her lashes mingling with the drops falling on her face. The journey back on the train seemed interminable. She felt used and cheap – and old! The girl Jack had been dancing with had been no more than eighteen, she guessed. Why had her life gone wrong, like this, she asked herself? What had she done to deserve all that had happened to her?

There was only one hope left for her now, and that was to re-marry. She thought there had been more than kindness in Alfred's attitude towards her and he had said that he was lonely at the shop. But would Alfred want to take on her little family as well? She didn't love him, but then, beggars couldn't be choosers. She did admire him, with his good manners and his kind ways. He wasn't short of money, etiher. She was grasping at straws, she knew, but if Alfred didn't propose, the future for her was going to be very black indeed.

Chapter Thirty

The Willows lay back in its own grounds off the main road running through Leyland, one of Preston's outlying villages. Beyond the curve of its driveway, the grey-stone Victorian building stood, solid and spacious, amongst stately trees and cultivated gardens. Lights illuminated several of the downstairs rooms, revealing luxurious interiors which spoke of easy, comfortable living. No wonder Reggie had been so anxious to come home, Janet thought, as Edward's car came to a halt outside the front entrance. She'd had no idea that his parents were wealthy and after seeing the house, she was beginning to wish she hadn't accepted the invitation, or that she had put on a more formal dress.

"Don't let this little lot put you off," Edward told her easily, as he opened the car door for her. "It's only leased. Dad hasn't put down roots here, yet. It belongs to a friend of his who has gone abroad. In Dad's business, people never stay in one place for too long. Come on in, and I'll introduce you."

Pushing open the heavy oak door, Edward led the way into a large, square hallway, from which doors led into the various parts of the house. One on the right was wide open, revealing the glow of lights and warmth and the comfort of deep armchairs and rich carpets. As they walked forward, an elderly woman wearing a spotless white apron and cap came forward out of the shadows at the back of the hall to take their coats. Edward introduced her to Janet as Mrs. Fitton, the housekeeper. "Thanks, Millie," he said, "will you tell Isobel we're here?"

So, everyone was on familiar terms here, Janet though, as Millie turned and disappeared. She began to relax and the next moment another woman appeared from the passage beyond. If Janet had been expecting someone svelte and sophisticated, she was quite mistaken. Isobel Knowles was quite the reverse. In fact, though expensively gowned, her figure was matronly and her face heavy – just like Reggie's, she realised.

"I'm sorry to have kept you waiting, Edward. I was just putting the finishing touches to the sole. So this is Janet, who was so kind to my son? I'm very pleased to meet you, my dear. Come along to the sitting room and I'll get us a drink."

As she let go of Isobel's plump hand, Janet's last reserve about the evening evaporated. She returned the other woman's smile with genuine pleasure. It was quite obvious that she was very welcome here and that it wasn't going to be a formal evening, after all.

As they entered the glowing sitting room, Janet saw another woman occupying one of the deep armchairs. In one glance Janet saw that this woman fulfilled all her previous expectations of what Isobel Knowles would look like, although she was much younger. Cut in the latest short style, her dark hair matched her simple, but expensively moulded dress and her silk-clad, slender legs, one crossed over the other, displayed their shapeliness to the best advantage. In her hand, between the long, pink-tipped fingers, a cigarette burned. As Isobel followed them into the room, the woman spoke in a lazy, casual way which Janet found intensely irritating. She couldn't have said why.

"Edward, darling! So this is Reggie's little friend?"

"Janet, this is Claire Randall, our neighbour here. She has just popped round for a drink and to meet you before we have dinner. What would you like, dear," Isobel asked, turning to Janet. "Can I get you a sherry?"

The drinks served, Isobel apologised for her son's lateness and her husband's non-appearance. "Reggie has just finished changing," she explained. "He has been at the Braille Institute in Preston all day and he had to wait for transport back. I'm afraid my husband is still closeted in a meeting with his fellow-directors. I've just had a message to say he will be later than he expected."

"Don't worry about it, we'll wait. We're not wanting to eat just yet," Edward assured her. Turning to the elegant figure on his right, he commented, "You're not staying to dinner, then?"

"No, I've someone coming to see me in an hour. Are you going to the Barclays on Tuesday?"

"They have asked me, but I haven't accepted, yet."

"I thought you could pick me up, if you're going?"

"Very well, if you need a lift," Edward said politely.

Janet felt a sudden resentment towards this woman, but it was no business of hers where Edward Knowles went, or with whom. Why should she resent the fact that he was going to escort Claire Randall on a purely social visit? Her thoughts were interrupted by the entrance of Reggie into the room. Edward rose to his feet, telling his half-brother who the people in the room were. He brought him over to sit near Janet, who was surprised and pleased to see how well he was looking. The change was truly astonishing, when she remembered the bewildered, acutely distressed boy who had been admitted to Ellswick two years earlier.

Janet was soon deep in conversation with him, giving him all the current news about his friends in the Home. He, in his turn, had plenty to talk about and Edward and Claire were left to their own small-talk. Isobel had left the room to go into the kitchen. She liked to supervise the cooking herself. She was a Cordon Bleu cook and her husband's associates knew what to expect when Isobel entertained. As Janet talked to Reggie, she heard Edward laughing with Claire. He evidently knew her well and although she wore a wedding ring, she didn't give the impression that she had a husband. Another War widow, perhaps? Janet speculated.

"I must be going now, darling," Janet heard her telling Edward. "My friend is coming over at eight. I'll see you on Tuesday evening, then. I look forward to it." Giving him a brilliant smile and perfunctorily taking her leave of Reggie and Janet, she hurried out to inform Isobel that she was leaving.

"Well, what have you two been chatting about?" asked Edward, as the door closed behind her.

"Mostly about the Home, and Reggie's been telling me all about his progress."

"Alright, brother," Edward said. "It's my turn, now. Have you been to any good fairs lately?"

He was trying to be kind, Janet realised but somehow, after the departure of the glamorous Claire, she felt awkward and gauche. Even her voice sounded stilted, she knew, as she answered him. What could she possible say that would interest a man like Edward Knowles she wondered? The more she tried to speak and act naturally, the more she seemed to dry up, and she prayed for Isobel to come to tell them that dinner was ready. She knew what was causing this lack of confidence. After meeting Claire Randall, she had seen how naïve she had been to think that Edward was interested in her at all. Of course, he had only asked her here in return for helping his half-brother – nothing more. And Isobel had probably suggested it!

Edward's father still hadn't returned when, the superb meal finished and the evening only half over, he suggested that he drive her back to the Home. She wasn't too surprised. She hadn't exactly scintillated, either before or after dinner. He had obviously had enough of her company.

"Mustn't have any loose talk about my bringing the staff home at all hours, must we?" he joked, as Millie brought her coat.

In the car, she couldn't think of a single thing to say and he asked, "A penny for them?"

"I'm sorry, I'm afraid I haven't been very good company tonight."

"I'm not complaining," he said, "and I'd like to see you again before I go back to the Regiment."

"Oh? I thought you had better things to do." The words were out before she could stop them.

"Mm… So you think that, do you? Well, Janet Crossley, we'll just have to see, won't we?"

After this cryptic remark, silence reigned once more inside the car. All he said, when he dropped her off at the Home, was "Perhaps you'll come again to Leyland, and meet Dad. I'm sorry he couldn't make it tonight."

Undressing slowly in her bedroom, her mind going over all that had been said during the evening, she reflected that it was her own fault that it had ended so badly. Picking up her hairbrush, she sat brushing her hair with long, aggressive strokes, knowing the exact moment when things had started to go wrong for her. It had been when Claire Randall had called Edward 'darling' in the familiar way. But why should that have bothered her? Edward didn't mean anything to Janet – he was a very presentable man, yes – but he had merely asked her to dinner because she had been kind to Reggie. And yet, it had ruined the evening for her.

If the other woman had not been there, speaking to Edward in that intimate way, she knew she could have acted quite naturally. But she had been comparing herself with Claire, knowing that she herself could never appear as smart and assured. Putting down the brush, she turned out the lamp and got into bed, closing her eyes, but sleep would not come. She found her mind going over the visit, once again. She imagined herself acting quite differently – sitting, poised and sophisticated beside Edward, holding him enthralled with witty, brittle chat, but she knew it was no use. She could never be like that. In the morning, heavy-eyed, Janet had to dress quickly to make up for having overslept.

"My goodness! Didn't you have a good time last night, then?" asked Dorothy, when they met in the corridor, "or did you come in very late?"

"No, Dorothy, I didn't, and I'm sure you've got more to do than stand here, talking to me," Janet answered, curtly.

"Oh, so that's the way it is, then!" Dorothy's eyebrows lifted in surprise, but she didn't comment further as she left Janet musing miserably on her own bad temper and manners.

What is the matter with me? She asked herself. Here she was, snapping at Dorothy when she was only showing interest. She must watch herself. This was no way to behave towards people who had become good friends and colleagues. During the days that followed, though, there seemed to be something strange happening to her. She found she couldn't concentrate for long on her lists without her mind wandering back to that evening at The Willows. She caught herself, very often, just sitting in her office, daydreaming. An image of Edward would come into her mind and she would experience a sudden contracting of the heart every time it happened. An intense longing to be near him accompanied the image – rapturous yet bittersweet, because she didn't for a moment believe he would want to get in touch with her again. That parting remark about 'coming again to Leyland and meeting Dad', had been purely politeness in an embarrassing situation. Why should he want to see her again? He was due back with his Regiment very soon. Every time she thought about that departure, an aching despair enveloped her. She tried telling herself that she was behaving in a completely irrational way and that Edward meant absolutely nothing to her. How could he? She hardly knew him.

But the daydreaming continued, and she wasn't sleeping well, either. She was going through every day like a sleepwalker and she was forced, finally, to analyse her feelings because her efficiency in her job was being undermined. In this short time, could she possibly have fallen in love with Edward Knowles? Now she had faced it, and asked herself the question, she acknowledged that she must be! The realisation took her breath away and her heart started thumping wildly. But if this was what it was like to be in love, it wasn't at all the way she felt about Harry. As for Peter, she admitted it to herself now – she had never loved him at all, if this was any criterion.

When she had considered carefully, it came to her that the kind of love she'd had for Harry had been almost maternal. She had wanted so much to be his wife so that she could care for him, look after him, protect him, rather like a mother. She would have been his wife in every way, of course, and she wanted children, but there hadn't been, on her part, any real wanting in a physical way. Harry hadn't made any sexual demands on her, either, she now realised. They had both been rather like two grown-up children. Their lives had been emotionally linked together for a long time and they had tried to carry on their childhood affection for each other into adulthood with disastrous results.

What of her feelings, then, for poor Peter? When she thought about that relationship now, she knew she had never felt anything warmer than friendship for him – at the most, affection. Even when she remembered that last golden day before he had been killed, she couldn't recall anything more than comfortable happiness. There had been no <u>desire</u> on her part for Peter, either. She would have been very wrong in marrying either of them!

Now she knew what it felt like to be really in love, any other feelings she had had paled into insignificance beside this rapturous stirring and awakening that was going on in her body. But it seemed impossible that she had fallen in love so suddenly. It was one of those things that you only read about in books. She didn't even know Edward Knowles at all, really. She had met him three times, and yet, ever since that first meeting in the post office in Preston, when she had first gazed into his eyes, there had been some kind of rapport between them. It had intensified with each meeting, short as they had been, until, after the dinner party at The Willows, her emotions had been in chaos. Now she felt as if she were on a cliff edge, about to go over any minute. Every time she thought about Edward, she experienced again that thrilling sensation in the pit of her stomach. When anyone came to call at the Home, her heart started pounding wildly, in case it should be him.

What was the use, anyway, she thought, despairingly. She could never compete with a woman like Claire Randall. She must try not to hope. It was foolish to think that he was really interested in her at all. Her visit to The Willows had been a purely social one and there was no reason why he should ask her out again. Both her previous attempts at making a life for herself in marriage had ended in misfortune, anyway. There was no reason to think that any future effort might be better. There appeared to be some kind of a jinx on her which was preventing her from finding happiness with a man. Perhaps she was meant to live out her life here, in this place, finally ending up a lonely spinster, like Maud. Sighing at her foolish imaginings, she pressed on with her work, trying to push Captain Edward Knowles to the back of her mind, but not succeeding. Her mind insisted on bringing her no respite from wild, romantic daydreams.

Alfred Simpkins had just parked his car at the end of Southgate Drive before walking up to Norman's gate and going through. He intended discussing his idea with Norman and he didn't think that Norman would be too enthusiastic. He must broach the subject carefully. When he was settled in the tasteful sitting-room with his drink, Alfred opened the conversation by asking, "Have you seen anything of your new neighbours, then?"

"No," Norman said, "but he's definitely a detective. Mrs. Bell, next door, was talking to his wife yesterday and she says he's with the Central branch – the station on Talbot Road."

"Look, Norman," Alfred began, "I've been giving it some very serious thought and you know, love, we never had to worry like this when Edna was alive. No one suspects a married man and it protected both of us. As two single men, meeting as we do, we're much more likely to be under suspicion."

"You're not suggesting one of us should get married, are you?" Norman protested. "I couldn't do it."

"No, of course you couldn't, but there's nothing to stop me from taking another wife, is there – purely for safety's sake, I mean."

""But, Alfred, who would you want for a wife, anyway?" Norman asked, visualising the thick-set, middle-aged matrons who formed the bulk of Alfred's customers. "You haven't met anyone who would fill the bill, have you?"

"There is someone, one of my customers, who reminds me very much of Edna. She's a young widow and she has a family to bring up. You know I've always wanted someone to take over the shop when I retire. She's expecting another child and if it's a boy, I'd have the son who would carry on after me. It wouldn't make the slightest difference to us, Norman. You know perfectly well that a woman could never come between us, don't you? It never made any difference when Edna was alive, did it?"

"No, I suppose not, but I don't like the idea of you taking on a family."

"Don't you see, love, that it would be the perfect cover for us if I had a wife and a family? I'm only thinking about protecting you, you know. I'd be able to come and go here quite openly, without tearing our nerves to shreds every time, if I was married again. We'd both be absolutely in the clear."

"Well, I'm not happy about it…."

"What else can we do?" Alfred asked. "Have you any ideas, then?"

"No," Norman admitted reluctantly, re-filling Alfred's glass, "and I've been very jumpy since you came last. I suppose we'll have to do something. My nerves are in a shocking state at the moment."

"Well, then, think about what I've said and see if you don't find it's the solution to our problem."

Later, as Alfred took his leave of Norman and clicked shut the gate, he turned, ready to walk back the way he had come, to the end of the street where he had left the car. As he glanced in the direction of the vehicle, his heart gave an uncontrollable leap. A policeman was standing by the car – a uniformed man, so he couldn't be Norman's new neighbour. He was obviously waiting for the car's owner. Abruptly turning round, Alfred walked swiftly up the street in the opposite direction until he reached a corner house, where he dodged round the side of the building, out of sight. The house was bounded by a low wall, supporting a privet hedge and he was gasping as he slowed and stood leaning against the wall.

Recovering his breath a little, he edged slowly to the front corner of the garden, peeping round into the street to where the car stood. The constable was still there! What was he to do? There was no back entrance to Norman's house. The kitchen entrance was at the side and reached by the front gate so he couldn't retreat there. In any event, he didn't want to involve Norman if he could help it. Should he then, leave the car where it was and walk up to the main road for the tram? What was the use, though – the police could find out who owned the car by the registration number. Alfred started trembling violently as the realisation hit him that he had no choice but to walk to the car and claim it as his own. Any other course would only incur more suspicion. Who had seen him, then, going into Norman's house, and presumably, informed a constable?

Suddenly, Alfred's common sense asserted itself. His meetings with Norman had been quite private and unobserved, so what evidence had anyone to accuse either of them with? He must calm himself and walk down the street in an unconcerned manner to claim the car. His legs felt wobbly and every step was a tremendous effort but, slowly, Alfred came near to the constable. As he got closer, he saw that the policeman was quite young. He approached cautiously, as the uniformed man addressed him.

"Is this your car, sir?"

"Er, yes, officer," mumbled Alfred, not looking the man in the eye.

"Well, sir, we've had a complaint from number forty-eight here," he indicated the house directly behind the car, "that you are in the habit of leaving your vehicle in front of their window for long periods. It obstructs their view, they say, and they have asked us to request you to leave it elsewhere. Perhaps in front of the house you are visiting, sir? That would seem to be the solution to the problem, I suggest."

"Oh, certainly, officer," Alfred gasped, relief flooding him in a great wave. It wasn't anything to do with Norman, after all! He almost collapsed onto the pavement as the policeman gave him a polite 'good afternoon, sir', and went on his way. His hands were shaking so much that he couldn't at first get the key into the car door but eventually he managed it and stumbled inside. Starting up the engine, he wondered whether his heart would stand many more shocks like this. If they were to avoid other incidents of this sort, he would have to act soon. He could no longer afford to delay, with the threat of ten years in prison looming over them both.

A few days after his visit to Norman, he called at Fore Street, bearing a bunch of flowers for Alice, who exclaimed with delight as she accepted them. The children were playing in the garden so they were free to talk without interruption.

"How thoughtful you are, Alfred," she said, indicating that he should sit in the best armchair.

Alice had been very busy with the carpet-sweeper, dusters and mops in case he should call, as he had promised. The house was looking cleaner and tidier that it had for some time and she quickly offered him a biscuit and a cup of tea as he sat down.

"Thank you, Alice, I'd appreciate that. And how are you keeping, my dear? Are you managing alright?"

"Not too badly, Alfred. I sometimes wonder what's going to happen to us all in the future, but we're alright at the moment."

"Your courage amazes me, Alice, but I've always found that if one has faith in the Lord, He will provide."

"Oh, yes, I've always found that, too," Alice agreed, smiling at him as she turned to go into the kitchen to put the kettle on.

Getting up from the chair, he followed her through from the sitting-room. "You go and sit down," he insisted, "I'll do that."

"Thank you, Alfred. The biscuits are in that tin."

"It's no trouble at all for you, my dear."

As he poured out the tea for her, he asked, "Well, then, when would you like to go out in the car?"

"Any time you choose, Alfred, will be lovely."

After he had gone, Alice resumed her seat on the sofa, pouring herself the last cup of tea from the pot. It wasn't very hot but she couldn't be bothered to get up again and make some fresh. The girls could stay outside playing a bit longer before she brought them in. She wanted to think seriously about her relationship with Alfred Simpkins. Admittedly, he was a lot older than she was but when she was with him, she always felt so <u>protected</u>. He fussed over her and made her feel important. It was wonderful to be carried around like that, after all the struggling she had done, looking after other people over the past few years.

The odd thing was, though, that he hadn't made any attempt to touch her or kiss her, as most men would have done. All he seemed to want was to take care of her and the children. Of course, he had mentioned during the conversations that marriage shouldn't be anticipated. By that she had thought he meant that unmarried people shouldn't be intimate. So perhaps that was why he hadn't yet made any advances to her. On the other hand, he had said that he was lonely and that he would like a wife and family in the house.

He would be well able to support them all, too, even when the baby came and there were three children to feed and clothe. Harry's capital was decreasing all the time – it was surprising how quickly the money went. They all needed new clothes and every week she had to take out enough for their food and all the other household items they needed. The money in the bank had shrunk at an alarming rate and there was nothing being put back to replace it.

She had had help from her own family and Harry's, of course, but she couldn't go on forever taking handouts, and her expenses would rise again when the new baby came. If she married Alfred she would be able to live in comfort and she wouldn't have to do anything but look after the children. Alfred had a woman who came in to do the cleaning and he did all his own cooking. His mother had taught him and he enjoyed trying new recipes, he had said. She herself hated cooking, so he wouldn't expect her to do much in the kitchen, either.

Alice had to admit that, in spite of all these considerations, she wasn't in love with Alfred. On the other hand, she liked him and respected him. What did love count for, anyway? It hadn't got her very far before, had it? She <u>had</u> loved Harry in the beginning and then look what had happened! She had soon gone in search of someone else. She thought of Jack Fenton and the coming baby.

No, she decided, it wasn't worth weighing love against all the material things that Alfred could give her. In fact, love was a luxury she just couldn't afford, any more!

Chapter Thirty-One

Four days after the disastrous dinner party, when Janet's spirits were very low, an envelope was delivered to the front door at Ellswick, addressed to Miss Janet Crossley. Her heart fluttering wildly, she slit open the envelope and lifted out the slim, folded sheet. I'd like to apologise for the other evening. I think we may have misunderstood each other. May I call for you tomorrow evening at eight o'clock. It was signed 'Edward'.

When she had read it, her spirits rose from complete zero to somewhere up in the clouds. It was miraculous! He wanted to see her again - and apologise! The thought of Captain Edward Knowles apologising to anyone seemed ludicrous. She felt as if sunlight was flooding through her whole body and her mind took off on its own crazy flight of fantasy about the meeting. After a few moments of re-reading the note, though, she tried to bring herself down to earth again. If he had to return to his Regiment soon, it was going to be a bitter-sweet sort of a meeting, knowing that he would be gone in a short time. But even this didn't diminish the pleasure that every thought about the rendezvous brought her.

She was ready the following evening, dressed in her favourite jade green silk suit – the same colour as her eyes – which complemented her shining auburn hair so well. She hadn't told anyone of her appointment with Edward. She'd had enough of their remarks the last time she had gone out to dinner with him at The Willows. This time she had kept it to herself. At five minutes to eight, she waited in her small office, in a flutter of anticipation. When the summons from the lobby didn't come, she told herself that she was too early, anyway. He had said eight o'clock and it was only seven fifty-five. Getting out her little handbag mirror, she checked that her hair was still tidy and that the combs which held it up were firmly anchored. Green eyes, lively and excited, stared back at her, the pink, lightly-freckled skin of her cheeks suffused by a rosy glow of elation and anticipation.

By eight-fifteen, she was beginning to panic. Was he, after all, not going to be able to come? The thought was unbearable, after the anticipation of the last twenty-four hours. Surely he would have sent another note for her, if he couldn't keep the appointment? Then, just as overwhelming disappointment was beginning to take hold of her, the duty nurses on the front desk arrived with the information that Captain Knowles was waiting for her in the lobby.

Instantly, her heart started pounding against her ribs and if she had had any doubts at all about her feelings before, she had none now. She flew to the door and out into the lobby. Something must have delayed him, that was plain. As she walked past the desk, Nurse Gordon caught her eye, her eyebrows lifting as she took in Janet's clothes.

"Have a nice evening," she said, as Edward, taking Janet's arm, led her through the entrance and out to his waiting car.

"I'm sorry I'm a bit late," he said, "but Dad was out and Reggie needed a lift from the village. I didn't realise I would have to wait for him."

"That's alright. I can spare a quarter of an hour for Reggie," she said, smiling.

"Ah, but can I spare a quarter of an hour of your company?" He opened the door and handed her in.

There seemed to be no answer to this cryptic remark and for a while they drove on in silence through the dusky lanes. Occasionally, as they passed through the flat countryside, a rabbit or other small wild creature scurried across the curving road in front of the car, unaware of death passing by on swift-turning wheels.

Although they hadn't spoken again, there was no embarrassment now in the mutual silence. Sitting beside him, Janet watched the long, lean hands on the wheel, noting the well-scrubbed nails, the flexible wrist with its gold wristwatch, the whole giving an impression of strength. For some reason, the hands did strange things to her emotions and she dare not shift her gaze to his face.

"Will you accept my choice of restaurant for dinner?" he asked her, breaking into her reverie. "I thought we'd be alone tonight, then we can talk."

"Of course. I don't mind where we go." She nearly added 'as long as I'm with you', but stopped herself in time.

"That's refreshing. We'll go to the White Hart at Chorley. They do a good steak there, and it's quiet. Do you fancy that kind of food?"

"Oh, yes, I'd love it. We don't get much in the way of steaks at Ellswick. It's more like rissoles, I'm afraid," she said, laughing.

"Good! He seemed pleased that she had accepted his suggestion so readily. "Now I must apologise for the way I left you after our last meeting. I went off like that because you gave me the impression you didn't want my company. Was I right?"

"Oh, no! I didn't want you to leave like that," Janet said, after a long moment, "but I thought you found <u>my</u> company boring. I know I wasn't very bright at your step-mother's. That's why you brought me home early, isn't it!"

"What on earth made you think that? You were the only bright spot in the whole of the evening for me."

"Well," Janet chose her words carefully after this astonishing statement, "I think it was your friend Claire Randall who spoilt the evening for me. She's so sophisticated and smart – I just didn't feel I had anything in common with her and she seemed to know you so well. I thought she was, perhaps, more than a friend…."

"Claire Randall! Good God! Whatever made you think I'm interested in Claire Randall!"

"She did call you darling, and you did make an arrangement to take her out that week."

He laughed then, a genuinely amused laugh. "My dear, funny girl. Claire calls everyone darling and I only offered to run her over to the Barclays as I had to go there myself. She dropped me the moment we arrived, much to my relief, and I didn't see her again that evening. I haven't seen her since, for that matter. In any event, what interest would I have in a woman like Claire Randall? I left The Willows early that evening so that we could have a little time to ourselves before I took you back to the Home. Didn't you realise that?"

"Oh, no! I thought you'd had enough of my company and I didn't blame you."

Turning towards her, his hands gripping the wheel, he surveyed her upturned face, pale in the moonlight which flooded the interior of the car. He didn't speak, but slowly brought the machine to a halt by the roadside beneath an overhang of trees from a small wood. Still without speaking, he turned to her, his eyes meeting hers, appraising and gauging before his hand reached for hers. The contact was like an electric current, sending little waves of desire flowing through her. It was quite enough just to sit there, her hand in his, believing that he, too, was feeling this rapture.

"I'm in love with you, Janet," he said softly, "and I've got to tell you now, before I go back. I was mistaken the other evening. I thought then that you were not interested in me, that you considered the visit as a purely social one. Now I think you feel the same as I do. I'm used to making quick decisions and I want you to marry me. You'll have to leave everyone – everything – though. You know we've been posted to Gibraltar and that we're leaving before Christmas?"

The question stunned her, taking her breath completely, but as she gasped, she already knew what her answer would be. It didn't seem to matter whether he was going to Gibraltar or Timbuctoo, she wanted to be with him. It was as simple as that.

"Edward," she said, when she had got back her breath, "I've been a complete fool. I've been attracted to you from the moment I saw you in the post office that day. I didn't realise it, though, until after the other evening. I've been miserable wondering whether I would see you again, knowing you were leaving soon.

Things have happened in the past which have affected me deeply. I'll tell you about them sometime, but they don't seem to matter at all now."

"You mean – you'll come with me?" His eyes searched her face, his hand firmly clasping her own.

"Of course," she said simply.

Releasing her hand, he put his arm around her waist, drawing her to him. "Darling," he whispered, "I hope you won't regret it. I shall try to make sure you don't."

His lips on hers aroused feelings she had never dreamed of. He seemed to be releasing from somewhere deep inside her all those long-suppressed urges that, up till now, she hadn't acknowledged she possessed. Putting her arms around his neck, her mouth opened to his and a melting of softness, sweet and insistent, spread over her limbs as, for the first time, she understood what it felt like to really want a man.

"Edward, Oh, Edward," she gasped, intoxicated by this wonderful new freedom from restraint.

"I know, darling, I feel the same. I want you too, but we're going to wait until we're married. Don't you agree that we shouldn't anticipate? It won't be long – I'll get a special licence."

How well he knew her already, Janet thought, trying to recover her breath. "Oh, yes, Edward I do agree, but the way I feel right now, I could forget all my principles. I've never felt like this before," she confessed, pliant and eager in his arms, wondering at the pure bliss of this blossoming of passion.

"We're going to be patient, my darling," he said, kissing her lightly now, before releasing her and turning back to the wheel. "But if we stay here a moment longer, I shalln't be able to guarantee it. Come on, we'll see if they've anything to give us at the White Hart. D'you feel you could eat, now?"

"I'm so happy, I don't care what we do," she said.

For the rest of the evening, everything seemed to go by in a blur of happiness – the drive, the meal, the holding hands and the final lingering parting at the Home very late in the evening. Heaven must be like this, she thought, as she made her way, starry-eyed, upstairs, through the quiet corridors and into her dark bedroom, to try to compose herself for sleep.

Mary Boothroyd had arrived in good time at Fore Street for the birth of Alice's third baby – a healthy boy. Sitting on the train during the journey, she had been wondering, with some anxiety, whether her daughter would be as depressed after this delivery. Alice, though, was up and on her feet very quickly. It almost seemed to Mary as if Alice had determined to get herself back to normal again as soon as possible, which was a great relief to her.

Alice had stubbornly refused to travel over to Bradfield to have the baby there, telling her mother that she couldn't make the journey with the children. Mary suspected that Alice had other reasons for staying in Lytham, which hadn't yet become apparent. She was overjoyed that she now had a grandson as well as two granddaughters. It looked as if the boy was going to be dark, like Alice, whereas both the girls were fair. Alice intended calling her son John, which pleased Mary because it was her own father's Christian name. She automatically assumed that Alice was calling the child after his grandad.

"He'll be ever so pleased when I get back and tell him you're calling John after him," she told Alice. "It will give him something to look forward to – a grandson being christened after him."

Of course, her daughter didn't disillusion her. It would never enter any of their heads, she thought, that John might be the other form of the name Jack. Alfred's approval, too, had been swift, and he had seemed delighted with the news. "Why, Alice, that's a very good biblical name," he had said. Since the birth, his visits to the house had been more frequent and Alice confided in her mother that she was sure he meant to propose.

"But Alice, he's nearly old enough to be your father."

"Well, what if he is a bit older than me? He looks after me and he's very kind to the girls, and he loves the baby – you can see that!"

"Yes, but Alice, do you love him?"

"Love? No, I suppose not, if you mean like Harry. But Mum, that doesn't last. I've found that out. And I'm quite fond of Alfred. I know he likes taking me out in his car and seeing that I'm comfortable – and he looks after the children, as well. They need a father and Alfred can give them things a young man can't. He's got a lovely house next to the shop and he's never had any children of his own. Oh, Mum, I do think he would be a good father to them."

"Perhaps he would, Alice, but you must know that there's more to marriage than money and a nice house. Suppose you don't get on with him, well, in bed. Has he made any advances to you yet in that way?"

"No, Mum, he hasn't, he's in the Church. He doesn't believe in it until you're married. I don't think he's bothered about it, anyway."

"Don't be silly, Alice! Every man's bothered about it! Are you sure he's, well, *normal* in that way?"

"I expect so, Mum, why shouldn't he be? Anyway, we get on well together, that's what matters. As I'm placed, with three children, I'll just have to take a chance on it, won't I?"

Mary sighed. This was what Alice had been waiting for, why she had recovered so swiftly after her delivery. It wasn't what she had hoped to hear, but then, as Alice had pointed out, she couldn't really afford to be choosey, situated as she was. A young man wouldn't want to take on Alice's ready-made family, and her bit of capital wouldn't last much longer.

"I just don't know what your dad will say about all this. He said at the funeral what a funny little man Alfred was. He thought he was a bit of a pansy. Are you sure he's got intentions?"

"Oh, yes, I think he's only waiting a decent time after Harry and the baby and everything. He likes things to be done in a Christian way. That's what he's always saying."

"Does Ellen know about this, then?"

"Yes, Mum, I think so. She's met Alfred a few times and I know she thinks he would make a good father for the children. Ellen and Maud go to the church as well, you know."

"It isn't always churchgoers who make the best husbands." Mary spoke sharply to her daughter. "Your father's never been in a church except for christenings and weddings, and he's been the best husband and father anybody could have."

"I know that, Mum, but you asked me about Ellen and I know that's why she likes Alfred. She thinks he's religious, like them, and she knows he can support me and the children. She has helped me with money for the children – like you, Mum – but neither of you can go on doing it forever."

"I've only got your best interests at heart, Alice. A mother wants to see her daughter happy. D'you think you could be happy with Alfred?"

"I think so, Mum, and it's my best chance. I shalln't be able to go on renting this house for much longer and there's plenty of room for us all at the shop. There are two spare bedrooms as well as the box room."

"Well, if you've decided on it, there's nothing else I can say, I suppose. I'll have to break it gently to your dad and what he will say, I just don't know. When do you think he'll ask you to marry him?"

"Oh, I should think, quite soon. Before Christmas, I should think."

"Well, you seem to have got it all worked out, love. I only hope that things work out well for you this time. You had a bad beginning to your married life, but perhaps this time things will work out better. After all, it's your life and you've got to make the decisions, not me."

"Don't worry, Mum, it will be alright, I'm sure of it," Alice said, picking up the baby ready to give him his bottle.

"He isn't like Harry, is he?" Mary commented. "He's much darker, like you, but his eyes are brown. I wonder who he gets those from? Come to think of it, your grandad has brown eyes – that probably explains it."

"Yes," Alice agreed, changing the subject quickly. "As soon as I'm feeling up to it, I'm going to buy a new dress with that money you gave me. I've nothing to wear after those maternity smocks. Are you going to stay and come with me to the shops?"

"I suppose your dad could manage for another day or two, if you want me to stay. You could do with the help for a bit longer. I'll write and tell him I'm not coming back until after the weekend. I don't like leaving him on his own, but he'll just have to manage. I don't want to upset him, but with a new baby to look after, you need me most."

Alfred, in fact, proposed to Alice two weeks later. She knew it was a special visit when he arrived with half-a-dozen long-stemmed roses which were, of course, now out of season. They had been grown under glass on the Moss and she knew they were expensive.

"You remind me of one of these, Alice," he told her, as she took the exquisite blooms from him. Blushing almost the same colour as the flowers, Alice gave him an affectionate peck on the cheek. He drew back quickly, ostensibly to remove his coat.

"They're lovely, Alfred. We'll have a little glass of sherry. I've got some in for Christmas." Alfred didn't approve of spirits but she knew that this would be acceptable to him.

Over the sherry, they settled in front of the fire. The girls were already in bed, while baby John slumbered in his pram. She would take him up to bed with her later on. She kept him by her own bedside yet, in the wooden cot Harry had made for Jenny.

"I'm glad to see you looking well, Alice. Blooming like those roses, like I said."

"Yes, I'm feeling fine now, and little Johnny's coming on a treat. He's taking all his food and putting on weight."

"He's a grand little chap. You have three beautiful children, Alice but it's a big responsibility for you bringing them all up, unless you're well provided for. It's a tragedy that your husband was taken when he was, but we mustn't question the ways of the Lord. Have you thought about the future at all, my dear?"

"I've been very worried about that, Alfred. I've been wondering what's going to happen to us when Harry's savings run out. I haven't spoken to anyone else, but you're a very good friend and I know you understand."

"Indeed I do, Alice, and I would like to be allowed to look after you and your family. Would you consider marriage, my dear? I know there is a difference in our ages, but I don't think that matters too much, do you? You don't need to give me your answer right away, but I'd like you to think it over."

"Oh, Alfred, I don't need to think about it, I'd be happy to be your wife," cried Alice, taking hold of his hand and pressing it gently.

"You think you could be happy with me, then, Alice?" He released her hand and took another sip at his sherry.

"I'm very fond of you, Alfred and the girls like you. Jenny's still missing her daddy, although Susan's beginning to forget. I'm sure we could all get along together very well. Pass your glass, Alfred, and I'll pour us another sherry. Let's drink to the future," she suggested, when they were refilled.

"Of course, my dear." Alfred raised his glass, delicately clinking it against hers. "And I want you to have a good engagement ring."

"Oh, you're too good to me, Alfred." Alice's eyes were wide and pleased.

"We'll go into Garrard's in Blackpool next week and you can choose one."

"Garrard's" Alice had occasionally peered into those glittering windows, gazing in awe at the rows of winking diamonds. She had never dreamed, though, that she would ever set foot inside.

"Nothing's too good for you, Alice, and when you're Mrs. Simpkins, you're going to have some of those nice things you've always wanted."

"You are kind, Alfred, I've always said so, and I think we're going to be very happy," she said, sipping her sherry and smiling at him over the rim of her glass. "Shall I fill you up again?"

"Why not?" Alfred replied, holding it up for her. "It isn't every day one gets engaged, is it?"

Chapter Thirty-Two

Janet, with Edward, travelled over to Blackpool almost at once, to tell her family the news. She had hinted in a letter that she had met an Army officer who had asked her to meet his own family. Apart from that, they knew nothing about the current situation between them. They had no inkling that she loved him or that he had asked her to be his wife.

When she introduced Edward to Florrie and then to her father as her fiancée, she smiled at the astonishment on their faces.

"Yes, it is very sudden, isn't it? You see, Edward's Regiment is going out to Gibraltar before Christmas. Oh, don't look like that, Dad, it won't be for long, you know. It's only for two years, and I'll write very often, I promise."

"I can vouch for her ability as a letter writer," Edward said smiling. "I'm sorry we've had to break the news in this way but it had to be a quick decision. Janet wants to come with me as my wife, and I think I can make her happy."

Looking at the Captain, Robert could believe him. Janet hadn't had much luck with her love-life so far. He prayed that this time she would be luckier. This man, he could see, was a gentleman. It was apparent in his manner and in his bearing. He was used to commanding men, too, but the way he was looking at Janet, another side to Edward's character was revealed. It looked like a tender, gentler side, which she probably knew better than the other.

She was very much in love with him, Robert saw, studying her face as she talked, her eyes soft and limpid, continually straying back to her fiancée.

"Well, you've given us a big surprise," he said, "but I hope this time my lass will find some happiness. She deserves it, because she's always been a good lass to her family. What we'd have done without her, I don't know."

Blushing a little, Janet told her dad not to be silly, and Florrie, agog to know what the couple's wedding plans were, asked, "And when is the wedding to be then, dear?"

"We're having the ceremony at the Registry Office in Preston," Janet told them, "a week before we sail, and we want both of you to come over, of course. Isobel, Edward's step-mother, is giving us our wedding breakfast at her home in Leyland, then we're travelling down in the car to Torquay for a week at Edward's house there, before we sail."

"I've asked Dad if he will come over and pick you up in the car for the wedding," Edward told Robert. "Save you a bit of trouble coming by train, then Isobel will put you up for the night."

"That sounds grand," Robert said, "and are you carrying on working until then, lass?"

"Oh, yes, I feel I ought to, Dad, until they get someone in to take my place. It's only fair. I couldn't let them down after they have all been so good to me, and Edward agrees."

"I have an interest, as well, in the welfare of Ellswick, and I feel that I can't very well run off with Janet without giving them due notice," Edward said.

"I'm so happy for you, dear," Florrie turned to Janet. "We shall both be looking forward to seeing you married, but if you can, you must come over to see us again before the wedding. It's such a shame that both Rose and Arthur are out – they've gone off on a Sunday school trip to Salmesbury Hall. Perhaps you could slip over next weekend, if you're not busy, and stay overnight?"

"Of course we will," Janet promised, "and then we can tell you all about the arrangements."

Janet did not go immediately to see Ann and her husband, at Bolton. She felt that it would be better, in the first instance, to write a letter to Ann to let her know she was to be married. Peter's death had been a severe shock for his friend, Donald. He and Peter had known each other for many years and Janet knew that he still wasn't over it completely. Her visits always reminded Donald of the happy days when they had all been friends, looking forward to the future. She didn't want to upset him, but, on the other hand, she wanted Ann to know that she had found someone she could love in a way she had never loved before.

She sent off a letter telling Ann that she was going to be married soon. 'You'll be very surprised when you receive this letter. You remember Edward Knowles, the Army officer I mentioned when I last saw you? We're going to be married very soon! I can't tell you how I feel about him. All I can say is that I've never felt like this about anyone and he's wonderful, Ann – a marvellous man, so masterful and yet so gentle. It has all been very sudden but I've never been so sure of anything in my life – just like you were about Donald. I understand now how you felt. The only thing is that we're leaving England at the end of the month for Gibraltar. Yes!

Edward's Regiment has been ordered there for two years. Perhaps we could manage to meet before we leave? How are you feeling, now that the baby is nearly due? I'm only sorry that we shall be gone before your baby is born, dear, if it comes to time, at the end of December. Write and let me know when we can all meet. Love, Janet.'

As she posted the letter, it struck her that Ann, now eight months pregnant, would have a two-year-old child when she returned home. Goodness, she thought, I might even have a child of my own by then!

During the period of waiting for her wedding day to arrive, Janet frequently visited The Willows, this time as Edward's fiancée. Claire Randall did not put in another appearance. Whether the news of Edward's engagement had put her off, Janet never discovered, but, to Janet's relief, she was not obliged to meet her again. She did meet Edward's father – for the first time, and got on well with him.

He told Edward, afterwards, "I always thought you had good taste, Ted."

"Glad you approve, Dad. I knew she was the girl for me the first time we met. Strange, isn't it? Since I've got to know her, I'm constantly telling myself how lucky I am to have found her."

"If I'm any judge, she's pure gold. She's quite different from some of these bored, languid young women I've met lately. Thank God you didn't choose one of those!"

"I think I've got a bit more sense than that, Dad. Now I've found Janet I shall try to make her happy."

"I'm only sorry your mother couldn't have seen your fiancée. She was just as good a judge of people as I am. You've got to be, in business, you know. And Janet has made a good start with Isobel. She isn't easy to please, but I can see she likes your fiancée! I think they could become good friends, given the chance."

"Yes, Dad, I know we shall be away for a while, but there will be plenty of time when we come home, especially if we make you both grandparents in the meantime!"

"It's about time you did, my boy. I was beginning to think you would finish up a crusty old bachelor. Now I can look forward to seeing my grandchildren growing up. Do you intend producing a large family, then?"

"I don't know yet, Dad. I haven't asked my bride-to-be, but I'm sure she has some ideas on the subject."

On the night before her wedding, Janet lay awake in her single bed at Ellswick, gazing at her wedding outfit hanging on the outside of the wardrobe door. Then she checked her new lacy lingerie, neatly folded on a chair beside her bed. She had set the alarm clock, which stood on the small chest of drawers, for seven o'clock. The ceremony wasn't until two o'clock at the Registrar's, but she wanted plenty of time to get ready. She didn't want to be in her usual rush on this day of her marriage to Edward. In the morning, when she first put on the clothes, she would still be Janet Crossley, but when she left the Registry Office, later in the day, she would be Mrs. Edward Knowles! She couldn't quite believe that this time she really was going to be married. It all seemed so unreal now that the time had actually arrived.

She had chosen a sea-green shade of soft wool crepe which exactly matched here eyes and which suited her so well. She would be able to wear the clothes afterwards in the chilly December weather, both in Devon and on the boat, before they arrived in Gibraltar. The dress had a coat to match of the same material, with velvet facings to the revers, and the high-crowned, broad-brimmed felt hat had a velvet ribbon around it in a deeper shade of green. It was now lying in its box, up on top of the wardrobe, waiting for her to wear it for the first time.

Across the room she could see her suitcase packed ready for the journey down to Torquay. This would be her last night at Ellswick – her last night in the place which had become her second home. She had tried to visualise her new home in Devon, but Edward had said very little about it, except that it was set back from the cliffs, high up, at Babbacombe. It would be completely different from Nelson Street, she imagined. Her mind went back to the time when she had been at home, waiting for Harry to come back from the War. Poor Harry! She had never loved Harry in this physical, demanding way. He had never kindled the passion that every contact with Edward's body brought her. The bliss of that intimacy swept over her again as she remembered Edward's last, exploratory kiss, as he had whispered, 'Tomorrow, my love, we won't be parting like this. You will be my wife.' Her body had cried out that she wanted him, this minute and that she couldn't wait much longer.

She didn't try to imagine their union. Her ignorance of lovemaking was complete but already she had recognised that once passion is awakened, there is little need for experience. Her body's demands had been natural and instinctive, she had found, as Edward had kissed her and held her.

Quite suddenly, a vision of poor, tragic Peter flashed into her mind. How could she ever have considered marrying him, she wondered. It seemed that there were many different kinds of love. This thing she felt for Edward was the sort that carried one along on a tide of passion. For the first time she began to understand the kind of feeling which must have existed between Harry and Alice. If it had been like this for them, nothing could have stopped them from falling into each other's arms, no matter what their other relationships might have been.

At that moment, Janet forgave Alice for taking Harry, and quite soon, sleep, deep and dreamless, overtook her.

The following morning flew by for Janet, in spite of her early rising, but by eleven-thirty, she was ready. Edward was to call for her to take her to Leyland. The two families were to meet at The Willows, Florrie and her father travelling with Mr. Knowles from Blackpool in his car. Isobel would have drinks and lunch ready for them before they all departed for Preston and the ceremony.

Surrounded by well-wishers, Janet sat in the visitors' waiting-room, nerves stretched, listening to the good-natured banter of the staff who were waiting for her fiancée to arrive.

"I should have snapped him up myself, that first time he came here," Dorothy laughed. "I missed my chance there, alright!"

The almoner, more serious, remembering Janet's previous disappointments, told Janet quietly, "This time, dear, you are not going to be let down. You nearly gave in your notice a couple of times, didn't you? If you hadn't stayed on with us, you know, you wouldn't have met Edward."

"Why, yes, of course!" Janet exclaimed. "I hadn't thought of it like that. If I'd left and gone home for good, things would have been very different. I wouldn't have met Edward again at the Fair. My goodness, it does make you think that these things are fated in some way, doesn't it?"

"Yes," Nurse Gordon reminded her, "and what about Harry Tomlinson being brought in here to the very place where you were working?"

"It's very strange how things work out, but I don't want to think about the past today. I'm being married in a couple of hours and Edward is the only one I shall be thinking about from now on. The past is dead and gone as far as I'm concerned."

"Oh, I'm sorry, dear. I didn't mean to upset you." Nurse Gordon's blunt manner was well-known to everyone and Janet knew she hadn't meant to offend.

"I'm not upset," Janet said, "the only thing I'm upset about is leaving you all. I've been very happy here, in spite of everything and you've all helped me when I've needed it, right from the first day I came here."

"Oh, stop! You'll have me crying in a minute," Dorothy said, jumping down from the table top where she had been perched and glancing out of the window. "I think your intended's car is at this minute coming through the gates. You'd better hurry to the lobby before he changes his mind."

Amidst laughter, the chattering group pushed Janet out into the corridor and through the door to the front lobby, where Molly set down her suitcase.

"Now – are you sure you've got everything?" she asked a flushed and suddenly nervous Janet.

"Yes, I think so." Janet picked up her kid gloves and handbag with trembling hands, watching, in fascination, the front doors. They suddenly opened wide and there he stood, handsome and immaculate, his eyes immediately finding hers and sending her an unspoken message of love. Breaking away from her friends, she ran to him, taking his outstretched hands in hers, while he bent to kiss her tenderly.

Molly, her eyes misty, came forward with the suitcase, closely followed by the others and one or two of the patients who had gathered to see what was going on. The formal leave-taking had long since been got over and this was a spontaneous send-off from her special friends and colleagues. They gathered round the couple, congratulating them and wishing them every happiness. Dorothy ran outside, to throw a horseshoe, fitted with satin ribbon, over the back bumper of the car.

"Am I allowed to carry my bride away now?" Edward asked, laughing as he picked up her suitcase. His hand in hers, he turned and led her through the entrance doors. The car was parked just outside, where he placed her in the front seat, putting the suitcase in the back, finally getting in himself behind the wheel.

The group around the entrance waved madly, calling out good wishes to the couple as the car pulled round the forecourt, making for the gates. Janet waved back to them until the car cleared the gates and moved out onto the Leyland Road.

"It's always rather sad saying goodbye," he said gently, as she sat silent beside him.

"Yes, Edward, I knew you would understand. I shall be alright in a moment. It's just that I'm so happy and yet I'm feeling sad at leaving them all. Oh, it's all so mixed up!"

"Don't worry, darling, you'll be feeling better when you see your family again. They should be at The Willows when we arrive. Are they thinking that I'm asking a lot of you taking you away from your family and all your friends?" We're going to a place you know nothing about, amongst strangers. Am I being selfish, Janet?" he asked her, serious now.

"No, of course you're not. I want to go wherever you go. It's just saying goodbye that's upsetting. I don't know why I'm crying when I'm so happy."

"Don't worry, darling, it's only natural that you should feel like that, but once the leave-taking is over, we have our whole lives to look forward to – together."

"Oh, Edward, I do love you."

"That's all I was waiting to hear," he said, putting his foot down on the accelerator and smiling at her, as the car shot forward in the direction of Leyland and The Willows.

Later, inside the Registry Office, the wedding party stood quiet and thoughtful while the bride and groom made their vows. When Edward finally placed the ring on Janet's finger and the Registrar pronounced the couple man and wife, Florrie dabbed at her eyes. Please God, she prayed, let Janet and Edward be as happy as Robert and I have been. She stepped forward as the Registrar asked her, as Janet's witness, to sign the book. Edward's father came forward to sign for his son, and Mr. and Mrs. Edward Knowles embraced as man and wife.

"Congratulations to you both," the Registrar, a dapper little man, said, shaking Edward's hand warmly. "And good sailing."

"Thank you. We appreciate your good wishes." Edward glanced at Janet's bemused face and gently squeezed her hand, which he had firmly in his.

"Congratulations, brother," Reggie said. "Do I get a kiss from the bride?"

"I might allow one." Edward relinquished hold of his wife, handing her over to his brother. Janet took hold of Reggie's arm and placed a sisterly kiss on his cheek. "You are the one who brought us together, you know," she reminded him. Beaming with pleasure, Reggie returned the kiss, telling her that she was the best thing that had ever happened to Edward. "It's about time he took a wife instead of living a selfish bachelor life," he said. Janet caught the underlying envy in Reggie's bantering remarks. She knew that he would dearly like to find someone to share his life with and she hoped that in the future he would so do.

"My turn now," Edward's father planted a firm kiss on her cheek as Reggie turned to speak to his step-brother. "Welcome to the family, Mrs. Knowles. I couldn't be more delighted about this, Janet. I know Edward loves you and he won't let you down. I'm so happy for you both."

Isobel, too, added her good wishes and it only remained for her father and Florrie to hug and kiss her to start the happy tears again.

"When you've all finished with my bride, I'm going to take her home," Edward announced. The party began to make its way from the room, happy and relaxed, earlier tensions dispelled, out to the waiting cars.

When the two families were seated at Isobel's elegantly laid dinner table, champagne toasts were raised to the bride and groom before the meal was served. Seated beside her husband, Janet confessed to him, "I feel a bit light-headed already but I don't really think it's the champagne."

"No," he agreed, "all this has knocked me a bit sideways, too."

"I've felt all day as if this isn't really happening."

"Don't worry, darling, we'll come down to earth again, once we're on our own." His hand found hers and its pressure was very reassuring. She had been much more keyed-up about the ceremony and its aftermath than she had realised. Once they were alone, though, they would both be able to relax and get back onto an intimate footing. That thought brought the blood racing through her veins and she turned her eyes to meet his, promising that she wouldn't disappoint him.

Isobel had excelled herself in the kitchen once again, providing a banquet fit for the most demanding gourmet. Millie, the housekeeper, had everything ready for serving the guests, and the meal was soon under way.

When they had eaten and were sitting around with their brandies, the two families began getting to know each other. Neither family had had the opportunity before and they soon found plenty to talk about. Reggie, sitting with the newly-weds, chatted and reminisced about past times with Edward, while Janet found herself wishing the hours away. Finally, Edward came to her rescue. "Don't forget, darling," he said clearly, "they are expecting us soon at the Midland. It won't take long to drive into Preston, but you have had a long day and we have the drive down to Torquay ahead of us tomorrow. I think we should say our goodbyes now."

"Of course, Edward," she said, turning to Isobel. "You've been wonderful, Isobel. You've given us a really superb meal and entertained us like Royalty. I can't thank you enough."

"There's no need to thank me, dear. You know I enjoy doing it, particularly when it's for my own family – you <u>are</u> my family now, Janet."

"I don't have to tell you how much I appreciate all you've done for us, Isobel," Edward said. "You've given us a wonderful send-off. Now then, Mrs. Knowles," he turned to Janet, "your turn, I think, to say goodbye while I go and see to stowing the bags in the car." He walked quickly away, but not before she had seen the emotion in his face. She must now try to control her own feelings, as he had done his. Suddenly she realised that two years was a long time. Two years away from her family! Throwing her arms around her father she hugged him while he planted a firm kiss on her cheek. His eyes, too, were misty as he released her, saying gruffly, "We're going to miss you, lass."

"It's not that long, really." She tried hard to sound cheerful, but she found herself swallowing hard. "Goodbye, Florrie, I'll write as soon as I get settled. I shall miss you all so much. You will send me all the news, won't you? And give my love to Arthur and Rose."

"Of course, dear, I've got your address so I'll get a letter off as soon as you've sailed."

"It will only be a small bungalow, you know – nothing luxurious – in the barracks, but I shalln't mind, if I'm with Edward."

"No, I can see you love him very much, dear. I hope you'll be very happy. You see – you've found the right man, at last, haven't you?"

"Yes, Florrie, you were right. Everything else that has happened has faded from my mind and now there's only Edward. I want to be with him for the rest of my life. You've been very good to me, Florrie – like a second mother."

"Oh, Janet, dear, I've been hoping you'd say that ever since Robert and I got married," she confessed. "It has made the day complete for me. It has been a wonderful one from start to finish. Goodbye, dear, and good luck."

"Are you ready, darling?" Edward had returned to the drawing room dressed in his great-coat and muffler.

"I've only got to put my coat on," she said, as Millie stepped forward to help her on with it.

The two families stood framed in the open doorway, the light behind them streaming out onto the driveway, illuminating the shrubbery and lawns. As the car came round to the front of the house, they all moved forward as Janet got into the front seat beside Edward. The vehicle waited for a moment while Janet settled herself then moved down to the gate. With both families waving and calling out good wishes, they turned in the direction of the Preston Road. Edward reached for Janet's hand. He knew that the leave-taking had drained her emotionally and that she needed a little time to get over its effects before he made demands on her of any kind. Janet, sitting silently beside him, had just wiped away the last tear. The pressure of his hand on hers was comforting and he seemed to understand that she didn't want to talk. They drove steadily on towards Preston in comfortable silence, each knowing that this was a beginning and that, already, they were getting to know each other.

Soon, they were entering the outskirts of the town, and, glancing at her, he asked softly, "alright now, darling?"

"Yes, Edward, I'm fine now."

"Good. We'll be at the Midland in five minutes, then we can relax."

The Midland, where they were to spend their wedding night! Her spirits lightened magically and when Edward handed her out of the car at the portico of the hotel, her eyes were bright and her colour high as they checked in at the desk and Edward received a key to their suite. Janet glanced around at the quiet opulence of the foyer. Everything here spoke of comfort and discretion. A boy came immediately to take up their bags as Edward suggested that they should both go into the lounge bar for a nightcap before they retired to bed. As they sat, sipping their drinks at an elegant little table, the dramatic events of the day slipped away from them.

"Happy now, darling?" he asked her, as one or two people came into the bar, seating themselves nearby. "It's a bit too public in here. I think we'll finish our drinks and go inspect our room – see what they have given us. I didn't ask for the honeymoon suite. I thought that might embarrass you too much, but I made it clear that we would like something special."

"I should think they're all special in this place, Edward," she pointed out as they made their way to the lift. "It must have cost the earth, booking in here."

"Ah, I can see I've married a prudent woman," he laughed, catching her to him as they entered the empty golden cage.

"You're laughing at me again!" She found her face was burning, partly, she thought, due to the effects of the brandy.

"Just admiring your good qualities, but don't speak for a moment – I'm going to kiss you." The lift began its silent ascent and when the third floor was reached, they made no attempt, for some minutes, to leave its gilded interior.

Eventually, the lift being summoned from below, they stepped out into the quiet luxury of a soft-carpeted passageway which wound round to their suite. Edward inserted the key in the lock and pushed open the door. At the touch of a switch, the bedroom was brought to sparkling life by a crystal chandelier. It revealed the spaciousness and elegance of the room, from satiny covers and drapes to the deep pile of rose-coloured carpet. One side of the room was given over to a long, fitted dressing table and stool, which ran almost its full length, over which ran an ornamental mirror. Rose pink shades masked two electric lamps placed at either end of the glass and these were echoed on each of the bedside cabinets, one of which held a house telephone.

"Oh, it's wonderful," gasped Janet. "I've never seen anything like it. It's just like a film set!"

"It's not exactly to my taste but then I'm old-fashioned, as you know. As long as you like it, darling."

"Oh, I do, Edward. I never dreamed I'd sleep under silk sheets."

"You've had quite a day, Mrs. Knowles," he said, drawing her over to the long dressing stool. Seating himself, he placed her on his knee. She put her arms around his neck, dropping her head onto his shoulder.

"I do feel a bit overcome by it all," she admitted, "and I'm so glad we're alone now – just the two of us."

"So am I, darling. I know all that has to be gone through, but this is the moment we start to forget everyone but ourselves. Now, I suggest you go and undress in the bathroom, through there." He indicated the door which she had mistaken for another cupboard. I'll wait for you in here. I'm going to get into bed. Don't keep me waiting too long, though!"

He watched as she gathered up a pale satin garment before disappearing through the door he had indicated. It was some moments later when she came back into the bedroom, momentarily standing in the frame made by the open door. Her long, lustrous hair gleamed in the glow from the lamp over the dressing table and the curves of her body were evident beneath the loose, creamy gown.

His voice came hoarsely, as he breathed, "Come over here to me, darling – now!"

Her feet took her swiftly over the thick carpet and as she stepped between the silky sheets at the other side of the bed, he reached for her, sliding the nightgown from her shoulders. With a little shock she discovered that he was quite naked. She held him in her arms as he nuzzled into her soft flesh, brushing her hair with eager lips.

"Oh, Edward," she cried, in rapture as his hands began their gentle exploration of her willing body. She found herself caressing him in return. She had never touched a man's naked body before, but now it seemed the most natural thing in the world as she took him into her soft, plump hands. She heard him saying, "I don't want to hurt you, my love – you must tell me…."

All her long-suppressed desire seemed to overflow in one great surge of passion as, at last, she took him into her body with an urgency which shook her by its strength. There was little pain, she was so ready for him. At last she knew the pleasure of having him hard inside her, coupled with the love she felt for this wonderful man – her husband.

As he moved within her, it was as if she was being carried up on a swelling wave which eventually expended itself on a sun-filled shore. Opening her eyes, she looked straight into his. "My own wonderful husband," she said, softly, brushing his lips with her own, the passion he had kindled in her expended, but the love she felt for him deepened.

"My own darling wife," he replied, kissing her very tenderly. "I love you so much. Did I tell you?"

Early next morning, Janet wakened and as soon as she stirred, Edward opened his eyes. "Good morning, Mrs. Knowles," he said, smiling and kissing her bare breast. "We didn't get much sleep, did we? Would you like to start early for Torquay as we'd planned, or shall we stay here for a while and set off after lunch?"

"Let's make an early start, shall we." As she spoke, she took him in her arms, nibbling at his ear, his neck, and finally at his lips. As she felt him harden against her, her own desire stirred again and she heard him murmur against her ear, "If we go on like this we shall never get started." Nevertheless, he didn't attempt to move and soon, they lay together, savouring the joy of being joined physically and emotionally as husband and wife.

At length, he said, "I shall have to tear myself away from you and see about getting the car ready. Would you like some breakfast sending up? All you need do is lift the house telephone and tell them what you'd like. Order the same for me and I'll be with you as soon as I can."

Dressing himself swiftly and kissing her lightly, he left her in the soft bed. She lay there, luxuriating in its soft comfort before getting up to run her bath. She felt like a sleek, well-fed cat, perfectly content with itself. She slid her hands down between her thighs, meeting wet stickiness and she wondered whether she had conceived from the night's love-making. How she hoped she had. There was nothing more she wanted now but to have his child. A baby! What a wonderful thing that would be. Edward's son – or daughter – it wouldn't matter which. Oh, her life was only just beginning, she realised, as she stretched, yawned and reached for the telephone.

When he returned to the bedroom, she was bathed and dressed for the journey. "You are wonderful, Edward," she told him, putting her arms around his neck and kissing him tenderly.

"Just keep on telling me that and I shalln't ask for more. Returning the kiss, he suggested, "Now, how about serving your lord and master with tea and toast, or whatever you've ordered. He grinned, glancing at the breakfast tray, which Room Service had just brought up for them.

The first leg of the journey, down to the Midlands, was taken steadily by Edward, the time passing mainly in happy talk, alternated by comfortable silences as he concentrated on the roads. At Shrewsbury they had lunch at a quiet old hotel in the centre of the town. They were both content in each other's company, their mutual love evident as they sat over the luncheon table.

By evening, they were in the Cotswolds and Edward suggested that they stay overnight in Bristol at a hotel he knew of up on Clifton Downs, close to the suspension bridge. As the car passed through the streets of the busy port, Janet gazed, fascinated by the scale and the variety of the buildings. Even in the dark, the white facades of the imposing Georgian houses loomed in splendour as they approached the Clifton area and the bridge.

"You can't see the bridge from here. We'll go across the Downs in the morning when it's light. It's well worth taking a look if you haven't seen it before."

"I feel now that I haven't seen *anything*. I haven't travelled much and it's all so wonderful and new to me."

"Wait till you get down to Devon," he promised her. "I don't think you'll be disappointed."

After a night at Clifton Towers, a hotel even more grand than the Midland at Preston, they crossed the Downs on foot and walked to the pylons of the bridge. It was a cold, pearly December morning and the structure hung across the tremendous depth of the gorge of the Avon, delicate as a strung web but strong as toughest steel could make it. Walking along the narrow roadway between the steel ropes, thick as a man's arm, Janet felt she dare not go near the edge to look below at the river.

Full of wonder, Janet was silent as they made their way back to the hotel before setting off on the last stage of their journey. As they drove down towards Exeter, she saw how lush the countryside appeared as they passed through wooded hills and down hidden valleys, with thatched cottages peeping above high hedgerows and fields splashed red, where the earth had been ploughed for winter crops. How different it was from the Fylde plain, her own home-land, with its flat fields and dykes and wind-stunted trees, its dark brown soil so different from this red, vibrant landscape through which they were passing.

But if the pastoral scenery of Devon enchanted her, the coast came as the crowning glory. As the car left the countryside behind, to join the coast road, the town of Torquay opened up before her, its hotels and villas standing high up, on a bluff, white and shining in the veiled sunlight which was trying to break through a sea mist. A gasp escaped her as they descended into the town, the purple water of the harbour broken up by dozens of small boats, their masts swaying in a light breeze.

"Wait until you see it in sunlight, in the summer," Edward said, "It's the next best thing to the South of France."

Driving slowly around the coastal road, past the elegant seafront shops, they took the steep road round the edge of the cliff which wound upwards towards Babbacombe. Janet had glimpses of the sea far below dashing against the rocks before they emerged onto Babbacombe Downs, where the road turned slightly inland. They rounded another bend, the road dipped and a large mansion came into view. Janet gazed in open-mouthed astonishment as her husband stopped the car at its gates, which were open, and prepared to negotiate the driveway. It was big enough for a dozen families, she thought, as the car came to a halt before a pillared entrance porch.

As she gazed in stunned bewilderment, he said, lightly, but with a touch of pride which he couldn't hide, "Yes, it is rather big, isn't it? I've been thinking of selling it for some time now. I've had one or two offers for it from hotel people but, so far,

I've hung on to it. Sentimental reasons, I suppose. I was born here and grew up here as a boy. Now I have a wife, though, the situation is rather different." He grinned at her suddenly, boyishly, Janet thought. "Are you thinking of filling it with offspring, Mrs. Knowles?"

"Edward!" She had managed to get back her breath. "I had no idea it was so – so –big! You just mentioned a detached house. I – I was imagining something a bit smaller than, well, The Willows, perhaps. Something *manageable.*

Her husband laughed. "My dear, sweet girl, Mother had a staff of eight besides the gardeners. Didn't I tell you?"

Janet rounded on him. "No, you didn't! You know very well you didn't even hint that the place might be a – a mansion!"

"Of course, they're all gone now. There are just Mr. and Mrs. Collins living in the annexe, keeping it in order. But we're not going to worry this week about the future of the place. We've come here for a honeymoon, not a director's meeting. Darling, I do love you when you look vulnerable and bewildered. Come on, let's go and see if Mrs. Collins had any lunch ready for us, as per my instructions."

Taking her hand, he led her up the flight of stone steps, past urns full of green plants, some of them still flowering in this mild climate. It took a few minutes for Mrs. Collins to come through from the back of the house to open the doors. A rosy-cheeked woman of robust appearance, she welcomed them with a great show of delight. On closer inspection, Janet decided that Mrs. Collins must be around seventy years old, although her skin was unlined as a fresh apple.

"And this, Mrs. Collins, is my wife, Janet," he told her, as they followed her into the marble-floored hall. Goodness, Janet thought, gazing in awe at the two curving staircases which rose on either side, a 'staff of eight' would be only just sufficient to run such a place!

"Very pleased to meet you, my dear." Mrs. Collins shook Janet's hand warmly. "I've set a table in the morning room, as you instructed, Mr. Edward, and lunch is nearly ready. I've put the champagne on ice and if you'll let me know when you're ready, I'll serve it up. Mr. Collins has just gone into the conservatory for fresh flowers for the table. As soon as he comes back, he'll take your bags up. Would you like to go into the morning room and I'll bring you some tea in? I'm sure you're ready for a cup. I've had a good fire going in there and I've taken the dust sheets off everything."

Taking their coats, she bustled off to the end of the hallway, disappearing through a door leading to the rear of the house.

"Well, Mrs. Knowles, is everything to your satisfaction?" Edward asked her, as they entered a beautiful room, its walls of eggshell blue decorated with gilt scroll-work. Long windows overlooked a section of the wood which, presumably, gave the house its name. She could hear in the distance a sound which was very familiar to her – the sound of the sea pounding against a shore somewhere below.

"Edward Knowles," she accused him, "you are a deceiver!" He had given her absolutely no inkling of the size and the magnificence of the house.

"I shouldn't worry about it," he said, "We can always sell it."

"But Edward, it's beautiful!"

"Oh, you like it, then?" Once again that dancing imp came into his eyes. He reached for her, drawing her into his arms, and for a while she was unable to answer him.

When the tea came it was on a silver tray and served in delicate old china cups. "Mr. Collins has taken up your bags and unpacked for you, Mr. Edward. I'll go now and put Mrs. Knowles' things away."

"Thank you, Mrs. Collins. We'll have lunch in half-an-hour."

Over a delicious meal, accompanied by champagne, Janet was just beginning to get used to her surroundings. That Edward's mother had been a very wealthy woman was certain and she had evidently lived in some style. In bringing her here, Edward probably wanted her to have a week in a semblance of the kind of luxury his family had been used to when his mother had been living here. And it would be only a week, because soon Army life would claim him again and Forest Lea would lapse into limbo until their return. All at once, she decided that she was going to forget that she had been a lowly housekeeper and become, for a short time, Mrs. Edward Knowles, mistress of Forest Lea. Perhaps that would please her husband.

"Edward," she said, "I'd like some more tea. Would you please ring for Mrs. Collins?"

"I thought you'd never ask," her husband replied solemnly, as he range the bell to summon the housekeeper.

The bedroom led off the long upper corridor, which ran the full width of the house, the rooms facing towards the sea. All Janet's clothes had been put neatly away by Mrs. Collins, either in one of the wardrobes or in the antique chests of drawers which matched the beautiful mahogany dressing table, with its three mirrors set in richly carved frames. The canopied bed had been turned down and Janet sat on the dressing stool at its foot, gazing around in disbelief at the splendid room with its heavy satin drapes and covers.

"This is one of the main bedrooms," he told her. "I usually use a small bedroom on the east side but as this is our honeymoon, I thought we might indulge ourselves a little. This room, too, happens to have all modern conveniences. Mother had the plumbing installed in that little room over there," he said, indicating a door she had failed to notice. "The dressing closet is over this side. I'll go in there and leave my clothes for Collins to valet for me in the morning. If you want to avail yourself of the modern facilities...." He finished, grinning. "I'll join you in a minute, darling." Kissing her tenderly, he strode away through a discreet door on the other side of the room.

After bathing in blessedly hot water, Janet slipped over her head the peach satin negligee, edged with rich lace, which she had bought as part of her trousseau. It had been very expensive, but she had loved it the moment she had seen it in the shop. Now she knew that it was the perfect garment to wear in this opulent bedroom on her first night in her new home. Glancing in the long cheval mirror, she knew that, her face flushed and her hair cascading down over her creamy shoulders, she complemented the room to perfection. She was sitting at the dressing table, brush in hand, when he came in to her. She heard him catch his breath as he saw her, mirrored, her hair shining in the soft light. Walking swiftly across the deep carpet, he took the brush from her hand, placing it down on the polished wood... Taking both her hands in his, he drew her up from the stool, turning her towards him and taking her into his arms.

"My darling girl," he whispered, "I love you so much."

His mouth came down hard on hers and, opening her mouth to him, she clung to him as he held her in those slim, strong hands.

"I love you, too, Edward," she gasped. "I can't tell you how much." The soft, sensuous surging had spread down over her limbs again, insistent and demanding, as he drew her towards the bed. She pulled desperately at the remaining buttons of the loose night-shirt he was wearing. The next moment they were lying on the bed and he was slipping off her nightdress and shrugging off his own shirt completely. The moment his bare skin touched hers, she was released once again from all propriety or modesty. She touched and stroked his body, revelling in her freedom from restraint.

His own hands, too, were bringing her to a peak of desire. When he could control his own urgency no longer, and he penetrated her, she expended herself, using him as he was using her, the two of them lost in their own passion, yet joined in union. Much later, he raised his head from where it had lain for a long time – on her breast. She, too, had slept and the room was very dark.

"Don't you think we should get into the bed?" he asked her, as she stirred under him. "The room's not cold, but I wouldn't like you to go down with pneumonia on your honeymoon, darling."

Laughing sleepily, they struggled down under the quilt, lying close together, entwined, as they settled down until the morning. Tomorrow, he was thinking, he would take her up on to the Moor, or along the cliff footpath. He would show her how beautiful his home county was – how beautiful….

Janet stood, on the first day of her honeymoon in Devon, on the lip of tremendous cliffs overlooking a crescent of beach below. Even today, when the sky was overcast, the sight of Oddicombe beach, with its almost vertical cliffs, filled her with awe. Now and then, the sun managed to break through, changing the sea to aquamarine and emerald where it lit. The golden finger touched the coastline as far up as Teignmouth in the north, before coming close to illuminate the beach below.

"Edward, darling, this is so very different from the Lancashire coast! It's so – spectacular and unspoilt."

He appeared thoughtful. "Yes, it is now, but there seems to be so many houses here being turned into hotels, these days."

"I love it already. I can't wait to see it all."

"Well, darling, I'm afraid we shalln't be able to see it all in one week, but we'll go where we can. Where would you like to go next?"

"I'd love to go to Brixham. You said it was a fishing village, didn't you?"

"Yes, it is and, as you'll see, it's not exactly like Fleetwood. Come on, it's only a short trip – we'll go and have some lunch there, at the Ship."

Brixham, with its quaint harbour full of fishing boats, nestling under the huge outcrop of Berry Head, was not in the least like her familiar home fishing port, as Edward had pointed out. Here there was an artist's picture at every turn of the head and she imagined that a colony of them would be setting up their easels come the spring and summer.

The weather remained calm, even kind, and they were able to go up onto Dartmoor, a bleak and inhospitable place in bad weather, finishing up at the old thatched inn in the village of Widdecombe. Wherever they went, Edward appeared to be known and respected and she was welcomed with warmth as the Captain's wife. The hospitality of the local people astonished her until she realised that her husband's family had been landlords in the area for several generations, and that he still owned property there.

Goodness, how little Edward had told her about his private affairs! Yet, how little they seemed to matter, anyway. She would have been as happy, she was sure, honeymooning in a tiny cottage with Edward as in the splendour of Forest Lea. What on earth were they going to do with Forest Lea, she wondered? Perhaps Edward would decide to sell it, after all, and they would settle for something like a normal house.

On the last day before they were due to leave for Southampton, her husband told her, "There's one place I haven't shown you yet. I've left it till the last, because it's the nearest, and we can walk there. You asked me where the sea was on that first night we arrived. You said you could hear it nearby, even though the house is high up on the Downs. You can't see the sea, for that reason, but it's just beyond the wood. There's a narrow, prickly path which runs through it towards the cliff, but there's a safe way down. It's a bit of a scramble, but I think we should manage it. Could you put on a thick skirt so that you don't scratch yourself, and a heavy jacket. It might be a bit cold down there."

The path was overgrown with dead branches and other debris and it evidently wasn't much used. Janet had also put on stout shoes so she found the going fairly easy, apart from an occasional snag on her clothes. Soon, they had descended to a level ledge of rock, where the trees thinned out. Below them the rock formed a series of rough slabs leading steeply down into a small cove. The green water was just visible in a small vee shape between the outcrops of rock, directly below them. "Come on, darling, follow me and watch your step. Give me your hand – these rocks can be slippery."

Taking her hand, he led her between the uneven slabs, selecting the best footholds on the natural stone stairway down into the cove.

She was watching where she placed her feet, but as they rounded one of the big rocks, the first complete view of the cove opened up and she looked about her. Her mouth dropped open in complete surprise and wonder. She gasped out loud, "Why Edward, it's the most beautiful thing I've ever seen!"

"Glad you like it, darling. I like to think it belongs to the house but, of course, it doesn't. The house is just built above it, that's all."

Special was the only word she could find for the place, she decided, gazing around her at the almost magical formations of the multi-coloured rocks which formed the furthest wall of the cove. A small white shingle beach completed the enchanting picture and on this, Edward spread a small rug from the picnic basket. They sat with tiny, transparent wavelets spreading slowly over the pebbles not far from their feet, before they receded again as the tide pulled them back. As Edward unpacked the basket, the familiar cries of gulls sounded from the cliffs above. The birds, encouraged by the prospect of titbits, wheeled nearer....

Sitting, perfectly contented, by her husband's side, neither needing to speak, with the clear sea lapping at her feet, Janet tried to imprint the memory of this idyllic, secluded place on her mind to take with her to the sun baked Mediterranean. She imagined that by the time their two years on the Rock was over, she would be longing to feel again its coolness and its calm.

She had insisted on doing her own packing before she and Edward left for Southampton, to embark. Mrs. Collins had waited on the couple the whole of the honeymoon week, causing Janet some secret embarrassment. This had crystallised in a strong urge to help the older woman in her work. She had actually asked Mrs. Collins whether she could do anything to assist her but the housekeeper had waved away Janet's appeals as inappropriate in the wife of Captain Knowles.

"Thank you, Mrs. Knowles, it's very good of you to be thinking of it, but I couldn't accept any help. I've been very happy to serve you and the captain. It's a pleasure to be able to cook for you both and wait on you, even if it's only for a short while – and on your honeymoon, too! It's what I've been waiting to do for a long time. Me and Mr. Collins don't get much chance to wait on people, with the Captain away so often."

"No, I expect the house seems big and empty, most of the time," Janet agreed, "and now we're going away again for two whole years."

"Yes, I was the cook and Mr. Collins the head gardener in the old days, when Mrs. Knowles, the Captain's mother, was living here. We had a full staff then. Taken out in her coffin, she was, long before her time. Mr. Knowles, the Captain's father, went right away afterwards, and I hear he's got a new wife, somewhere up north."

Janet watched Mrs. Collins' eyes mist over at the reminiscences. "Well, Mrs. Collins, I don't know what the Captain intends to do with the house," she said.

"If the house is sold," Mrs. Collins continued, "the Captain has promised us a cottage, so we shalln't go without a roof over our heads. But maybe the Captain will see his way to keeping the place on, now he's married?"

"We shall have to wait and see," Janet said, privately wondering how Edward could possibly be expected to keep up such a place. On the other hand, she knew with certainty that she would love to live here! The fact was, that she had not only fallen in love with Edward, she had fallen in love with his house, as well!

Now, their final night in this wonderful place was here. Tomorrow, they would drive to Southampton and she and Edward would set off on the longest journey she herself had ever taken and cross stormy seas. He had warned her that the Bay of Biscay could be very rough. What kind of a sailor would she prove to be? But in a couple of days, she would be there, trying to settle into a new life as the Captain's wife.

After her experience with Mrs. Collins at Forest Lea, she had realised that, as an officer's wife, she would be in a very different social position from the one she had occupied until her marriage. It was only now that this fact came home to her with full force. In future, she wouldn't be waiting on anyone. She would have people to do things for her, instead. Remembering her impulses to help Mrs. Collins during this past week, she wondered how soon she would adapt to her new role and accept it all as something quite normal.

It would probably take a long time, she decided, as she placed each garment neatly in the suitcase before getting ready for bed. Her husband was making final arrangements for the morning with the Collinses but he had promised to join her very soon. Her heart started to beat a little faster as she heard his footstep outside the door....

Chapter Thirty-Three

It was just before Christmas when Alice Tomlinson and Alfred Simpkins became man and wife. Walking down the aisle on the arm of her father, Alice smiled at her mother, sitting in one of the front pews of Lytham Parish church, together with her mother-in-law, Ellen. Beside them sat Doris, the children's godmother.

Mary had been right about Joe's disapproval of the marriage, but he had had to abandon his objections in the face of Alice's determination. Mary had suggested that Alice herself should tell Joe of her plans, knowing that her husband would not be as angry face to face with his daughter.

"But, Alice," he had argued loudly, "he's not much younger than me."

"I know, Dad, but I need someone who can look after the children, this time. You don't want me to be struggling again for money, do you?"

"No, I don't, but I think you could have found someone different to Alfred. He doesn't look very manly to me."

402 / Sally Redmayne

"He's going to support us all, Dad. Don't go on about it. I've thought a lot about things and I know what I want. I want to be secure and not have to worry about whether I can afford to buy clothes for me and the children. Alfred won't let us go short of anything. You've seen the ring he bought me when we got engaged and that's only the start. He's letting me choose my own wedding ring, too, and I know I shall only have to ask him if I want anything else."

"Well, I've said my piece, so don't come complaining to me if it doesn't suit you when you're wed," her father had warned her, "and I think your Mother feels the same way about things. He looks a bit of a cissie to me."

"Oh, Dad, don't talk like that. Say you're happy for me and give us your blessing – please!"

"Alright, lass, I never could stay angry with you for long, but I only hope you're doing the right thing." Joe had conceded reluctantly, putting his muscular arms around her and kissing her roughly.

Now, as they approached the alter and Alfred stepped forward, Alice was aware of her father's set face as she stepped up to stand beside her husband-to-be. Alfred, joining his future wife in front of the vicar was congratulating himself on his decision. He thought she looked very beautiful in her new lavender wool crepe coat and dress. He was going to be a very proud man to have her as his new young bride. Norman, of course, had been a bit difficult about things at first.

"How do you think I feel, then, about you taking another wife?" Norman's hurt face had told Alfred that he was taking it worse than he had expected.

Alfred had taken hold of Norman's hand and squeezed it. "You know perfectly well, love, why I'm doing this. It's for our safety – that's all. There won't be the same suspicion if I'm married, with a wife and three children, will there? You know what could happen, if the law got on to us. We'd be arrested – we'd go to prison, Norman. Prison! For ten years at least! It isn't as if it's going to make any difference to us, is it? Surely you don't imagine that a woman could come between us, do you? That's silly!"

"Yes, I suppose it is, Alfred, but your family are going to take up a lot of your time and attention, once they are living with you," Norman had pointed out, his mouth sulky.

"Well, what do *you* suggest, then?" Alfred had asked. "We can't meet openly as things are, without raising eyebrows, so it's no use thinking that we're ever going to get on a different footing, is it? Not until the law's changed, anyway – and when is that going to be? Never, at this rate! With any luck, I should have twenty years left yet at the shop, but when I'm ready to retire, I want someone to leave it to, and she has a son. I don't want it all to go to waste. He'll be just the right age, when I retire, for taking over, and it isn't as if you're interested in it – you've told me that often enough."

Oh, no, Norman hadn't like the arrangement, but he had come round in the end, as Alfred had known he would. After all, what was their alternative? In the end, Norman had admitted that this was, perhaps, the only way when you really came down to it.

Alfred glanced at the girl by his side as the vicar started on the familiar ceremony and her eyes met his. They were calm and sure. Alfred realised that his future wife was quite aware that she was sealing some kind of a bargain. He didn't think, though, as he took the ring from his pocket and placed it on her finger, that she knew exactly what she was getting. But then, what did he really know about her, either?

As the ceremony ended, he briefly placed his cheek against hers before they made their way into the vestry to sign the register. Whatever the outcome, for better or for worse, they were now Mr. and Mrs. Alfred Simpkins.

It was very strange, Alice was thinking later, as she and Alfred found themselves alone at last in the sitting room at the back of the shop. The guests had all departed, her mother and father, with Doris, on the late train to Bradfield. Ellen had also left them earlier, to travel on the local train to Blackpool. The children were upstairs, asleep in their new bedroom, and the baby slumbered peacefully in his pram, ready for Alice to take him up to the smaller room which was to be his, next to his sisters. Her husband hadn't taken her into his arms or attempted even to touch her, never mind kiss her. That peck on the cheek at the end of the ceremony, when it was expected of him, had been the only time he had come close to her. Not that she was longing for him to do so, but it was only right and proper she thought, for a new husband to want to kiss and hold his bride.

On the other hand, Alfred was being very pleasant to her, asking solicitous little questions. Was she tired of the day's events? Was she comfortable? Would she like a drink, or something to eat? Because if she did, he would be only too pleased to see to it.

"No, I don't want anything, Alfred. I'll just take Johnny up to his cot and then get undressed upstairs while you finish off down here."

"Very well, Alice. I shalln't be long. I'll just make sure everything's alright before I come up."

As she entered their bedroom after seeing that Johnny was tucked up in his cot, Alice walked over to her own bed by the window. It had seemed strange to her when Alfred had first shown her over the house to find that he preferred single beds to the old style double bed. He had said that they were more hygienic and that he was used to them. Oh well, she thought, I suppose I can get used to them as well. After all, it's not the same as it was with Harry. Harry would have been scornful, she knew, of the idea of single beds. Well, she was Mrs. Alfred Simpkins now, not Mrs. Harry Tomlinson, and she must try to adjust to Alfred's ideas of what was right and proper.

It did seem a very long time before she heard her husband mounting the stairs. She herself was already in bed, sitting back prettily against the pillows, her low-cut satin nightdress revealing the soft curve of her breasts.

"That's a lovely nightgown, Alice," Alfred commented, as he began to remove his clothes, one by one and place them on the clothes tidy which stood near to the wardrobe, ready for the purpose. His shoes he placed neatly on the bottom shelf of the wardrobe to join a couple of other pairs, sitting there, side by side. Alice was surprised to see that her husband didn't remove his undervest before putting on a pair of heavy pyjamas. The only parts of his body she had glimpsed had been his white arms and legs in the moment before he had pulled on the pyjamas. He didn't make any move to come near her, and the next moment he was getting into his own bed, placing his thick-lensed spectacles on the bedside table in their hard case. He got down into the bed straight away. What sort of a man could have resisted the sight of her, she wondered, shoulders uncovered and all-but-bare breasted? What man wouldn't have fondled or kissed her before eagerly setting foot in her bed? But Alfred had done none of these things.

Alice couldn't believe that her husband was not going to consummate the marriage that night, like any other normal man. Her whirling thoughts brought a memory of Alfred telling her that people should not have sexual relations before they were married. Well, they were married now, and he still didn't seem to think that they should be having relations. What could be wrong? She knew that she herself was attractive to men. She'd never had any difficulties in that direction, and she had gone to some trouble in choosing her wedding trousseau, meaning to please him, both dressed and undressed, in her nightwear.

But her had treated her more like a sister – affectionately, not passionately. Oh, well it was all too hard to figure out. Suddenly, her mother's words came back to her, "Are you sure he's quite normal in that way, Alice?" Was there something wrong with Alfred? Some illness that had made him unable to perform the sexual act? God! Had she got herself married to a man who was impotent? If she had, her mother and father must never find out. They had both warned her, too, hadn't they, about his age?

Turning instinctively to look at her husband, Alice tried to imagine what his physical deformity might be. Then she realised that he was already sleeping peacefully. Why hadn't he told her, then, that he had problems on the sexual side? Why, in fact, had he married her at all? Had he been like this when he had been married to his first wife, Edna, or was it something which had developed since that time? Perhaps that was why they'd had no children?

Slowly, her mind whirling, she lowered herself into the sweetly-scented luxury of the bed, but sleep was impossible. The questions kept chasing each other across her mind. She lay wide awake, trying to come to terms with her situation. What if he *never* attempted to exercise his rights as a husband? Of course, she had been a widow now for some time, living only with her children since Harry had died, and she hadn't missed Harry's lovemaking all that much. Just occasionally, she had thought of Jack Fenton, with appreciation, but she'd neither the time nor the opportunity to seek another relationship with a man. When Alfred had courted her and he had finally proposed, she had automatically assumed that they would be living as man and wife as soon as the ceremony was over.

How wrong she had been in thinking that! A comforting idea came to her as she turned her face into the soft pillow to ease her aching head. Perhaps he merely meant that they should refrain from union tonight, and that they should rest. Perhaps he thought the day had tired her and that she needed sleep. He had been so considerate and solicitous in the past that she could almost believe it – almost! Sighing bitterly, hot tears trembling on her lashes, she rubbed wet eyes into the pillow as she lay – fretfully going over once again the possibilities inherent in Alfred's behaviour until, a long time later, sleep finally came and released her from her torment.

When Alice awakened the following morning, she found she had overslept because she hadn't got off to sleep until the early hours. When she looked across, she saw that the other bed was empty. Alfred, then, had got up – probably hours ago. It was a Sunday, so he didn't have to open the shop and the day appeared to be overcast, as she turned towards the window. They had decided against going away for a honeymoon, not because Alfred couldn't afford it, but because it would have been difficult, taking away a baby. She was just wondering why she couldn't hear any of the children when there was a tapping on the door and her husband, a pleasant smile on his face, put his head round the door and addressed her.

"Ah, Alice, my dear, I see you've awakened. I thought you might like to sleep on this morning. I've given the girls their breakfasts and seen to little Johnny's bottle, and I've got your breakfast on the go downstairs. I'll bring you up a cup of tea first, then you can have your breakfast in bed. Did you sleep well?"

Struggling with very mixed feelings, Alice decided that Alfred was being extra-solicitous towards her. She decided not to mention yet her agitation of the previous night. Perhaps there would be a chance later in the day to discuss things with him. She did feel very hungry, she found, as the aroma of frying bacon came in through the open bedroom door.

"Thank you, Alfred," she said, "that would be nice," trying to appear unconcerned and to smile. He, for his part, seemed not to notice that she was at all perturbed by the situation.

"I'll bring your tea up, then." He went down the stairs, to return very soon with the fresh cup. It tasted delicious, and had just the right amount of milk and sugar. Then came her breakfast, on a tray set with an embroidered cloth, on which was placed a single rose in a finger vase. When she saw it, she was almost ready to overlook his shortcomings of the previous night.

"Now then, my dear, take your time with that. I've told the girls to stay downstairs with me while you enjoy it and Johnny's sleeping in his pram, so you've nothing to worry about."

Good heavens! Impotent or not, when it came to being capable around the house, Alfred would take some beating, she thought, as she tucked into the savoury bacon and the buttery toast. He was as good as any woman! Her mind was already beginning to reassess her position here and to adjust to the fact that she could, in fact, be better off as things were.

What did it matter, anyway, if her husband was impotent? There was one good thing about that, she realised, as she relished the tasty meal. If she wasn't having sex with Alfred, she wouldn't be having any more children. Smiling slightly, Alice finished off the breakfast, wiping her lips daintily with the crisp serviette he had placed at the side of the tray. She was feeling a lot better today, already, as he had suggested she would, the night before....

Chapter Thirty-Four

The great bulk of the liner 'Himalaya' lay beside the dock at Southampton, looming as high as a three-storey building and as long as Nelson Street. Walking up the passenger gangway, holding on to Edward's arm, Janet felt a tingle of excitement as her feet touched the deck. Up until now, the fact that she was leaving behind England and all her family and friends hadn't seemed real. She had thought about it fleetingly during the wonderful days of the honeymoon, but now that she was actually embarking with Edward, she realised fully that she was leaving behind familiar things and starting completely afresh on a foreign shore with her new husband.

There were twenty-six officers making the trip, Edward had told her, but only half-a-dozen of their wives. Others could not leave England, either through family ties or for health reasons. Most of the commissioned men were, in fact, still bachelors, as Edward had been until this last month. Besides the officers, five hundred men from the ranks were going on the ship to St. John's barracks, to garrison the Rock, as her husband called

Gibraltar. He had assured her that, even though Spain was their next-door-neighbour, the Rock was very British, with a few hundred British people living there permanently.

As they stood on the deck with their hand luggage – the trunks had been taken on in advance – a steward came to take them to their cabin. The officers, of course, were the lucky ones. Their cabins were up on the deck, while the men had to occupy the rabbit warren of rooms down below. Looking round at the neat, orderly beds and seeing the economical use of the available space in the furnishings, Janet exclaimed in surprise.

"I didn't think the cabins would be as pleasant, Edward, and look, everything's got the name of the ship on it, S.S. Himalaya."

"Yes," laughed her husband "that's so that nothing's stolen."

His merry eyes became serious as he took her in him arms, gazing down at her. "No regrets?" he asked lightly?

"Not the tiniest," she assured him, her arms sliding around his neck, as his mouth came down over hers.

A deferential knock sounded on the door, and he released her. She sat down on one of the beds while he went to open it. Outside stood a sailor in the uniform of the ranks. Seeing Captain Knowles hatless, he removed his own cap, placing it under his arm.

"Ah, Owens. I shalln't need you until after we sail. At ease, man. Had a good leave?"

"Yes, sir," Edward's batman replied, his eyes straying to the bunk where Janet was sitting. So – the captain was entertaining a lady before they sailed:

"And this, Owens, is my wife. You will have the opportunity of meeting her later. For the moment you can go and see that our trunks have been safely stowed. I take it that they have given you a berth near to this cabin?"

"Very good, sir. Yes, sir."

"Very well. Report to me after we get under way."

The dark little Welshman turned and retreated in the direction of Storage.

"Why, Edward, is Owens your personal servant, then?" Janet asked him in surprise.

"My batman, yes," Edward said, smiling. "He valets my clothes and puts my things out for me when I'm on duty."

"But, Edward, I thought I was going to do all that for you," she cried, seizing his hand, her eyes puzzled and anxious.

"You'll have a lot more important things than that to do, darling," he assured her, bending and kissing the tip of her nose. "And anyway, I intend that you should do all the more personal tasks that I shall require doing, Mrs. Knowles." He pulled her up from the bed. "Don't let it bother you, my love," he told her gently. "Owens knows his place and he is very discreet. He wouldn't be my batman if he weren't!"

"You mean, you've had other women visiting you in the past?"

His arms encircled her waist. She pulled away a little, watching his face, while he answered, "Well, I can't say I've lived like a monk – you don't think any soldier could do that, do you?" His eyes met hers squarely.

"No, of course not. It's just that the thought of you with another woman is unbearable, even if it is in the past. I know it's unreasonable. I've had other loves, too, but I love you so much, Edward, I want to think I'm the only one."

"You *are* the only one, darling," he assured her, kissing her eyes, her throat, her hair. "I didn't ask anyone before to marry me, did I?" he pointed out. "Anyway, we're not going to worry about the past. We've both put all that behind us now."

His lips claimed hers in a kiss that seemed to settle things once and for all. Now there were just the two of them, together in love, and now in marriage.

"Shall we go out on deck and see her cast off?" he asked, letting her go. "She's due out very soon, now."

"Oh, yes, I'd like that. We'll wave to everybody from the rails."

As they walked out of the cabin, a steward approached, telling Edward, "I was just coming for you, sir. There are visitors for you in the mid-ship saloon."

To Janet's amazement, Edward seemed to receive this piece of news without surprise. Whoever could have come aboard to see them off? They weren't expecting anyone.

"Dad!" she exclaimed joyfully, as Robert came out of the saloon to meet them, closely followed by Isobel and Leonard. She ran to Robert, throwing her arms around his neck. "Oh, what a wonderful surprise," she exclaimed, as her father hugged her tightly. As he released her, she turned to Edward, "Did you arrange this, then, darling?"

"I have to admit that I did. I asked Dad if he would pick up your father and Florrie and bring them along in the car with Isobel. I can see that I did the right thing. I know we've all said our farewells, but I though it would be good if we had a proper send-off from both our families. I expect they took their time, travelling down, probably made a bit of a holiday of it." He grinned at his father who confirmed that the four had indeed used the opportunity of staying at a couple of good hotels en route for Southampton.

"My – you're looking bonnier than ever, lass. Married life must be suiting you," Robert said, holding his daughter at arm's length, her hands in his.

Blushing furiously, Janet laughed, telling her father that she was happier now than she had even been in her life.

"I can see that, lass – you don't have to tell me," he said, releasing her.

She turned to Florrie who after embracing her, pressed her hand saying, "Don't forget to write, dear, as soon as you get settled."

As she spoke, the ship's whistle for 'all visitors ashore' sounded and there were quick embraces all round before the two families parted, the older generation to retrace their steps down the gangway onto the dock, to stand in front of a gesticulating, waving crowd. The Regiment Bank struck up a rousing march tune and everybody gazed upwards as the ship got under way. Up on deck, Janet and Edward waved harder than ever as the S.S. Himalaya swung slowly away from the dock, the distance between the ship and the quayside increasing with every minute.

With passengers above and their families below waving frantically, the ship pulled further out into the Solent, eventually turning fully and heading out past the Needles, to sea.

Janet pulled her coat collar up around her neck as the ship turned into the wind.

"Cold, darling?" Edward asked her. "Shall we go down to the cabin, then?"

"I haven't thanked you yet, Edward, for that last, lovely surprise."

"I thought you might be pleased." Edward smiled. "Well, Mrs. Knowles, this is where our married life together really begins......"

About the Author

Freda Gregory (writing as Sally Redmayne) was born in Blackpool and lived there for 23 years until her first marriage took her inland to Radcliffe in Greater Manchester. Unfortunately, the marriage failed and Freda set up her own successful hairdressing business there, only retiring on the death of her second husband. She has one daughter Sally, from her first marriage who shares her love of clothes and fashion and who is currently working as a freelance costume designer for television and drama. Freda came to writing quite late in her life attending Creative Writing Courses at Bury Adult Education Centre where she obtained the skills necessary for writing a novel. She is at present at work on a sequel to this book set twenty years later during the Second World War.

Printed in the United Kingdom
by Lightning Source UK Ltd.
116519UKS00001B/4-33